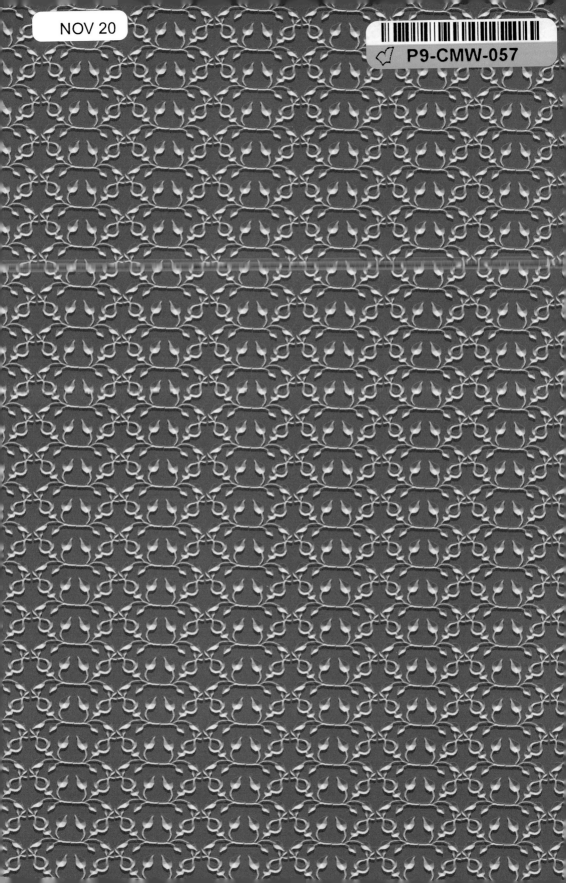

TSARINA

TSARINA

Ellen Alpsten

ST. MARTIN'S PRESS
NEW YORK

Published in the United States by St. Martin's Press, an imprint of St. Martin's Publishing Group

TSARINA. Copyright © 2020 by Ellen Alpsten. All rights reserved. Printed in the United States of America. For information, address St. Martin's Publishing Group, 120 Broadway, New York, NY 10271.

www.stmartins.com

Design by Meryl Sussman Levavi

Library of Congress Cataloging-in-Publication Data

Names: Alpsten, Ellen, 1971– author.
Title: Tsarina / Ellen Alpsten.
Identifiers: LCCN 2020019385 | ISBN 9781250214430 (hardcover) |
    ISBN 9781250214454 (ebook)
Subjects: LCSH: Catherine I, Empress of Russia, 1684–1727—Fiction. |
    Russia—History—Catherine I, 1725–1727—Fiction. | Peter I, Emperor of Russia,
    1672–1725—Fiction. | GSAFD: Biographical fiction. | Historical fiction.
Classification: LCC PR9110.9.A47 T73 2020 | DDC 823/.92—dc23
LC record available at https://lccn.loc.gov/2020019385

Our books may be purchased in bulk for promotional, educational, or business use. Please contact your local bookseller or the Macmillan Corporate and Premium Sales Department at 1-800-221-7945, extension 5442, or by email at MacmillanSpecialMarkets@macmillan.com.

Originally published in the United Kingdom by Bloomsbury

First U.S. Edition: 2020

10 9 8 7 6 5 4 3 2 1

To Tobias:
Thank You

TSARINA

PROLOGUE

He is dead. My beloved husband, the mighty tsar of all the Russias, has died—and just in time.

Moments before death came for him, Peter called for a quill and paper to be brought to him in his bedchamber in the Winter Palace. My heart almost stalled. He had not forgotten, but was going to drag me down with him. When he lost consciousness for the last time and the darkness drew him closer to its heart, the quill slipped from his fingers. Black ink spattered the soiled sheets; time held its breath. What had the tsar wanted to settle with that last effort of his tremendous spirit?

I knew the answer.

The candles in the tall candelabra filled the room with a heavy scent and an unsteady light; their glow made shadows reel in corners and brought the woven figurines on the Flemish tapestries to life, their coarse faces showing pain and disbelief. Outside the door, the voices of the people who'd stood there all night were drowned out by the February wind rattling furiously at the shutters. Time spread slowly, like oil on water. Peter had pressed himself into our souls like his signet ring in hot wax. It seemed impossible that the world hadn't careened to a halt at his passing. My husband, the greatest will ever to impose itself on Russia, had been more than our ruler. He had been our fate. He was still mine.

The doctors—Blumentrost, Paulsen, and Horn—stood silently around Peter's bed, staring at him, browbeaten. Five kopecks' worth of medicine, given early enough, could have saved him. Thank God for the quacks' lack of good sense.

Without looking, I could feel Feofan Prokopovich, the archbishop of Novgorod, watching me, along with Alexander Menshikov. Prokopovich had made the tsar's will eternal and Peter had much to thank him for. Menshikov, on the other hand, owed his fortune and influence to Peter. What was it Peter had said when someone tried to blacken Alexander Danilovich's name to him by referring to his murky business dealings? "Menshikov is always Menshikov, in all that he does!" That had put an end to that.

Dr. Paulsen had closed the tsar's eyes and crossed his hands on his breast, but he hadn't removed the scroll, Peter's last will and testament, from his grasp. Those hands, which were always too dainty for the tall, powerful body, had grown still, helpless. Just two weeks earlier he had plunged those very hands into my hair, winding it round his fingers, inhaling the scent of rosewater and sandalwood.

"My Catherine," he'd said, calling me by the name he himself had given me, and he'd smiled at me. "You're still a beauty. But what will you look like in a convent, shorn, and bald? The cold there will break you, your spirit, even though you're strong as a horse. Do you know that Evdokia still writes to me begging for a second fur, poor thing! What a good job you can't write!" he'd said, laughing.

It had been thirty years since Evdokia had been banished to the convent. I'd met her once. Her eyes shone with madness, her shaven head was covered in boils and scabs from the cold and the filth, and her only company was a hunchbacked dwarf to serve her in her cell. Peter had ordered the poor creature have her tongue cut out, so in response to Evdokia's moaning and laments, all she was able to do was burble. He'd been right to believe that seeing Evdokia would fill me with lifelong dread.

I knelt at Peter's bedside and the three doctors retreated to the twilight at the edge of the room, like crows driven from a field: the birds Peter had been so terrified of in the last years of his life. The tsar had called open season on the hapless birds all over his empire. Farmers caught, killed, plucked, and roasted them for reward. None of this helped Peter: silently, at night, the bird would slip through the padded walls and locked doors of his bedchamber. Its ebony wings blotted the light and in their cool shadow, the blood on the tsar's hands never dried. His fingers were not yet those of a corpse, but soft, and still warm. For a moment, the fear and anger of these past few months slipped from my heart like a thief in the night. I kissed his hands and breathed in his familiar scent of tobacco, ink, leather, and the perfume tincture that was blended for his sole use in Grasse.

I took the scroll from his hand—it was easy enough to slide it out, although my blood thickened with fear and my veins were coated with frost and time like branches in our Baltic winter. It was important to show everyone that I alone was entitled to do this—I, his wife, and the mother of his children. Twelve times I had given birth.

The paper rustled as I unrolled it. Not for the first time, I was ashamed of my inability to read, and I handed his last will to Feofan Prokopovich. At least Menshikov was as ignorant as I. Ever since the days when Peter first drew us into his orbit and cast his spell upon us, we had been like two children squabbling over their father's love and attention. *Batjushka* tsar, his people called him. Our little father tsar.

Prokopovich must have known what Peter had in mind for me. He was an old fox with a sharp wit, as comfortable in heavenly and earthly realms. Daria had once sworn that he had three thousand books in his library. What, if you please, can one man do with three thousand books? The scroll sat lightly in his liver-spotted hands now. After all, he himself had helped Peter draft the decree that shocked us all. The tsar had set aside every custom, every law: he wanted to appoint his own successor and would rather leave his empire to a worthy stranger than his own, unworthy child.

How timid Alexey had been when we first met, the spitting image of his mother, Evdokia, with his veiled gaze and high, domed forehead. He couldn't sit up straight, because Menshikov had thrashed his back and buttocks bloody and sore. Only when it was too late did Alexey grasp his fate: in his quest for a new Russia, the tsar would spare no one, neither himself, nor his only son. You were no blood of my blood, Alexey, no flesh of my flesh, and so I was able to sleep soundly. Peter, though, had been haunted by nightmares from that day on.

My heart pounded against my lightly laced bodice—I was surprised it didn't echo from the walls—but I met Prokopovich's gaze as calmly as I could. I wriggled my toes in my slippers, as I could not afford to faint.

Prokopovich's smile was as thin as one of the wafers he would offer in church. He knew the secrets of the human heart; especially mine.

"Read, Feofan," I said quietly.

"Give everything to . . ." He paused, looked up, and repeated: "To . . ."

Menshikov's temper flared; he reared as if someone had struck him with a whip, like in the good old days. "To whom?" he snarled at Prokopovich. "Pray tell, Feofan, to whom?"

I could hardly breathe. The fur was suddenly much too hot against my skin.

Feofan shrugged. "That's all. The tsar didn't finish writing the sentence." The shadow of a smile flitted across his wrinkled face. Peter had liked nothing better than to turn the world on its head, and, oh yes, he still had hold of us from beyond the grave. Feofan lowered his gaze. I snapped back to life. Nothing was decided. Peter was dead; his successor unnamed. But that didn't mean I was safe. It meant quite the opposite.

"What—that's it?" Menshikov snatched the paper out of Feofan's hands. "I don't believe it!" He stared at the scrawl, but Prokopovich took the scroll from him again. "Oh, Alexander Danilovich. That's what comes of always having had something better to do than learn to read and write."

Menshikov was about to give a stinging reply, but I cut him off. Men! Was this the moment for rivalry? I had to act fast if I didn't want to live out my days in a nunnery, or be forced aboard a sled to Siberia, or end up facedown in the Neva, drifting between the thick floes of ice, my body being crushed and shredded by their sheer force.

"Feofan—has the tsar died without naming his heir?" I had to be sure.

He nodded, his eyes bloodshot from the long hours of keeping vigil at his lord's bedside. In the manner of Russian Orthodox priests, he wore his dark hair plain—it fell straight to his shoulders, streaked with gray—and his simple, dark tunic was that of an ordinary priest. Nothing about him betrayed the honors and offices with which Peter had rewarded him; nothing apart from the heavy, jewel-studded cross on his breast—the *panagia*. Feofan was old, but he was one of those men who could easily serve many more tsars. He bowed and handed me the scroll. I thrust it into the sleeve of my dress. Feofan straightened up.

"Tsarina. I place the future of Russia in your hands." My heart skipped a beat when he called me by this title. Menshikov, too, raised his head, alert, like a bloodhound taking scent. His eyes narrowed.

"Go home, Feofan, and get some rest. I'll send for you when I need you. Until then, do not forget that the tsar's last words are known only to the three of us," I said. "I hope you will serve me for many years, Feofan," I added as he rose. "I bestow upon you the Order of Saint Andrew and an estate outside Kiev with ten—no, twenty thousand souls." He bowed, looking content, and I thought quickly about whom to send into exile, whose property I would have to appropriate. On a day like today, fortunes were made and lost. I gestured to the servant standing guard next to the door. Had he understood our whispers? I hoped not.

"Order Feofan Prokopovich's carriage. Help him downstairs. No one is to speak to him, do you hear?" I added in a whisper.

He nodded, his long lashes fluttering on his rosy cheeks. A handsome young boy this one was. His face suddenly recalled that of another. One I'd thought the most beautiful I'd ever known. Peter had put a brutal end to that. And after, he'd ordered that the head, that same sweet head, be set at my bedside, in a heavy glass jar of strong spirit, the way apples are preserved in vodka in winter. The gaping eyes stared sadly out at me; in the throes of death the lips, once so soft to kiss, now shriveled and drained of blood, had pulled back from the teeth and gums. When I first saw it and, horrified, asked the maid to remove it, Peter threatened me with the convent and the whip. And so there it lived on.

Feofan laughed softly, his face splitting in so many wrinkles that his skin looked like the parched earth after summer. "Don't worry, Tsarina. Come, boy, lend an old man your arm."

The two of them stepped out into the corridor. The footman's pale, narrow-legged silk trousers clearly showed his muscular legs and buttocks. Was there any truth in the rumor that Prokopovich liked young men? Well—each to his own. I blocked the view of the tsar's bed with my body. Pale, frightened faces turned to me: both noblemen and servants sat there like rabbits in a snare. Madame de la Tour, the scrawny French governess who watched over my youngest daughter, Natalya, was hugging the little girl close. I frowned, as it was much too cold in the corridor for her and she'd been coughing since yesterday afternoon. Her elder sisters, Elizabeth and Anna, were there beside her, but I avoided their eyes. They were too young; how could they understand?

Nobody knew yet whether I was the one they had to fear. I searched the crowd for young Petrushka, Peter's grandson, and the princes Dolgoruki, his followers, but they were nowhere to be seen. I bit my lip. Where were they—busy hatching plans to seize the throne? I had to lay hands on them as soon as possible. I snapped my fingers and the closest guard leaped to attention.

"Send for the privy council—Count Tolstoy, Baron Ostermann, and Pavel Jagushinsky. Look sharp, the tsar wants to see them," I ordered, making sure that my last words were heard the entire length of the corridor.

Menshikov pulled me back into the room and closed the door.

"Come," I said curtly. "We'll go next door, to the little library." Menshikov picked up his embroidered coat of green brocade from the chair in which he had kept watch at Peter's bedside for the last days and weeks. A peasant household could easily have lived for two whole years on just one of the silver threads woven in its cloth. His ivory-handled walking stick he clamped underneath his armpit. At the hidden door that led to Peter's small library I turned to the doctors. "Blumentrost. You are not allowed to leave this room and you are to summon no one."

"But . . ." he began.

I raised my hand. "It cannot become known that the tsar has passed away. Not yet."

Peter would have approved of the tone.

"As you command." Blumentrost bowed.

"Good. You shall be paid later today. The same goes for your colleagues."

Menshikov swayed a little. Was it tiredness that made him unsteady on his feet, or fear?

I walked ahead of him into the cozy little library. Menshikov followed, but only after seizing the tall carafe of Burgundy he had been drinking from, as well as two Venetian goblets. "This is not a moment to be either sober or stingy," he said with a lopsided smile before kicking the door shut like a common innkeeper. The fire had burned down in the grate, but the wood-paneled walls retained its heat. The colorful silk rugs we had brought from our Persian campaign—easily adding a dozen carts to our train—brimmed with all the flowers and birds of God's creation in their full splendor. The plain chairs standing by the desk, the fireplace, and near the shelves had been made by Peter himself. Sometimes I would hear him lathing and hammering far beyond midnight. Carpentry drove out his demons and gave him his best ideas, he used to say. His ministers feared nothing so much as a night Peter spent doing carpentry. He would fall asleep, exhausted, across his workbench. Only Menshikov was strong enough to hoist the tsar onto his shoulders and carry him to bed. If I was not there waiting for him, Peter would use the belly of a young chamberlain as his pillow. He always needed skin against his skin to keep his memories at bay.

The high windows were draped with lined curtains that he had bought as a young man on his visit to Holland, long before the Great Northern War, those two decades of struggle for survival and supremacy against the Swedes. The shelves sagged beneath the weight of the books, which I was told were travelogues, seafaring tales, war histories, biographies of rulers and books on how to rule, and religious works. He had leafed through each and every one of them time and time again. It was a world where I could never follow him. Scrolls still lay open on his desk or were piled up in heaps in corners. Some books were printed and bound in thick pigskin; others were written by hand in monasteries. On the mantelpiece stood a model of the *Natalya,* Peter's proud frigate, and above it hung a painting of my son, Peter Petrovich. It was painted months before the death that broke our hearts. I had avoided this room for years because of it; the painting was too real, as if at any moment my son would throw me the red leather ball he held in his hands. His blond curls tumbled onto a white lace shirt; his smile hinted at a row of little teeth. I would have given my life to have him here, now, and declare him tsar of all the Russias. Still a child, certainly. But a son of our blood, Peter, mine and yours. A dynasty. Isn't that what every ruler wants? Now there are only daughters left, and a dreaded grandson, little Petrushka.

The thought of Petrushka took my breath away. At his birth Peter had cradled him in his arms and turned his back on the unhappy mother. Poor Sophie Charlotte. She had been like a nervous thoroughbred, and like a horse her father had sold her to Russia. Where was her young son now? In the Dolgoruki Palace? In the barracks? Outside the door? Petrushka was only twelve years old and Peter hadn't even granted him the title of tsarevich, but I feared him more than the Devil.

In the library, Menshikov said: "You did well, calling for the council and getting rid of Feofan, the old fool."

I turned to look at him. "We're the fools. I hope he keeps his word."

"What word did he give you?" he asked, astonished.

"You see! You only hear what is spoken, but so much more than that is said." I seized him by the shirt collar and hissed: "We're both in the same boat. God have mercy on you for every second you waste right now. I saw neither Petrushka nor his charming friends in the corridor, did you? And why is the rightful heir of the Russian empire not here at his grandfather's deathbed, where he belongs?"

Beads of sweat appeared on Menshikov's forehead.

"Because he's with the troops at the imperial barracks, where soon they'll hoist him on their shoulders and give him three cheers as soon as they find out the tsar is dead. What will happen to us then? Will Petrushka remember the people who signed Alexey's judgment, albeit just with a cross next to their name, as they couldn't write?"

I let go of him. Menshikov filled his goblet and took a large slug of wine, his hands trembling, his strong fingers weighted with several heavy rings. His natural wiliness was blunted by the fatigue of the wake in Peter's chamber, but I was not finished with him. "Siberia will be too good for us in their eyes. The Dolgorukis will feed the four winds with our ashes. No one but us knows that the tsar is dead," I whispered. "Our secret buys us time." Time that might save us. We couldn't keep the tsar's death secret for too long; it would be out by morning, when a leaden dawn broke over Peter's city.

Menshikov, the man who had turned so many battles in his favor, whose neck had slipped so many times from even the most perilous of nooses, seemed dazed. My dread was contagious. He sat heavily in one of the cozier armchairs, which Peter had brought from Versailles, and stretched out his still-shapely legs. A marvel that the dainty piece of furniture was able to bear his weight! He took a few sips and then turned the colored glass this way and that in front of the fire. The flames warmed the goblet's smooth, tinted surface; it looked as if it were filled with blood. I sat down opposite him. Tonight was no time for drinking games.

Menshikov raised his goblet to me in jest. "To you, Catherine Alex-eyevna. It was well worth gifting you to the tsar, my lady. To you, my greatest loss. To you, my greatest gain." Suddenly he laughed, laughed so much that his wig slipped down over his eyes, his laugh like the sound of wolves in winter: high and scornful. He pulled the wig off and flung it away. I calmly took his insolence, while Peter would have had him flogged for it. Menshikov was suffering like a dog: it was his lord and love, too, who had died. What was in store for him now? His suffering made him unpredictable. I needed him now; desperately. Him, the privy council, and the troops. The tsar's last will and testament was wedged up my sleeve. Menshikov's face was red and bloated under the shaggy, still dark blond mop of hair. He stopped laughing and looked at me uncertainly over the rim of his glass.

"Here we are. What an extraordinary life you've lived, my lady. Divine will is the only explanation."

I nodded. That's what they say about me at the courts of Europe. My background is the joke that always puts envoys in a good mood. But for Peter, whatever he willed at any given time was normal and so nothing was extraordinary any longer.

Suddenly, Menshikov's glass slipped from his fingers, his chin dropped onto his chest, and the wine spilled, leaving a large red stain on his white lace shirt and blue waistcoat. The last weeks, days, and hours caught up with him and a moment later, he was snoring and hung as limp as a rag doll in the chair. I could grant him some rest before Tolstoy and the privy council arrived. Then he would be carried back to his palace to sleep off his stupor. Menshikov already held the Order of Saint Andrew, as well as far more serfs and titles than I could grant him. There was nothing left to promise him. He had to stay of his own accord: nothing binds people more powerfully than the fear for survival, Catherine, I could hear Peter say.

I walked over to the window, which looked over the inner courtyard. The golden icons sewn to the hem of my dress tinkled with each step. When little Princess Wilhelmine of Prussia back in Berlin saw the way I dressed, she had laughed out loud: "The empress of Russia looks like a minstrel's wife!"

I pushed aside the heavy curtain that kept the inky chill of a Saint Petersburg winter night—our city, Peter, our dream!—at bay. Alexander

Nevsky Prospect and the Neva were shrouded in a darkness that now held you forever in its arms, a darkness that hid the breathtaking beauty of what you created: the icy green shade of the river's waves blending to perfection with the rainbow hues of the flat façades of both palaces and houses, which were such a novelty twenty years ago. This city that you conjured out of the swampy ground, by force of your sheer, incredible will and the suffering of hundreds of thousands of your people, nobles and serfs alike. The bones of the forced laborers lie buried in the marshy earth as its foundations. Men, women, children, nameless, faceless; who remembers them in the light of such magnificence? If there was a surfeit of anything in Russia, it was human life. The morning would break wan and cool; then, later, the palace's bright, even façade would reflect the day's pale fire. You lured the light here, Peter, and gave it a home. What happens now? Help me.

Candlelight moved behind the windows of the fine, tall houses, gliding through rooms and corridors, as if borne on ghostly hands. In the courtyard a sentry stood hunched over his bayonet, when with a clatter of hooves—embers flying off the hard cobblestones—a rider dashed out through the gate. My fingers clenched around the catch of the window. Had Blumentrost obeyed my order? Or had the rider left to confirm the unthinkable? What would happen now? *Volya*—great, unimaginable freedom—or exile and death?

My mouth was dry with fear: a feeling that knots the stomach, turns sweat cold and bitter, and opens the bowels. I hadn't felt it since— stop! I mustn't think about these things now. I could only focus on one thing at a time, whereas Peter, like an acrobat, would juggle ten ideas and plans.

Menshikov was mumbling in his sleep. If only Tolstoy and the privy council would come. The whole city seemed to be lying in wait. I bit my fingernails until I tasted blood.

I sat down again close to the fire and took off my slippers, stiff with embroidery and jewels. The warmth of the fire made my skin prickle. February was one of the coldest months in Saint Petersburg. Perhaps I should order some mulled wine and pretzels instead of the Burgundy; that always gave me a swift boost. Was Peter warm enough in the room next door? He couldn't stand the cold and we were always freezing on the battlefield. Nothing is frostier than the morning after a battle. I could only keep him warm at night, when he struck camp in the folds of my flesh.

People asleep look either ridiculous or touching. Menshikov, snoring open-mouthed, was the latter. I drew Peter's last will from my sleeve and the scroll lay in my lap, so close to the flames. Its letters blurred as my tears came: real, heartfelt tears, despite the sense of relief. I still had a long day and longer weeks ahead of me and I would need many tears. The people, and the court, would want to see a grief-stricken widow with tousled hair, scratched cheeks, a broken voice, and swollen eyes. Only my show of love and grief could make the unthinkable acceptable, render my tears more powerful than any bloodline. So I may as well start weeping now. The tears weren't hard to summon: in a few hours I might be either dead, or wishing I was dead, or I'd be the most powerful woman in all the Russias.

1

My life began with a crime. Of course I don't mean the moment of my birth, nor my early years. It's better to know nothing of life as a serf, a "soul," than to know but a little. The German souls—*nemtsy*, property of the Russian church—were more wretched than you can ever imagine. The godforsaken place in which I grew up is lost in the vast plains of Livonia: a village, and country, that no longer exist. Do its *izby*—the shabby huts—still stand? I neither know nor care. When I was young, though, the *izby* that lined the red earth of the village street in rows, like beads on a monk's rosary, were my world. We used the same word for both: *mir*. Ours looked just like many other small villages in Swedish Livonia, one of the Baltic provinces under the rule of Stockholm, where Poles, Latvians, Russians, Swedes, and Germans mingled and lived together more or less peacefully—in those days.

Throughout the year, the road through the village held our lives together like the belt on a loose *sarafan*, the wide gowns we wore. After the spring thaw, or the first heavy rains of autumn, we would wade knee-deep in ox-blood-colored slush from our *izba* to the fields and down to the Dvina river. In summer, it turned into clouds of red dust that ate their way into the cracked skin of our heels. Then, in winter, we would sink up to our thighs in snow with every step, or slide home on ice as slick as a mirror. Chickens and pigs roamed the streets, filth clinging to their feathers and bristles. Children with matted, lice-infested hair played there before they came of working age, when the boys stood in the fields, chasing away the wild birds with rattles, stones, and sticks; the girls worked the monastery's looms, their little fingers making the finest fabrics. I myself helped in the kitchens, since I was nine years old. From time to time a loaded cart, pulled by horses with long manes and heavy hooves, would rumble through the village to unload goods at the monastery and take other wares to market. Apart from that, very little happened.

One day in April, shortly before Easter—the year 1699, according to the new calendar the tsar had ordered his subjects to use—my younger sister, Christina, and I were walking down this road, heading down through the fields toward the river. The pure air was scented with the greatest wonder of our Baltic lands: the *ottepel,* the thaw. Christina was dancing: she spun round in circles, clapping her hands, her relief at the end of the darkness and cold of the winter palpable. I clumsily tried to catch her without dropping the bundle of washing I was carrying, but she dodged away.

Through winter, life in the *mir* was on hold, like a bear's shallow breathing as he lives off the fat beneath his fur until spring. In the long season, the leaden light dazed our minds; we sank into a listless gloom, soaked with *kvass*. No one could afford vodka, and the bitter, yeasty drink fermented from old bread was just as intoxicating. We lived on grains—oats, rye, barley, wheat, and spelt, which we baked into unleavened flatbreads or made into pastry on feast days, rolling it thin and thinner before filling it with pickled vegetables and mushrooms. Our *kasha,* the gruel, was sweetened with honey and dried berries, or salted with bacon rinds and cabbage; the cabbage of which we prepared vast amounts every autumn, chopping, salting, and pulping it, before we would eat it every day. Every winter I thought I'd be sick if I had to eat sauerkraut one more time, but we also owed our lives to it. It helped us withstand a cold that would freeze the phlegm in your throat before you could hawk it up.

Just as the snow and frost were becoming unbearable, they would slowly fade away. First, it might stay light for a moment longer, the time it takes a rooster to crow, or the twigs straightened with the lighter load of the snow. Then, at night, we woke to the deafening crack of the ice breaking on the Dvina, the water spurting up, free, wild, and tearing huge slabs of ice downstream. Nothing could withstand its power; even the smallest brooks would swell and burst their banks, and the strong, scaly fish of the Dvina leaped into our nets of their own accord. After a brief, scented spring, feverish summer months followed and our world was drunk with fertility and vigor. Leaves on the trees were thick and succulent, butterflies reeled through the air, bees were drowsy on nectar, their legs heavy with pollen, and yet too much in a hurry to linger on any one blossom. No one slept through the white nights; even the birds sang throughout, not wanting to miss any of the fun.

* * *

"Do you think there's still ice on the river, Marta?" asked Christina anxiously, calling me by the name I was known by back then. How many times had she asked me this since we'd left the house? The spring fair was tomorrow and just like her I longed to scrub the stench of smoke, food, and the dull winter months off our skins for what was the highlight of the year. There would be amazing sights, delicious foods of which we might afford some, and all the people from the neighboring *mir,* as well as the odd handsome stranger, a thought that was never far from Christina's mind. "Shall we race each other?" she asked, giggling. Before I could answer, she set off, but I tripped her up and just managed to catch her before she stumbled and fell. She shrieked and clung to me like a boy riding a bull at the fairground, pummeling me with her fists; I lost my balance and we fell onto the embankment, where primroses and rock cress were already blooming. The sharp young grass tickled my bare arms and legs as I struggled to my feet. Oh, wonderful—the clothes were strewn all over the dusty road. Now we really had good reason to wash them. At least we could work by the river: only a few weeks ago, I'd had to smash the ice on the tub behind the *izba* with a club and push the icy lumps aside as I scrubbed. My hands had frozen blue with cold, and chilblains are painful and slow to heal.

"Come on, I'll help you," said Christina, glancing toward the village. We were out of sight of the *izba.*

"You don't need to help me," I said, though the laundry was heavy on my arm.

"Don't be silly. The quicker we wash it all, the sooner we can bathe." She took half the washing from the crook of my arm. We didn't usually split the chores, because Christina was the daughter of Tanya, my father's wife. I'd been born to him nine months after the summer solstice to a girl in the neighboring village. He was already engaged to Tanya when my mother fell pregnant and he was not forced to marry her: the monks had the final say in such matters, and they, of course, preferred to marry my father to one of their girls. When my mother died giving birth to me, Tanya took me in. She had little choice: my mother's family had stood on the threshold of the *izba* and held my bundle of life toward her. They would have left me on the edge of the forest as fodder for the wolves if she had refused. Tanya didn't really treat me badly, all things considered. We all had to work hard, and I got my share of our provisions, such as they were. But she was often spiteful, pulling my hair and pinching my arm over the slightest mistake. "You've got bad blood. Your mother would spread her legs for anyone. Who knows where you really come from?" she'd say if she was feeling malicious. "Look at you, with your green, slanted eyes and your hair as black as a raven's wing. You'd better watch your step." If my father heard her, he wouldn't say anything, but just look even sadder than usual, his back hunched from working in the monastery fields. He could only laugh his toothless chuckle when he'd had a few mugs of *kvass*, which brought a dull light to his sunken eyes.

Before we walked on, Christina took my arm and turned me toward the sun. "One, two, and three—who can look at the sun the longest?" she said breathlessly. "Do it. Even if it scorches your eyelids! Between the spots that dance in front of your eyes you'll see the man you're going to marry."

How eager we were to know him then: at midnight, we'd light three precious candles around a bowl of water and surround them with a circle of coals; we'd stare and stare, but the surface of the water never reflected any faces but our own. No midsummer ever went by without us plucking seven types of wildflower and placing the spray beneath our pillows to lure our future husbands to our dreams. I felt the afternoon sun warm on my face and spots danced senselessly golden on the inside of my eyelids, so I kissed Christina on the cheek. "Let's go," I said, longing for the warm rocks on the bank. "I want to dry off when we finish bathing."

In the fields, souls were bent double at their work and I spotted my father among them. Only part of the land was cultivated in spring, for the first harvest. In summer, turnips, beets, and cabbage were planted in the second part: all crops that could be harvested even in winter, when the earth was frozen solid. The last third of the ground lay fallow until the following year. The time we had to make provision for the rest of the year was short, and a few squandered days could mean famine. In August my father might easily spend eighteen hours in the fields. No, we didn't love the earth that fed us: she was a merciless mistress, punishing us for the slightest mistake. Six days of the week belonged to the monastery, the seventh to us. God gave no day of rest for us souls. The monks walked back and forth between the workers in their long, dark robes, keeping a sharp eye on their property, both the land as well as the people working it.

"What do you think is underneath a monk's robes?" Christina asked me now, saucily.

I shrugged. "Can't be much, or you'd see it through the cloth."

"Especially when they see you," she answered.

Her words reminded me of Tanya's insults. "What do you mean by that?" I asked tersely.

"Aren't you meant to be older than me, Marta? Don't say you haven't noticed the way men look at you. They'll all want to dance with you at the fair and no one will pay me any attention."

"Nonsense! You look like an angel. An angel in dire need of a bath. Come on!"

Down by the river we settled at our shallow spot from the previous year. A little path wound down through a birch grove and some low bushes. Early buds were on all the twigs; wild iris and bedstraw would bloom here soon. Down on the riverbank I sorted the laundry, putting all the men's good linen shirts and trousers on one side and the *sarafans* and linen blouses we women wore on feast days on the other. We had spent some of the long winter evenings embroidering colorful, floral motifs on the flat collars and tucks; the patterns were like a secret language and passed on within families and villages. Perhaps we could swap some of Father's woodcarvings—small pipes and cups—for new thread at the fair tomorrow? I wound my hair into a loose knot, so it wouldn't dangle in the dirty foam, and folded my faded headscarf to shield me from the sun. Then I knotted the hem of my *sarafan*, even though it was quilted and lined against the cold, and tugged at the long ribbons threaded through the seams of the sleeves of my blouse, gathering the cloth into countless pleats. From afar I must have looked like a cloud on long, bare legs.

"Let's begin." I reached out for the first linen and Christina handed me the precious bar of soap. I dipped the washboard in the clear water and painstakingly rubbed the soap over its sharp ribs until they were thickly coated with a slippery layer. Making soap was hard work; your whole body ached afterward. Mostly Tanya gave me this task in autumn, when the monks had been slaughtering to pickle, smoke, and salt meat for the winter larder and had bones to spare, or in spring, using ashes gathered throughout the winter. All the women would help mix rainwater and ash with pig or cow fat and the ground bones of animals to make a caustic lye, which they boiled for hours in great cauldrons. The gray, slimy brew—its big, hot bubbles bursting on the surface with a loud splash—thickened but slowly from one hour to the next. We had to stir it constantly until it felt as if your arms were about to fall off. In the evening we poured the goo into wooden molds. If we could afford to add salt to it, we ended up with a solid lump of soap. But mostly we needed the salt for the animals, or to pickle meat and cabbage for the winter: the soap remained more of a slime that you added to the washing water.

The river glittered and Christina and I worked fast: the prospect of bathing spurred us on as we dipped the clothes in the water, scrubbed them hard, beat them on the flat stones—"Imagine it's the abbot," I said, goading Christina to beat them harder. She threw her head back and laughed, her blond hair slipping out of her bun. We wrung them out, and hung them to dry on low-hanging branches along the shore. "On your marks, get set, go!" Christina shouted suddenly, as I was still straightening and smoothing the last of the shirts. She undid the lacing of her dress, pulling the simple *sarafan* and rough tunic over her head as she ran, and then she stood naked in the spring sunshine. How different she looked from me. Christina's skin was as pale as skimmed milk, her body slim, with narrow hips and high, budding breasts that looked as if they fit just so in the hollow of her hand. Her nipples were like little raspberries. She was already able to bear a child: her blood had started to flow the previous year. I, on the other hand—well, Tanya was probably right about me looking like my mother. My hair was thick and black and my skin was the color of wild honey—or dried snot, as Tanya used to say. My hips were wide, my legs long and strong, and my bosom large and firm.

Christina was splashing about in the shallow stream close to the bank. Her head bobbed up and down between the rocks where water gathered in pools. The sand of the riverbed shone white between her feet when she rose. "Come on, what are you waiting for?" She laughed, then dove headfirst into the waves, allowing the current to sweep her off into the deep. I undressed as fast as I could, loosened my hair, and hurried after her. We splashed and dived and—deliciously forbidden!— scrubbed our bodies with the precious soap. I opened my eyes underwater, grabbed at water snails, broke off sharp reeds from the riverbank trying to spear an eel, and tweaked Christina's toes, pretending to be a fish—anything to have a laugh after the dreary winter months! The water was still icy and when I was the first to get out, goose bumps instantly rose on my skin. I shook my hair and watched the flying drops sparkle in the sun before I wound it into a bun.

"Better than the bathhouse," gurgled Christina, still drifting in the shallows. "At least you don't get whipped with twigs till you're all sore and almost bleeding."

"Oh, I can see to that," I said, snapping a twig off a bush. Christina squealed and had just ducked underwater when I heard sounds from the road: horses neighing, stones crunching under cart wheels, men's voices. "Stay in the water," I ordered Christina, and looked up at the road. Three riders encircled a cart decked with pale canvas while the man on the coach box was still holding the reins. In spite of the distance I felt him scrutinizing me, and I desperately wished I could reach my *sarafan*.

"Who is it?" Christina whispered, drifting back and forth in the shallow water.

"Shh! I don't know! Stay where you are!"

To my alarm I saw the man get down from the coach box and throw the reins to one of the other riders. I counted three armed men while he turned down the little path toward our riverbank. I ran to the bush where my clean blouse was drying. It was still damp, but I slipped it on nonetheless. I had just managed to pull it down over my thighs when the man stood before me. He must have been the same age as my father, but he had certainly never worked as hard in his life. His long Russian coat had a dark fur collar and his breeches were cut from soft leather and held by a richly embroidered belt. His high boots were spattered with mud and dirt. I shielded my eyes with my hand. Sweat glistened on his forehead, although his face was shaded by a flat beaver fur hat.

He had a full beard, as all Russians did in those days. He looked me up and down, judging me, then took off his gloves. He wore several rings with bright stones on his short, thick fingers. I'd never seen anything like it: not even the abbot wore this much jewelry. I took a step back yet, to my dread, he followed.

"Can you tell me the way to the monastery, girl?" he asked in harsh German. He still had all his teeth, but his gums were stained dark red from chewing tobacco, and he smelled of sweat from the long ride. It would have been rude of me to make a face, and an offense to a travel-ing stranger, so I stood there uneasily while he looked me up and down. I sensed that the outline of my breasts was visible beneath the thin, wet linen. Feeling my hair slipping its knot, I instinctively reached up to tighten it, and the blouse slipped, baring my shoulder.

His tongue darted across his lips, which made me think of the snake my brother Fyodor and I had spotted the previous summer in the un-dergrowth of our vegetable patch. It was pale green and we could almost see its intestines shining dark beneath the skin. It had slithered toward us, slowly at first. Although he was smaller than me, Fyodor pushed me behind him. The snake looked poisonous, and deadly, but my brother bent down and picked up a heavy stone. At the very moment when the snake shot forward, jaw agape, he smashed its head in. The nerves in the reptile's dead body made it go on twitching and wriggling.

The man took another step toward me, and from the water Chris-tina screamed: "Marta, watch out!"

He turned his head and I bent to grab a mossy stone. I may have been a virgin, but I knew all too well what he wanted. We had a cock and hens in the backyard, after all, and my father had to hold the mares for the stallions in the monastery stables. Besides, in the *izby,* where families all slept together on the flat oven, bodies and breaths mingling, there was little room for secrets. I knew what he wanted and I wasn't going to let him have it.

"The monastery's straight ahead, just down the road. You'll be there soon if you hurry!" I said curtly, even though my shaking voice gave me away.

He didn't respond, but took another step toward me. "Your eyes are the same color as the river. What else is there to discover about you?" he asked. There was little more than a breath separating us.

I stood firm and hissed, "If you come any closer, I'll smash your skull in and bake a pie of your brain. Get back to your coach and go to the damned monks." I weighed the stone threateningly in my hand. Out of the corner of my eye I saw his three companions dismounting, shaking out their limbs after the long ride and allowing their horses to graze. I bit my lip. One skull I could smash, but we didn't stand a chance against four men. My heart pounded in my breast as I tried not to give in to the fear of what might happen. The first of the men seemed to head down the path. The stranger smirked, sure of an easy victory. Christina sobbed in the water and the sound made me furious: an anger laced with strength and courage. "Get out of here, Russian!" I snarled at him, and he hesitated; then, all of a sudden, he held up his hand, stopping the other man in his tracks.

"By God, girl, you amuse me. We'll see each other again, and then you'll be kinder to me." He stretched out his hand as if to touch my hair. Christina screamed. I spat at his feet. His face grew hard. "Just you wait," he threatened. "Marta, eh? That's what she called you, the little minx in the water?"

I was mute with fear as he turned and walked back up the embankment. Only when he had urged on his horses with a flick of his whip, and the clopping of hooves and the clattering of wheels had died away, did I breathe and let the stone slip from my sweaty, sticky fingers. My knees buckled and I fell onto the rough, gray sand, shivering. Christina waded out of the water; she wrapped her arms around me and we held each other tight, until I was only shaking with cold and not fear anymore. She stroked my hair and whispered: "Marta, you're so brave. I'd never have dared to threaten him with a silly little stone." I glanced down at the stone at my feet. It really did look silly and little.

"Do you think we'll see him again?" she asked, while I struggled to my feet. I bit my lip in worry. He'd asked the way to the monastery to which all of us belonged—our *izba*, our land, the shirt on my back, we ourselves.

I chased the thought away. "Nonsense," I said, hoping I sounded surer than I felt. "We'll never see that tub of lard again. Let's hope he falls off his coach box and breaks his neck." I tried to laugh, but couldn't. Christina didn't look convinced either. Clouds covered the sun, veiling the daylight with the first blue of dusk. I was shivering in my damp shirt, which was covered in dirt. What a nuisance: I would have to wash it again tomorrow, early in the morning before the feast. I brushed sand and pebbles off my shins. "Let's go." Silently, we slipped into our old clothes and gathered up the still damp washing to hang it over the flat oven at home to dry, though it would make the air in the hut even more humid and worsen Fyodor's cough.

"Let's not tell anyone about this, shall we?" I asked Christina, hoping I could pretend the meeting by the river had never happened. But in my heart I knew this wouldn't be the end of it. Nothing in this world happens without a reason. That afternoon my life changed course, like the weathervane on the monastery roof spinning in the first blast of a sudden storm.

2

It rained the night before the fair. The monks didn't make *nemtsy* attend their church on Sunday like the other souls: I had been baptized Catholic but to me faith was just mumbled prayers and a constant crossing of yourself with three fingers. On the day of our death, this—or so we hoped—was supposed to gain us entry to the freeborn Heaven.

As we walked to the fairground by the monastery, our feet sank into the warm mud of the road, a soft sucking sound accompanying each step. We carried our sandals of wood and raffia in our hands so as not to ruin them. My youngest sister, Maggie, who was only four, could barely keep up with us, so I took her hand and slowed to match her scuttle. The morning had been damp, but now the afternoon was sunny, the sky big and blue. At the village green, men were still leveling the ground for the evening's dancing, and women were stretching ropes between high birch trees for children to swing on. Others were standing around in groups in their long, bright dresses, laughing, talking, singing songs, and clapping along. The fairground was already a lively hubbub, as people from all over the province had come for the market. A bear was tethered to a post outside the first tent I passed, his pelt dirty and disheveled, and the teeth in his jaws were filed down, as well as his claws. Still, better to keep away from the captive animals: their angry, unpredictable natures were merely slumbering, unbroken by their chains. In winter, the traveling merchants who kept them would freeze to death by the roadside; the bears would rip their chains from the dead men's hands, driven by hunger to the nearest houses and farms. So Maggie and I gave Master Bruin a wide berth as he uselessly whetted his claws on his post. Maggie glanced round quickly for her mother, but Tanya was at a stall, looking at necklaces and bracelets. Putting her finger to her lips, the little girl curiously lifted the flap of a tent, its cloth mended and darned with colorful patches.

"Maggie . . ." I was about to tell her off when she gasped and shrank back in dread. I took her place and peered inside: a gruesome creature with two heads, four arms, and two legs was tied up in the middle of the tent. I suppressed a cry as one head turned to look at us, while the other hung helplessly to one side. Saliva dribbled from one slack mouth, while something like a smile spread across the other sad, slightly crooked face. A hand stirred; fingers reached out to me. I counted them: there were six! I shrank back. It was horrid, but I couldn't take my eyes off it. Maggie squeezed in again beside me. At that moment a voice boomed behind us: "Aha, young ladies, so curious already about my Tent of Wonders?"

We were so startled, we almost tumbled right into the tent. Behind us, a man held on to a dwarf by a short chain wrapped around his neck. On his other side stood a girl in a dress of bright green and blue patches with a rope about her waist; her hair was wrapped in a torn fishing net. I had not seen makeup before and she looked frightful to me: her face seemed to have been pressed in lumpy flour, two garish red patches were painted on her cheeks, and she had outlined her eyes and eyebrows with a lump of coal.

The man bowed. "I am Master Lampert, bringing the wonders of the world right here to your sorry little village."

I frowned: only we were allowed to badmouth the *mir*, not some random stranger! Master Lampert now kicked the dwarf in the side, whereupon he did a somersault and the bells and dull coins on his jacket clinked cheerfully. "No one has dwarves, mermaids, and ghastly creatures like mine. Come to my show this evening, ladies!"

Ladies! Maggie and I giggled. No one had ever called us that. Master Lampert ignored our foolishness and carried on. "There's a fun competition planned, throwing rotten fruit at my monster. Who hits it bang smack in the face, wins." He pointed at the miserable being in the middle of the tent. Timidly, I glanced at it again. Both its heads were hanging once more, and its arms dangled uselessly. The "mermaid"—

whatever that was supposed to mean—smiled at me, revealing black gaps in her teeth. Dear God, I was glad when at that very moment an angry Tanya dragged Maggie and me out into the open.

"What are you doing loitering with the traveling folk? Are you one of them?" she snapped. "Come, Christina and I are watching the fire-eater." In spite of the harshness of her tone, she pressed a few honey-roasted nuts into my hand. God knows how she'd smuggled the money for them past Father, who'd surely feel we'd deprived him of a drink or a dose of chewing tobacco. This was a feast day, no mistake. A troupe of musicians came down toward us along the muddy paths between tents and stalls, and the jolly noise of drums, flutes, and bells mercifully swallowed Tanya's scolding. I fed a few nuts to Maggie and followed Tanya and Christina to the stalls with the fire-eaters, jugglers, and a magician in the midst of plucking a red ball from a farmer's grubby ear. The crowd cheered and clapped furiously. Other men pressed forward, wanting to have balls conjured from their ears, too. Christina pointed to the fire-eater "Have you seen those muscles? He eats fire all right," she said, giggling. I sighed inwardly. If the monks didn't find a husband for her from among the serfs in the village soon, we would be the ones leaving a little bundle on the edge of the forest. I strolled on a few paces to a juggler with a long white beard and a bare chest weathered by the sun. A vermilion dot was painted on his forehead, heavy rings made long loops of his earlobe, and his white hair was slicked back and plaited: still, his eyes shone bright and clear. He must have seen so many things in his life! I, on the other hand, would always stay here in this village. The crowd fell silent as he added a fourth and fifth club to the three he already held and said in broken German: "Two clubs— for bunglers! Three clubs—for fools! Four clubs—is good! Five clubs— for masters!" Christina squeezed in beside me and Maggie's little hand snuck into mine. Tanya joined us, too. The clubs flew straight up in the air, high and fast, their wood shimmering in the sun. As he juggled, the old man got his helper to throw him a sixth club, and a seventh. I gasped and then watched breathlessly; the colorful musicians marched noisily past again. When the juggler took off his cap to ask for money, we walked on, past the barber-surgeon, where people with all sorts of aches and pains queued up. I heard a man's horrified gurgle as the barber pulled the wrong tooth. There was cheering from the puppeteer's stall:

I headed toward it. The play was in full swing, and we sat down on the grass with the other onlookers. Surely we could watch for a little while without having to pay? It seemed to be set in a fortress. One puppet wore a glittering round cap, and had the Russian double-headed eagle embroidered on its jerkin. That must be the young Russian tsar. A soldier puppet stepped out in front of the tsar puppet and the man beside me burst into laughter.

"What's it about? Is that the tsar?" I whispered.

He nodded. "Yes. Two years ago, Tsar Peter wanted to visit the fortress in Riga. He's hardly ever in Moscow, did you know that?" I shrugged, and he carried on. "But the Swedes wouldn't let him. An ordinary soldier barred the way to the tsar of all the Russias, and the king of Sweden"— here he pointed to a third puppet, sitting on a stool—"refused to punish the man. The tsar is said to still be furious. He's sworn revenge on all Swedes." He blew his nose into his fingers. The tsar puppet was having a temper tantrum, stamping wildly on its crown. I laughed loudly along with the others, and was feeding Maggie the last of the sweetened nuts when a shadow fell across me, blocking out the light. A voice said, in Russian, "That's the girl." I looked up. It was the man from the river.

3

~~~

S urrounded by his three helpers and a group of monks, he looked
even wealthier today, amidst us souls, peasants, idlers, and scoundrels. His low-slung belt was richly embroidered and despite the warm
spring sunshine, the wide collar of his dark green velvet coat was again
trimmed with fur. Tanya jumped up, dragging me to my feet along
with her.

One of the monks pointed to me. "Tanya, is that your daughter?"

"No, *otets*." We addressed everyone who had power over us as "father." "Marta is my husband's daughter. But I've raised her. Or tried to,
anyway," she added bitterly. Her grip on my wrist was painful. "Has she
done something wrong?"

The Russian stroked his beard and smiled at me. I couldn't see his
eyes; they were shaded by his flat hat made of beaver fur. The monk
seized me by the chin. He stank of pickled onions and vestments that
had been too long in the wearing. I wrinkled my nose. Couldn't priests
wash themselves, or at the very least change their underwear? The
monk stared at me brazenly before releasing me. He turned to Tanya.
"Go home. We'll come to your *izba* early this evening."

"But it's the dance this evening," Christina cried out. "I've been
looking forward to it all winter." All of us had been looking forward to
it all winter.

The monk gave Tanya a searching look. She shrugged, her face
now plain. It was the serfs' only and oldest weapon against our masters,
whose power inevitably made them our enemies. We had to bear their

constant meddling, be it in matters of family or work. How often were orders frustrated by the mental void in which we took refuge?

On the way home Christina sulked and Tanya's face was pinched with anger. She spat noisily, and repeatedly, as she walked. When I tried to tell her what had happened beside the river, she just said, "Shut your mouth. I knew it—all someone like you does is make trouble for us!" Maggie cried, and fell over three times on the short walk home. After the third time, I picked her up and carried her on my hip, her warm little body pressed close to mine. Already I sensed it was the last time I would hold her like this.

I was almost relieved when at last, toward evening, there was a knock at the door of our hut. The silence in the *mir* was eerie, as everything that was able to walk was at the fair. Waiting for the unknown is a punishment in itself. My father had asked what had happened, but all he learned was that the monks wanted to come and see me. He sighed, got up from the oven, which took up the whole corner of the *izba,* and poured himself more *kvass* in a shallow bowl. Then he sat on the bench in the "red" corner of the hut—meaning the good, clean corner—dusting the icon of Saint Nicholas that was painted in cheap, earthen colors on a rough, flat wooden board. Then he looked at the plain wooden cross beside it and frowned, as if thinking for a moment. In the end he shrugged his shoulders and left them both hanging there, side by side. My father patted the bench next to him, and I sat down.

"What have you been up to, Marta, hmm? It's all right, you can tell me." To my surprise, he was smiling.

I shrugged. "Nothing special. A Russian who's staying with the monks wanted to grope me by the river yesterday. So I threatened to smash his skull in."

My father laughed so hard he began to cough. The smoke from the flat oven that filled our hut had made him sick a long time ago. "You call that nothing special, eh? Good," he wheezed, when he was able to breathe again. Tanya eyed me coldly. Nothing more was said, until they came.

* * *

The men pushed the door open themselves. As they stepped over the raised threshold my father's face suddenly emptied, just as Tanya's had done earlier. He rose briefly, crossed himself with three fingers in the Russian manner, and then sat down again. The Russian covered his nose with his elbow for a moment—coming in from the outside, the stench of six people living together in a small space hit him full-on. He looked around in disgust at the *izba,* whose four walls held our pitiful life together. Boiled moss was wedged between beams to keep cockroaches away. His gaze took in the modest heaps of clothes and blankets we left folded on the floor. Our six coarsely carved wooden bowls were stacked in the corner, beside the vat of water. We relieved ourselves in a second bucket, which we emptied onto the street. The corners of his mouth twitched, then he wiped his muddy heel on the straw that covered the floor of our *izba.* I hated him for this haughtiness. This, after all, was my home.

"*Brat,*" said the monk to my father. Brother.

My father murmured, "Welcome, *otets.*"

The monk bowed to our icon and crossed himself. "Good that you keep your icon clean."

My father smiled and the monk continued: "We have a guest at the monastery. Vassily Gregorovich Petrov, a merchant from Walk. He needs a maidservant and has been so gracious as to think of your family."

Gracious! I almost choked with fury, but Tanya leaped up and pushed Christina forward. She curtsied clumsily to Vassily and licked her lips. "My lord. Big houses need servants. I'm telling you, my lord, no one works as hard, no one is as skillful as my Christina. Look at her, my lord, isn't she an angel?" She tugged at Christina's plait until her blond hair fell loose over her shoulders. "Her delicate skin, and such beautiful teeth!"

She forced open Christina's slender jaw to reveal her teeth, like traders did at the cattle market in spring! It was revolting; even the monk raised his eyebrows. My father turned his face to the wall. Vassily seized Christina's wrist, where the veins shimmered blue through her pale skin. He shook his head.

"She'll die after a single winter. I can't afford to feed useless mouths." He pinched her narrow hips, making her wince. "She's no good for childbearing, either." The monk stroked his matted beard. "No, I want that one. She's healthy and strong as a horse." He pointed at me. I felt faint.

Tanya cut in again: "She has bad blood and she's stupid and lazy to boot." She didn't want to give up that easily.

"Shut your mouth." Vassily reached into the leather pouch that hung on his belt beside a dagger and pistol. With a cart full of wares, the journey was long and dangerous. He gave the monk a few coins. Tanya pushed forward one last time. "And what about us? We lose a worker if she goes!" She held out her hand. My father's face darkened. Vassily hesitated, but the monk shrugged, so he gave Tanya one silver coin. She bit it quickly and pocketed it.

Vassily turned to me. "Pack your things, girl. My cart's already outside. We're leaving right away."

Tanya nudged me along. I was wearing my good linen blouse, with the embroidered flowers at the neck, beneath a clean *sarafan*. Walk was about a three-day ride away; my clothes would get ruined on the journey. When I undid my lacing, the monk turned away. Vassily, however, appraised me from top to bottom as I slipped out of my shirt and put on my simple, old *sarafan*. My cheeks burned with shame as I wound my braid in a knot and tied my scarf tight around my head. I swore to myself that I wouldn't make it easy for him.

"I'm ready," I said. My father hugged me, for the very first time.

"Look after yourself, my child. Your mother was a good woman. We'll see each other in the next life, God willing," he whispered in my ear.

"What am I to God," I hissed, to stem the tears. Vassily seized me by the wrist. Maggie started to wail. Tanya slapped her face, which only made her scream even more. The monk made the sign of the cross over me and I snarled at him. Then I was out of the door and sitting beside Vassily on the coach box. His three helpers, who hadn't even dismounted, eyed me briefly. They must have known beforehand that the deal would not take long. I felt sick with humiliation.

* * *

Most of the journey to Walk I spent crying beside Vassily. He didn't say a word to me, but clicked his tongue at the horses, driving them into a fast trot along fields where the clods of earth were already dry and gleaming. In the flat, open countryside his companions rode in front of and behind the cart, so that from afar we must have looked like a skein of wild geese in the sky. In the forest, though, they shielded the cart with the horses' bodies so they would be in a position to ward off thieves and wolves. I hardly dared look around. I knew nothing beyond our *mir*. In the guesthouse where we spent the night, I was given my own room. Vassily locked me in. I had never been in a room alone before. The straw bed was more comfortable than the hard oven I slept on at home. One of his men settled outside my door, while the other two guarded the cart. Was Vassily afraid I would run away? But where would I go? There was no way back.

4

The first sight of Walk was overwhelming. Noise and smoke rose up into the dense blue of the sky and the houses were much bigger than the ones in our *izba*. Most were crowded inside the town's walls, while others sat large and comfortable on wide plots of land between the road and the river and were built on stilts against the yearly flooding during the *ottepel,* like the houses in my *mir* that stood close to the Dvina. I tried to count all of Walk's chimneys, but gave up as we trundled through the town gates. I had never seen so many people in one spot before: the bustle on the streets reminded me of the anthills we used to smoke out in autumn; the insects would flee, running all over the place, in all directions, which always made me laugh. Farmers were carrying cages of geese and chickens on their shoulders, or driving calves and pigs before them. It must have been market day. Well-dressed gentlefolk placed their shiny leather shoes carefully, avoiding the muck on the streets. Women hurried home with their purchases from the market and red-cheeked boys hawked fresh bread and pastries from loaded trays hung around their necks. Beggars and riffraff hung about such as I had seen at the fairground before, probably ready to pilfer an apple here, or a bulging purse there. Dogs fought, barking and yelping over the rubbish thrown in front of the houses; coachmen on other carriages cracked their whips and cursed one another. This beat Master Lampert's Tent of Wonders hands down, even though my nose was already numbed by the stench. In our *mir* all smells—slops, stray cattle, rotting vegetables—were lost in the vastness of the plain.

Here, the midday sun gathered the air in the alleyways in suffocating clouds. The people of Walk, I later discovered, simply emptied their chamber pots out of windows, right onto the heads of passersby. But the smell of human waste was blunted by the smell of delicious foods, soups and sauerkraut, cabbage- and meat-filled *pirogi,* roast chicken, fresh flatbread, and many, many more things that I, in my poverty, was unable to name but would get to know in coming weeks.

Vassily saw me staring at a group of men. "Those are Tartars from the east. Bloodthirsty, lazy scoundrels, all of them." They frightened me with their slanting eyes, high cheekbones, and the rough pelts wrapped around their calves. "Those men over there?" he said, pointing to fairer-skinned men in tight, knee-length breeches, silver-buckled shoes, and narrow jackets. "They're Poles." The tall, blond soldiers were Swedes from the town's small garrison; they winked at me before eyeing up the good German girls going from stall to stall with their mothers and maids. Their hair was neatly tucked under stiff, puffy bonnets, yet the bodices of their high-necked dresses were laced almost indecently tight, molding their bosoms and slim waists. I felt like a savage beside them. A group of Orthodox priests greeted Vassily, and I saw other Russians, too, in their trailing, belted robes with the wide collars, their matted beards still sticky with their lunchtime soup. They grinned at me brazenly. I stuck my tongue out at them behind their backs.

"Is it far?" I finally dared to ask, as I had lost all sense of direction. The sky above us was a mere square; where was the horizon, where a forest or a river? How should I ever find my bearings in such a place, I wondered, when Vassily pulled on the reins. He whistled and a gate opened in a long, high wall. With a clattering of hooves the horses turned into a cobbled yard.

"We're here," he said curtly.

* * *

His house was inside the town walls, yet near the river. It was so big that I thought surely several families must live in it. Underneath the house, pigs and chickens were penned in among the wooden piles. To the right and left were stables for the carriages and horses—I caught a whiff of animals' bodies and a vast vegetable garden was laid out behind it. Vassily tossed the bridle to a young serving boy and lifted me down from the coach box, brushing my breast with his hand as he did so. I jumped, but he said calmly, "Here's Nadia. Go with her into the house and do as she says."

I looked up, clutching my bundle. A woman was coming toward us across the yard. Her dark hair was streaked with gray and her eyes bulged slightly in their sockets, like the toads we children used to blow up with straws until they burst. Three hairs sprouted from a wart on her chin, and fresh blood and feathers were stuck on the apron around her comfortable waist. "Who's this, my lord?" She frowned, didn't even look at me, and placed her hands on her hips.

"A new maid, Nadia." Vassily avoided her gaze. "She's called Marta."

"Marta what?"

He shrugged. "I don't know. Does it matter?"

* * *

Nadia showed me to my room. She was short of breath after having climbed a ladder that led up to a small, drafty chamber. The floor was bare and between two bedsteads stood an open Russian chest made of oak and studded with iron bands and slate. In the corner, I spotted a bucket. When we entered, another girl rose from her bedstead in the corner and hastily placed a tunic that she was embroidering into an open chest. As she curtsied to Nadia I could not help but notice the fine, colorful thread she used.

"Move your stuff, Olga, there's a new girl. Her name is Marta," Nadia said, and turned to me, snorting: "What? Did you think you'd have a flight of rooms for yourself? Olga is also a kitchen maid. She can break you in and teach you a thing or two." Olga lowered her eyes, blushing. I noticed how scrawny she looked next to Nadia. Her clavicles were a hard edge toward her slender neck and her wrists were mere bones as she clutched her hands close to the tips of her long, thick, blond plaits.

"Settle in, girl, and don't give me reason for complaint," Nadia said, ready to leave.

"I will not," I said hastily, as I knew that I had to get along with these women. "I work hard. In the monastery, I cleaned the ovens and the floors and kept store for the monks . . ."

"Good. I have no time for idle hands," Nadia said curtly. "Olga, make some space in the chest, will you?" Olga obeyed, shoving her things to one side of the open chest. My blouse and spare *sarafan,* which I had worn at the fair, certainly would not take up much space. But when I folded my clothes inside the chest I was surprised: next to Olga's neatly folded clothes lay a dress in Western style, balls of wool tinted in the color of the sky, a comb in a dark and shiny material, as well as softly gleaming large buttons, which were tied up for later use, like a bunch of posies. Where did she get such treasures from?

"Any more questions?" Nadia jangled the bunch of keys on her belt. She certainly looked in charge, and was impatient to get on with things.

"Yes," I dared to say.

She raised her eyebrows. "What?"

"How will I not get lost here? The house is so vast," I said, yet I felt it might not be vast enough for me to hide from Vassily. The look of the narrow bedstead terrified me: Would he come for me, there, tonight? Did the other women know why I was here?

Olga smiled at me, but Nadia's reply was curt. "You country bumpkin. Do your work and you will not lose your way. Olga, the fire needs rekindling for the master's samovar and *tchai.* Don't forget the vodka, will you? Two lugs in the cup to warm his bones." Olga slid out of the room. When Nadia made a decision, there was no contradicting her. Trying to stay on her good side, as well as sharing the bedchamber with Olga, might shield me from Vassily, I hoped, yet my stomach clenched with fear. How should I sleep a wink and then be strong enough to do my chores? I remembered his words from the river all too well, and he did not seem like a man who made vain threats.

5

Nadia, Olga, and I cured meat and fish; pickled mushrooms and root vegetables; marinated fruit, vegetables, and herrings in alcohol and vinegar; and stuffed *verst* after *verst* of sheep's intestines with spiced meat to make sausages. Chickens, geese, and piglets ran around my legs, and the huge, glowing oven added to the summer heat, making it unbearable. As soon as Nadia turned her back on me, I would nibble at things and stick my fingers in all the saucepans, which made Olga warn me only half-jokingly: "Stop eating, otherwise you'll grow all fat and Nadia might slaughter you in autumn as well." But I'd never dreamed such delicacies existed. True, I had worked in the monastery kitchen on feast days, but what was the monks' simple food compared to this heavenly fare? Vassily's pantry had to be kept well stocked for his many guests, who stayed several days. The shelves were stacked with vinegar, oil, and gherkins. Milk was left in barrels to sour into kefir, or hung in muslin cloths to make cheese, if I didn't have to skim it and churn the cream into salted butter. Greaves, flour, red and white onions, nuts, lentils, peas and beans—thin green ones, as well as the fat white ones Tanya used to boil into a slimy stew—were all stored in sacks. Hanging from the ceiling, beside lightly salted sides of ham, were bundles of herbs and spices, all except the saffron, which Nadia locked away in a casket. When I'd asked why, she'd told me it came from a country far, far away in the east and was weighed on the market in gold. "Once we had a maid who pinched a bit and Vassily had me break her fingers. They didn't quite grow back together again, so we had to chase her," she said casually.

The rest of the time I beat skins and carpets, turned or changed the straw on the floor, or waxed the floorboards until they shone and smelled of honey, and dusted the gilded frames of the icons on the wood-paneled walls. I was uncomfortable about having to air the bed in Vassily's room in the mornings—so far he almost seemed to have forgotten about my presence, yet the cruelest hunter puts its prey at ease before striking suddenly—but I would touch the starched and herb-scented sheets in awe. Nadia taught me to spray the washed and thoroughly dried linen with a brush of feathers dipped in the water in which she had soaked the peeled and sliced potatoes. Even the monks' cells that I had cleaned in the monastery just offered bare planks or stone coves as beds. At home I'd slept together with my family on top of the big, flat oven in our *izba*, burrowed deep in warm straw, like a sow in its sty. I tried not to think of them and of days past, as it made me too miserable. I longed so much for my family that in hindsight even Tanya's steady stream of nagging and slights seemed bearable. Often I cried in my cushions, and at first Olga would leave me be, folding her hands as in prayer on her thin blanket.

Vassily traded in anything that made him money: linen from Russia, French velvet, and another cloth called silk. Once, Olga held one of the bales against her cheek, sighing at its shine and softness: "Did you know that its threads don't come from fields, like cotton, or from animals, like wool?"

"No?" I snorted. "So do they fall from the sky, or what?"

"Well, almost. Vassily told me that it is spun by big, fat caterpillars that do nothing all day but hang around on certain trees, munching leaves."

I laughed. "How stupid do you think I am? Show me a caterpillar like that and I'd swap places anytime!"

"True," she said, her voice plain, as she carefully placed the bale of silk back on the shelf.

Vassily kept careful records of his goods: wax and honey; salt, sugar, and flour; meerschaum, fats and oils; leather—and little pouches of a strange white powder that had a powerful effect. I could always tell when he had snuffed of it. He would then be in high spirits, and go to town together with friends to a *kabak*—an inn that served only vodka—his whip dancing playfully on his shiny, freshly polished boots. There was a second storeroom that Vassily kept tightly locked.

"What's in there?" I asked Nadia on my first visit to the warehouse.

"Why should I risk my neck in telling you?" she asked, before telling me anyway, proud of her knowledge. This was where Vassily hid forbidden treasures: sable, ermine, vodka, and caviar in buckets of ice to keep it cool. Only the tsar was allowed to trade in these goods and even here, outside the Russian empire, Vassily could have his nose cut off for it, or be broken on the wheel. No tsar was to be trifled with where his income was concerned—not even Peter, despite the strange things we heard about him. When Nadia didn't look, Olga and I would lure the servants of Vassily's customers into the kitchen, calling to them from the window, laughing and teasing them by blowing kisses. Then, over a mug of *kvass,* they would tell us everything that was going on in the world.

"You won't believe it, my girl. They say the tsar is no longer in Russia, but traveling around Europe. He calls himself Peter Mikhailov, lives on cabbage like you and me, and is learning how to build boats in Holland."

What nonsense, I thought, but politely held my tongue. No one in their right mind would swap the richest of lives for our daily drudgery.

Or: "If Peter carries on like this, Charles, the king of Sweden, is going to show us what for. He's still a child, but he exercises with his troops from morning to night. They're great towering fellows who adore Charles and obey his every order. Now *that's* a real king."

Their tsar bewildered them: he had just issued a decree ordering them to cut off their beards. For a Russian, being clean-shaven was sheer blasphemy: all their icons showed Christ with a beard. Had Peter lost his mind? Was he a changeling after all that his mother had smuggled in from the German Quarter on the outskirts of Moscow, desperate after the birth of a daughter? Or was the influence of his German whore, Anna Mons, to blame? He was with her in spite of his marriage to a good and God-fearing Russian noblewoman, who'd given him a healthy son and an heir to the throne. Even I had heard rumors that Peter was a false tsar.

* * *

One night near the end of May, however, as not only my tears, but also the first white nights full of birdsong and longing kept me awake—had

I really been looking forward to them only a couple of months ago?—I heard the floorboards creak in our room and sat up, so startled by the noise that I even stopped sobbing, my heart pounding. Was this Vassily coming for me?

Olga stood at my bed, moonlight pooling around her thin feet, and her threadbare nightshirt hanging like a limp flag on the pole that was her body.

"What?" I asked, sitting up, wiping my nose and feeling almost defiant. Was my unhappiness something to snitch about to Nadia? One could never be sure. I was almost becoming a Russian. In the tsar's realm no one trusted the other one little bit. But instead of mocking or betraying me, Olga reached out and her long, slender fingers caressed my hair. Her touch was floating, like a young bird's wings touching my tresses, yet it did more to me than a long drink of water in summer or a fur coat in winter.

"Stop crying, Marta. You exhaust yourself and you have to be strong," she whispered. "For us serfs, things are as they are."

I wiped my eyes, too proud to open my arms, embrace her, and ask her to hold me tight. I could only hope for the best, whatever that meant in this house, where I was at Vassily's mercy, I thought with dread. She smiled at me one more time—a mere shadow clinging to the corners of her mouth—and her face was like a veil when she turned and climbed back into her bed. She could only offer words to comfort me, but I fell deeply asleep as I had never before in Vassily's house, exhausted from all that had happened and all the new things I had to learn. Perhaps it was for her tenderness and her comfort that I neither heard the steps coming up our narrow flight of stairs, nor the feet coming along the corridor, heavy with drink and lust. I only woke when the door was wide open, shrieking in its hinges in a way it never seemed to do in daytime. I startled. Vassily stood on the threshold, the milky moonlight showing him a clear path into our chamber, right up to my bed.

I was unable to move, though my thoughts raced. An icy chill spread in my veins: the moment I had feared so much had come. His waiting, I knew now, was part of the game, and the game was up. What exactly would happen, what would he do? If he only let me live, I hoped, biting my lip to not whimper for dread, and I started to shiver as Vassily stood there, swaying a little in the door, steadying his heavy body on the frame with one hairy hand. I did not stand a chance against him, I knew, and pulled my knees up, despite my legs shaking like blubber. Vassily was still catching his breath after the climb and I pulled the blanket over my head, curling up like a kitten, shielding my eyes against the sight of him and my head against blows, or him taking me by the scruff of the neck. At least I did not want to see him come for me; it would be awful enough to feel him and to suffer his wrath. Had my waiting been part of Vassily's punishment for defying him?

"Come here," he said hoarsely, his voice thick with stupor. "Or shall I come and get you, girl?"

6

No, please not, I thought, shoving my fingers so deeply in my mouth it made me gag, but it also stopped my teeth from chattering. I tasted salt from both my sweat and tears and perhaps also blood—in my terror I bit myself, and winced at the pain, because I knew there was more to come. Despite the tender May air, sweat prickled all over my body. Perhaps it would be better to give in. I feared pain and could not expect any help: from Olga's bedstead all was quiet. How could she sleep through this, or was she gagged by sheer terror, as I was? Against all reason I wanted to crawl over to her and hide behind her—together we might be stronger!—when she sat up and said: "I'm coming," her words as brittle as last autumn's leaves.

I held my breath, stunned, and then hiccupped with surprise as I peered out from beneath the edge of my blanket and between my spread fingers. She rose from her bed as if dressed in a flaxen sheet: her light blond hair was flowing to beyond her hips as she stepped toward him. I flinched as he seized her tresses, yanking her head and wrapping his fist in the silvery mass. She let out a short, pained scream. In a twist, he dragged her out of the door, which he did not care to shut, and into the corridor.

And so I lay wide awake and heard it all.

When Vassily had climbed back down and Olga stumbled into our chamber, her thin legs trembling, and clutching her torn nightshirt like a drowning person might a piece of driftwood, I was by her side before she fell down on her bedstead. I held her head, felt her tears on my throat and her slender body heaving, caressed her hair and dabbed her burst lip until the blood clotted. "Why is he doing this?" I asked, hearing the helplessness in my voice.

She tried to shrug, but winced: I saw bruises at her shoulder. "This is nothing. It gets him going. If I put up a fight, it's even worse." Her blue eyes were huge in the moonlight. Was this what Nadia had meant by saying Olga was to "teach me a thing or two"? Perhaps she was right, I thought, while holding her: for us serfs, things were as they were. Her hot cheek melted into my palm as she whispered, "Don't help me. You can't. Help yourself."

The following day, I saw Olga dip her fingers in a tub of pork lard and sneak to our room, where she greased the door's hinges. I understood: the shrieking sound when Vassily came for her made her shame worse.

A couple of weeks later, I did not wake from my ever more restless slumber when Vassily came for her, but from her retching over the bucket in the corner of our chamber. In our chest, I spotted a pair of soft green gloves on Olga's pile of clothes, next to her other treasures.

* * *

"Have you been in Vassily's service long?" I asked Nadia one afternoon in August in my still choppy Russian, which caused endless laughter in the house. We were shredding cabbage for a pie of bacon and vegetables. The kitchen was sweltering in the summer heat, my hair stuck to my forehead, and I had shortened the sleeves of my *sarafan* as much as possible, pulling the strings threaded through its seams. I took care to do my chores swiftly, and with a smile, so Nadia would not cuff me. That day, she seemed in a good enough mood to chat.

"My family belonged to his father so I grew up in his service." She gave me a short, sharp look. "Even though I wasn't pretty or charming, I was allowed to work at their house. I could be trusted. When Vassily's mother died giving birth to him, I raised him."

I almost dropped the cabbage stalk I was holding. "So you are like a mother to him?"

Instead of answering, she just cast me a glance, and I busied myself with the cabbage, guarding my tongue. Nadia was at Vassily's beck and call, as any housekeeper worth her salt would be, bowing to his every demand, but mercilessly keeping us in check. That she had raised him as her child shocked me, nevertheless, as I only knew my love for my younger siblings, especially Maggie. How close was Nadia to Vassily? "Doesn't Vassily have any family, then?" I asked, sluicing the cabbage bits that floated in a shallow bucket of water, cleaning it thoroughly, as both earth and small slugs loved to stick to its layered leaves.

"He's a widower and childless," she replied. "His wife died three years ago of consumption." She checked another cabbage stalk for blemishes and then shredded it in the blink of an eye.

"What about Olga?" I dared to ask. Olga, who wore her *sarafan* more loosely these days and who nibbled from the sour gherkins and the pickled Baltic herring when she thought no one was looking.

Nadia split the next cabbage stalk with a single, powerful blow, which made me jump. "Olga was bought a year ago, a bit like yourself. Our lord made her pregnant."

"Our lord?" I lowered my own knife. "But that only happens in the Bible."

"Stupid girl," scolded Nadia. "Vassily's a man like any other. And Praskaya can't keep an eye on him all the time." She chuckled, which made the hairs on her wart quiver in rhythm. "But she'll be back soon."

"Who's Praskaya?" I gathered the discarded leaves to feed to the chickens and pigs later.

Nadia clicked her tongue. "Praskaya's a snake. She's Vassily's mistress, can hold her own in any drinking game, and her jokes would make even a soldier's ears burn. She allows Vassily to stray, but only as long as no other woman is a threat to her . . ." She fell silent, because at that moment Grigori, the young stable boy, came into the kitchen, followed by Olga herself, who had been washing and darning the horse blankets. Grigori was about fourteen or fifteen years old, with arms and legs that seemed too long for his skinny body, and angry pustules blooming across his cheeks and neck. He was a mix of a puppy and a colt, like my brother Fyodor had been.

"I'm starving, girls. Can I have some of the vegetable soup already?" He eyed the cauldron where the pea soup—lunch for everyone—was bubbling on the open fire. Its scent was heavenly and thick with bacon rind.

Nadia growled, "Cats and maids eat in spades, servants and dogs wait by the bogs," but then filled a wooden bowl for him anyway. Grigori sat with us, slurping his soup contentedly. I was tempted to cross two fingers to ward off the evil eye, because Olga crossed herself with three fingers behind Grigori's back, and I noticed scratches and deeper marks like cuts on her arms. As little as Olga spoke about herself, she knew much about others, and she had told me all about Grigori. "Keep well away from him; he's got the evil eye," she'd whispered. In the milky darkness of our chamber her words had crawled across my skin like spiders' legs.

"Really?" I'd sat up, pulling the threadbare blanket up to my chin. "It comes over him all of a sudden, when he's exhausted. He screams and twitches and thrashes about before throwing himself on the ground. Then he foams at the mouth, as if Satan himself were in him."

"Has he always been like that?" I'd shivered, in spite of the blanket.

"Yes, he used to have these fits as a child. But he's been much worse since Vassily punished him."

"Punished him? What for?" My throat had suddenly gone dry, thinking of the maid who had pinched saffron. Severe measures were taken for small mistakes.

"Grigori wasn't paying attention and Vassily's stallion scraped its flank on a rusty hook in the stable and died of blood poisoning. Vassily whipped Grigori senseless. Since then we've often had to tie the boy up to stop him hurting himself."

Did I really think that Vassily would forget and forgive something? Least of all a girl who had threatened him in front of his men? Though in the bright sunlight of the warm kitchen, all these stories seemed hard to believe.

"Some soup, Olga?" Nadia offered, but she shook her head, turning her face away in disgust. "You have to eat." Nadia scowled, while Grigori sat hunched on his stool, eating his soup and smiling shyly at me whenever I caught his eye. Nadia glared at us, sieved the rest of the flour, chucked tiny gravel and husks, and weighed out the precious salt before giving me my orders. "Go to the chicken shed and collect the eggs," she said, and I sighed, thinking of Vassily's chickens, who were foul beasts that put up a fight for each and every egg, when Nadia added: "Then chop the white onions." White onions. They always made me cry my eyes out.

* * *

When Praskaya returned from her journey, she hated me on sight. I had to tie my hair back tightly, hide it under a scarf, and keep my eyes lowered at all times. She gave me the hardest tasks she could account for to Vassily. "Carry the coal bucket!" "Sweep out the fireplaces—look at the state of them!" "The pigs have to go out in the field—don't dawdle, go on, go, go, go." If I showed the slightest clumsiness, she would box my ears, dig her nails in my arm, or pinch me hard, twisting my skin, leaving blue and blackish bruises. Once she pushed me as I was carrying boiling water for her bath; I stumbled and almost scalded my hands and feet. In the evening, she would lock our bedroom door. Olga and I were prisoners every night, which also meant that Vassily wouldn't come. Thank you, Praskaya." We laughed, before, despite our fear, we sank into deep, dreamless sleep.

* * *

It was the hottest, driest summer in living memory. Under the burning sun the corn caught fire in the fields and the harvest failed. I worried desperately; from all over the country we heard horrid stories. Souls died during their work in the fields, and their masters—against every law of man and country—closed first their ears to their suffering and then their cellars and pantries to their begging. Corpses lay bloated in the *mir* or floated downstream, to be eaten by fishes and bears. Still, I also heard that those who could, made it away. At night I left the curtain undrawn and looked up to the starry sky, hoping for my family to do the same elsewhere, in peace and safety.

* * *

Olga gave birth to a boy: Nadia chased me from our chamber as labor started. All I was allowed to do was heat vat upon vat of water. For hours her agony pierced both my soul and the kitchen walls, where I sat, my head buried in my elbows, my hands on my ears. Her son, Ivan, was never christened. Praskaya let the newborn slip from her hands while bathing him in her tub. Perhaps it was for the best. With a bit of luck, a nice young man might still marry Olga and make an honest woman of her.

But a few months later, during a late, windy spring with the river frozen longer than usual, she was pregnant again. Clearly, Vassily did not need the key to our chamber to get to her. When I wanted to comfort her, her pale eyes welled up and she turned away. When Vassily left on his travels, using the warmer months to fill his storerooms, Praskaya found some ridiculous reason to give Olga a whipping.

The next morning, Olga's bed was empty. How and when did she tiptoe out? I cursed her greasing of the hinges. We looked everywhere for her, but in vain. Two days later the Dvina washed up her body. Weeds hung in her hair, and fish had nibbled away her eyelids. Her big blue eyes stared out at nothing, and her little hands were clenched above her lightly swollen belly as if in prayer. As Olga had taken her own life, she wasn't buried in sacred ground, but thrown into a clay pit outside the city walls, where animals dug the corpses up and ate them. I felt like clinging to Nadia as the town warden sent two coarse men who threw Olga's corpse on their cart, but the housekeeper just turned and went about her work. The following week, Vassily drove Praskaya away. What became of her, I do not know. Then, at night, he came for me.

7

My fear would not let me sleep properly. Still, the floorboards creaking under Vassily's feet woke me from an exhausted, unsteady slumber. He was on top of me before I could scream, and pressed his hand over my mouth, pulling me to my feet. I felt wide awake with terror, and bit down on his stubby fingers. He let go, but slapped me so hard that I fell backward onto my bed. I tasted blood on my lips, and gave a sob.

"Whore! I've been wanting to do that ever since that day by the river. I told you then that you'd be nicer to me, and my waiting makes this the sweeter." He sat on my thighs, pinned my hands above my head, and tore my nightshirt from my body: my breasts shimmered pale in the moonlight. Panting, he tweaked my nipples and sucked greedily at my flesh, biting me and gasping, "By God, you're beautiful. Your Tartar slut of a mother must have drunk absinthe, your eyes are so slanted and green. And how splendidly you've fattened up. Olga felt like poking a bag of bones."

I struggled under his weight, but he slapped me again, and harder than before. I thought of Grigori, and kept still: Did I want to be beaten foolish, like him?

"I knew it. You want it too," said Vassily smugly, taking off his nightshirt. His naked belly hung down over his small penis. "Besides, I like a wildcat like you. Praskaya had got old and boring and Olga just lay there like a piece of wood."

"Please, don't," I begged, although I knew it was pointless. Vassily's cock was bent and wrinkled; he rubbed it, but it stayed tiny and red, like a stray dog's. He saw me staring at it and screamed, "You've hexed me!" He yanked me to my feet and cursed, probably praying in vain to all the saints in Russia to make him go hard. I was flooded with relief: perhaps he would go away again and leave me in peace for good. But no. He dragged me off the bed and pushed me on my knees, forcing open my jaw. I felt sick. Surely he couldn't—! Yes, he could. He shoved his limp thing into my mouth, grabbed my head, and dug his fingers in my hair.

"Lick it. Suck it, my little witch; nice and slow, deep and firm. That's how I like it." He pushed himself deeper and deeper down my throat until I gagged, but he tugged my hair and threatened, "If you bite me, I will beat you to death."

I knew he meant it. I closed my eyes and timidly sucked and licked at the disgusting thing in my mouth. Vassily began to groan and I felt him swell. I was so miserable I wanted to die. Hopefully it would soon be over—whatever "over" meant. Just then he pulled away and said hoarsely, "Turn around, now." Vassily threw me facedown on the bed, spread my thighs, and shoved two fingers between my legs. He gave a satisfied laugh.

"You're like a bitch in heat, and yet you're still a virgin." Then he opened my legs wider, spat on my most secret spot, and forced himself inside me. I screamed. He thrust a second time; I clawed at the sheet and wept with pain. Please God, if only he would stop! He was right on top of me, scraping me raw inside. Still he thrust, again and again, panting and slapping my buttocks. He spanked me harder and harder, so that I bit my pillow, before kneading my breasts and burying himself mercilessly inside me. Had Olga had to endure this, over and over again? Perhaps Praskaya wasn't the reason she had killed herself after all. My voice cracked; I could neither scream nor cry. Vassily reared up, then fell on top of me. His breath rattled as he slid out of me and it felt sticky and damp between my legs. Olga had told me that this was when it was most dangerous. His weight was almost crushing me. Time dripped past; everything inside me ached with pain and unwept tears. When Vassily finally started snoring, I wriggled out from underneath him. He grunted, and I limped over to where a bowl of water stood in the corner of the room. I leaned against the wall and held on to the door handle before sinking onto a stool. All my limbs were shaking. It was a while before I stroked my tangled hair off my face and licked at the dried blood on my swollen lips. Vassily lay sprawled across my bed. I couldn't look at him, but broke the thin crust of ice on the water and washed carefully between my legs. The rag was soon red with blood.

Suddenly, I remembered something else Olga had told me. I silently opened the door and groped my way to the kitchen in the dark. The coals smoldered quietly in the oven; beside it, on the worktop, next to the pestle and mortar and under the long rows of scoured and shining copper pots, I found the vinegar. I moistened my fingers with it and pushed them up inside myself. It burned like fire. Olga had sworn to me that if you did this you wouldn't fall pregnant. Had she tried it on herself? The thought was not cheering. I rinsed myself three or four more times with the vinegar. In my room, Vassily was probably slumped on my bed, passed out, and sleeping soundly until the morning. I couldn't bear going back to my chamber, so I curled up like a baby on the warm floor by the oven and cried myself to sleep.

* * *

Maybe the vinegar really did help. Every month, thank God, the blood still came. On that first, terrible night, after Vassily left my chamber, Nadia turned a blind eye to me sneaking into the room where Praskaya's bathtub still stood, and left the kitchen as I stoked the fire to heat bucket after bucket of hot water. As I carried the last bucket to the tub, a piece of camphor-scented soap lay on its rim. I ladled the hot water over my body countless times, hoping to cleanse my soul.

In the kitchen afterward she glanced at me, before saying in a matter-of-fact way: "It won't be nearly as bad from now on."

I wasn't sure that was really a comfort.

* * *

Vassily visited me almost every night. I learned how to give him pleasure, which disgusted me, but made him come more quickly and leave me sooner rather than later. He gave me presents as he had done with Olga, which made me feel like a whore: another dress in the German style, which I put on a scarecrow in a field, or boxes of sticky sweets from somewhere far south of the Black Sea. I burned them in the oven; the sugar melted and I breathed in the bittersweet smoke with flared nostrils. Sometimes, at night, I dreamed of Olga. Had it been her who had kept me at bay, or had I stayed away, lest her bad luck might spread, trying to survive just as everybody else here? During my rare breaks from my chores, I walked to the riverside where her corpse had been found. Where she was now, no one could touch her anymore. It was a tempting thought that made me sad, but also angry. Several times I waded out into the waves until my skirt grew wet and heavy. But I didn't have the courage; or perhaps I didn't feel the true, deep despair needed to give myself forever to the waters of the Dvina.

* * *

In November of the same year the air crystallized the breath on my lips and the blue ice on the Dvina glistened in the bright sunshine. I wrapped a blanket over my woolen quilted *sarafan*, slipped into the servants' boots standing next to the door, and went out to the stables to bring Grigori fresh, hot *tchai*. The poor lad had to make sure the water troughs for Vassily's horses didn't freeze over. To stop himself falling asleep he always held a sack full of pieces of metal. If he nodded off too deeply, so that his muscles relaxed, the sack would fall to the ground with a clang. Then Grigori would shake himself awake, seize his club, and smash the thin layer of ice that had already formed on the water in that brief moment of rest. Two of his toes had already frozen off, and he was constantly exhausted from the lack of proper sleep. I hurried, because the bowl of *tchai* was very hot, but at the stable door I stopped. What was that strange noise? I heard a whistle, and rattling breaths.

"Grigori, are you there?" I asked, but shrank back as Vassily flung open the stable door. He was wearing nothing but trousers and knee-high boots, and despite the cold he was drenched in sweat. In his hand he held his long horsewhip with the silver pommel.

"What do you want?" he snarled. For the past two days he'd had an infected tooth that must have been hellishly painful. His cheek was red and swollen.

I held out the bowl. "I've brought *tchai* for Grigori. It's so very cold . . ." Then I looked over Vassily's shoulder and fell silent, horrified. He had tied Grigori to a wooden beam with his arms stretched above his head, and had ripped the boy's shirt—already far too thin for winter!—right down to his belt. Was Grigori still alive? The skin on his back hung down in bloody strips. My stomach turned and I retched at the sight of it. What could the poor boy possibly have done?

"Oh my God." I dropped the clay bowl; it smashed, and spattered *tchai* all over Vassily's boots. "Why have you done this?" I asked, aghast. I pressed my fingers over my mouth to force back the rising bile.

Vassily spat out, "Lazy, useless creature. He fell asleep, and now the troughs are frozen. How are my horses supposed to drink!"

"You've beaten him half to death because he fell asleep? He's just a boy. Stop—" These days, I could get away with a good number of things with Vassily, but instead of answering he went back inside the stable. Grigori merely sighed as the whip sliced down on his raw flesh once more. He was still alive, but barely so, and Vassily was about to strike again. I couldn't stop myself; I hurled myself onto his arm and tore the horsewhip from his hand. "You animal! You're killing him," I shouted.

Vassily shoved me; I stumbled, fell over backward in the straw, and dropped the whip. Vassily grabbed it and hit me with it, two or three times. I curled up in the straw, shielding my head with my arms. The whip licked across my hands. It felt like an animal clawing at me, and I howled. Vassily wiped the sweat from his brow and his eyes almost popped from their sockets. "Just you wait until tonight. I'll teach you to behave like that with your master." Then he left the stable.

I sat up slowly. The whip had torn both the blanket and my dress. Warm blood trickled down my arm, but I could deal with that later: Grigori's head was hanging back, his whole body slumped, and he was gurgling and foaming at the mouth. When I loosened the rope he collapsed on the straw with a sigh. Vassily's shirt lay nearby—I folded it to make a cushion for Grigori's head. Then came the seizure, more terrible and more violent than I could ever have imagined. His face twisted and his eyes bulged; he did look possessed as he thrashed about, arms and legs jerking, gurgling incomprehensible words. Suddenly a stream of blood mingled with the foam at his mouth and he spat out a piece of pink, spongy flesh. I shrank back and crossed myself, before taking pity on him and overcoming my fear. What could I do? I thought of how I used to calm my younger siblings when they screamed, and I grabbed his lolling head. His eyes rolled back until only the whites were showing. I mastered my dread and pressed his face firmly against my breasts, rocking him back and forth, crying silently as he gradually quietened in my arms. At last he lay still. His life was now in God's hands, and I felt his breath go cold between my breasts, in fits and starts, before it stalled.

Moments later, Grigori was dead.

8

For the rest of the day, I was strangled with a fear that curdled my blood and twisted my guts. Never before and never again have I known such terrible foreboding. I saw Vassily neither in the house or yard, and Nadia and I watched as Grigori's body was dragged from the stable. I wept: What would Vassily do with me? Nadia eyed me, but said nothing. She knew well enough what was going on, and tonight, of all nights, it was my turn to keep watch over the fire in the kitchen, which in winter could not be allowed to go out. I couldn't lock myself in the maids' room; I was utterly at Vassily's mercy. When Nadia wanted to go to bed, I clung to her against all reason.

"Can't you stay with me, Nadia? Please."

She loosened my grip. "What on Earth have you done? I have never seen him so angry." My heart sank. She should know, as she had raised Vassily, after all. He ought to be like a son to her, and for that she loved him, as monstrous as he was. I couldn't expect more from her than those words.

I was doomed and moved around the dark kitchen like a sleep-walker, pointlessly scrubbing the top of the stove again and again with a sprinkling of ash and a coarse brush. As long as I was doing some-thing, no one could do anything to me, I thought foolishly. Eventually I wrapped myself in my blanket, exhausted, on the warm floor in front of the stove. I couldn't sleep, and listened wide-eyed in the silence. Pic-tures were chasing madly through my mind: Olga's heavy belly, swol-len with Vassily's bastard. Ivan's little limbs sinking into the depths of Praskaya's tub. The terrible sight of Grigori's battered body. I didn't want to die: not like that, not now. Then I heard Vassily's footsteps approaching, swift and threatening. Before I could hide, he grabbed me, dragged me to my feet, and pressed me against the wall.

"You'll pay for your haughtiness now, girl," he hissed, his breath stinking of vodka. There was no guessing what he might do—and there was no escape. "Look what I've got for you. This'll make you wail like the cat you are." He dangled a whip with several knotted straps before my eyes. I hiccupped in horror. Executioners used lashes like these to flay thieves and swindlers alive. A single blow would tear off layers of skin. "Yes." He enjoyed my despair. "Do you know what Regent Sophia did with disobedient souls? She flogged them, rubbed them with vodka, and set them on fire. I am still her loyal subject, and I spit on the false Tsar Peter. You're going to make a beautiful torch, Marta." He pulled me over to the big kitchen table and bent me across its heavy wooden top. His mouth was twitching with laughter as he kissed me, which made me gag, and bore down with all his weight. "I'm the last thing you'll remember, girl. Enjoy me, whore—"

His weight squashed me. Whore! What had I ever done besides defend myself, or Christina, back then at the river? Had my mother been a whore for lying with my father, and dying in childbirth, giving her life for mine? Should I end like this, and why? The weight of Vassily's head on my throat and chest almost choked me and I gasped for air. In his haste, he wasn't pinning my hands down, but was too busy pushing up my dress and spreading my legs. He didn't think I'd put up any real struggle. In the dim light I frantically swept over the table, first beside me, then behind my head. That afternoon, Nadia had been crushing herbs, right there where I was lying; she'd used the heavy brass pestle and mortar, because the frozen greens didn't give up their flavor lightly. Vassily pulled my hips up. As he threw himself on me, my fingers stretched back as far as they could and brushed against the cool metal of the mortar. Quickly, I pulled it toward me.

"Turn over," Vassily groaned, and started yanking me onto my stomach. No! I'd be lost. And so I raised the pestle with all my strength and brought it crashing down onto his skull. There was a hideous crunching sound, like cart wheels on frozen snow. In the faint glow from the fire, Vassily's face changed: first astonished, then empty. He opened his mouth and spat over me, spilling not words and hatred, but blood. His head split in two like a walnut. But that was no longer enough for me: I hit him again, and a third time, spurred on by my fury, my helplessness, and the shame he had made me suffer. He should not go to the next world with the face of a man.

Vassily slumped, fell sideways, and lay still on the cold stone floor. I slid off the table and knelt beside him. His face was pulp. I was still holding the pestle; I smashed it down one last time, just to be sure. I felt so sick; the kitchen spun all around me and I passed out on the floor next to him.

9

Someone was wiping my face with a damp cloth. I came to, and blinked: Nadia was kneeling over me in her nightdress, her hair braided in two long plaits. Her night-light—a piece of rope dipped in rancid pig fat—flickered on the floor beside us. It gave off an evil stench, but there was another, more nauseating smell: the kitchen reeked of blood and death, just like slaughter day in the village.

Nadia shook me. "Marta, wake up."

I tried to sit, but everything hurt. Then I saw Vassily: all that was left of his face was a bloody mess. Had I done this? I pulled myself onto my knees, closed my eyes, and rubbed my temples with trembling fingers. My whole body shivered now and I felt so weak I could barely move. "He wanted to kill me, Nadia. He threatened to flog me, rub me with vodka, and set me on fire," I stammered, looking up to her. The night-light drew strange shadows on her face with the bulging eyes and the lips pinched in steady disapproval. What had I done? The kitchen closed in on me and spun. I tried to steady my head by holding it and gasping as if coming up for air after having been held underwater. "Please, Nadia—" I started, and cowered, but she stood, glaring at me. What awaited me? Vassily had been her master and she his true and faithful servant, unflinchingly breaking a young maid's fingers for pinching saffron. More so, he had been the son she never had. I could only hope that things would go quickly: the town warden's henchmen seizing me for my sentence. I had committed the worst kind of *volnenye,* any form of disobedience by a soul toward their master. Men were broken on the wheel for it, women were buried alive up to their heads and left to die of thirst and starvation. Only in milder cases were they condemned to a life of hard labor in the spinning mills. But killing Vassily was no milder case. My teeth were chattering. I wrapped my arms around my knees to hold them steady, but my legs were trembling too much with cold and fear. "Please," I said again as she took a step closer, ready to seize me. On her face, emotions gave chase: stunned surprise, shock, and then, sheer hatred. I wrapped my hands around my head, ready for her blows. Would she finish Vassily's work and pour vodka over me before setting me alight? I peered through my elbows, sobbing.

Nadia kicked Vassily's faceless body with all her might, first once, and then again. His ribs crunched and she stomped on his fingers. "Serves him right, the dog. He should be fed to his sows." She stopped, breathing heavily, and looked at me, thoughtful and stern. I hiccupped with surprise. "Someone should have done this long ago," she said. "What are we going to do with you? They'll torture you, and then you'll be executed."

"Come with me," Nadia said, pulling me to my feet. I stumbled up, wiping snot and tears off my face with my sleeve. "We have to be fast. It's almost morning."

I tried not to step in Vassily's blood, which was all over the kitchen floor. Nadia shuffled ahead of me down the corridor, her candle dancing like a will-o'-the-wisp, and I followed. She was leading me not back to my room, but deep inside the house.

"Where are we going?" My voice cracked.

"Come" was all she said. Finally, she stopped outside the room where Vassily met his customers. Only he and Nadia had access to it. She pushed the door open and raised her night-light. The curtains were drawn and the last embers glimmered in the iron grate. On a wide, wooden desk a quill stuck in an inkwell. The letters and numbers on the papers and scrolls looked to me like mouse droppings. Next to them I spotted an empty carafe of vodka. Nadia sniffed it scornfully: Was this how Vassily had summoned his courage, and his cruelty? One of the small bags of white powder lay beside it, open and still half-full. Nadia moistened her finger, dipped it in the powder, sniffed it hard up her nose, and rubbed some on the roof of her mouth and her gums. Then she grinned, and swept her arm across the desk, making Vassily's bills and papers whirl

up into the air. His books flew across the room; their pigskin bindings came off and they lay there, tattered and open, as she kicked them
about. Dust danced in the darkness and made me sneeze.

She shoved me. "Help me," she said, tipping the contents of the desk
drawers onto the floor. Quills, slide rules, coins, knives, inkpots, leather
pouches, bullets, and pipe tampers tumbled out at my feet. I gawped,
too surprised to cry, as Nadia finally tore down one of the curtains and
kicked over the chair behind the desk.

"What are you doing?" I stared around at the chaos in the room.

Nadia shrugged. "We've had burglars in here, Marta."

"Burglars?" I was dumbstruck.

"Yes," she said, as if speaking to a hapless child. "The ones who killed
Vassily. Such a terrible thing. Our good and generous master." Her big,
bulging eyes glittered with cunning. Suddenly, she seemed capable of
anything and was no longer a servant, but the one who gave the orders.
"What are we going to do with you, Marta? You have to leave, right now,
and never come back. You've only got until dawn."

"Where would I go?" I begged. "I have no one, Nadia."

"I can help you with one thing. After that, you'll have to trust in
God." Her hand slipped under a shelf; she unearthed a little key and
unlocked the casket on Vassily's writing desk.

"How do you know . . . ?" I was stunned.

"I know everything that goes on in this house, Marta." She counted
out a small handful of coins, although the casket was full of them. "Do
you have another dress, apart from those rags?" She pointed at my torn
and bloodstained *sarafan*.

"Not a plain one. Olga's clothes are still in our room, but her dress
is not made in the Russian fashion."

She pressed the coins into my palm. "So much the better. Pack your
bundle. No one will remember one maid more or less in Walk. The carts
set off from the town gates at daybreak for Marienburg. You'll take one.
Do you understand? That's far enough away. I'll wait till sunrise to call for
help. The money's enough for the journey, and to live on for the next few
weeks. After that you'll have to fend for yourself." Nadia grabbed my chin
and stared me down. "I never, ever want to see you here again, Marta. Is
that clear?"

"Marienburg?" I said dully. The city was many *versty* and many worlds away.

"No one will think to look for you there," she repeated.

"What will happen to you?" The coins lay cool in my hand; only a few, but it was more money than I had ever seen.

Nadia smiled. The candlelight flickered in the draft from the open door, drawing lines on her round, smooth face. She pointed to the casket. "There's enough here. When all this is over, I'll move in next to my sister's *izba*, with a little garden. I shall die honored and loved. That's all I want," she said. "It's more than I could ever have wished for."

There was nothing else to say. Our paths were separating. I was alive, and that was what mattered. No spinning mills for me; no breaking wheel, no agonizing torture, no being buried alive. Instead: life— and freedom, albeit an uncertain one. What more could I ask for?

Nadia led me back to my room through the silent house. She watched while I hastily washed my face and packed a good *sarafan*, my woolen tunic, and a last pouch of sticky sweets that Vassily had given me just a few days ago. "I'll have these," Nadia decided, and took Olga's buttons, the balls of wool, and the dark, shiny comb. "These you'll have better use for," she said, and gave me the green gloves. "Let's get you dressed and out of the door." Putting on Olga's dress was harder than I'd expected, as Vassily had had it tailored for her when she was not pregnant. Nadia squashed my flesh into the bodice and laced me up. The bones in the seams pinched my waist, and I could hardly breathe. Then I put on the *tulup*, a heavy sheepskin coat—another of Vassily's presents—as well as two pairs of thick, woolen socks so I could wear the boots that were kept by the front door for the menservants. I twisted my hair into a knot and tied the scarf tight around my ears and chin.

Nadia clapped her hands. "How wonderfully ugly you can be. Nobody's going to look at you twice. But be sure to lower your eyes, my girl," she said. "There's not another pair like them in all of Walk. Slanted, and green, like a cat's."

I nodded, forgetting to lower my eyes, and Nadia cuffed me. We walked in silence to the front door, where she gave me a blanket of double-knitted wool that I rolled up under my arm. Then she grabbed me by the shoulders. "This night, Marta, will forever be our secret. If ever you should speak of what has happened, the Devil may cut off your ears, nose, and hands and roast you alive."

Nadia's curse was real and frightening. She kissed my forehead and unbolted the front door. An icy gust of wind made me shrink back, but Nadia forced me over the threshold, out into the dark and the cold. I clutched her tunic, in vain; she pushed me away. I watched her pick up a stone and walk around the house to beneath Vassily's study. She hurled it and I heard glass crack and shatter. "That's how the burglar came in," she said before pointing to the gate. "The carts for Marienburg are at the town gates. Go now. Farewell. It's people you should fear, not the Devil."

Those were her last words to me, before the door of Vassily's house closed behind me forever. As ever, there was no contradicting her.

* * *

I stood there, alone in the night, in possession of nothing but my life. Thick clouds smothered the stars, and the snow was falling like a curtain, hiding Nadia's tracks. I could barely make out the stable where Grigori had died that morning. It felt like a lifetime ago. I trudged down the icy steps to the courtyard, crossed it, and, using all my strength, pushed back the iron bar on the gate. When I stood in the empty street, snowflakes stuck to my eyelashes and the tears froze on my cheeks. An icy wind cut through the seams of my coat. I couldn't see, or work out which way to go. Where were the town gates? I trudged on and when I looked back, snow was already filling my footsteps as if I had never existed. Had I ever been so lonely? Still, I took a deep breath and stopped crying, because it only wasted my strength. With a handful of snow I rubbed the last of Vassily's blood from my face, making my cheeks burn.

Then I set off.

10

The wind cut right through me, biting down to the bone. By the time I reached the town gate, my lips were white with rime. I was comforted neither by burying my fists deeply in the *tulip's* fur-lined pockets nor by the memory of poor Grigori's frozen feet. The thought of them made me wiggle my toes in my much too large metal-capped boots.

Despite the early hour, the gate was teeming with life: horses bit on their snaffles, their breath steaming up into the clear winter air and their heavy, hairy hooves scraping on the icy cobblestones. Torch flames cowered in the freezing wind, hot tar dripping and sizzling in the snow. Men drenched with sweat despite the biting cold heaved bundles and bales onto carts, shouting orders and cursing. Swedish soldiers grouped close to the wall, leaning on their weapons and keeping an eye on everything and everyone. Their uniforms looked like they were cut from cheap, thin cloth and they warmed themselves with crackling fires. A couple of weeks earlier a footman of one of Vassily's customers had told me that Augustus the Strong, elector of Saxony—was it true that he squeezed an apple to sauce with his bare hands and bent horseshoes straight?—had declared war on Sweden. Along the Swedish Livonian border to Courland the first skirmishes were said to have taken place, but it felt very far away. Still, Augustus had more than once tried to take Riga from the Swedes; among Vassily's staff everyone believed that it wouldn't be long before he came knocking on our door, asking for his due. Being Russian, they didn't mind, as he was a puppet of the tsar; a puppet with a mighty army at his back.

No wonder the mood in Walk had been sullen and downcast in recent weeks and people in both the streets and the market had been going about their business hurriedly.

Along the wall, old women sold hot *tchai,* boiling up the bitter broth in huge black cauldrons on beds of smoldering coals. The tea's coarse leaves drifted in maelstroms on the simmering surface: you had to strain them through your teeth when drinking it. Other *babushky* offered flat sourdough bread, topping it sparsely with salted meat and sauerkraut. I felt faint with hunger and while I wanted to stretch out my money as far as possible, I bought both the *tchai* and the bread. When I counted the coins into her palm, the woman raised her eyebrows: my raggedy appearance in my ill-fitting clothes and too-large boots didn't go with someone walking around with a small fortune in their pocket. Better to have counted it earlier, out of sight, I scolded myself, suddenly panicked. What if someone knocked the coins out of my hand? Both dawn and the crowds, who were all on their way to somewhere, made the town gate a target for pickpockets and other loafers all too ready to pilfer.

I greedily first ate the salty meat and the sauerkraut. When that was gone, I dipped the chewy bread into my *tchai* and sucked hungrily on the softening crust while looking around. "Not so greedy, my girl!" The woman laughed toothlessly as she poured me more tea. "Keep your ardor for your lover, as long as you are young and beautiful and men will still look at you."

I barely heard her. My muscles ached with tiredness but also with fear and apprehension. Had Vassily's body been found yet? What if Nadia didn't stick to her story; and who, after all, believed a serf? Crimes of souls against their masters—especially a master such as Vassily— were commonplace and the punishment was usually swift and brutal. The dread made me feel even colder. I fingered the coins in my pocket again. Their weight and number reassured me.

The first carts were ready to leave, and the drivers pulled themselves up onto the coach boxes. Soldiers circled them, asking their origin and destination so loudly I could hear it from across the road. They seemed to inspect the load repeatedly. They, too, were not wholly welcome in Walk anymore. Vassily had hoped that very soon not only Saxony but also Russia, too, would fight the Swedes. But when I listened to gossip in the market that meant only one thing for the Baltic people: we'd be helplessly caught up in a war that was neither ours to fight nor to win, and we'd be crushed when those powers clashed. Every day I survived from now on would be a miracle that I had to cherish.

The heavy-hooved cold-bloods were ready to pull, neighing and flicking their ears, and the coachmen shouted out their destinations, hoping for last passengers.

"Pernau!"

"Dorpat!"

"Marienburg!"

I hurried to the cart, which was just about to leave. "How much will it be?" I asked, grabbing the reins and craning my neck.

The coachman grinned and tapped a stubby finger on his cheek. "It's for free, my girl, if you add a kiss and a night."

I frowned, even though he seemed harmless enough to me. "Tell me, old man, or I'll ask someone else."

He shrugged. "If you squeeze between the barrels it will cost you a denga."

A denga. That was half a kopeck! For squeezing between barrels in a cart! It was daylight robbery but I had no choice, so I picked out a coin; the money was all warm and sticky, as I had held it so tight. The man bit into it with one of his three yellow teeth and slipped the coin out of sight. "Let's go," he said, and pulled me up on the coach box. I crawled inside the cart. When it jolted forward, I leaned on the barrels and stretched my legs. Apart from some crates of chickens and a young couple, I was the only passenger. The woman was very pregnant and her husband would hold her steady whenever the cart shook or plunged into a pothole. They seemed to only have eyes for each other and this suited me fine; I was in no mood to chat and answer questions. When I lifted the waxy flap of the cart, the morning mist and a curtain of snowflakes swallowed both Walk's town walls and the patrolling soldiers. Soon we were out in the open. The next time I looked, the sun was shining, dull as a copper coin, in a sky that hung low and menacing. The villages we passed were dark dots against the snowy, shrouded plains.

11

In the day, the couple and I shared a goat's skin full of sour milk and some pieces of cold oatcake with the coachman, Misha. At night we stopped at a guesthouse that was hardly better than a pigsty. I sat at the open fire with the coachman. I was too fretful to sleep anyway.

We reached Marienburg late in the afternoon. As evening fell it started snowing and didn't look like it was ever going to stop. Nadia was right: nobody would notice me here. The alleyways were crowded and when we splashed soggy slush onto passersby, they jumped, stepped in filth and on beggars' fingers, and cursed us with raised fists. Swedish soldiers were everywhere: Were they the heros who would stop the mighty tsar? They looked like any other men to me; a bit more handsome, I'll allow, tall and blond in their blue uniforms and cloaks with a certain pride and confidence to them.

The cart stopped outside a *kabak* just as the innkeeper kicked out a drunkard. The man fell in front of us and was in no fit state to get up again. Punters downed as many glasses of vodka as quickly as they could to reach a profound stupor. Misha threw the reins to a stable boy, got down from the coach box, shook his legs in his coarse linen trousers, which were tucked into sturdy, knee-high boots, and took off his high rabbit-skin cap.

"Marienburg. Off you go, hurry up or I'll kick you," he said, eager for his visit to the *kabak* after looking after his cart and horses. The husband helped his pregnant wife out of the cart and then extended his hand to me.

"May God protect you," I said when we parted ways, him standing between his wife and the mucky road. I felt a crushing sadness at their care and tenderness. Hardship and need make for vain hope and deep sorrow. Loneliness lunged at me like a wolf at a lone traveler, burying its claws into my soul. I swallowed my tears and grabbed my bundle. Where should I go? Who needed a maid, and how to find out about them?

Misha had his horses fed and watered and their hooves searched. He eyed me, while picking between his teeth, checking now and then to see what he had found. "Don't you know where to go, girl?" He tucked a pinch of chewing tobacco underneath his upper lip and sucked noisily, then spat red saliva into the snow.

"No. Yes," I said. "Well, I am looking for work. I don't ask for much . . ."

"Come over here."

I walked up to him gingerly. He raised my chin with a dirty hand smelling of leather and tobacco, pushed back my headscarf, and felt one of my dark locks. He grunted and said, "I didn't even notice how pretty you are. Don't lower your eyes like that. And what has happened to your lips? Has a bee stung you in the mouth?"

I blushed and grabbed my bundle, but he seized my elbow. "Where is your family?"

I didn't answer, forcing back my tears that welled up. "I'm looking for work as a maid," I said instead. He hardly looked the type to know a family in need of staff but I didn't know how else to start.

"Do you know how to read or to write?"

"No."

"Perfect. Too much learning spoils a pretty head," he said with a laugh. "I might have work for you. Come, follow me," he said, before telling the stable boy, "Watch the cart and keep me a bottle of vodka, or I'll have your hide."

I hesitated. But could I afford not to try in case it was true? I followed him blindly through the streets of Marienburg, one leading off into another, for what felt like forever until we finally reached a small door with a candle glowing cozily behind the red glass casement. The coachman knocked, waited, and then pushed the door open. When I peered inside, seeing only a dark and dingy corridor, he shoved me in. When I turned in surprise, Misha bolted the door behind us.

12

Somewhere in the house I heard a woman's shrill laughter. Misha barred my way out with his body and forced me up the narrow, creaking stairs. It was warm inside and I tried to loosen the belt of the *tulup,* without losing my grip on my bundle. I could hear first another woman scream, and then the sound of a hand hitting flesh. The sound reminded me of Vassily and I froze in my tracks but the coachman pushed me along farther until we reached a dingy upper floor.

"*Matushka*? Sonia?"

Could this be his mother? Had he brought me home? Did she need a maid? Even vain hope is better than no hope. One of the doors on either side of the corridor opened, and then another. Girls peered out of all the doors, their faces painted as garishly as the mermaid in Master Lampert's Tent of Wonders. But now there was no Christina to swap glances with. The girls' hair was loose and unkempt. I saw naked breasts, shimmering pale in the house's dusky light, and thighs in graying lace drawers.

"A new girl," one of them chirped, licking her lips. I looked more closely. She was a Tartar girl and had a firm and lithe body.

A Swede poked his head out of the door, wrapping a sheet around his nether region. "Can I try her?"

"You'd think you'd be busy enough with me," she scolded, and smacked him. He laughed, and dragged her back into the room.

I froze. Olga had told me about a house of sin in Walk, but I hadn't believed her. That was surely what was going on here. I looked around quickly and saw no way out. The girls closed in on me, taking off my scarf and touching my hair.

"Look at that hair, all thick and shiny . . ." one girl said.

"And she's all nice and fleshy. Who has fed you so well, my dove?" another one said, with a giggle.

They stopped and scattered when a woman came down the corridor. This had to be Sonia. I took a step back, bumping into the coachman. Compared with her, even the portly Nadia had been skin and bones. Sonia's red dress was laced tightly around her belly blubber. On her wide, sallow face little hairs sprouted in a fine mustache on her upper lip. A lacy cap covered her bald head and her eyebrows and eyelashes were almost white. I shrank back with fear, but the coachman grabbed my arm and bent it back. White-hot pain shot through my shoulder.

"Sonia." He grinned. "It's been a while."

"Indeed." She slapped him hard. "The culprit always returns to the scene of the crime. Don't think that I have waived your debts." Then, she hugged him and kissed him on both cheeks. All the while she was looking me up and down. "Who's this?" she asked, eyeing me.

"She comes from some godforsaken place to Marienburg. She doesn't have a family, but is hardworking, she says . . ."

The girls giggled. Sonia pushed me underneath a night-light, taking my bundle and tossing it to Misha to hold. There she held me still, so close I could smell her sour breath, and squinted at me.

"You have eyes like a cat and nice full lips. My men like that." Sonia forced my mouth open. "You still have all your teeth, nice and white"— and loosened what remained of my braid and unlaced my dress to weigh my breasts. "A bosom like a milkmaid. Delicious. I have new Swedish recruits coming tonight. They won't believe their luck."

Despair washed over me. Was this the punishment for killing Vassily?

"Are you a virgin?" Sonia asked.

I didn't know what to say and I lowered my eyes. Sonia grinned. "Ah. Butter wouldn't melt, eh? Who was it? A stable boy? Your former master?" I blushed, all of a sudden grateful for the twilight of the corridor, when Sonia slapped me so hard that my ears rang and tears welled up in my eyes. "Stupid girl. But we'll sort that out. Men are so easy to fool." She turned to Misha. "How much do you want for her? I'll forget about your debts, if you like?"

Misha grinned. "I knew it. She is just what you are looking for. But she doesn't come cheap."

"Let's see," Sonia said, taking a key from the ring at her belt and opening a door. "There is better light in this room. Come in here." I clamped my feet to the floorboards—not even ten horses would drag me into that room.

"I want to go," I said. I don't know what I was hoping would happen.

Nothing, of course. Misha, who still held on to my bundle, pushed me into the room, which was musty and windowless and which smelled of mold. The stench reminded me of our *izba* at the end of the long winter. "You are going nowhere," he said. I saw a mattress, a few chairs, and a table with several candles as well as several empty vodka bottles on top of it. A rat scurried through the open door into the corridor. Sonia breathed heavily as she lit the candles with her night-light. A dull shine spread through the room: What was to happen here?

"I want ten rubles," Misha said. "And—"

"And?" she asked with suspicion in her voice. "There is to be more?"

"Yes. I want to be the first to take her. Here and now."

Sonia pursed her lips, but the girls tittered and clapped their hands. "That's his due, Sonia. He should be good at breaking her in . . ."

"Please, Sonia. Can we watch?"

She shrugged. "Do what you have to do. But we'll watch. I don't trust you—what if you disappear with her afterward, to sell her else-where?" She slumped on one of the chairs. "At least we'll know if she's any good. My men like girls who wail like cats. But don't bruise her, otherwise I'll train my new whip on you."

"No!" I cried when he grabbed my arm. "Let me go, you swine!" I shouted, pushing against him with all my might.

It didn't stop him. It barely slowed him down. My mind raced as Misha pushed me toward the filthy mattress. After striking out blindly a few times to no avail, I tried to take control of the panic bubbling up inside me. There had to be some way out and I had nothing to lose. Looking up, I could see Sonia counting and recounting the rubles in her palm. The gaggle of girls that had followed us were standing behind her, lacing their arms around each other's shoulders and waists.

My mind raced. I had to make it out of there, or I'd be lost, damned for all eternity. Misha let go of one of my arms to fondle my breast, weighing it in his palm. Now or never! I twisted out of his grip with a jerk, stretched, and hit Sonia's hand from underneath as hard as I could. She screamed: the rubles flew high up in the air and rained down all over the creaky, pitted floorboards. I heard them clink and saw them shine. Misha stopped groping me and the girls lunged for the coins like vultures going for a carcass. Sonia jumped up and started pulling them by their hair, her mouth foaming with curses. Misha kicked them and shouted, all while also trying to grab some coins. I bolted up and ran down the corridor, my hair loose and my dress undone, stumbling down the stairs. The bolt crashed on the floor when I pulled it aside, and with a strength that was born out of sheer dread, I tore the door open and ran outside.

* * *

The icy air of the Marienburg winter night hit me like a cudgel. The snow fell so thickly that I couldn't see farther than a couple of steps ahead. I kept running, through now-empty roads, not looking behind me, paying no attention to where I was going, slowing only to lace up my dress. When I finally felt far enough away I stopped. I had a stitch, the icy air stabbed my lungs, tears blinded me, and I could hardly breathe for fear. I sank up to my calves into the snowy, wet slush of the road where it had been torn open by cart wheels. The soles of my old boots as well as my two pairs of socks and the hem of my dress were soaked. I was freezing. I leaned against a wall of a house and wiped tears and snot from my face. My limbs now felt like lead, my teeth chattering so hard that it made my whole body tremble. Only then did I understand my utter misery: I had left not only my bundle and my gloves in the whorehouse, but also my *tulup* coat. I quickly checked my belt: the little purse was also missing. I was as good as dead.

I sank onto the threshold of the house and buried my face in my arms, too spent to even think. This was it. I had killed and now I should die. I hoped for a quick, merciful death. Perhaps I'd just fall asleep and feel nothing? Already a drowsiness came over me, and I curled up inside the house's entrance.

The street was empty, bar a group of patrolling Swedish soldiers who walked past without spotting me. I had withdrawn into the house's entrance before the light of their lanterns touched me. At this hour, only loafers and beggars were out. The brave burghers of Marienburg sat around their dinner tables, folding their hands in prayer, even if the little wooden church opposite my resting place was still lit for the evening service. My stomach growled. I couldn't remember the last time I'd eaten. All that wouldn't matter anymore soon. As my eyelids closed, I tried to think of something nice, such as Maggie's weight hanging on my arms when I swung her around, her little face splitting with laughter in the spring sunshine. It was a memory from a lifetime ago.

With every shallow breath I took my leave from life, my hands and feet totally numb. My mother had died to give me life, and my life was going to end on some street corner in Marienburg, where I knew no one and was no one. It hardly seemed worthwhile. In the past three days my life had turned into a nightmare, so death didn't scare me. Just let it be quick, I prayed, and I shut my eyes for what I thought would be the last time.

13

I heard voices so beautiful that I thought death had come and I was at the gates of Heaven. Though what business would God want with a murderess like me? I opened my eyes almost unwillingly. The chanting grew louder and I tried to sit up, yet my limbs were painfully stiff. The chorale was so elating it gave me goose bumps: the voices and lyrics felt like a cloak in the cold. I gave an involuntary sob. I couldn't even die properly and in peace.

The hymn stopped and the church door was flung open. Warm light fell onto the icy pathway leading up to the little wooden building. Candles were lit in the low windows, banishing the cold and the darkness. As well-dressed gentlefolk left the church, I moved deeper into the shade of my threshold. I was cast out and damned.

A tall man stepped outside the church. Despite the bitter cold, he wore no coat over his Lutheran black gown with its small white collar. He seemed to have a friendly word for everyone leaving the church, accepting what looked like small gifts and alms and shaking hands with all the men before parting. People chatted on the street and then took their leave. Even though I pulled in my stiff knees and made myself as small as possible, some of the churchgoers spotted me as they walked past, the women hurriedly—and somewhat disgustedly—pulling up their wide, thick skirts so as not to touch me and the men crunching through the snow as if they'd not seen me.

Through the open church door I caught a glimpse of the inside. Simple wooden pews stood aligned on both sides of the well-lit nave, braziers smoldered, and fresh straw was scattered on the wooden floorboards. Someone had taken the trouble to adorn the altar with Barbara branches: their cat-paw buds reached up to a painting of the Holy Trinity. In the monastery, the sheer number of icons staring down on me with stern, knowing eyes had been as threatening as the swathes of myrrh and incense were suffocating. This Lutheran church looked so homely that I was overcome with longing; it was a true light in the darkness.

The pastor pulled the door shut, ready to lock the church. His duty was done: Were a well-deserved dinner and a loving family awaiting him? My heart ached at the thought of everything I'd never have, and I curled up even more. The movement must have caught his eye, for he hesitated on the church's threshold.

"Who's there?" he called out in Russian, raising his lantern. Its light ate into the night, but didn't quite reach me, when I started coughing. I gasped for air, covering my mouth with my fingers, but he could hear me. He came down the pathway, crossed the road, and touched my shoulder.

"What are you doing out here at this ungodly hour? You'll freeze to death, girl," he said in German. "Look at me." He lifted my chin, but my head dropped listlessly. He touched my cheek and then took my wrist, checking my pulse. "Good God! Get up." He pulled me up to my feet, though I was so limp he had to drag me up the narrow pathway toward the church. I stumbled after him, trying not to think of Misha forcing me into the house. My clothes as well as my heart were unbearably heavy. The pastor more or less carried me behind the nave to a small chamber hidden behind the altar. He took a cloak from a hook on the wall, wrapped me in it, but then frowned and took it off me. "Get that wet dress off," he said, and tugged my lace bodice. I didn't resist and put my arms up like a child so he could slip it off. He began to unlace the bodice of my German dress and then rubbed my bare arms and back with his hands. I tried to cover my breasts but he shooed my arms away. "Don't be stupid," he said curtly. "I am married with three children. Do you think I've never seen a woman's breasts before?"

He covered me with the cloak anew; its cloth was itchy, but I felt as warm and safe as in a womb. He left the room and returned with a bowl filled with a steaming, scented drink. "Here. Drink this, but watch out. Don't scald your tongue."

I sipped and swallowed, which made my throat hurt, but never before had I tasted something so delicious. Its scent was heady with wine, cloves, and cardamom, and the drink itself thick, hot, and sweet.

"What is this?" I whispered, and took another sip. It was like drinking life itself, and the heat of the braziers made my face burn. Still, he blurred when I tried to look at him. Was there only one man, or were there two? I wasn't sure and couldn't care. I squinted, but it didn't help. I had a splitting headache.

"It's mulled wine. My wife makes it for me and for the congregation, if they are lucky. It's one of her many secret recipes. Some work, others don't," he said with a smile, before asking me, "What's your name?"

"Marta."

"Marta. What's your family name?"

I shook my head, avoiding his gaze.

"Hm. You don't have to tell me if you don't want to," he said. "I am Ernst Gluck, the pastor of this Lutheran church. Where are you from?"

"I came from Walk today." I answered with what I felt was not an utter lie. "I am orphaned and I am looking for work."

"Honest work, that is?" he asked with raised eyebrows, and helped himself to a bowl of the hot spiced wine, eyeing me over the rim of the cup. I held his gaze; it wasn't difficult, as he had a friendly, honest face, and I hadn't seen too many of those recently. His hair and mustache were the color of honey and his skin was weathered by the Baltic seasons. The little wrinkles around his blue eyes and his mouth—fine, white lines in his tanned face—spoke of a happy, good nature.

Or even worse. His words rang in my ears and my grip weakened. The bowl of spiced wine slipped to the floor. Its clay broke and a deep red puddle spread on the flagstones, just like Vassily's blood on his kitchen floor. The crimson footprints I left in his house spun around me, treading all over me and marking my soul, just as Misha's grip and his greedy fondling had branded me. Sonia and her girls had been women, but of no help for the likes of me. He was right: How could a girl like me, after all I had done, hope for honest work? I shivered at the thought and then trembled uncontrollably. Chills seized me, yet I felt boiling hot; my hands searched in vain for a hold and my teeth chattered so hard that I couldn't speak anymore. The last thing I remembered was Ernst Gluck catching me before I fainted.

14

For the next weeks I was at death's door. The Glucks weren't sure if I wanted to live, they told me later, when I opened my eyes on a day in February. It must have been noon: early spring sunlight fell into the friendly, bright room I was lying in, its rays drawing patterns on the carpet woven from many colorful strips of cloth. The walls were painted in a sunny yellow and all the furniture was stained white. I turned my head. Next to my bed stood a low chair with a bunch of early crocuses blossoming in a small vase. A woman sat at a dainty desk, her blond hair plaited into a thick braid, big brown eyes scouring the open book in front of her. She frowned and moved her lips silently—was she counting up numbers, ticking them off with a flick of her quill? Next to her stood a girl, her serious little face a smaller copy of the woman's. Her way of leaning on her mother's chair made me think of Maggie, and it hurt deep inside. She felt my gaze, looked up, and nudged her mother gently.

"She's awake, Mother," she whispered.

The woman rose, her blue-gray cotton skirt swishing around her slim waist and hips. "Can you hear me? Do you understand me?" she asked me, her large eyes full of worry.

I nodded. Swallowing hurt so much, I didn't even want to think of having to speak. She touched my cheek lightly, smiled, and slipped out of the door, returning minutes later with a bowl of hot, thick soup. It smelled heavenly. "Help her to sit up, Agneta. She has to eat, otherwise she'll die on us after all," she said, and Agneta placed her hand behind my neck, while her mother pulled me up, stuffing two cushions behind my back. Then she spooned a soup of comfrey with fleshy lumps of fish into my mouth. Even though it hurt to swallow to begin with, I gladly finished it and then wiped the bowl clean with the crusty brown bread she offered me.

"Welcome back among the living, girl. There isn't much you'll have to fear in life after surviving this," she said, smiling.

* * *

I can only marvel at the Glucks' kindness and generosity. The war was close, I learned; both armies awaited further orders, growing nervous and tetchy. This was not the moment to take in strangers. As soon as I was well enough I did everything I could to thank them, even if I hadn't much to offer but my work. I darned socks and turned collars on Ernst Gluck's shirts, as well as on those of his two sons, Anton and Frederic. After supper, I scrubbed the pots with ash and soap until they sparkled, and following each service I swept the church, and gathered wilted branches from the altar's adornment to burn in the braziers of the cozy small vicarage I shared with the Glucks. On market day I drove a harder bargain than Caroline Gluck herself, and each Sunday afternoon I ladled pea or barley soup into the beggars' wooden bowls outside the church, for every week their number grew. During Mrs. Gluck's visits to old or sick members of their congregation, I'd carry her bag with medication or alms, and hold her lantern if things got late. Last but not least I played with Agneta in all my free time, giving in to her every whim. Caroline gave me a chamber behind the kitchen, which was wonderfully warm, as the oven was on the other side of the wall. I had it all to myself, as the cook went home in the evening once her work was done. I felt like a part of the family and ate at the table with them, watching, listening, and taking everything in.

* * *

"Marta? Come and see me when you have a moment," Caroline said one afternoon, peering out of her study. I had been wiping the floor, so I wrung the cloth and wiped my hands on my apron. My heart pounded. For a while I'd known I was strong and healthy again. It was only a matter of time till this life of peace and happiness would come to an end. How should I brave the world without the Glucks' warmth and kindness?

If she asked me to leave, I hoped that she'd give me a recommendation, or, in the best case, knew of another family who needed help. On the threshold of the yellow room that looked like sunlight itself I curtsied, waiting for her to ask me in. I wore one of Caroline's old, high-necked dresses, which I had widened a bit in the seams and tucks to suit my curves. The Russian way of dressing made me feel like a peasant now compared to the more tailored Western style.

"Sit down." Caroline smiled, patting the stripy fabric of the sofa. A fire crackled in the tiled oven—it was April, but winter still had a hold on the weather—and the basket next to it was filled with logs. I waited for her to speak when she closed her accounts book: those numbers were a source of despair because of her husband's generosity—soon, they'd have to pawn the vicarage, she'd say—but they were also a good way of catching a cheating, thieving cook. The rows of numbers looked like poppy seeds on a bun. She took my hand; her fingers felt warm and dry.

"How are you, Marta? I'd say you're back to full health now?" she asked, her gaze searching my face.

I nodded, but forced back tears of fear. I did not want to leave this place. I had had no idea that any family as friendly and welcoming as the Glucks could exist. It couldn't be easy to turn me out, but I'd make it easy for her.

"You have been with us for almost twelve weeks. What are your plans, Marta?" she asked.

"I'll have to look for work, I suppose," I said, swallowing my tears and steadying my voice.

"Ernst tells me you have neither friends nor family in Marienburg. These are no times for a young woman to be on her own. You are a good, hardworking maid. Why don't you stay with us?"

I sat bolt upright.

She laughed. "You should always keep yourself so straight, Marta. You have nothing to hide. Do you want to stay with us, take care of Agneta, and keep the house and the church tidy? You don't have to cook, but you can do the shopping. Your bargaining skills have saved me quite some money," she said, smiling. "You'll get room and board and a small salary, which might serve you well as pin money. And when our ways part I'll give you a good recommendation."

I threw myself on my knees, kissing Caroline's fingertips, but she hastily pulled away her hands. "You are more Russian than I thought. So we have an accord? I am happy for you to stay."

I nodded so forcefully that my bun came loose. "Of course I want to stay."

"Good. The maid's chamber next to the kitchen is yours; it's nice and warm. But let me tell you two things—"

"Yes?" I looked up in surprise.

"I suffer neither lies nor fornication in my house."

I shrank back, shocked by the openness of her words, but she patted my hand. "That's just a general rule, no offense. Everyone's heart has its secrets and God has spared me from the sin of curiosity. But if you speak, it has to be the truth. And I see how the young men on the street ogle you. It's not your fault, but I would not suffer an unmarried, pregnant maid, and my Ernst, too, is but a man."

My cheeks burned like fire, but I swore to myself I would be up to her standards.

"Off you go now. There is a lot to do." She took up her accounts book again. "Tell the kitchen we'll have fish pie and bread for supper. No beer, just water and *tchai*."

I left her to her numbers. The rectory was the first house built of stone I had ever set foot in, and the cold of the granite seeped into my bones when I kneeled on the floor beneath the simple wooden cross hanging on the chalked walls. I botched the Paternoster, which I had heard again and again in the past few weeks, but had never learned properly. My God had sold me to Vassily, but the Glucks' God had saved my life and, more importantly, had given me a home and a purpose.

I believed that I could live like this forever.

15

My time with the Glucks was as busy as it was happy. Agneta, an afterthought in the priest's marriage, was spoiled, but I was happy to indulge her. I hardly saw Anton and Frederic; they were a bit older than me and handsome boys—Anton especially, with his curly, honey-colored hair and bright blue eyes. The girls who'd marry them would be lucky, I thought. The pastor taught them together with the sons of the town's many well-to-do burghers in a cold room on the upper floor of the rectory, where they scratched on slates with styluses and leafed through one of the many books from his library.

Sometimes I'd linger outside the door to listen: How could a single man know as much as he did? Every day he received a dozen or so letters, and when I cleaned the room I spotted scroll upon scroll filled with his tiny, neat handwriting. The sheer number of books on his shelves made me despair; once I had finished dusting them I could start all over again. He taught his pupils from the Bible, but also about history and geography; they knew about places called England or France. Also, they spoke, wrote, and read German, Swedish, Russian, Greek, and Latin. The pastor's true passion, though, was numbers and mathematics. Handsome Anton seemed to have taken after him, as he once calculated the number of liters in my bucket with no effort.

Of the many amazing things in Pastor Gluck's schoolroom, the most intriguing to me was the drawing of a man. He wore no clothes, and so I had avoided looking, embarrassed. But then one day while cleaning the room, there was no one else there and I stood right in front of it and stared. He looked nothing like our saints, but had several pairs of arms and legs that were spread like wings; his body as sheer as a veil. He looked ready to fly. I could see everything inside his body, everything I had never known. The picture had been drawn by a master who lived in Italy, one of the countries Gluck had told me about. It didn't sound real. He said the sun always shone and the air smelled of honey. I was stunned; were we all like this, on the inside: veins, heart, and brain, blood flowing and muscles bulging? I frowned and asked, "But where is the soul, Pastor Gluck?"

He looked at me in surprise. "I can't tell you how often I have thought of that, Marta. The soul is God's masterpiece. We have it but on loan; it belongs to him in eternity. Be careful with it; it's fragile and invaluable, the one thing that makes man a man. Nothing is more precious."

"Nothing? Not even the truth?"

He hesitated. "Telling the truth might not always save you. But maiming your soul will destroy you for sure. What good to conquer the world if you damage your soul? I can spot such a man from a hundred yards away."

* * *

In my first summer with the Glucks, Tsar Peter of all the Russias declared together with August the Strong war on mighty Sweden. I remembered the puppet show I had watched at my last spring fair, about a soldier refusing him entry to the fortress of Riga: Peter used that slight as a pretext for war. He also claimed that he wanted to free the Baltics, provinces of "olden Russian lands" from the Swedish yoke, which Reverend Gluck said felt like mocking us all, as the tsar's words were not based on history, religion, nor language. "We are but a pawn," he'd say at the dining table on days when news came. "Our peace is broken without waging a direct war. I have heard that Peter has tens of thousands of men in his army. Who over time can oppose such a power?" His words worried us and we prayed longer than usual before dinner, thanking God for his provisions and asking for peace and prosperity. As long as I could remember, people from Russia, Poland, Sweden, and the Baltics had lived together and gone about their business. Was our world coming to an end?

* * *

At first, our lives didn't really change. The harvest had been good and the barns and pantries were filled, ready for the long winter. Merchants, minstrels, roving tradesmen, and handymen were out and about, as they had always been. But the news they brought to Marienburg was worrying. The skirmishes had spread and were said to also have reached the *mir* where my family lived. I just hoped that they had left with the great famine of the last summer and were spared the war, living in safety and health. It had been three years since I'd left home. I had turned nineteen. Maggie would be seven years old by now, Fyodor almost a man, and Christina for sure married and a mother herself. Every night, I hoped that their lives were as blessed as mine was with the Glucks.

* * *

In late October, shortly before the big autumn storms were unleashed, Charles of Sweden, the mythical warrior king, crossed the Bay of Riga and set foot on the Baltics. We heard that he jumped from the prow of his ship into the spray of the shoreline to claim our countries for good. By late November his army had reached Narva, a Swedish stronghold, which had been under siege by the Russian army for over a month, as the priest told me while pointing out Narva on the map. Forty thousand Russians had struck camp outside the city's mighty walls, I heard, but was unable to imagine such a horde or what it meant for Narva. The men were exhausted from the long march, short of ammunition, and food was as scarce as clean drinking water. Any *izba* or *mir* had been plundered and the people had fled, hiding their livestock in the deep forest. Supplies and reinforcements promised from Novgorod never arrived and the generals were at odds with each other. There were drunken brawls every night and the troops' morale was at an all-time low when their cannons, which were cast from thin, cheap metal, exploded in their faces when they tried to fire them. King Charles arrived with nine thousand men, a fraction of the Russian army, but nature was his ally: a thick fog drifted in from the sea, followed by a heavy snowstorm, swallowing his men and horses from the enemy's sight. The Russian soldiers ran into the Swedish bayonets like crazed, scared deer.

The tsar only survived because he was in Novgorod on the day of the battle. The Swedes scornfully minted a coin showing a crying Peter sitting outside Narva, his crown slipping from his head and the words *He sat in the snow and sobbed like a child* engraved underneath. The priest showed it to me, laughing despite his admiration for the young tsar. "Look at his face! It's so well done. The poor man, the very picture of thwarted ambition." The following Sunday, he held a special service saying grace, for the order of things as we knew them was kept, and we thought the war was over. In truth, it hadn't even started.

16

Food became scarce shortly before the Battle of Narva, as there were now two big armies who took what they thought was their due, plundering farms and stopping merchants to relieve them of their goods. Fewer and fewer traveling tradesmen dared to be out and about. In the market, I heard women exchange heated words or even saw them getting into fisticuffs over butchers' bones, shriveled-up beans, stale bread, and bags of sprouting dry peas. Thankfully, I did not need to take part in those, as there was always a good loaf as well as a bunch of unblemished vegetables left under the counter for the priest's household, as all the farmers attended Gluck's service on Sundays. The cook served us a pie of wild mushrooms and red onions for dinner, which was filling, but the difference to the bounty of summer was stark. The November mist shrouded the town and drifted into our hearts.

We bowed our head for the table prayer: the priest, whose family stemmed from Germany, asked for peace and prosperity in the Baltics, for the health of both Tsar Peter and King Charles XII, and for the salvation of the soldiers' souls. Caroline sliced the pie and served the largest piece to her husband, then to her sons, Agneta, and then me. The last and usually smallest piece went on her plate. We ate in silence and heard nothing but the scratching of wood spoons on pewter plates and the autumn wind whipping the empty roads of Marienburg, making the rectory's shutters rattle.

All of a sudden Agneta looked up, and said in her most solemn tone, "Is it true that the tsar of Russia is a two-headed giant who eats children for supper?"

We all laughed, grateful for the lighter note, while Agneta looked confounded.

"Yes," Anton said, smiling, "and little priests' daughters with blond braids and blue eyes, crispy yet tender, are his favorite." As he teased her, I noticed how dark his eyelashes were in comparison to his very light eyes. Yet when he looked up, I lowered my gaze.

Agneta frowned, realizing she was being teased, but looked relieved at the shift in mood and returned to her plate. We all glanced at the priest. We had heard so much about the tsar of all the Russias and his strange decrees, the *ukazy*. They were set to change his country, cost what it may. His subjects seemed less than happy with his ideas: despite his law from two years ago that had forced the Russians in Walk to shave their beards, I'd still spotted bearded Russians in Marienburg, who also still wore their long, belted gowns, sleeves dragging in a puddle. Surely, in Russia itself it was a different story? There, I had heard, beards were to be shaved under threat of hefty fines or hard labor. Also, at every Russian city gate, dolls showed how men or women had to dress, and tailors took orders for new wardrobes there and then. If the Russian weather was not conducive to tight trousers, short jackets, and low-cut dresses, the tsar didn't care.

"Peter wants to take the eastern Muscovy and turn it into a western Russia. One should admire him," Ernst Gluck finally said.

"Admire? And why is that?" Anton said, sounding astonished, as ever ready to verbally cross swords with a man as learned as his father. His confidence, spirit, and fire added to his looks and his presence, and I had noticed how Marienburg's young maidens lingered after services to catch a word with him, or a glance.

"You'd think I have explained that often enough in my lessons," Gluck said with a sigh. Anton rolled his eyes. He caught me looking at him and shot me a smile. I quickly looked away, blushed, and swallowed a jolt of pleasure.

"Anton," his mother scolded, but with a gentleness reserved for her favorite child.

"No, Mother, let me speak. The tsar is our enemy and if he gets his way we'll be but a footnote in history, a story to scare children with at bedtime. Since when does Russia ever give up what it has conquered? Look at how the kingdom of Rus has spread to the east from Kiev, swallowing everything along its way. We have centuries of slavery ahead of us. What nonsense to give the fact that we were 'always' Russian lands as a reason for war? Why doesn't he stay in his Muscovy, where he belongs? He's got no business here in the West."

Ernst shrugged. "You are right. We are but a pawn. Neither Peter nor Charles have a true claim on our lands. But without the West, Muscovy in doomed, Anton. The tsar needs an ice-free harbor, to trade and to fight, which Archangelsk doesn't guarantee. Azov, on the Black Sea, really belongs to the Porte in Istanbul, who will get it back as soon as they can. Peter and Russia risk to be crushed between the Ottoman Empire in the east and the Swedes in the west, No, he *has* to fight; and he needs the Baltics to breathe and to prosper. Considering Peter's heritage it's no surprise that he's looking west."

"Why is that?" I asked.

"His mother grew up in the household of an open-minded man, who corresponded greatly with Western thinkers. And don't forget his half sister Sophia, the regent. She, too, looked to the west for Russia's good."

"The slut," Frederic spat out.

His mother raised her eyebrows. "And why's that? Because she wanted an education and a life for herself instead of rotting in a *terem*? She was a good ruler as long as Peter was too young to reign, and his half brother Ivan, God bless his soul was, frankly, an idiot."

"What is a *terem*?" I asked. God, I felt like such a country bumpkin, but the Glucks answered me with never-ending patience.

"A part of the Russian house where the women of the family live. The only men allowed in are relatives. Women live there in hiding, until they are able to marry, and receive no proper lessons. If they are ever allowed to leave the *terem*, then it is only in closed carriages and in wide, concealing clothes. But somehow Sophia convinced her father, Tsar Alexis, to allow her to learn. At his death, she was the eldest and healthiest of his surviving children and seized power as a regent. Peter was but a toddler of three years then, and his half brother Ivan so ill that he couldn't keep the tsar's tiara on his lolling head, it was said. Sophia did good work, especially by knotting diplomatic ties with the

West and corresponding with rulers and thinkers. Really, compared with her, Peter can't count to three. But she's a woman. That's her true, unforgiveable fault."

A woman had ruled Russia, I thought with wonder. How could that be? "Is she still alive?" I asked.

"Yes, but in a convent somewhere, probably cursing every day she has left. She and her lover, Prince Gallitzin, thought far, yet not far enough when they were in power."

"Prince Gallitzin! This—" Anton stopped, unable to find a word that showed his contempt for Regent Sophia's lover.

"Past," Caroline said, covering Agneta's ears just in case. The girl immediately wriggled free to hear more.

"Think before you speak, Anton," his father said.

Anton threw his spoon onto his plate, rose, and left the room, slamming the door. A look of thunder settled over his father.

"He's such a hothead," Caroline said, but not especially disapprovingly. Frederic mashed up the mushrooms on his plate, shifting them from right to left, and Agneta looked at everyone's faces, trying to work out what had made everyone so angry. The room felt darker and colder without Anton.

"Prince Gallitzin," Caroline said, helping her husband to find the thread of his last thought.

He smiled at her. "He lived with Sophia, but was far from, well, whatever Anton wanted to call him. He is a soldier and a diplomat. Without his work and his thoughts, Peter wouldn't have half his ideas: the military and administrative service for the sons of his nobles; building a navy; his travels to Holland, Berlin, England, and Vienna to see life and the progress of the West with his own eyes. Since then, Peter is restless and his goal is clear: he wants Russia to be a true player in politics, a global power, if you want. I bet that he is already looking for a foreign bride for his son Alexey, even though it's unheard of in the house of Romanov."

"But why didn't Sophia think far enough ahead?" I asked, keen to return to the topic of this woman ruler. Had she also been beautiful? It all sounded like a fairy tale, albeit with an unhappy ending. How awful to be banned to a monastery after such a life, and such a love.

"Well, her hold on power wasn't safe as long as Peter lived. But she never threatened him, even when he was but a boy, and it would have been so easy. Who knows why she didn't. I doubt it was her love of family. Her clan and the family of Peter's mother were forever at odds. Perhaps she simply didn't take him seriously."

"Where was he while she was the regent?"

"At first he lived in the Kremlin, until he set fire to it. He is said to love arson, and, more than that, extinguishing flames. So Sophia sent him to Moscow's German quarter, the Nemezaja Sloboda, outside the city's gates. There, he was playing. Playing at being a soldier, playing at being at war, and playing at ruling as a tsar. That's where they say he met people from all over the world, and from all walks of life. tradesmen, merchants, artists, thinkers, doctors, and pharmacists. This is where they believe he picked up his passion for all things Western. Have we ever before heard of a ruler who leaves his country for three years just to travel and to learn? Russians usually hold foreign ways in great suspicion."

"Did Peter meet Anna Mons in the German quarter?" I asked, and Caroline shot me a warning glance. This was not for Agneta's ears.

Ernst smiled. "Ah, women, always interested in love stories. Yes, I suppose that is where he met her, just before Sophia banished him to a village far from Moscow and far from any power, or so she thought. He, however, took his friends along and built up an army to counter hers, a state within the state. Before she knew it, he had men and arms, was married to a daughter of a respectable Russian family, had a son and heir and had reached majority."

"What happened to Peter's wife?" I continued.

"Evdokia Lopukina? The poor soul. From their three sons, only Alexey was to live. Some years ago Peter sent her to a remote nunnery after she refused a divorce. He is said to have pleaded for hours with her, but to no avail. She's rat fodder for all her pride, and Anna Mons has the time of her life. But she's given Peter no heir so far, so who knows what will happen."

Caroline shivered. "Poor Evdokia. How terrible, to bury such a young woman alive. Why didn't he send her back to her family?"

Which brought the Glucks to one of their favorite subjects of conversation: whether divorce should be allowed or not.

17

We decorated the church to say grace for the harvest, all the women together. Despite the shortages, people brought in bundles of grain, stewed fruit, pickled vegetables, smoked fish and meat, and scented wood, which we tied together with colorful ribbons. The dozens of homemade candles burned brightly: we had sat together in the evenings, turning them from bees' wax. The best fat for candles was to be found in whales' heads, but was very dear and hard to come by.

The pews and floorboards were shiny and clean when the congregation flocked in, and the church air was fragrant with the offerings. The men and women were well dressed, though you could only tell that from the cut of the cloth and the thickness of the fabric, for Lutherans didn't dress like Russians, who praise their Lord by dripping with velvet, gold, and silver. Cleanliness was more important than riches, and the only signs of vanity on show were the vast white lace collars the married women wore. Young girls tied colorful scarves around their waists, and pearls shimmered in their earlobes as well as around their necks. Their hair was braided and wrapped around their heads like crowns. The girls entered the church with cheeks blushed from the winter cold and pretended not to even notice the young men, though I saw a few of them discreetly casting glances at Anton and Frederic. I had polished their boots to a shine and their breeches were so tight that you could see the muscles of their long, strong legs. They and their friends in turn pretended not to notice the girls, only to later eye them up when they took their places in the pews among their families.

It was a world I would never be part of. The Glucks were kinder than I could have hoped, but I would never be courted by these boys from their respectable families, I would never be a bashful maiden guarded by her family, would never be sold for a piece of silver, or carry bitter secrets. I was feeling sorry for myself to be sure, and it must have shown on my face. When I looked up, I saw Anton smiling at me. He winked and a light shot through me. I *did* belong here. Maybe someday I would belong even more.

* * *

I was sitting with all the pastor's children during the service. Agneta's little hand stole into mine while she leafed through the hymnal with the other. I knew all the chorales by heart, so I wouldn't be embarrassed by not being able to read one. Anton and Frederic chuckled and whispered to each other; Anton, it was recently decided, was about to start work with a Marienburg merchant in spring. Only then could he think about having his own family. Anton, leaving the house, ready to settle down with another girl, whom he loved and honored? The thought was crushing, and the feeling was the stronger, as I had not been ready for it at all, like a river that had been dammed until it burst.

Anton was looking right at me; his gaze scalding. I didn't hear a word of the service after that. When the voices joined in a hymn, I heard it as if from far away. I rose with the congregation, without thinking, my knees trembling; when I sat down again, Anton's fingers touched my hand. I bit down my smile. I had no strength left to fight this feeling. His fingers held mine hidden in the deep folds of my dress, so no one around us could see, not even Agneta or Caroline at the end of the pew. My heart was racing behind my tightly laced bodice but I was trying to keep a pious face, when my eyes met the gaze of a tall blond stranger seated in the pew behind Anton and me. I blushed even deeper: Had he watched us? I turned without giving him another glance. The priest stepped out of the small altar chamber, the people rose, and the service started. Only when the last hymn was over, and we knelt in prayer, did Anton let go of my hand.

I turned around and caught Caroline's eye. God was giving me more than what I could hope for, I thought. A family.

18

In the following days Anton and I lived for every moment that we could snatch to spend together. He spent the mornings studying with his father while I cleaned, and then he'd wear his best attire to present himself to one Marienburg merchant after the other. But with a war declared and the armies camping, waiting for orders and ready to strike and making all travel and trade dangerous, finding employment wasn't easy. Still, somehow he could leave the house just when I had to go on an errand or come to the church when it was just me tidying it. I'd drop my work there and then: we'd talk, laugh, murmur little sweet nothings to each other, hold each other tight—and yes, we'd kiss, kiss, kiss, our lips brushing and our breaths lacing in the cold nave.

Shortly before Christmas—the busiest time in the year for the Glucks—we were alone in the rectory and Anton prowled through the rooms and corridors, catching me at every corner, at every staircase, snatching kisses and embraces. He held me tight, cupped my face, and covered my face and throat with kisses, before he sighed: "Marta. I can't go on like this. I hate all this secrecy and following you around like a randy dog. Be mine. Marry me. Come spring I'll have work and then I can feed us. We can have a small house together and . . ."

"What nonsense!" I said, though they were the words I most longed to hear. "Your parents will never allow us to marry. It is one thing to take in a girl off the street as a maid, and I am eternally grateful for their kindness, but it is quite another to welcome her as a daughter-in-law."

"But as soon as I have an income, it shan't be their decision to make." How I loved his pride and confidence! "It's *my* life, and I want it to be with you, every day and every night," he said, kissing me again and again, holding me tight, till I felt his desire through my dress and apron. "Be mine, entirely," he begged, his breath hot on my skin. "We love each other. Being together is part of love; part of a love like ours."

My heart leaped with excitement and plummeted with shame. I thought of the things Vassily had made me do. Could I forget the pain of Vassily raping me, of Misha holding me down in that hellish house? Was there something else? Yes, there had to be. He raised my chin and I met his deep, honest gaze. Anton was what Christina and I had thought of when we plucked flowers and lit candles seeking out a future husband's name. Just then we heard Mrs. Gluck's voice calling me and jumped. He snatched a last kiss before I hastily straightened my dress, smoothed my hair, and began walking toward the study, from where she ran the rectory's household.

Anton held me back, his fingers hot on my skin. "Don't lock your door tonight," he said, before letting me go.

"I have to go," I said to him, numb with fear, and happiness.

* * *

I sleepwalked through my chores that day, thinking only of the night ahead. My fingers trembled so much that I broke the Christmas cookies to crumbles when turning them from their copper cutters and had to start all over again, wasting butter and flour. I cut myself while hollowing the apples' cores to fill them with raisins and nuts. I was unable to tie a single wreath, but dropped all twigs of fir and holly. Seeing Mrs. Gluck startled me, though she behaved as she always had. I remembered her words of warning: "I will not tolerate fornication in my house." But surely a soon-to-be husband and wife lying together was not fornication, as such? Wasn't I entitled to marriage, happiness, and a contented life, just like her? If I might not have been their ideal daughter-in-law, I would make up for their kindness and my good fortune for the rest of my life, I swore while touching my lips, swollen from Anton's kisses. I couldn't fight my feelings any longer. For the first time in my life I knew the power of passion, a flood which tears away all reason, just as the big melt crushes the last ice floes in our rivers.

* * *

He came to me when I had almost fallen asleep, after folding my hands in evening prayer three times over, and then tossing and turning on my straw sack. The door opened but a gap, and mercifully without creaking, and a moment later he held me in his arms. I stiffened on my straw sack when I first felt his weight upon me, but everything was so different to Vassily! Anton's body was warm, his hands were smooth, and his breath was sweet when we kissed. I pressed myself against him, wanting to feel him everywhere, and almost helped him when he gently took off my nightshirt, letting it drop on the floor, and covered us with his coat. Lying so close to him, I dared to discover him. I was hesitant at first, but then I grew more daring: his muscles, the dark and curly hair on his chest, and his flat, hard belly. The straw felt spiky on our naked skin, but we giggled and his skin on mine was a caress in itself; how long had my body waited for this delight?

"How beautiful your breasts are." He sighed, cupping them gently. "And your skin is as white as milk." His lips followed my throat, nibbling my tender skin, making my breath fly. Lightning shot through my veins when his tongue found my nipples, sucking and teasing the tender flesh. I sighed and spread myself open, as all I wanted was him, more of him: much, much more. My whole being gathered in my limbs, spilling into my belly and then between my thighs. I wrapped myself around his hips and pulled him toward me, trying to guide him. Vassily had always been in such a hurry, once he finally had gotten hard. But Anton's fingers met mine, stopping me, and he smiled. "Not so quickly. You, too, want to enjoy this, don't you?"

I was not quite sure what he meant, but Anton kneeled between my thighs, spread them, licked his fingers, and gently caressed me, fondling my curly hair. "What a sweet dark fur you have there, my little cat. I'll like that as long as I live, I promise." He bent over me, kissed my belly, and then gently raised my hips to his mouth. "Don't move." His whisper sent shivers over my skin: What was he doing? I felt embarrassed seeing, feeling, knowing him so close to my secret spot, and I wanted to push him back, when I felt his tongue: I rose with a muffled scream and my whole body arched with shock at what he was doing and at what I felt. He traced my wetness, again and again, deeper and deeper, before caressing me in tiny circles. Vassily had shoved himself so many times into my mouth—I had had no idea that it could be the other way around as well. Heat shot through my body and my limbs went as soft as butter in August; my fingers laced themselves into his fair hair. I moaned, then all of a sudden his tongue stopped and he held still. All I felt was his hot breath on my moist, swollen flesh.

"Please," I sighed.

Anton's tongue tip brushed my softest, most secret spot, a spot I hadn't even known existed. I felt a wave building up in my body, mighty and powerful, and I was ready to throw myself into it with abandon. Molten gold seared my veins, I called out and then fell back, my face sweaty and my throat dry. My skin glistened pale in the moonlight, droplets pooled like liquid starlight between my full breasts. Anton slid up to me and kissed me, so that I briefly, greedily tasted my own scent on his lips, before he slid into me, gently, carefully, feeling his way where I was so wet and swollen. Vassily had always been nothing but pain, but I moaned when Anton thrust into me more forcefully, right up to the root. Closing my thighs around his hips I met his every move, wanting more and more of him. I held his neck, his back, his bottom, and finally he stifled a scream and fell on top of me, panting, and his heartbeat racing. I stroked the hair from his moist forehead and blew the glistening sweat from his face. He smiled, his eyes closed, his lips searching for mine, his hands still cupping my body. This was how we fell asleep.

When he slipped out of my chamber shortly before sunrise, my lips were swollen from his kisses, my breasts longed for his tenderness, and my heart was full, yet it felt as light as never before.

* * *

The following Sunday in church I folded my hands in prayer and asked God for one thing only: to live a long and fulfilled life at Anton's side. When I raised my head during the last hymn, my gaze met the eyes of the tall, blond stranger whom I had already seen at the harvest service. He was not old, but his sinuous body was haggard and his weathered face lined with countless small wrinkles and scars. He looked just as many of the Swedish soldiers of the Marienburg Garrison did. He stared brazenly at my mouth, as if he knew what had happened. I lowered my eyes, but his look burned holes in my lids.

19

Anton couldn't sneak out to see me for the next few days, and at mealtimes I understood that he had to behave like always and pay me no attention. In the kitchen I heard that yet another Marienburg merchant had turned him away. Ernst Gluck was said to be angry and helpless. I couldn't believe that: a man like him, with his faith and his patience? The same afternoon, Mrs. Gluck called me into her study. Had Anton spoken with his parents already? That was why he wasn't coming to see me: he wanted to put our love on a formal footing. My fingers trembled as I plaited my braid anew, and I felt my blood rush through my veins; surely I wouldn't dare to look at her when I entered the room. Would she treat me like family now, or would she be disappointed in the choice her son had made? I knocked on the door with my heart in my mouth.

The Glucks were in the room together. I was surprised to see the pastor, as he was so busy shortly before Christmas. But then, of course he'd be there to welcome me into the family! They smiled as I entered, and she set her sewing aside. "Come in, Marta, and close the door. It's such a cold and windy day. We'll have more snow later, what do you think, Ernst?"

The only person missing was Anton himself. Was he too nervous to sit through this? He wasn't meant to speak to his parents till he had found work. I could forgive him his haste, I thought with a little smile, as I, too, couldn't wait to be with him forever.

"Mulled wine?" Ernst Gluck asked. "It's delicious."

Mulled wine, at noon, in these times? We definitely had something to celebrate. I sat next to Caroline, sinking into the stripy sofa. The bowl warmed my hands; the bits of apple and pear bobbed on the surface, soaking themselves full of the steaming red liquid and sinking to the bottom of the bowl.

Mrs. Gluck broke the silence as her husband stoked the fire in the tiled oven. I saw embers fly. "Marta, something absolutely wonderful has happened. I'd never have dared to hope for such luck and happiness for you."

I blushed deeply. "What has happened?" I asked, my voice husky with feeling. Indeed, how could I have hoped for such happiness? Oh my strong, honest, and most beloved Anton. He had kept his word.

"You know that there are some Swedes in my congregation? Men who live in the garrison? Honest, good men, such as a dragoon called Johann Trubach," said Ernst Gluck, leaning against the warm oven.

"Yes?" I said, nodding. Had this Trubach some link to a merchant and had given Anton a job?

Caroline smiled and took my hand. "A soldier will never be a rich man, but Johann has his own room in the garrison, steady pay, and a warm heart. That is all that counts, isn't it?"

Well, yes, but what for? My fingers clenched the bowl so as not to drop it. Where was Anton, and why was he not here at my back to speak up for us?

"Believe it or not, yesterday Trubach asked for your hand in marriage. He was not to be deterred," the priest said, and his wife beamed at me. "It's true. He spotted you in church and fell in love, there and then."

"But that's impossible," I stammered. All this was a mistake—I was promised to Anton. Another man could not ask for my hand in marriage; I was spoken for. Surely the Glucks had sent that silly dragoon packing?

"I know," he said. "And I've been very open with him. You have neither parents nor a dowry. God knows, you don't even have a family name." He winked at me. "But for him it's enough to know that you share a roof with us."

"Can I think about it?" I asked, dry-mouthed. I had to buy time to tell Anton and make him stop this. Together we'd find a way out!

"What is there to think about?" Caroline asked. "We have accepted his proposal in your name. Nothing better could happen to a simple girl like you," she said, and hugged me. "Congratulations! Ernst will marry you in the New Year."

"So quickly? Don't you need my help anymore?" I asked, instead of blurting: *No! I love your eldest son and he loves me. We are engaged to marry!*

"Not so much anymore, Marta. Agneta will join Ernst's classes, and Anton has finally found work, albeit with a merchant in Pernau. He left this morning but he'll visit us for Easter, and then Johann and you have to come for supper, too. Anton was sorry not to see you, but he sends you his warmest regards."

Anton had left without saying good-bye to me? He sent his *warmest regards*? I swallowed hard and tears welled up. I tasted bile: by Easter I'd be dead from longing for him. Of course he had not known that I was to be married off! I saw concern in Mrs. Gluck's eyes and she took my hand. "There, there," she said. "I know, it's all such a surprise. Why not marry soon, at Epiphany? Trubach is coming for supper tomorrow evening. He is a nice man, you'll see." She took up her sewing again and the pastor smiled at me as a father would, proudly and kindly. The talk was over. I turned to leave and saw a quick glance passing between the Glucks: a silent look of agreement and understanding. Were they getting rid of me? No. They had wanted only the best for me, always. Could I disobey them, to whom I owed everything? The answer was clear in both my heart and my mind: I could.

* * *

That night I only waited for the right moment. I had no time to lose and checked my bundle twice. I had enough money to take me to Pernau; the first carts were leaving at dawn. I'd walk if I had to. The Glucks would be hurt, insulted, too. I couldn't care. Just as I rose for the third time to check my belongings, I heard a tapping against the window-pane. Someone was throwing pebbles against it. I almost stumbled in my haste to reach the window, tearing the lead lock open. A horse was tethered outside the rectory, its breath steaming. The winter night hid the rider's face—his coat collar was turned up and his hat was pulled deep over his forehead—but my heart knew what my eyes couldn't see:

it was Anton, who had come to take me with him. He got off the horse and hastened over.

"Marta," he said, embracing me. "I have to go, but I can't just leave without saying good-bye to you."

The clouds moved across the moon and in the sudden light I saw him clearly: his blue eyes and his strong white teeth. "No need for saying good-bye, Anton. I have packed. Let me get my boots and my coat and I'm ready. I shall sit behind you on the horse. We can do this," I whispered, my voice choked.

"It's not safe to travel with a young woman, Marta. There are two large, marauding armies out and about, just waiting for their next orders. Do you know what bored soldiers do with a girl like you?" he said. "And, besides, what will we live on? Give me time to build my life in Pernau and I'll come and get you."

"But time is running out . . ." I pleaded.

"I love you," he said. "You are best here, with my parents. We have time aplenty."

"Far from it. They are marrying me off to a Swedish dragoon and your father wants to wed us at Epiphany, in only a couple of weeks. But I only love you and I will only ever love you." I heard the fear in my voice. Men can sense a woman's despair like bloodhounds their prey, I thought, remembering something Tanya had said a lifetime ago. Still, I couldn't stop myself. "Isn't the war almost over? After Narva there shouldn't be any more reason to fight, should there? That's what your father says, at least. The Swedes have won and are keeping their hold on the Baltic provinces." I sounded unsure.

"My father knows nothing," Anton spat out. "What is Narva to Charles but another feather in his cap? He is crazy about war and France and England are only happy to know he is busy here. Charles will only stop when he reaches Moscow." The church bell tolled and he looked around. "I have to go, Marta."

I clung to his neck, crying. "Don't leave me."

He loosened my grip, caressed my face, and whispered, "Don't cry. Let's wait and see, shall we? Perhaps this isn't the worst way forward? After all, I wasn't the first with whom you—well, you know—"

"How do you mean?" My voice was hoarse with hurt.

He shrugged. "Well, like this we can always meet without anyone being suspicious. You will be an honest woman then, and we can do what we want . . ." He kissed me, his warm tongue in my mouth. To my anger my body answered his embrace.

I pushed him away. "Take me with you," I said at last, through tears, grabbing his cloak once more with my fists and clinging to him.

Somebody stirred in the rectory's door and he hastily shrank away from me, relief in his face. "I ought to go. Don't despair, Marta. We'll meet again." He mounted his horse, tipped his hat, and galloped away through the narrow alleyways of Marienburg, his horse's hooves thundering on the cobblestones, toward a town that was by the wide, open sea, far away from me. Why had I wasted those last moments to quarrel with him? I should have smiled and lured him in, saying, *Come, my love, let's talk about this inside, shall we?* Pain and shame tore me apart, but I held my breath when the Glucks' cook, who worked late, stepped out onto the snowy street.

"Who's there?" she asked, raising her lantern and squinting into the darkness.

I shrank back, fell onto my room's cold stone floor, and cried helplessly, clawing at the straw, writhing and heaving with sobs. Anton's betrayal stabbed me with icicles. Only when I shivered with cold—despite my warm clothes, which I had wanted to wear traveling to Pernau—I got up and closed the window. The flagstones were covered with rime as I opened my bundle and unfolded my dresses, just to fold them again. I did this over and over again before finally falling asleep.

20

I was sick for the first time between Christmas and the New Year, and threw up in a kitchen bucket. The cook had surprised us with a heavy goose liver pie for Christmas dinner: surely, that hadn't agreed with me. When I didn't bleed I thought of Olga's despair. I was pregnant with Anton's child.

* * *

Whenever Johann Trubach came to see me, my eyes were red and swollen from crying, and I hardly even thanked him for the small gifts he brought each time, be it some colored yarn; new, pointed needles; or boiled sweets. The day before Epiphany—the day Ernst had set for our wedding—I was resolved: I had to end the engagement.

Johann fetched me for a walk in town. As the war, and what might happen next, was ever on our minds, I was glad that he didn't wear his uniform, but instead a simple, dark knee-length jacket with tight breeches and sturdy, high boots. His shirt was spotless, and he even wore a silk neckerchief and a warm fur-lined coat. Dressed like that he looked like a well-to-do burgher—not that such a man would ever marry the likes of me.

"Lift your hands up high in the air, so they are nice and white," Caroline told me, and pinched my cheeks rosy before Johann came. "There you go. Now you look healthy again. Don't be too long, will you? We have a lot to prepare for tomorrow."

Marienburg was busy but joyless. The stench of sewage on the icy streets gathered in the clear January air. I took care so the muck wouldn't spoil the boots Caroline had lent me for the walk. Coachmen still drove their oxen and mules on with their whips, even though their carts only carried light loads. Baker boys with frozen red faces sold meager rations of bread, pie, and Epiphany cake, in which a lucky charm was hidden: I bought a cake for the rectory, as we all needed some good fortune in those days. Farmers hawked poached animals such as skinny hares and small deer; they were freshly hunted, blood still trickling from their ears. Well-dressed men tipped their hats to each other, trying to hide their axes and dragging along little handcarts full of freshly chopped firewood. I counted more and more beggars in town, squabbling with the girls of easy virtue for the best places to loiter. A man sold hot chestnuts, turning them on the spit, his fingertips charred by the smoldering coal. Johann bought me a handful and we walked on, enjoying the soft, sweet, and mushy taste in silence. Once we had eaten, his fingers sought mine in the muff that Mrs. Gluck had loaned me. I hastily withdrew my hand and he looked at me, saddened. "May I not hold your hand? Do I disgust you so much? What can I do to make you like me more?" he asked.

I felt ashamed: at our few meetings, he had treated me with more kindness than I could have asked for. "You don't disgust me—" I started, but he would not listen to me.

"Why do you then always look so sad when I come to see you? It was your own free will to marry me, wasn't it?"

"Yes. And no."

"No?" He stopped, stunned, and looked at me, his hands hanging by his side. It was as if I had stabbed him right into his heart.

I touched his arm. "Please. You are a good man, Johann. But I simply can't marry you."

He smiled, which surprised me. "Oh, I see. It's the priest's son, isn't it? I have watched the two of you in church. I know it's hard, but forget about him. He will marry a Pernau girl who will further his prospects, such as a merchant's daughter."

I blushed. Had this been clear to everyone but me? Perhaps I was being foolish. It would be easier to get married and raise this child as ours. Which man in love notices a month here or there? But I didn't want to be a liar, like Anton.

"I am pregnant, Johann," I said, lowering my voice. "You won't want to marry a girl who carries the child of another man, will you?"

He stopped and stared at me. My courage gave way to dread. What would he do? Slap me? Drag me back to the rectory and shame me, for the Glucks to throw me out? I'd be on the streets again, but this time pregnant. I felt breathless and light-headed from fear, and stepped back, when Johann embraced me in full view of all Marienburg, kissing my forehead and laughing. A minstrel lifted his pipe from his frozen lips, just to smile at us. Johann tossed him a coin.

"How wonderful, Marta!"

I was dumbfounded.

"I, too, have something to tell you before we get married."

I looked at him. What could it be?

"I will not be able to satisfy you as a husband. It's all over, be it due to an old wound, or due to the cold in the field and the fortress of Riga. I'll only be half a husband to you, but a full father to your child, I swear."

What was there left to say? The following day Ernst married us in his church. I wore a high-necked dress cut of pale gray cotton and held a small bunch of snowdrops so tightly that my knuckles turned white. For our wedding breakfast we ate chicken stuffed with offal and drank wine and beer: it was the best the Glucks' kitchen had to offer. When we shared the Epiphany cake as dessert, I found the lucky charm inside my piece.

* * *

Johann kept his promise and was a good husband, who never raised his voice or hand against me, liked the food I cooked, and only came home drunk on a Friday, when I agreed for him to spend part of his pay to go to a *kabak* with his friends. We laughed together—not a lot, but enough—and for that time in my life, his good nature gave me what I had longed for: peace at heart. If this was to be my life, so be it. His room in the garrison was sparsely furnished with a table, two chairs, and a narrow bed; our few clothes hung on two hooks on the wall; and I tried to make it pretty by placing flowers in a bowl on our windowsill. But a month after our wedding, he left for the field. I felt very lonely after the warm chattiness of the Glucks' household, but visited Caroline as rarely as possible without being impolite. Everything there reminded me of Anton, my feelings for him and how he had humiliated me.

The only friend I had in the garrison was my neighbor, Lisa, whose sons and husband were away in battle. One evening in May we sat together in her room, turning collars and darning socks for the still-wealthy customers who liked her needlework. We sipped *kvass* and Lisa chewed tobacco—her only joy in life, she said—but I found the spitting of red saliva as off-putting as the tinted gums and the rotten teeth the habit gave you. In a break from sewing she spat for once neatly in her bucket and then took my palm in her hands.

"Let me read your hand, my sunshine, and see what life has to offer a dove like you. Haggard old Johann can't be all, can it?" She giggled tipsily and looked at my palm, where lines crisscrossed, starting low down at the wrist and leading up all the way to my fingers. She shook her head. "Who are you trying to fool, or have you borrowed your hand from another woman?"

"Why? What is it you see?" I asked eagerly. "Will I be happy? What about my baby, what will it be?"

She glanced at my palm again. "I see a big, strong love and many, many travels. I see a long life—you are as strong as a horse, aren't you, Marta?"

"Travels?" I said, laughing. "Impossible. And what about that big, strong love? Will it be fulfilled?" I honored Johann, but would not speak of love when thinking of him.

She bent my hand and counted the small folds that formed beneath my little finger. "Indeed. I see thirteen pregnancies."

"Thirteen? Good Lord!" I said, but then fell silent. Johann had to content himself with caressing my body while I lay on my back, my eyes closed. I felt so lonely and miserable in those moments: Where was Anton now, and was he ever thinking of me? I was even ready to forget his ugly last words and his betrayal, if he came back for me.

I rested my hand on my only lightly swollen belly; I did not show much. "What about this baby then? Is it a boy or a girl?"

She dropped my hand. "I can't see that. Stop asking nonsense and get on with your work," she said, picking up her needlework again.

* * *

Two days later I met Mrs. Gluck in the market. By now, farmers only sold what they didn't need to survive, and there were no more foreign merchants and traveling salesmen to be seen. One year with foraging armies had sent the province into famine: the people of Marienburg paid with strings of pearls for a pound of butter and with emeralds for a side of bacon; most burghers had swapped their flower beds for vegetable patches. With Mrs. Gluck was a pretty young woman, who carried her basket as I had once done. The pastor's wife embraced me. "Where are you hiding, Marta? Finally we meet again." Her joy at seeing me warmed my heart.

"Well, you know how busy marriage keeps you," I said, and glanced at the stranger. She carried herself proudly in her well-cut blue cloak, the color flattered her light eyes and her blond hair that was wrapped in a heavy bun at the nape of her neck. Small pink pearls shimmered in her earlobes: this was a young woman from a good family.

Caroline linked elbows with her. "Meet Louise. She is Anton's fiancée and has moved in with us. As soon as Anton met her—he works for her father—they were head over heels in love. I hope to be a grandmother soon as well."

She glanced at my belly, smiling, while Louise met my gaze calmly, her gray eyes gauging me, before she gave me a hint of a smile. I was sure that Anton hadn't so much as touched her fingertips in his wooing of her. He'd be the first man to have her, not like the maid in his parents' house. I nodded curtly and just wasn't able to wish her well, as politeness demanded. The sight of her stabbed me right in the heart.

21

After meeting Louise and Caroline in the market I had a mad longing for a hot bath, wanting to scour the memory of Anton from myself. I dragged bucket upon bucket of water up to our room and lit a fire, neither counting the kindling wood nor the coals, but when I poured the last of the steaming water into my wooden tub, a searing pain shot through my lower belly. I bent over double and my knees buckled; I felt a warm gush between my legs before my skirt turned red with blood. I wanted to get up, but pain floored me: it felt as if a giant were squashing me in his fist, breaking my back there and then. I crawled out of my room on all fours and was just about able to knock on Lisa's door before I passed out on the gallery that ran around the garrison to a narrow flight of stairs down into the courtyard. She lifted my feet, told me to breathe and to push. I'd have bled to death without her. Anton's son was stillborn at five months, and with him died my love for his father. Days after, Lisa still spooned hot broth and *kvass* into my mouth to help me gather strength. Lisa had read such nonsense in my palm. During these lightest months of summer my days were as dark as a midwinter night.

* * *

King Charles of Sweden loved war for war's sake. Yet after the first successes, such as holding Swedish Livonia and taking the neighboring Courland, the war turned sour for him. The tsar of all the Russias seemed to have learned from his first defeats. Rumor was rife all over

Marienburg: "Have you heard? General Boris Petrovich Sheremetev is approaching with tens of thousands of men. He's a son of one of Russia's oldest families and has war in his veins. So far, he has lost no battle, they say. The Swedes don't stand a chance."

"Huddle up in the garrison. By July we will be under Russian siege!"

"No, hide in the rectory, it's solid and built of stone. The garrison will burn like tinder."

The rectory? I would not live under one roof with Anton's fiancée, and held out in the garrison, together with other women and children.

On the 25th of August, 1702, Sheremetev attacked Marienburg. To me it seemed as if the day of reckoning, with which Ernst Gluck had threatened us, had truly come. Seen from the garrison's tower, his armies were a flood darkly coming to swallow us whole; shouting, screaming, and shooting. Hell opened its gates. The cannon maws roared and spat death and destruction, the cannonballs howled like wolves in the air—the sound scared me witless the first time I heard it and I hid underneath the table, trembling and crying, pressing my hands to my ears—and they tore open town walls, roads, and the market square. People were rushing around, crazed with fear, bundling their possessions and dragging children and animals along. The wooden houses were ablaze; thick, gray smoke made people choke and hindered them from saving what they could; there was no quenching of the fire. The town lay in ashes, the air reeked of sulfur, and the siege's steady thunder deafened our heartbeats.

By noon the Russians stormed the town: when I watched the dirty, ragged Swedish banner being torn from the main gate, my stomach clenched. To a serf, one master was like the other, but what would it be to live with the Russians once more? I heard the whooping and shouting of their army: they fired round upon round into the air and I knew that Marienburg had capitulated. What had happened to Johann? Was he still alive, and if not, what was to become of me? Lisa mourned both her sons and her husband, who had not returned from battle. Her wailing haunted the empty garrison. I dared to leave my room to plead with her, but she would not open the door.

The next morning, all was silent next door. I hoped she had made it away in the dead of the night, as in the following days no one in their right mind would go outside any longer. The Russians locked captured

Swedes inside stables and set them alight. They plundered and looted, marveling at the riches, and practiced their knife-throwing skills on the Holy Trinity above the altar of Ernst Gluck's church, before melting down the church silver, guzzling the wine of the Eucharist, and lighting bonfires with the pews. I felt weak with hunger, as if an animal sat inside me, slowly and steadily gnawing from my guts to my stomach. I rummaged through any cupboard, shelf, and pot in the deserted flats and rooms, but found nothing but some moldy dry beans and rock-hard bread: in my despair I soaked both in saved rainwater until there was only pulp, then devoured it, but it gave me stomach cramps. Whoever stayed in town would starve: hunger finished wars' dirty work, upending your body once all life was ruined. The Russians ruled the town like a trinity of fire, storm, and death.

* * *

Three days after the battle I heard a knock on my door, which I had barricaded with our table and chairs. The hour of curfew was close and I was just about to cut a carrot for a thin soup—I had dug in a forgotten spot of a vegetable patch in the garrison like a squirrel looking for last autumns' acorns—and halted, knife in hand. The garrison had no more gates and the rest of the building began to serve as firewood. Even I had lit a fire using cladding from the stables. Who could it be? Dusk and even the early hours of the night were but a thin gray veil, which made it hard and very unwise to break the Russians' law. I hid my carrot and grabbed the knife harder.

"Who's there?" I hissed, my ear close to the door.

"Marta Trubach?" a man asked. "I have word from Caroline Gluck. It's about Johann."

Johann! Was he alive after all? I thought of my neighbor Lisa's wailing and even more terrible, the silence behind her door. I moved the table and chairs aside and opened the door, albeit hiding the knife in the folds of my skirt. Outside stood a haggard man: many Sundays ago I had filled his bowl with the rectory's soup at lunchtime and had sometimes given him a forbidden second helping. He hadn't forgotten that, it seemed.

"What is going on?" My eyes swept the gallery. He seemed to be alone, as he, too, looked around carefully. The Russians had their own sense of humor, liking to cut off ears and noses of hapless folk they caught in the street, or branding them like animals. I had also heard stories of caps being nailed to heads or burghers who had had to run the gauntlet.

"Johann is in the town hall. That's where the priest's wife has found him. He is wounded and she doesn't think he'll make the night. But he calls for you in his fever."

My husband was alive: true, we had only lived together for a brief month. But what childish love had I felt for the caddish Anton, and how had I thanked Johann for his kindness! I hesitated: the town hall lay on the other side of town. Curfew was almost upon us and Marienburg's ruins swarmed with Russian soldiers. Despite General Sheremetev's strict orders, they raped anyone in a skirt, be it a seven-year-old girl or a toothless grandmother.

The man slipped away. "I'll be on my way. I hope you see Johann again before he dies." He hastened down the narrow flight of stairs and then out of the garrison.

I remembered Johann's smile and understanding during our fateful walk shortly before our wedding. He had taken me, and loved me, as I was. I wiped my face and hands, twisted my long hair into a hasty bun, and wrapped myself into a cloak that Johann had given me shortly after our wedding. Underneath, I wore a long linen skirt and a belted, sleeveless tunic, which I had embroidered with a pleasant floral pattern during my long, lonely evenings. Even if it was for the last time, Johann should see me neat and pretty. If God protected me and I lowered my head, running fast, I might see Johann while he was still alive. He had given me some peace in life, perhaps I could do the same for him just before he died.

That was the least I owed him.

22

Marienburg was eerily empty. Afternoon had given way to a pale dusk, but the air still reeked of vodka, gunpowder, and smoke. The roads and alleyways were torn open, and I ran whenever I could, avoiding the worst potholes and hiding behind smoldering ruins. If I saw no one, I hoped childishly, no one would see me: I held my cloak tightly so it wouldn't flap and give me away. Soon, I found myself close to the town hall and felt relief: just one more corner and I'd be with Johann. I pressed myself against part of a blackened wall: all seemed quiet. I took a deep breath and prepared for the last spurt across the open square to the town hall and makeshift hospital. I set off—and was jerked back, smashing into the wooden wall.

"Look what we have here!" Three Russian soldiers grinned at me, forcing me against the timber. Their uniforms were dirty and torn and made up from all sorts of clothing: stolen, found, or given—who knew? They all had teeth missing and the one who held me wore a dirty eye patch. Pus seeped from the wound over his face and his hair was caked with mud and blood. The stench of sweat and shit made me retch.

"Let me go, you pig. I have to go to the hospital," I spat at him in Russian.

"To the hospital? Are you a nurse? I have a burning wound that needs urgent seeing to." He laughed and forced my hand between his legs. I snarled at him like an angry cat, but he covered my mouth with his filthy hand, forcing up my head. "Of all the girls I've seen in this damn town you are for sure the prettiest, all clean and nice. And none of the others have complained."

He forced me against the wall; my cloak slipped and splinters dug in my neck and back. I wriggled and tried to scratch him, going for his face and hands with my nails.

"Damn it, Andrey, hold her. She's a wild one. Juri, you go and look out for Sheremetev's men. I'll go first; I spotted her," he grunted, pressing my fists above my head and shoving his tongue in my mouth. He stank so much, I felt bile rise, and bit his lips as hard as I could. He shrank back, cursing and shouting. I tried to break away, but he caught me by my hair and tore me back. Pain shot through my scalp and I burst into tears when he forced me back against him, wrapping my loosening hair around his fist.

"You witch. You'll pay for that, girl." He slapped me so hard that my head flung to the side, straining my neck, and my vision blurred. I felt him tear my tunic open and rip my skirt off.

"Breasts like a wet nurse and legs like Menshikov's mare," he cheered, while his friends grabbed me from behind. They lifted me up and forced my thighs open. My tormentor's pants hung around his knees and he pushed into me with a single hard thrust. I screamed until my voice cracked, when the second soldier turned my head and forced his tongue into my mouth. The first man thrust and thrust, laughing, swearing, and digging his hands into my backside. These would be the last moments of my life; the world closed in on me. Everything was erased by blinding pain. I would die as my stepmother had predicted: slowly, and in pain and shame. I heard Juri, the lookout, scream, "Guards!"

He ran away as fast as his bent, hairy Tartar's legs would carry him, but the two others howled with fury when a crop hit them hard over their heads and shoulders. Horses neighed and voices shouted; the one who had been raping me stumbled backward, his eye patch torn off and blood and pus trickling down his face. I sobbed and curled up against the wall, so as not to be trampled by the horses' hooves, and covered my head with my arms. How many men there were I couldn't say for all the shouting and whips cracking. One guard gave one of the soldiers an uppercut, before grabbing them both by the hair and thundering their heads together. Their skulls crunched like gravel under feet, but it sounded like music to me.

"Stand to attention!" the guard shouted, himself straightening up. "The general marshall, Boris Petrovich Sheremetev. Rape is punishable with the whip and hard labor."

I made myself as small as possible, gasping and wiping tears, snot, blood, and dirt off my face. Both my rapists tried to stand to attention but wobbled because they still felt dizzy. Hooves thundered on the cobblestones and a black stallion circled. In the dying light of the day I tried to see the face of the rider who towered high above us: the legendary General Sheremetev, the hero of the Russian army.

My rapist held his hurting head and tried to bond with the guard, winking at the men.

The marshall sat straight on his shiny leather saddle. His silver breastplate sparkled in the evening sun and his fur-lined coat was fastened with a diamond-studded miniature portrait. I squinted my eyes: it showed the face of a man. A blue sash ran across Sheremetev's chest, but he wore neither hat nor helmet, and was clean-shaven. His stallion reared as he ordered, "Cut out his tongue. Catch the third one that made it away. Thirty lashes each with the knout should do."

The guard grabbed the man by his jaw, forced his mouth open, and sliced his tongue cleanly at the root. The sight of him throwing the piece of pink, spongy flesh in the dust made me gag, but I loved it all the same. "If you survive the knout, you can fry your tongue for dinner. If it was up to me, I'd add your cock to that stew," the guard told him.

My rapist held his throat with both hands, his eyes wide with shock. Blood spurted from his mouth—like the most stunning fountain— and his knees buckled. Well, now he knew what pain felt like, gargling and writhing like a worm, I thought, and almost wished the guard would make his threat true and castrate him, though thirty lashes with the knout should see to that. The men mounted again and Sheremetev was ready to carry on. I tried to straighten, but pain shot through my lower body, and I cowered again. I couldn't walk. How should I make it to the hospital? Johann had died by now, I feared, but I still wanted to reach him. Perhaps if I just waited for the men to leave?

I wanted to give them a weak smile as if I was fine, when the guard

said, "What about the girl? We can't leave her behind. It's too dangerous."

I froze. Sheremetev looked down at me. "Get up, girl," he said curtly.
I swayed and I felt the blood trickling down my thighs. Embarrassed, I
tried to cover myself with the shreds of my tunic.

"Those swine," Sheremetev said, and got off his stallion. The world
blurred as the tall man came toward me. He lifted my face into the
white night and cursed again, then took off his dark green cloak and
wrapped me in it. I had never felt anything as soft and ample. The fur
lining caressed my skin and I buried my face in it, sobbing. Sheremetev
mounted and reached out for me. "Give her to me. She is too hurt to
get on by herself. As for the three rapists, fifty lashes will do after all,
twenty-five of them on their cocks."

He placed me behind him on his horse and I held on to him. Sitting astride like that was painful but I leaned on his back. The uniform's
cloth was scratchy; silent tears ran down my cheeks when I buried my
face in it. I heard the soldiers plead for mercy, but in vain, as the guard
lifted his arm for a first round of lashing. I turned my head to see as
much as I could of it.

"Hold on tight, girl," Sheremetev said. "We are riding back to my
camp."

I heard my rapists scream until we were well outside the remnants
of the town walls: the guard was doing his work properly. Was there
some sort of justice for once in my life? When I had a final look at
my life as I had known it, smoke billowed out of the garrison's ruins,
as flames devoured the rest of the walls and the watchtower. The fire
turned the sky a rosy shade of ash and made the horizon glow, giving Johann a hero's burial. There was no way back, but once more God
in his wisdom and mercy had let me live, I understood, just before I
passed out.

23

Somebody gently slapped my cheeks and lifted my legs; blood rushed into my brain and I came to, looking into the worried but friendly face of a young man. He raised my head by the nape of my neck, dabbing my face with a cloth soaked in spirits.

"The soldiers. Johann . . ." I tried to sit up, when the memory hit me and I felt burning pain: Johann was dead and I had been raped. I might as well die, too.

The guard dabbed my face again, and said with a soft Ukrainian lilt, "Do you remember what happened? You are in General Sheremetev's tent. He has saved you from . . ." He stopped, blushing. I meekly raised my hand.

"I know, please don't remind me," I said, and looked down on myself, which made him blush even deeper. Had he stopped my bleeding, then washed and wrapped me in the cloak once more? I tried to sit up, but felt so dizzy that I grabbed his arm to steady myself.

"I have to go," I said, trying to stumble to my feet. "I have to see if my husband is still alive."

"You are going nowhere. Marienburg is aflame. The people are fleeing. Sheremetev will be here any moment and he wants to see you strong and healthy. When did you last eat? Are you hungry?"

I couldn't care less about what the Russian wanted, but my stomach growled and I remembered longingly the carrot I had peeled hours earlier. What had happened to it? "I am starving," I said, and smiled for the first time in what felt like days.

The guard left the tent and when he lifted the waxed cloth that served as a door, afternoon sunshine flooded inside. How long had I been asleep? I had a good look around: the tent's floor was covered with layers of rugs, uneven in some places, as the weaver had held them across her knees while working. I cocked my head: their patterns reminded me of fabric I had seen in Vassily's stockrooms. A desk was drowning in scrolls and maps, and one of the three chairs around it was covered in a throw made of shiny, dark furs. I had never seen anything like it: Were those sable skins? Next to the foldable campaign bed on which I lay stood a chest studded with slate and iron bands. It was locked with a bar and a chain: Was that the war chest? Just then I spotted a tray with some leftover food on the floor, right next to my bed. Had Sheremetev sat here, eating, watching me in my sleep? The thought troubled me, but I bent down and sniffed at the food like a dog. Some wine was left in the brass goblet, a slice of cumin bread was untouched, and half of the succulent meat still stuck to a chicken leg. I smelled the crispy skin covering it and felt ill with hunger. I just couldn't wait for the guard to return, and lunged at the tray. I gulped the wine and stuffed the bread into my mouth, crunching the cumin between my teeth. The juicy meat melted in my mouth, which was just as well, as I didn't take the time to chew. I almost choked with embarrassment when I heard laughter at the entrance of the tent. I looked up, my lips and chin covered with cumin and crumbs, holding half a chicken leg in my hand and my face red from lack of breath.

Boris Petrovich Sheremetev's skin was tanned and shiny, as if he had just had a shave. As victor of Marienburg his uniform was freshly laundered and pressed, and his long black cloak had a big white cross embroidered on its back.

"Well, that's a good sign, girl, if you are hungry," he said, grabbing another bottle of wine from the table to refill my goblet. "Drink. It heals and helps you to forget what you have seen and what has happened. Believe me, I know what I am talking about. Next to a battle lost, there is no greater misery than a battle won."

He must be joking, but he sounded very serious as he pulled himself a chair close and crossed his legs in his tight breeches and high shiny boots. I eyed him from under my lashes: he was older than I had thought. The dark hair at his temples was sprinkled with white and his wrinkled, scarred face reminded me of the dry, brittle earth of our Baltic summers. Deep lines carved down from his nose, which was as bent as an eagle's beak, to the corners of his thin lips. It wasn't a mouth that smiled easily.

More chicken, bread, pickled fruit, and sour gherkins were brought by the young Ukrainian; Sheremetev and I ate in silence, until I dared to ask, "Why did you save me, General Marshall?"

He looked at me warily. "I don't know. I have seen it happen a hundred if not a thousand times, what happened to you today. Perhaps I am just tired. I have not been home for three years. Who knows? We'll see."

He leaned forward, clenching his fingers, as if he was undecided what to do with me. I shrank back. Sheremetev laughed. "No worries, girl. I have never forced a woman to do anything she didn't want to do. What's your name?"

I felt ashamed: without his help, I'd be dead, torn to pieces by those animals in the alleyways of Marienburg. "Marta," I said, embarrassed, wrapping the cloak tighter around my bare shoulders in the torn tunic.

"Get some more sleep and then let's decide what should happen with you." He made to rise, when the tent's flap was flung open and the young Ukrainian stumbled aside, because the tall man who entered the tent shoved him out of the way.

"Stay, Sheremetev," the stranger said. "Don't we always enjoy each other's company?" His hair was ruffled and the same color as a stray dog's coat, a dark, dirty blond. His features were choppy, almost as the dolls' faces my father had carved from a log for my sisters and me. A steady, curious smile sat in the corner of his thin-lipped mouth and his eyes were too dark to tell the pupil from the iris.

Sheremetev turned and sighed: "You again, Menshikov. Haven't we discussed it all for the moment? I have agreed that you have the first pick of the loot."

The stranger didn't answer, as he had spotted me. He placed his hands on his hips and blew his cheeks. "Sheremetev, you old devil. A girl in your tent! Now that's a first. Have you finally forgotten that hag of a wife of yours? And are you not much too noble for this sort of hanky-panky? Who is she? Well, well, to the victor, the spoils, I say—" He grinned and placed his hands on Sheremetev's shoulders. His fingers were laden with rings from the roots to the knuckles; their gemstones broke the sunlight into prisms. Meanwhile, Sheremetev's guard had steadied himself. Indeed, he stood more rigidly to attention than I thought was possible.

"What do you want, Menshikov?" Sheremetev said wearily, but rose, standing between Menshikov and me. He wasn't as tall as Menshikov but carried himself with pride. I sensed the guard's worry; sweat glistened on his forehead, but Menshikov laughed.

"The usual things. Eat, dance, laugh, and love," Menshikov said, plunging into a chair, which almost buckled under his size and weight He eyed me shamelessly; I hid in the cloak and lowered my eyes.

Sheremetev went to gather some maps. "Do you want to fetch the maps we have spoken about?" he asked, but Menshikov brushed them aside.

"Forget about your maps, they are only good to light a fire. I have the best ones in my tent and will send them over later"

"Too kind. I wonder what you're doing with all these maps if you can't even read, Alexander Danilovich."

"Careful, Sheremetev," Menshikov said, only half playful. "But let me get on with important business, will you?" He tugged on my cloak, which I clutched in front of my breasts. "What's your name, girl? Where did Boris Petrovich find you? I thought my soldiers had scoured every corner of this godforsaken town for pretty faces. Open that cloak, so that I can see more of you. You are one hell of a woman."

Sheremetev looked up from his maps. "That is what I thought, too, when I found her. Perhaps not quite in those words, Menshikov."

I met Menshikov's gaze and wrapped the cloak even tighter. "And who are you to stare at me like that? Do you really think I'd show you my body like a whore? Never. You'll rather see black snow." Who was this man to walk into a war hero's tent and behave like he could take what he wanted? I looked at Sheremetev to see if I had gone too far, but he coughed lightly to hide laughter, studying a map.

Silence reigned. The guard stared at the tips of his boots, his head as red as the apples growing in the orchards outside the town. Menshikov stared at me, openmouthed. Then he threw back his head and laughed until he had to wipe tears from his eyes and gasped: "Who I am, you want to know, you dirty little tramp?"

"I am only dirty because the moment doesn't allow me to be otherwise. And my name is Marta."

Menshikov grabbed my chin hard. I stifled a wince and met his gaze. I would not lower my eyes, whatever the cost. "I, Marta, am Alexander Danilovich Menshikov, the most powerful among the powerful, the tsar's most loyal and absolute friend."

"Who loyally and absolutely fills his pockets whenever possible, behind the tsar's back of course," Sheremetev added.

"Shut it. We don't need you here."

"It's my tent, Alexander Danilovich. And I am the victor of Marienburg, not you."

Menshikov grunted and wrapped one of my dark curls around his fingers and sniffed at it. "You smell good, though a bath wouldn't hurt. Show me your neck." He pushed back the hair that covered my shoulders and forced my chin up. "Ah, it's nice and long. And you seem strong and healthy. Just what I need when I'm in the field."

Both Sheremetev and I startled, but Menshikov just slapped my hip and got up. I pulled my legs in and glowered at him.

"Your wine is sour, Sheremetev. I'll send you some Rhine wine together with the maps later on. Give the girl a bath, so she can follow my scribe to my tent. I wouldn't trust your soldiers to let her walk alone through the camp. Perhaps she can sleep on the floor next to Daria's bed, as long as they don't squabble. I'm not so much into girls wrestling, unless it happens under the open sky, in the mud." Menshikov grinned at me, nodded to Boris Petrovich, and was gone: the waxed cloth hit the pillars a couple of times, then all was silent. I swallowed and tasted the salt of my rising tears.

Sheremetev shrugged and sighed. "So be it then, Marta. He truly is the most powerful among the powerful, after our tsar. If he wants you, I can lay no claim on you. You heard that I granted him first pick of all the Marienburg loot. Let's have you bathed and find some clothes that might fit you, shall we?"

If even a Russian marshall and victor of an important battle could not act at will, what could I hope for? I buried myself in his cloak like a stubborn child, trying hard not to cry. "No. I don't want to. I am not a toy."

I saw understanding in Sheremetev's eyes. "Being born a girl is a punishment. Look, Marta, I am not saying I like it, but if Menshikov orders you to his tent, let me tell you, many other girls would give an arm and a leg for that. Use life's surprises to your advantage. See your power over men like a hand of cards; play them, to trump your life." He laughed before he added, "And, by the way, Menshikov can be all words and no pants. If his mistress cottons on that he is interested in you, she'll scratch his eyes out. Try to be careful of her."

"Who is his mistress?" I asked, my skin prickling with fear. Had I stumbled into a wasps' nest?

"Daria Arsenjeva. She is a daughter of an old Russian boyar family; be sure to be on her good side or you'll need a very strong protector. She's been with Menshikov for years, and though she looks the other way as expected when she has to, you can never be sure how she'll react. At some point he'll do the honorable thing and marry her, I suppose."

He had just taken his map over to his desk and sat down, leaning his head in his hands, when the guard led in a maid. She curtsied, which almost made me choke, and then led me to a tub in a curtained corner of the tent. While I waited, she filled it with bucket after bucket of hot water. The poor thing had to run endless times between the fire and the tent as I asked her to splash more and more hot water over me. I cleansed myself of my old life and its memories.

When Menshikov's scribe came with his arms full of maps I sat on the bed, ready and waiting for him. The borrowed clothes were a bit tight around my chest and hips, but my wet hair was braided and my skin burned from being scrubbed. I felt like a new woman. When the guard lifted the tent's waxed flap, I thanked him with a nod and turned one last time to Sheremetev, who feigned not to see me leave.

"General Marshall Sheremetev," I said. He looked up.

"What is it, Marta?"

"You have saved my life and you have been very kind. I shall not forget that, and if it's ever possible, I will pay you back."

If the victor of Marienburg found those words strange coming from a penniless young woman, he did not let on, but bowed his head and answered solemnly, "Gratefulness is a forgotten virtue these days. I am sure we'll meet again and I am looking forward to it."

24

The stench of sweat and latrines, dysentery and gangrene, pus, blood, dirty clothes, cabbage soup, bean stew, cold gunpowder, and swathes of smoke lay like a bell jar over the wide field where Sheremetev's army was camped. The smell stuck to my skin like nettles to a shirt. The Russian tents met the horizon, housing tens of thousands of men. It was an unforgettable sight; the sheer size of the tsar's army was truly shocking: I had never seen so many people in one spot. While I walked, the sun set upon the camp and the soldiers lay around campfires in their torn and dirty uniforms, stirring heavy cauldrons and playing cards and dice, as the tsar had forbidden all other games of chance. Men cleaned their weapons, checked minor wounds, spooned up thick brews, or downed liters of beer and *kvass*, which had been given to them every evening since the siege that had ended in their favor: to the victor, the spoils.

I thought I saw a familiar face moving through the crowds, though I couldn't be sure. I squinted and then ducked behind Menshikov's scribe: it was *matushka* Sonia and her sorry band of girls, offering themselves. She was, if possible, even more portly than before, and spoke with the Russian soldiers as she had done previously with the Swedish dragoons, before pushing the naughty little Tartar girl forward. Her gums were toothless, angry pustules bloomed on her neck, and her dirty, ragged dress hung on her skinny frame. I was far from safe but I felt pity still for their wretchedness—how easily I could have ended up just like them. I noticed that even the washermaids, their arms heavy with linen, gave them a wide berth. I lowered my head until I had passed them. There was enough to deal with.

All around us the fields had been crudely harvested to feed the tsar's hordes. In the vicinity of Marienburg there wasn't a head of corn left to grind, no livestock to slaughter, no chickens to pluck, no orchards with cherries, pears, and apples to be picked from them. From the remnants of the town, fresh smoke rose into the wide sky, and despite the late hour of the day a steady stream of people moved out of the city, out into the white night and an uncertain future. The Russians took off them what they pleased, sharing it among themselves there and then, ridding the wealthier burghers' carts of everything they could, or liked, be it a jar of pickles, a rolled-up rug, a fine piece of furniture, a last plump chicken, or a wailing girl, maids and burghers' daughters alike. Only the crippled, the beggars, and the loafers plodded on, as what they had to offer was too lousy even for the least of Sheremetev's soldiers. I searched the people who made it away: Were the Glucks among them? If they were alive, where would they hide from the Russians? We were like ants getting crushed under the tsar's feet. It was horrid: things had come to pass as the Glucks had predicted. I felt like a swimmer caught in the rapids of a river after the *ottepel,* the current almost crushing me and just a branch to hold on to. If I as much as tried to come up for air and to think, I would drown for sure. So I looked ahead, as this was the only way I could go.

I closed my ears to the crude jokes and the wolf-whistling of the men; every step still hurt and I hoped that my rapists had died under the whip. Nobody survived fifty lashes; I knew that as well as Sheremetev had done. When we arrived at Menshikov's tent, I braced myself and carefully considered Sheremetev's words, which I had soaked up like one of his sponges did the bathwater just a few hours earlier. Tar dripped from the torches stuck to the pillars on both sides of the entrance where two guards stood, bayonets slotted onto the ends of their muskets, and the tent's lanterns glowed warmly in the pale dusk.

"Wait here," the scribe said, and went into a side room of the tent, which was more like a house made of canvas, with an entrance and several rooms. I was stunned: there was no sign of war or hardship; these were the most beautiful things I'd ever seen. Menshikov's tent made Vassily's home look like a hovel. I saw beds carved from black, shiny wood, standing on curved, elegant legs that ended in animals' heads. The beasts' mouths were wide open and manes flamed around them. What on Earth were they? Richly embroidered cushions and fur-lined velvet blankets lay carelessly piled up on the daybeds, and my naked feet—which were dirty once more after crossing the camp—sank into the deep pile of the colorful rugs on the floor. On Menshikov's desk, two high candelabras shed a flickering light on bowl upon bowl of nuts, candied fruit, biscuits, fresh cherries, and apples. I also spotted piles of maps and stepped closer. In Ernst Gluck's schoolroom I had seen similar ones, albeit drawn a lot cruder. When the war had begun, the priest had followed the campaign by sticking Caroline's sewing pins into the thick paper, trying to guess both the Swedish and Russian strategies. The memory of it made me smile.

Across the maps lay a freshly sharpened quill in a heavy, golden pen holder. I picked it up and twisted it in my fingers before sniffing at it. Mmh, fresh ink—what else smelled so beautifully of learning? It reminded me of the Glucks' rectory. I weighed the pen holder; its value would have freed and fed my family a hundred times over and we'd never have had to work again. I calmly put it back where I had found it. Just then, the skin on my neck prickled. Was somebody watching me? I looked up and met a man's rigid gaze, fixed in oil on canvas. I shrank back in horror: he didn't look like our icon of Saint Nicholas or the Holy Trinity above the Glucks' altar. His face looked so real with the fine, pale skin and rosy cheeks; his dark, curly hair seemed shiny enough to touch and his blue eyes gazed at me, sparkling and bright. His eyebrows reminded me of a raven's wings, high and dashing, while the fine mustache led my gaze to his well-cut mouth. His breastplate of gold and silver, his white coat and the bright blue sash across his chest turned him into a warrior; one elbow rested on his helmet, which was topped with a bunch of red feathers; the other hand pointed far ahead, to the west. In the lower right corner the double-headed eagle swooped, as I had seen it a thousandfold on the Russian flags during the siege of Marienburg. Perhaps this was Alexander Nevsky. This was the only Russian saint I knew next to Saint Nicholas. There was something about the man's eyes, though, which didn't look very saint-like. "What are you doing, girl, ogling like that at our tsar?" a woman's voice asked sharply behind me. I spun around, blushing. I didn't want to look nosy: the sin of curiosity, as Caroline had called it, and I surely didn't want to be caught staring at a man. But I lacked all words, so stunned was I by the woman's beauty. I shoved one mud-crusted foot underneath the other and hitched my too-tight coarse linen skirt higher, trying somehow to look more in place, though it was hopeless.

She watched me gleefully, savoring my embarrassment, and the corners of her small, rosy mouth twitched. Her blond mane fell loose on her shoulders like a shimmering fur and the tightly laced blue silk dress matched her eyes, which reminded me of violets. It was very deeply cut and showed half of her firm, white breasts. Close to one nipple a tiny, naughty mole rose and fell each time she breathed. She circled me like a hawk does a mouse and I didn't dare to move, as each of her steps doused the air with rosewater and a heavier, headier scent I had no name for. But with the flick of a wrist she broke the spell by pulling a lacy handkerchief from her tight sleeve and pressing it in front of her tiny upturned nose. "God, you reek, girl. Don't you ever bathe? And it's you Menshikov wanted in his tent? I was worried when I heard about you, but now that I see you—" She giggled and stopped midsentence, which felt like a slap. "I suppose he just wanted to get one up on Sheremetev, which is just as well. I can do with another maid. Or did you flirt with him?" she asked, grabbing my wrist and digging her nails into my flesh. I met her eyes calmly, freed my wrist, and shook my head.

"For sure not," I said. For some reason, I was not afraid of Daria— for that was who she must be—in spite of Sheremetev's warning. The way she carried herself, so sure of her beauty, reminded me of my little Christina. My heart ached with loss.

"Are you Daria Arsenjeva?" I asked.

"How do you know?" she hissed.

"Well, General Sheremetev said that you were very beautiful and very witty—and that Count Menshikov is utterly besotted with you."

Her smile was catty. "Well and wisely spoken, my girl, even though Sheremetev would never say anything like that. He despises me and thinks I am a whore, living with Alexander Danilovich. But who cares what the uptight ass thinks?" she said, smiling, as she sank onto one of the daybeds, spreading her wide skirt, which was embroidered with pearls and gemstones and lined with lace. Her small, silky slippers matched the color of her dress and she patted the seat next to her. "Come, sit down. How did you come here? It must have been quite a story, and I love a good yarn!"

I told her, skipping the details of the attack. But by the way she looked at me I understood that she knew anyway. I was a prisoner of war: What else could have happened to me? Daria Arsenjeva listened to me while nibbling on some cherries in a way that made me blush. Then the curtain to a side room was torn open and Menshikov entered the main tent. I sat up, but Daria stayed as she was, half lying among the cushions, sucking on a cherry, the mole near her nipple reeling in Menshikov's gaze like bait would a big fish. She lowered her long, dark lashes, but her eyes never left him. He patted my head and tousled my hair.

"Ah, Sheremetev's little find. How do you like her, my darling Daria?"

Daria poked me with her sharp elbow. "Not bad. She's a bit buxom for my taste, but we have had a bit of a laugh already."

"I like a bit of buxom. What shall we do with her?" He took an apple from the bowl on the desk, threw it in the air, caught it again and bit into it, chewing and crunching it as loudly as a horse, every bite an explosion of spit and apple flecks.

Daria moved as swiftly as a squirrel, slapping Menshikov's mouth with her lacy handkerchief. I held my breath as his face reddened with anger, but Daria casually said: "She can work as a washermaid. More hands truly make for lighter work. In the evenings she can be with us. If I catch you near her, I'll kill you both, and I am not joking."

I curtsied, grateful for Daria's jealousy. We'd get along just fine: if Menshikov was all she wanted, God, she could have him. Daria pulled him with her into the side room, drawing the heavy, velvet curtain with gold tassels shut and smiling at me. "The guard will show you the washing place. You can sleep in a corner here; take all the cushions and blankets you need. My maid will bring you some of my dresses that she can alter for you. Those rags you wear are an eyesore."

Somebody else should alter my dresses? I curtsied once more and kept a straight face. Daria's scent still lingered long after she was gone.

25

By day, I scrubbed, rinsed, dried, and pressed the general's shirts and those of the many nobles camped around Marienburg. The tsar had drafted the offspring of the Russian nobility for military service for years, and the sons of the realm's best families spread their long limbs in the Baltic sun in a well-deserved break from warfare. Most of them had seen neither their families nor their holdings for years, as the huge distances did not allow short breaks. In the evenings I joined Menshikov's tent and watched Daria very closely: her way of dressing, of moving, of treating people and of speaking to them. She'd chat to men in a low voice, so they'd have to lean in in order to listen. She seemed to keep Menshikov on his toes with a mix of crude humor, servility, and flashes of naughtiness. Her moodiness kept him in thrall, as he was never entirely sure of what she would do next. Thankfully, that kept Menshikov too busy to pay me more attention than was necessary, or healthy. I could get on with surviving. If life in the Russian camp could be like quicksand, my friendship with Daria was a rope that a merciful God had thrown me.

"Your lips are chapped. Here, smooth them with this paste of beeswax and honey. Before you go to sleep put some sour cream on your skin. There's nothing like a bit of *smetana*. And just look at your hands, they are as red and callused as a serf's," Daria chatted on, handing out advice, bottles, and jars. "Keep your hair shiny by rinsing it with beer after each wash." In our *izba*, father had only had sips of beer on high holidays; if we spilled a drop he'd wallop us. Daria herself rinsed her hair in a chamomile brew before bleaching it strand by strand with the juice of a fruit I had never seen before: shiny yellow and shaped like an egg. "Have a bite," she said, watching me when I bit into the waxy skin and then pulled a face: the taste was sour and acidic. Daria laughed so much she had to hold on to her chair; she liked a practical joke. What she didn't share with me was a smelly gray paste she ordered from a city called Venice, which kept the pallor of her face. "It's so expensive you could live for a decade off the price of one jar, but believe me, it's no good," Daria's maid told me while cleaning the tub. "The Moscow *damy* who use it, are always sick, have headaches and no appetite. Worse still, their skin looks like it was eaten by maggots. It's rotting away, and just when the tsar has forbidden them to wear veils in public. So you know what they do?" She chuckled. I shook my head. "They wear even more of the stinky stuff. Beats me." Daria's skin looked fine to me, I thought; perhaps the maid was telling tall tales.

Daria's life in Menshikov's palace in Moscow seemed like a steady feast, filled with light and laughter. If the court calendar with the many royal birthdays and saints' name days didn't give a reason to celebrate they'd meet for a forbidden game of cards, a big dinner, or a dance.

"Whom do the *damy* feast with if the men are all in the field?" I wondered, but she laughed.

"That makes them the merrier, silly. The tsar has freed them from the prison of the *terem,* he wants us to live and gamble with the men."

"What an idea," I said, somewhat shocked. What next, should we light up pipes?

"I know. He has seen it all in a palace called Versailles, in a faraway country, France, which he had visited during his Grand Embassy. I tell you, the ideas he brought home! We women were not *bojaryni—*the boyar's wives and daughters—any longer, but *damy.* Our families were scandalized, but the tsar threatened us—my father as well!—with hard labor should he dress in the old way, refuse to send my brothers to school, or lock my sister Varvara and me up until we were married off."

"I hope I'll see Moscow soon, Daria," I said.

"Oh, me, too, Marta. I can't wait to go home! The sight of Moscow takes your breath away: a thousand spires and cupolas glitter in the sun and the mightiest houses sit right next to huts of mud and clay. It's the mix that makes it so special. But the Moscow of my childhood is no more, Marta. Moscow was once the center of a world, the meeting point of East and West; never mess with a Muscovite. We are full of tradition and custom and yet so wonderfully wild, for at heart, Marta, we are all Tartars." She pulled her eyes slanty.

I giggled, but then asked: "Why is the Moscow of your childhood long gone, Daria?"

"Well, what will happen if Peter really builds his new city, here, in the West?"

"A new city? Impossible, Daria. How would he do that, just stomp it out of the ground? Where, and how, and when? In the middle of war?"

Daria just shrugged sullenly. "The tsar can do anything. Whatever Russia has, is his."

I fell silent. If a noblewoman like Daria, who was so close to the almighty tsar, felt sad and torn by his measures and at times like a stranger in her own country, what, then, did the merchant, the farmer, and the serf in the field think?

* * *

Everything but boredom was welcome in Menshikov's tent. Mornings might start with Mass for the generals and nobles, while a second service was held under the open sky for the tens of thousands of soldiers: Alexander Danilovich and his friends would pray, bow, and cross themselves with three fingers as custom demanded, and they'd kiss the icons and ask for God's protection. But in the evening an unbridled joy at life reigned; a haunted merriment, which was the other side of war's terror: live today, as you'd meet God and Saint Nicholas soon enough for the day of reckoning. The tsar was said to have given new marching orders, so the brief respite in Marienburg was soon to be over. What would happen to me? I'd be looking for a roof over my head yet again, and the thought filled me with dread and also a fatigue so deep it felt like a bottomless well. So all I could do was smile sweetly when Menshikov tugged my hair and drawled, "You never sleep, are radiant with beauty, and drink every soldier under the table. Where do they bake girls like you? I'll order ten of your sort."

The endless evenings were fueled by wine, vodka, and beer. No one here would drink *kvass*. I had never laughed and never drunk so much in my life—as Daria's friend I was one of theirs by night, even if I washed shirts by day.

"Hurry, Marta," Daria would call, clapping her hands. "Alexander Danilovich offers us a world of wonder tonight," she said, squashing my flesh into my bodice and lacing me up brutally to save time.

"A world of wonders?" That sounded like Master Lampert's tent.

"Yes, he has ordered in a group of Tartar acrobats that cartwheel and somersault and dwarves that leap through rings on fire," she said. "I also asked for storytellers—nothing like a good yarn, don't you think?"

"Indeed," I said smoothly, but she pinched me.

"I know you are one for a story or two? I just love how you ran away from the merchant's house after he died of smallpox and then refused the lusty priest's son. I am sure you have so many more to tell me. With you, I am never bored."

I crossed my fingers that my altering of the truth would never come to light and smiled. "Never. I promise. And if I run out of stories, I shall invent more. Just for you."

No, we were never bored: already the evening before a Ukrainian magician had baffled us, and for tomorrow's masquerade, Daria had some men's clothes altered for us. "Stunning," I called, when I saw her dressed up as a man. "You look so much better than I do," I said, though I knew that the tight, knee-length breeches showed off my long, slender legs as well as my round hips. The men were less lucky, their broad shoulders bursting out of a dress's bodice, chest hair showing, and big, clumsy feet tearing hemlines. Still, the sight of them left us in stitches. Whoever didn't drink enough for Menshikov's liking was forced to do so; he'd pick his unfortunate victim and order, "You, over there, hold him down. Marta, force his mouth open, yes, grab his jaws. Daria, fill that boot with vodka and pour it into his mouth. A true Russian needs nine days for a proper stupor."

Menshikov downed a huge cup himself to keep the gargling and writhing man on his tent floor company, before he shouted: "Nine days. Three to get drunk, three to be drunk, three to get sober again."

We roared, "Nine! Nine! Nine!" and it seemed like the world's best word, while Menshikov's guest passed out and was dragged out of the tent to freshen up for further fun. Everybody who could feasted with us: young boyars' sons who had hardly grown mustaches yet, as well as old, dignified princes who shouldn't have left their hearths anymore. Peter hounded them all into his war. Apart from *matushka* Sonja's whores, and the washermaids—mostly girls taken prisoner at sieges such as Marienburg—Daria and I were the only women in the camp, but living in Menshikov's tent meant I was lucky. Once Daria trusted me to not even try to catch his eye, I could guess myself lucky: most of the girls, bless their souls, were easy meat for any soldier who cared. Still, sometimes while I was soaking and scrubbing the clothes in the buckets, a man would sneak up from behind and grab both my breasts with his grubby paws: "Lovely, they jiggle like an udder, but are as firm as Crimean melons"—or smack my bottom: "God, I can crack a nut on that one!" I would slosh them with a bucket of the dirtiest water around, which made them smell even worse than before. If someone made a rude joke, I came back with a quick, jesty answer that left them red-faced. So I found my place in the camp and stored whatever I saw or heard in my mind like a farmer would his grain: my life was linked to my Russian captors. Then, in late autumn, word reached us that Daria's sister Varvara and Menshikov's sister Rasia were to visit. I was excited, but also a bit wary. Would they treat me with the same ease as Daria did? To her, I was neither a maid nor a prisoner of war, but a friend.

26

Rasia Menshikova was no beauty and, like Daria, covered her face in the fashion of Moscow in a thick layer of chalk-white paste and powder, while crimson dots marked her lips and cheeks. Her eyebrows and lashes were tinted black. But she had a kind word for everyone, listened more than she spoke, and held herself straight, so her bodice would push up what little cleavage she had. She was a wise woman.

It was the end of October when I joined Daria, her sister Varvara, and Rasia in Menshikov's tent after my day's work. "Come, Marta," Daria said, and patted an empty cushion next to hers. I saw Varvara, who was all white skin and dark red hair, raise her eyebrows and shoot Rasia Menshikova an I-told-you-so look. It was clear that she would never have invited me in as Daria did, but now it had to be fine for everyone else. So I sat comfortably with them, who were all linked to the most powerful of the powerful in Russia. How had this come about? Life left me no time to marvel at its miracles; all I could do was run along and try not to lose breath. I spotted Sheremetev among the guests, which was rare, and waved at him. He raised his glass, smiling, before he went on talking with the other generals. The camp was buzzing, like bees ready to swarm. Were the marching orders well and truly given? The air in the tent itself seemed to be crackling: Which choice merriment might Menshikov have ordered tonight, I wondered, looking around with joy and curiosity.

So far, people sat and ate. Rasia Menshikova, too, nibbled on a pastry filled with goose liver pâté and then had some grapes, before wiping her fingers and sipping some beer. She leaned in. "Have you heard about the tsar and Anna Mons?"

Daria and Varvara shot each other a quick glance. "No. What is it, Rasia? Is Peter fed up with her? Has he finally realized she'll never give him a child?"

I sensed Rasia's heavy Persian perfume when she giggled. "Yes! Finally. My brother says that the tsar is looking for a husband for Anna Mons, which is quite generous, really. He could just send her to a nunnery, like Evdokia."

"She doesn't have an ounce of nun's flesh about her," Varvara sniggered.

Rasia said, "If he's marrying her off, she's lucky. The German whore is as barren as a tundra bush; I have smuggled a loyal maid into her household, who knows her potions, so I am sure of it. It's about time she stopped that whoring on her father's behalf, like all her siblings. Incredible, how far that innkeeper from the German quarter rose."

"Anna Mons has siblings?" I asked.

"The Mons are worse than rabbits, but one is more beautiful than the other. The old Mons has thrown Anna into the tsar's arms, and if it weren't for her golden thighs, Peter's wife Evdokia might still be at his side."

I looked around. The food had been served, but of course vodka and schnapps flowed as if there was a secret fountain somewhere. I yawned—what else would happen tonight? I saw neither magicians nor trained dogs and jugglers. Menshikov clapped his hands at the Arsenjeva sisters, and they rose, coming to him. He took them on one knee each and pulled their dresses off their shoulders, stripping them half-naked. The music played up and Menshikov swayed them in the rhythm; he roared a song and fondled their full, dangling breasts while the other guests watched with hungry eyes. Rasia watched hawk-eyed as Daria and Varvara started to kiss and caress each other: the flames of countless candelabras bathed their bare skin in a soft, shimmering light and made their jewelry sparkle. They moved slowly, writhing their bodies and licking each other's lips, throats, and breasts, lacing tongues and savoring each other's full, rosy flesh. Daria closed her moist lips over her sister's nipple, sucking it, while she teased the other breast with her fingertips, and Varvara arched backward, sighing and moaning. Lust burned in the surrounding men's eyes and even Menshikov held his knees still, watching with intent.

"But Rasia, they are sisters!" I whispered, shocked.

She shrugged. "The Arsenjevas are wild things, unbridled, and there is nothing they haven't done. Rumor has it that they have even slept with their brothers and their father! Perhaps that is why my brother and the tsar like them so much. Our boundaries are lost; we live in new times and we need a new kind of man, Marta," she said, never taking her eyes off her brother and the Arsenjevas.

"The tsar likes the Arsenjevas as well?" I asked carefully. Had Daria set her goal higher than I had thought?

"Well done, Marta. Chatting like a woman and listening like a man. Daria and Varvara hope to marry my brother and the tsar, while sleeping with both. If Anna Mons's reign is well and truly over, then of course this is their moment. Perhaps we'll see the sisters fight? What fun." Rasia gave me a brief, bloodthirsty smile, and her eyes sparkled, just when Daria hitched up Varvara's skirt and spread her sister's naked thighs. "Any of them could be the next tsaritsa. The tsar's first wife, as you know, is in a convent. Evdokia would refuse to talk to either my brother or me, or dine at the same table as us. Now rats and nuns keep her merry company."

She rose and left. I sat alone next to the curtain of the tent's entrance, watching her leave. Why was Rasia Menshikova herself here—on her brother's orders? Was she also here to make use of the moment that Anna Mons left the tsar available?

It would certainly fulfill Menshikov's—or anyone's—wildest dreams.

27

The half-naked Arsenjevas were enlaced in Menshikov's arms, Daria's head buried between her sister's thighs and Varvara sighing and writhing. I didn't want to look—watching them sent my blood racing— yet I simply couldn't help it. When I finally averted my eyes, I spotted Sheremetev: he, too, sat alone in the shade of a tent post. Both his plate of food and his jug of vodka were untouched. What did he think of all this? His face was calm and unreadable as he watched the crowd. I couldn't help but think that he'd approve.

I was rising to join him across the heaving tent when hooves thundered outside in the camp. It was far beyond midnight. Only a madman would travel in these times at such an hour, I thought. But, yes: horses neighed and snorted and men called out, cheering and clapping. Before I could step aside, the tent's waxed flap was flung open and hit me so hard that I stumbled and almost fell, but a man grabbed me by the upper arm. He was so tall that I saw nothing but his chest in the dark green uniform jacket and the bright blue sash adorned with an order of sparkling diamonds. I wanted to free myself from his grasp, looked up—and gasped. It was the man from the painting in Menshikov's tent. Peter, the tsar of all the Russias, stood seven feet tall in his boots, and his powerful body darkened the candlelight, while their flicker lengthened his shadow even further. His hand, which held me firmly, looked too dainty for his mighty frame. Still, when I tried to curtsy, he steadied me with astonishing ease and smiled. "Stop bobbing about, girl, that's a waste of time. Can I let go of you now? Don't fall. You might still be needed later on tonight." He winked, let go of me, and stepped into the tent, a scruffy, laughing, and shouting bunch of men in his wake.

I leaned against a tent pillar, as I would not trust my feet. Silence fell when the tsar stood among his soldiers and raised his arms. Then, all hell broke loose: I heard shouting, laughing, cheering, and whistling. The princes and generals leaped to their feet, bowing and running to him; some of them sobbed and even hugged him, getting a pat on the back or kisses in return. Corks flew from bottles, the cupbearers shouted, the cook and his helpers dragged in more food, servants raced, and the music played a wild, joyous tune. Menshikov's merry court had found its true master.

I moved away from the entrance, next to Sheremetev, and settled on my haunches. The tsar greeted some of his princely childhood friends before he stepped up to Menshikov, who had set the Arsenjeva sisters down. When Menshikov opened his arms wide, the sisters watched the tsar like a mouse does a cat.

"Brother of my heart. I have missed you so much. Without you there is no joy," the tsar called out in German. German! I was startled. Was that their secret language, ever since they had traveled together in the West? Well, if so, I, a serf, shared their knowledge—the thought stunned me.

Menshikov sobbed, speaking German as well. "My beloved. A day without you is a day wasted."

The two men embraced, laughed, cried, and swayed in their own secret rhythm, smelling at each other and kissing each other's cheeks again and again. Menshikov's tall, muscular body was dwarfed by the tsar's powerful frame; how could a man of his build exist? Jugs were raised and voices cheered: "To our tsar, the victor of the Great Northern War! To the battle of Marienburg; death and destruction to all Swedish worms!"

Daria, as always a quick thinker, clapped her hands. "Long live the tsar! To the victor of Marienburg!"

Sheremetev almost choked on his beer and I gently patted his back to ease his cough. "No worries, Boris Petrovich," I said, "we all know who the true victor of Marienburg is."

He pulled a face. "I could win a thousand battles, and give my life for Peter, but his heart will still always belong to Menshikov. Such love cannot be summoned. On the contrary. You go looking for it and it flees you." His words gave me goose bumps, and he took off his cloak with a rueful little smile and covered my shoulders against the night chill with it. Then he cleared his voice. "There you go. That's better. No, Menshikov alone is the brother of his heart."

"Where do they know each other from?" I asked, clutching the cloak that had once before warmed me so wonderfully. How could I ever forget what this man had done for me? I moved a bit closer and took a piece of cold lamb from his plate, nibbling on it. "Is Menshikov of old noble stock, like you?" Though I guessed the answer from what I had watched and heard in the past weeks.

"That's the best joke I have heard in a long time. Nobody knows where he really stems from. Perhaps he was a pie boy in the streets Peter grew up in, or possibly his father was employed to drill Peter's toy army—your guess is as good as mine. The higher Menshikov rises, the more he sweeps his traces, and the crueler any punishment for jokes about his low birth get."

"How could he ever win the tsar's heart like that?"

He watched the two men. "They were young together, Marta. Sharing our youth links us more than we can tell. Soon, the tsar himself might marry one of those Arsenjeva whores, and Menshikov the other. Then they'd be family," he said, shuddering. I looked up: Peter and Menshikov were kissing the Arsenjevas. Menshikov took Daria's breast in his mouth, his lips making her moan. I lowered my eyes, cheeks burning, as it reminded me of the lust I had felt in Anton's arms. The tsar swung the half-naked Varvara over his shoulder like a sack of flour—fox-red locks flowing and her dress torn—and her laughter rang like a silver bell as they all disappeared into the tent's side room.

Well, at least we now had time and calm to talk, I thought, and poured more vodka into both our jugs. Sheremetev smiled at me. "You are quite astonishing, Marta. Look at you: sitting here, laughing and drinking with the nobles of the Russian realm. Just some weeks ago things were very different for you." I blushed: he had forgotten neither my torn clothes nor my bare flesh. No man would. In the tent's dusk, the look in his eyes was unreadable. I lowered my gaze. The night was still young.

If anyone would still want me, I thought, but toasted him.

"What were we talking of?" he asked, clearing his throat.

"Menshikov," I helped him, as I wanted to hear all about the man that I could.

"Menshikov is a mystery. Last week he had a Prince Lopukin flogged, a brother of Peter's first wife, because he had joked about Menshikov's low birth. He can do what he likes and Peter allows it to happen. The two of them are always, always together." His voice sounded bitter.

"I have even heard that . . ." I began, but Sheremetev raised his eyebrows.

"Watch your pretty ears, or they'll be cut off, and that would be a shame. Who has said that? Menshikov and the tsar are close, but I'll dare anyone to speak ill of my ruler."

I sipped some beer, ashamed, but he squeezed my shoulder, pulling me a bit closer. "I am not surprised if people think such nonsense. They share everything, be it a plate at a dinner, a tent, or women. Menshikov went with Peter on his Grand Embassy and studied with him in Holland. Well, or at least he kept him company, as he can't even read. It was the uprising of the Streltsy guard that affirmed Menshikov's standing. It was he who hurried back to Russia on his own, and put it down mercilessly, by beheading one Streltsy after the next, hundreds of them, until his arms ached and he waded in blood. That's just one more reason why Peter loves him so much . . ."

"Who were the Streltsy soldiers? And why should Peter love Menshikov for executing men?" I nicked a piece of roast pheasant from Sheremetev's plate. Its skin was hot, crispy, and tasted a bit sweet, as it had been marinated in mustard and honey. I licked my fingers, listening to Sheremetev.

"The Streltsy soldiers were once the most respected regiment in Russia. When Peter was born they feared the hold that his mother had over old Tsar Alexis, especially after she had given him a healthy son. At Alexis's death, they stormed the Kremlin and at Regent Sophia's order killed Peter's uncle and grandfather and made the boy watch: both men took two days to die, spiked on halberds." I closed my eyes in horror. Ernst Gluck's words came back to me: "Sophia kept him in the Kremlin, at least, until he set fire to it . . ." Sheremetev's voice continued: "The Streltsy called Peter a son of a bitch and spat in his mother's face, letting them live, but just about, and hailed Regent Sophia. So when Menshikov beheaded them after that second uprising, he in truth was killing Peter's demons—at least some of them."

"What do you mean, at least some of them?"

"There are others, and they make him ill, and torment him with fits and seizures," Sheremetev said. His face was very close to mine. "But you know, I could never have done what Menshikov did. Killing on the battlefield is one thing, but executing a man with my own hands? Never."

I huddled in the cloak. How strange the Russians were, forever caught between a zest for life and seeking penance for their sins; filled with deep religious belief, yet capable of heathen violence and full of disdain for common decency, swaying between hair-raising cruelty and deep, tearful regret that might haunt them for years. A Russian soul knew no calm, no balance, and no peace, ever.

I touched Sheremetev's arm. "No, Boris Petrovich, You are too good a man for that. You save girls who are about to be raped. Menshikov would have joined in with those loafers, who knows?"

"Yes, who knows?" he said, and downed his vodka.

28

We spoke until the dark morning hours of that October night. We were alone in the main tent, as all the other guests had staggered away, grateful for some rare hours of rest before sunrise. But for me, with the tsar present, everything had changed. It felt like ants crawling in my veins. How much longer would we camp here, and what would happen to me then? I had to be ready and know as much as possible about Russia and its people. Sheremetev laughed at me when I thought the tsar's changes to his country stopped at shaving of beards and ordering a new way of dressing.

"God, girl, that's just the beginning. The tsar says that traveling has opened his eyes to how backward Russia and its people are. Ever since his return from Europe he is a man possessed, as if time is running out for everything he wants to achieve. Nothing is safe from him, be it pleasure, agriculture, education, religion, administration, marriage and heritage, the army, food—just about anything that touches a Russian's everyday life. Russia is Peter's dough, yet the yeast doesn't quite want to rise..."

"But does he really need to do all this? It's such an effort, the war and all..."

"This war is a struggle about life and death for Peter's realm. It forces us into the future, but the tsar lacks everything: money, men, and equipment, which he needed at best yesterday, or rather last week. War is terrible, but it also brings progress," he said, and gently prodded me when my eyes closed. "Stay awake and drink more, Marta. I love talking to you. You listen so well to an old man's chatter."

The beer did refresh me, and I licked the foam off my lips, keeping them moist and shiny. Sheremetev's gaze lingered on them, before he averted his eyes. "I see no old man. Go on, tell me more."

"You flatter me." He smiled at me warmly. "Russia is like an old mill wheel, rotting away in a backwater, until a new, young, spirited miller takes over, wanting to grind more grain or sell more sacks, and so he makes the water rise. The wheel spins faster and faster, until the blades break and even the millstone cracks."

I chuckled. He had a way of putting things that even I understood.

"You laugh, but Peter won't stop at anything. The country is not up to his demands. His orders can't even reach the people—we have the *voivody*, the counsels and the tax collectors, but since Peter keeps on asking for more of everything—men, money, planning, leadership, and support—they can't keep up. He is looking for new sources of wealth, all while kicking the old manufacturing into new shape. Every family, be it a serf's or a nobleman's, has to give him their sons, either as workers or to travel abroad and study, learning for Russia and bringing their knowledge back home. Have you heard that the tsar is building a fleet? A fleet! Fifteen years ago nobody here had as much as seen a ship. All a Russian knew was a ferry to cross a swollen river and, possibly, a fishing boat. His will is our fate, even if it might take a hundred years for us to thank him for his efforts," he said bitterly.

"But the war is over, isn't it? You have beaten the Swedes?"

He wiped his eyes and I felt his tiredness. "Marienburg is nothing. The tsar wants a harbor that is navigable throughout the year and not hampered by ice in winter. He wants the conquest of the West, a pact with other European powers. As long as both Charles and Peter live, they'll go on fighting, even if the war lasts for twenty years. We count for nothing in this. Do you know what Peter did after the trouble with the bad cannons in the Battle of Narva?"

"No."

"He had all the church bells melted down in order to cast new, better, bigger cannons."

I gasped—a man who touched the possessions of the church?

Sheremetev saw my shock and said: "Yes. I, too, wonder what is still sacred to him." He lowered his voice. "And then this idea to build a new city in the middle of the swamps of the Bay of Finland . . ."

He stopped mid-sentence. The curtain to the side room was torn apart and Peter swayed into the main tent, belting his trousers and tucking his sweaty shirt into the waistband. Did he see us sitting so closely side by side in the shade of the tent post, or didn't he care? A man like him was never truly alone, I thought, and to acknowledge people or not was surely a matter of choice. The last of the candlelight drew shadows on his face, making it look gaunt and tired. His bright blue eyes lay deep in their sockets; he rubbed them, his forehead glistening with sweat.

Sheremetev and I sat as still as if we were watching a shy animal. The tsar slumped into a chair, which buckled under his weight, and stretched his legs before grabbing a jug from the table next to him and drinking deeply once more. He closed his eyes, let his head tilt, and hummed a little song, then fell silent and started breathing heavily. Was he asleep?

Sheremetev and I looked at each other: it was time to retire, him to his tent and me to whichever corner I rolled out my bedding in tonight, as Daria's room was busy. I was about to get up when Sheremetev grabbed my arm. Peter had startled from his slumber and sat bolt upright, his eyes unblinking and wide open. All of a sudden, he flung the clay jug at a tent post. It smashed, splashing beer onto the rugs and cushions below. Peter bent over and buried his head in his hands, moaning and whimpering, but then rose, roaring like an angry bear. His eyes rolled until I saw only their whites, and he leaned heavily on the table, which gave way and broke. In a clatter, plates, glasses, and jars fell to the floor. He stared and then his knees buckled; he cradled his head in his too-fine hands and sobbed, foam bubbling on his lips, before he reared up, thrashing about, hitting the furniture and writhing in his fit.

Sheremetev held me and pulled me back.

Peter groaned. "What have I done, Mother? What have we done?" The mighty man bent over double, his tongue pushing between his lips and teeth. I thought of Grigori and felt no more fear: there was no time to lose; we had to help him.

"Hold his legs, I'll take care of the rest," I said, and tore away from Sheremetev, who had shrunk back in horror. I was not afraid, and in this moment Peter was not the mighty tsar who had ravaged my homeland and destroyed my life. He was just a helpless man who suffered. If I hadn't been able to help Grigori, I could help him.

Peter curled at my feet, slavering and foaming, his eyes wide and rolling. Sheremetev grabbed his boots and weighed him down, but the tsar rose and hit out at his much smaller general, smacking him so hard that Boris Petrovich groaned, but he didn't let go. I took a deep breath and lunged between those thrashing, bulky arms, grabbed the tsar's twitching head, pulled him close, and forced his forehead between my breasts, holding his ears and neck so tightly that he couldn't move away. We sank to the ground and his breath rattled, his body cramped up a couple of times, before he lay still. His breath was hot on my skin and he sucked in my scent before he grabbed me around the waist, so that I could hardly breathe. After a long time he lay still and his breath steadied. I dared to look at his face: he had fallen asleep peacefully and I rocked him like I would a baby.

"This was bound to happen." Sheremetev sighed, slowly taking his weight off Peter's feet. "The long ride, the girls, and all this drink. Peter likes to see himself as a Titan, but he is just a man."

I had no idea what a Titan might be, but put one finger to my lips in warning. Peter's face was drenched in sweat and his hair smelled of dust, smoke, leather, and the love he had made to the Arsenjevas. His curls stuck to his temples when I tenderly stroked his head, blowing some air onto his face. He sighed and burrowed his nose deeper in the gap of my cleavage; his breathing grew heavier again and he held me even tighter than before. I never stopped caressing him and perhaps even kissed his forehead without thinking, while he started to cry softly, soaking my bodice with his tears.

When Sheremetev got up, I saw the tsar's feet: like his hands, they looked too dainty for his huge body.

"Don't let go of him, Marta, will you? Everything hangs on him," Sheremetev said, and slipped out into the darkness, which was alive with fires and songs from all over the vast Russian realm: melodies that started slow and sullen, before gathering speed and culminating in clapping and chanting. Peter's coming had rallied their spirits; they took fresh courage and gained new strength. Voices asked Boris Petrovich some questions before all fell quiet.

My back hurt from holding the tsar so steadily, but only when he seemed truly asleep did I dare to reach for some cushions. Yet when I shifted, he grabbed my waist so hard that I gasped for air. "Stay," he murmured. "Stay with me. Hold me tight, *matka*."

"I will, *starik*," I answered in German, with a little smile. If I was his old girl, he'd be my old man: that seemed only fair. His eyelids fluttered and he looked at me in surprise, but then fell back asleep, this time deeply and calmly. I grabbed all the cushions I could reach, stuffing them behind my back and under my bottom and thighs. The darkness in the tent paled into dawn when I, too, fell asleep, holding the tsar of all the Russias in my arms as if he were a baby. Just before my eyelids closed I remembered a supper from days long gone by, and Agneta Gluck's high-pitched voice asking, "Is it true that the tsar is a two-headed giant who eats little children for breakfast?"

* * *

I woke on my own, feeling drowsy after the all-too-short and uncomfortable hours of sleep. There was no sign of the tsar anywhere, but the tent was swarming with people clearing up after the night's feast and packing things away, with chests open and everything piled topsy-turvy. For a moment I wondered if I had dreamed all that had happened. Neither Menshikov nor the Arsenjevas were anywhere to be seen. All the flaps were fastened open and a fresh breeze swept through the tent. When I stepped outside I shivered, the blue, cold morning light blinding me. The camp was in upheaval, and Daria and Varvara watched hawk-eyed as their maids loaded all their treasures onto carts, even though we'd need sleds soon. I tried not to look at Varvara's throat, where she wore her love bites as proudly as trophies of war.

She arched her eyebrows when I approached. "Ah, Murta, too, is finally awake. What a lazy little thing you have plucked from the gutter, Daria." She turned to me.

Daria looked up, surprised. Varvara had never been friendly, but not outright hostile either. What had gotten into her?

"You really are unlucky, girl, missing out on everything: the tsar is long gone, without taking his leave from anyone. When I woke, he had already left my bed," Varvara added. With her shining auburn hair and glittering eyes she looked like the cruel, cunning vixens in the forests of my childhood. "You be off now, Marta. A maid like you has her hands full when the camp is packed up," she chirped, and reached out her fingers for me to kiss.

Daria looked on, embarrassed, and not knowing which side to take. "No, Varvara, Marta, really, please don't . . ." She was torn and I knew that this could be my undoing. And so I kissed Varvara's fingers, yet in my heart I knew that it was I, and not her, who had held the tsar in her arms last night and who had possibly saved his life.

When I looked up, I met Varvara's gray, cold eyes. She, too, knew the truth, I understood, and felt a chill. Who would protect me from her?

* * *

Peter's new marching orders were a surprise to everybody. The Russians had to take the fortress of Nyenschantz on the shores of Lake Ladoga, which was surrounded by vast, empty marshland.

"Must we?" wailed Daria while her dresses were folded in oak chests studded with slate and iron bands. "I swear, nothing good comes from it. In summer, countless gnats eat you alive, while in winter that damn river Neva rises, swamps the land, and drowns all life. What fun."

But the fortress's dank walls and high turrets were key to controlling the estuary. The siege took Menshikov two weeks, until it fell after a skirmish at sea. Peter, I heard, was bursting with pride: he had won a first naval battle. Menshikov was made governor of the strait—*obergshathalter*—and the tsar changed the fortress's name to Schlüsselburg, as it was key to the future as he saw it. Menshikov had Peter's letter to him read aloud at dinner every evening for days on end following the victory: *By God, this nut was hard to crack, but you have done it, my beloved brother.*

When the first snowflakes fell, Daria's steady moaning about the wet and the cold—it snowed and snowed—paid off and Menshikov gave in to her nagging. He sent her, Varvara, his sister Rasia, and me back to Moscow to get ready for the Yuletide. When I helped Daria to pack I wondered if the tsar, too, would then return to Moscow, which was foolish, of course. What was I to him?

IN THE WINTER PALACE, 1725

The snow fell like a curtain, slanted and silent, shrouding streets, quays, and prospects up to the axles of the carts already making their way into town for the morning market despite the awful weather. Outside the city walls, beyond the reach of the lantern light, paths and roads had disappeared. It would still be a while until the late and heavy dawn arrived and wedged a brief day between the hours of darkness, its time marred by the steady snow and the dullness of the black ice on the river and the roads.

I feel that your city knows, Peter, and your death is our secret. The high houses with their flat façades mourn their master's passing in silence; the waters flowing underneath the four hundred bridges murmur their loss. Only the winter winds, as untamable as ever, chase down the Nevsky Prospect and dodge my orders, carrying the news with them to the utmost corners of the realm. The vast, endless plains of your empire always had to endure the whims of *batjushka* tsar; your people followed orders they could not hope to understand. The tsar was as God-given as day and night, winter and summer, the sun and the moon: there was no questioning him.

In the wan morning light, all the bells of Russia will be tolling, somber and uniform, for hours on end. Your people will drop whatever they do and kneel, caps in hand, tears streaming down their faces, praying for your soul, crossing themselves with three fingers. It would make you happy to see how Europe, too, will pay you and your city their respects. This is what you always wanted, isn't it, for Saint Petersburg, your paradise?

Thanks to Feofan Prokopovich there is no lack of legends about how you chose the spot for it. Was it true that Saint Alexander Nevsky had beaten the Teutonic hordes in battle here? Or did you go hunting, my love, when an eagle circled above your head, settling on your shoulder, showing you the way with its beady eyes and its hoarse cries? Might you have wandered through the swamps of Lust Eland—as one would never do, really—when the very eagle guided you to its heart and you cut a cross from beech branches, marking a spot and shouting, "In the name of Christ the Almighty, I shall build a church and a fortress here to honor the saints Peter and Paul."

* * *

All this belongs in the realm of legends. The truth was much simpler, yet much grander: to strengthen his hold over the Neva strait, Peter built a Russian fortress. The hard-fought-for new lands should never be lost again. The tsar chose Lust Eland as the driest spot of all in the Ladoga swamps. When Peter had the bones of Saint Alexander Nevsky re-entombed, clouds of gnats set upon us. During the endless hours of the ceremony we went on swatting the insects and cursing the useless serfs who were told to kill them before they bit us and flew off, their bellies heavy with our blood. Peter alone stood without blinking, never moving, watching stone-faced as the saint's coffin was lowered into its new tomb. For him, this was the beginning of a new Russia.

In the evening, I treated my many bites with *kefir,* which cooled the skin, and Peter told me to stop moaning and went on talking about the paradise he'd build here. By then I was ready to take every step along the way with him, even though I was just one of many girls whom he'd toss a coin or two to after a night of merriment. I smiled and urged him on; Evdokia's sour face and her unwillingness to follow him in his flights of fancy had been her downfall.

Prokopovich's claims that the tsar's chosen land was empty, waiting for his blessed touch, are untrue as well: Swedes had settled all around the shores of Lake Ladoga in big, well-to-do farmsteads and I spotted many *mir* like my own had been. The first real house in Saint Petersburg was a hut, which Peter and I shared as a cozy home. He left the fort one morning, walking all alone into the forest, his ax on his shoulder and throwing stones and insulting the guards that Menshikov had sent out to follow him, as bands of marauding Swedish mercenaries had been sighted. Peter chose the trees he deemed right and chopped their trunks to the length he needed, before building our hut with his own hands, sweating, laughing, and loving every moment of it. I held the nails as well as other bits and bobs and played pranks on him by hiding his hammer and chisel. Once finished, the little house was barely wider than it was long, lodging a small hall, a kitchen, a living room, and a bedroom. The hearth was fired up throughout the year, as Peter hated the cold, and I cooked our *kasha* and *tchai* on the open fire, stacking our bowls as I had done as a child in our *izba*. Peter made our wooden furniture himself: a table, two benches, and our bed, as well as a lockable chest studded with slate and iron bands. The only sign of Peter's wealth and rank was an icon of heavy gold, studded with pearls, rubies, sapphires, and emeralds, which hung on our bedroom wall, right next to a map of Europe.

This hut was the root from which Peter's paradise was to grow and blossom; his New Jerusalem, glowing in all the colors of the rainbow. If he himself was content with his hut, he drove his architects and stonemasons mercilessly to build bigger and better, a city such as the world had never seen. He wanted nothing for himself, but everything for the fame of Russia.

Peter ordered orange and lemon trees to be brought in from Persia, and had roses, mint, and camphor planted in the gardens to smother all evil smells. He was beside himself when a messenger brought a sample of the first-ever blossom from the Summer Palace's gardens out to the field, when we stood once more in battle. The gardener had soaked the flower in olive oil to keep it fresh, but instead the petals were rotten and slimy. The tsar knouted the messenger and ordered his gardeners to send him proof of the next blossom, with the flowers wrapped one by one in tobacco leaves instead. The first streets and prospects were lit by lanterns with candles and oil—their glass was of course made in Menshikov's workshops—such as had never been seen in Russia, so the police could spot any loafers more easily. Heavily guarded barriers—*shlagbaumy*—were put up on the main roads and the bridges linking the forty islands. Nobody but doctors on their way to an ailing patient, or people whose visit was expected, were allowed to drive through without a pass. But when I looked out of the window, shortly after Peter's death, I knew that just behind the splendor of the palaces lay the first modest wooden houses, followed by row upon row of *izby* made of straw, clay, and moss and finally the squalid, ragged tents of the poorest of the poor, trying to claim their bit of paradise for them. This city mirrors your world, Peter, whether you want it to or not.

Saint Petersburg grew quickly in the first twenty years of the new century. I remembered our senseless joy when the first Dutch frigate, bobbing on the already icy waters, weighed anchor. It delivered salt and wine for the long winter ahead, and its visiting sailors were reason enough for a feast so wild that it even stunned Menshikov and shocked the visiting Dutch. Peter mercilessly plied the men with drink, then asked us all to go out for a sail on stormy waters in the morning. The rolling waves sobered us up real quick and the Dutch were happy to leave with a present of five hundred gold ducats in their pockets. Peter promised each ship anchoring in the bay within the year the same generous gift.

*   *   *

I cooled my forehead on the windowpane. My thoughts were racing and I was laughing and chatting with Peter as if he were still alive; as if I could place my feet on his thighs and he'd squeeze and rub them, until they cracked and popped back into place, and tickle me until I squealed. He'd do that until I had fire in my thighs, which he liked.

The glass mirrored my feverish face, with its shiny eyes and burning cheeks. Some strands of hair had come undone and I gathered myself for the long wait that still lay ahead, before Russia could begin praying for the soul of its new ruler, its first-ever tsarina.

For the time being Menshikov snored like a bear, sprawling his heavy body in the tiny chair, his head lolled to the side and his mouth open. The fire had burned down and a chill crept through the thin windowpanes. I still waited for the privy council: Ostermann, Tolstoy, and Jagushinsky. Why were they not in the palace at their dying tsar's side? Did they avoid my call? I had saved them all from Peter's anger countless times, but people forget so easily when it comes to saving their own skin.

Had it been safe to entrust my secret message to the young servant?

The Winter Palace looked so welcoming and gay during the day, its stunning shades of blue and green mirroring the Neva in springtime. Yet at night it had its own life of countless dark corners and secret passageways that led to the dark icy waters of the river. Not even the rats turned their heads when a body splashed into those floes. Fishermen would find the corpse, or what was left of it, in their nets much later, once the *ottepel,* the big thaw, had been and gone. How stupid of me. I chewed my wrist with anger. If my messenger had been caught, questioned, and killed, then the Dolgorukis knew about my plan and, even worse, I'd have lost valuable hours. I should have sent Menshikov and the Imperial Guard. Just then Menshikov coughed and sat up, shook himself awake like a dog casting off water, rose, and then stretched all the sleep from his tall body. A short slumber refreshed him as much as a whole night's rest, as I knew from the many times I had been in the field with him.

When he stepped up to me, the vodka, sweat, and the tiredness of his long wake at Peter's deathbed blended with his perfume of musk and sandalwood. His hair was messy, his full lace collar had slipped, and a red wine stain shone brightly on his crumpled shirt. I smiled and tenderly straightened his collar. He kissed my hand, surprised. This was the man I had shared everything with, even my husband's love, and now we shared a fate. We were forever linked, whatever happened.

Menshikov tore the window open and rubbed his face with some snow. "Brrr! Cold. Looks as if we are in for a storm, don't you think?" he asked, eyeing the sky. "Winter in these swamps is always to be relied upon." Now wide awake, he shivered, closed the window again, and stoked the fire with logs from the basket. The flames licked over the wood, burning brightly and spreading a dry scent, like a walk in a summer forest. He raised his eyebrows.

"Where is the privy council? I thought you had sent for them?"

I pursed my lips and he stared at me. "By God, Catherine. How much time do we have left? Say something."

The tone of his voice angered me: at least I had done something, while he had been lost in his stupor. "If you hadn't been so drunk I wouldn't have needed to rely on a little soldier, would I? Perhaps the lad had his throat cut and we can scramble onto a sled heading to Siberia. Or I can just as well shave my head already now, ready for a nunnery.

Do you think I have fought so hard for this to happen?" I heard the fear in my voice, but Menshikov placed his hand on my mouth to silence me.

"Psst," he whispered. "Do you hear that?" He looked at the little door that led over to Peter's bedroom. I frowned and listened. He was right: somebody was sobbing in there, sounding desperate and lost. Menshikov stayed by the fire when I tiptoed to the door and opened it soundlessly.

Peter's chamber was bathed in candlelight: he looked as if he was asleep, even if death already spread its sickly sweet-smelling shroud over the room. In front of Peter's bed kneeled a girl wearing a long, dark, hooded velvet cloak. Her shoulders heaved as she kissed Peter's fingers, which were beginning to stiffen.

The doctors Blumentrost and Paulsen startled when they saw me and cowered in the corner: they had failed to obey my strict order to protect the tsar's corpse. I felt cold anger, but grabbed the girl, pulling her to her feet and forcing her to face me. But then I let go of her in surprise, as she looked at me fearlessly and stubbornly, as had ever been her way, her pretty face swollen and her light blue eyes—Peter's eyes—reddened with tears.

"Elizabeth!" I said. "What are you doing here? Why are you not in bed, like your sisters?" I shook her and snot ran from her nose to her lips. Her plump body lay heavy in my hands, until she wriggled herself free from my grasp.

"Stop it, Mother," she hissed. The dark cloak made her look regal: I still saw her as being like one of her own dolls, yet she had grown into a young woman.

"How did you get in here?" I asked. If she had managed it, others could too.

"Easy," she said. She licked her lips, her shining eyes as lively as a young bird's despite her sorrow. "The corridor was as good as empty and Madame de la Tour was guarding little Natalya. The poor thing is coughing like death itself and so the French locust stayed away. And Anna . . ." Her voice trailed off. I knew that my eldest daughter was busy dreaming of her wedding with the German duke Charles Frederic of Holstein, who, with his narrow shoulders and his terrible stammer, wasn't handsome, but his wider family ruled over all the north of Europe. At first, he had asked for Elizabeth's hand in marriage, but when he did so, Peter was so pleased that he gave him our elder daughter instead. Their wedding day was close and Anna would speak of nothing else.

Elizabeth was hell-bent on angering me. "There was only a young and handsome guard outside my father's door and I have my ways . . ." she said, showing her small, sharp teeth like a cat that got the cream. My heart sank. My daughter, the tsarevna of all the Russias, behaved like an innkeeper's harlot. From playing with dolls she had moved on seamlessly to life-size "toys" in her father's barracks. She was only fifteen, a year younger than when I had been sold to Vassily all those lives ago, but she already had the worst reputation of all the royal princesses of Europe. Being born out of wedlock to a former serf and washermaid didn't help. Peter had sent her portrait to every court with an eligible crown prince, and the painters didn't even need to flatter my daughter. Elizabeth was a beauty, with no cleft lip and no pockmarks for a gifted brush on canvas to have to hide. Peter was puzzled when no engagement came to pass; why did Versailles keep on delaying an answer in such an insulting way? Who else could the young king of France be happy to marry than his Lizenka, all lively and beautiful as she was? Yet in the end, young Louis settled on the daughter of the deposed king of Poland, a dull girl with no dowry. Peter saw in Elizabeth what he wanted to see: his strength and his zest for life, his ruthlessness and his sensuality. Contrary to all her brothers she had simply refused to die, neither at birth nor all through the illnesses that blighted a child's early life.

Her birth had been the most difficult of the eleven times I had actually been brought to bed: she was born with her feet first, the very day that Peter celebrated his biggest victory of the Great Northern War. The midwife had crossed herself with three fingers, all pale with fright, when she spotted Elizabeth's tiny soles where her head should have been. "Holy mother of God. Not this, as well!" she had called, her face smeared with blood and sweat. "Born feet first under the December stars. Those are the worst signs for a woman. She'll be a wolverine."

* * *

"What will happen now?" Elizabeth asked. "Who will be the next tsar? Did Father settle on little Petrushka after all? He's not even the tsarevich."

He decided nothing, I thought, but said, "Yes, but he is Alexey's son. And soon, he will be a man. That's enough of a claim."

"A man!" Elizabeth said gaily. "Do you know what the dark cells of the Trubetzkoy Bastion or the dank cellars of Schlüsselburg can do to a *man's* body and mind?"

It seemed Peter's soul had slipped into his daughter's body. She'd make love to a soldier standing up outside this door, she'd sob her eyes out at her father's deathbed, and she'd banish her little nephew for life into a musty dark cell. She was a true Russian, of wild beauty, harsh cruelty, and deep pity for the plight of others, overwhelming lust for life, and a shocking ruthlessness. She was a stranger to me.

"Whatever happens, Elizabeth, nothing is to befall Petrushka. Whoever hurts him will be a murderer in the eyes of all other European courts. Do you want to start a reign like that?"

She shook her head, albeit gingerly, and said, "Well, if Petrushka is not even the tsarevich, if my elder sister marries to Germany, and all my other brothers have passed away, then . . ."

"Then?" I asked icily.

She shrugged and smiled brightly. "Then I should be tsarina next! Father loved me and he made Anna and me crown princesses. Why shouldn't I rule?"

I felt like crying: a whim of nature and chance had made this lazy, plump, sensuous being my daughter and the tsarevna of all the Russias. She wanted to be tsarina, with all its burdens, as well as blessings? Peter's vast realm with its millions of people, its unbelievable riches, and its terrible plights of poverty and squalor, should have to listen to her? Its fate, be it war or peace, should hang on her playful fingertips, which men liked to kiss after a masterfully danced minuet or a quadrille? Her little head that had so far mainly been used to show off the latest fashionable hairstyle should think politics?

"Elizabeth!" I giggled instead, then laughed so hard that the doctors looked worried, but she lunged at me like one of the small monkeys she kept in Peterhof Palace, and was battering me with her fists when Menshikov hurried into the room.

"What's this din," he hissed, and grabbed her arms. "We are not in a *kabak.*" She winced in his grasp, but he held her around her plump waist and lifted her up, carrying her over into the other room. She wriggled and kicked; her red-hot anger left me speechless, yet I remembered a ball where Elizabeth had slapped another girl and had torn a fistful of her hair out in front of the whole court, just because both of them wore pink dresses and the other one looked prettier in it. Peter had laughed tears at it, but I had had the fight stopped and married the girl off well, topping up her dowry. Perhaps I was more a mother to my dead sons than to my living daughters?

Elizabeth calmed down, but Menshikov wanted to be sure. "Will you behave now, Tsarevna?" he asked, lifting his hand off her mouth. Elizabeth smoothed her cloak and raised her chin, which made her heavy diamond earrings sparkle. I closed the door to the other room, glowering at the doctors. My order was to be upheld and no one was to see the dead tsar's body. They nodded, pale with dread.

Menshikov, Elizabeth, and I were alone.

* * *

The fire had warmed the small library and when Menshikov served us wine, Elizabeth downed hers in one go, smacking her pink lips.

"You drink like a peasant," I scolded her.

"Well, *you* must know," she said.

"Stop it," Menshikov cut in. "Tsarina. Elizabeth. We don't have time for pettiness."

She spun and stared at him, her eyes icy. "*What* did you say? *Tsarina*?" She lengthened the word to its full size and power before she turned to me. "But of course. That's it. Now I understand: you want it all for yourself. Being just my father's wife and crowned consort is not enough. Finally, no one will prevent you if you want to take yet another chamberlain to your bed . . ."

I slapped her so hard, her lip burst. She gave a muffled scream and touched the wound.

"Don't," Menshikov pleaded, and handed Elizabeth his lacy handkerchief. We sat in silence, while some logs crashed in the fireplace, making embers fly. Elizabeth dabbed her lip, looked at me darkly, and slipped off her cloak, stuffing the handkerchief into the seam of her tight sleeve. In her richly embroidered emerald-green silk dress and the foaming lace of her bodice her shoulders looked like polished alabaster. Following the fashion of Versailles the dress was so deeply cut that I could almost see her nipples, and diamonds rained down from her neck into her cleavage. Countless peasant families could survive for centuries on these jewels alone. Was she on her way to a feast? I had long since lost track of her comings and goings, lost interest in the healthiest and merriest of my children. How did I allow this to happen?

Elizabeth moved her chair closer to the fire, kicked off her silk slippers, and warmed her feet in their sheer silk stockings. She seemed happy to be here, in the middle of things, and asked, "So, tell me, Menshikov. What is it that you want to do? You are never short of an idea or a plan, are you? Do you want to rule together with my mother, or do you want to seize power all by yourself? Shame on both of you: this palace still breathes with my father's soul. The water on the windowpane is not dew, but the sweat of your fear. Do you sleep with each other, now and then?" She smiled and I wanted to slap her. Menshikov's face darkened, but he stayed calm. "One day, Tsarevna Elizabeth, you will understand how hurtful and stupid those words were," he said.

"No, Alexander Danilovich. I shall always sleep with any man who takes my fancy. I shouldn't hesitate if you wanted to be the lucky one," she teased him.

I held my breath: Did she truly offer him her bed, her birthright, in return for his support? How would he resist that? God, couldn't I even trust my own flesh and blood? A ruler's world was made of only friend or foe, even in his own family. I looked beseechingly to the door, begging for the privy council to come. Ostermann, Tolstoy, and Jagushinsky—I needed them all, but I calmly sipped some wine and said, "Prince Menshikov is right. One day you'll learn that it might be better not to sleep with a man just to secure his loyalty."

"One day? When I am old and no one wants me anymore?"

I didn't want to have heard her; she knew how to wound. The flames danced, soothing my spirit and making me tired. "The Dolgorukis will try to enthrone Petrushka. If that happens, we are all done for," I said curtly. "Siberia is the best we can hope for."

"But Vassily Dolgoruki is my godfather. He would never . . ." she started.

"He would, though, wouldn't he?"

"But why?"

"Because of Alexey, of course," I said.

"Oh yes." She eyed Menshikov, who twisted and turned the colorful Venetian goblet in his hand as if he had nothing to do with all this. But Elizabeth wasn't finished with him. "Because of Alexey. My brother. Oh, Alexander Danilovich, your sled to Siberia won't even have a cushion or a blanket. You'll burrow in straw like a pig in winter. Perhaps, just perhaps, you'll get enough kopecks to buy an ax once you make it there. If not, just chew the wood off a tree, build a hut, and get on with it. But you'll have to wait until summer, when the ice melts."

Her laughter rang out like the silver bells she tied around her dwarves' necks to find them in the darkness of the palace corridors. Menshikov pulled his fingers until the joints cracked. He, too, felt like hitting her. Welcome to my world.

"If Petrushka gets to be tsar, he will free his grandmother Evdokia from her nunnery and shave our heads instead," I said. "I will be nothing but the late tsar's whore and you, Elizabeth, will be a bastard born out of wedlock. Petrushka might still have to fear your bloodline and your birthright, but he will leave Saint Petersburg forever . . ."

"No!" She shot up. "Never! That would be the betrayal of everything Father lived for," she gasped. "It would be like a second death for him. That's horrid."

What a strange girl she was: betraying her father's dream was worse than being buried alive in a nunnery.

"Well, then, you will have to sit and wait with us," I said.

"Wait? What for?" she asked, eyeing me over the rim of her glass.

"The privy council," Menshikov said.

She laughed. "Those old fools. Ostermann has the gout whenever he sees fit, Tolstoy is so fat he needs two or three chairs to support his big bottom, and Jagushinsky stinks as if he's rotting from the inside out. Which one of them will share your hut in Siberia, Menshikov?" She dug her toes in his thighs. "Who's the least fun? I'll see to that."

"Stop it!" I scolded her. The privy council had been the wisest heads in Peter's empire. God protect Russia from Elizabeth, I thought. She shrugged her bare shoulders and hummed a tune before getting bored with that as well, looking sullenly into the flames.

I glanced at the window, trying to guess the time. The inky night was putting up a struggle against the morning hour with its wan blue shine and the day's short hours of sparsely measured gray light. The city lay in wait, shining in its cloak of sparkling white; ice crystals adorned the windows of the palaces and houses. As children we'd suck on icicles, surprised that they tasted of dust. Just then, Elizabeth asked huskily, "Have you ever loved my father?"

And I just don't know the answer to that anymore.

29

My first journey to the heart of the realm seemed endless: How could a country be so vast? The winter was severe and our sledges were stuck right in its merciless cold. Birds froze in mid-flight, falling like stones from the sky, and travelers perished in sudden snowstorms, never reaching shelter. The wolves lost all fear of man and came right up to the *izby* doorsteps, snatching children and small livestock, crazed with hunger. How my family could have survived this, I did not know, having to shake the thought out of my head, lest it eat me up. My Baltic fatherland was no more, as from Reval to Riga everything had fallen prey to the war's terror. At the end of our time in Marienburg, Sheremetev was said to be clueless as to what to do with all his loot, and prices for either a sheep or a child sank to a denga apiece. Half a kopeck for a human being!

There was no time to think as impatience drove the sisters Arsenjeva on. They'd have the drivers whip the small spotted ponies mercilessly to win *verst* upon *verst,* until the animals' mouths foamed, and their backs were covered in weals. At every postal station we changed ponies, taking our pick from the innkeeper's and other travelers' stables, without ever paying for them. What belonged to any Russian belonged first and foremost to the tsar and his friends, and Menshikov took full advantage of that. When I had first heard about traveling to Moscow, I had pictured a modest number of sleds and possibly a guard making their way through Russia. All I knew, after all, was the drive with Vassily to Walk and then the smelly cart to Marienburg. Instead, we left in a train with hundreds of people. Menshikov sent ahead everything he deemed necessary for the Yuletide festivities in the capital. I did not know where to look first, stunned by his splendor, and also by him being so spoiled. Behind our sled traveled a good hundred sleds laden with luggage, food, and people, such as Menshikov's political and military advisors, as well as two chamberlains and three page boys, a cauldron maker and two trombonists, a Moor and a family of dwarves, three scribes, a dozen castrated choir singers, a pope, and two cooks with their chubby kitchen boys. When I asked Daria about it, she just shrugged: "Alexander Danilovich needs what Alexander Danilovich needs."

The closer we got to Moscow, the more handsome were the houses and inns, where all life centered around a big hearth with a mantelpiece made of stone or tiles, and the kitchen served hearty cabbage stews, chicken broth with dumplings made of offal and *blintshiki*, little pancakes filled with molten cheese or salted and smoked meat. Pigs and poultry were locked in sties and coops and would no longer stray among the guests in the main room. When we stepped into the cozy warmth our dank furs steamed up the small windows. The heat and the stench of the many people eating and drinking and sleeping hit me like a slap, but it took only a couple of glasses of vodka to get used to it all. At night, the men of our train burrowed in the straw like pigs, while I relished having a room in the inn, where I joined the Arsenjevas. If Varvara minded—"Shouldn't Marta sleep in the stable with the other serfs?"—Daria's friendship protected me. The maid first warmed our bed with her body, before curling up on the threshold of our door for the night. Before I fell asleep at night I would pray to the God who wanted to listen, thanking him for my fate, such as it was, even if my future hung on Daria's mood and goodwill. What if Varvara started to talk even more against me? Already, no day passed without a stinging word or two.

The seven hundred and seventeen *versty* from Schlüsselburg to Moscow could take anything from six days' to four weeks' travel: we hardly ever saw daylight, as we got into the sleds in the early-morning darkness and stepped out of them long after sunset. They were like small, colorful houses on skids, painted gaily on the outside and stuffed with cushions and fur blankets, where we lay and chatted the day away, relishing the warmth of the copper pans full of smoldering coals that the maids had placed there as their first duty of the day.

The sun made it up into a leaden sky by late morning, and we craned our necks, longing for its first rays. My belly was filled with hot, sweet, and salty *kasha* and the bitter *tchai* we'd had for breakfast in the inn. This was so different from the cold and lonely trip from Walk to Marienburg just a few years ago, and I relished the comfort, the good food, and all the laughter and the stories the sisters had to tell. Depending on whether Rasia Menshikova felt like company or not, she shared our sled or kept to herself, though I was sure that nothing escaped her attention. She guarded herself from joining in with Varvara's needling, but wasn't as close to me as Daria, either.

The landscape flying by the small barred windows of the sled looked alike from one day to the next. Forests, hills, and plains were shrouded in snow, and only adventures and mishaps marked time's passing, such as the heavy snowstorm that forced the driver to sit with us—the sisters plied the man with vodka and told jokes to make his ears burn—or the wolves that attacked our sledge, circling it one afternoon well before we'd reached the safety of an inn. When Varvara heard the first long, dragging howl that made my blood chill, she shouted at the coachman, "Whip those beasts away. They are Tsaritsa Evdokia's faithful servants and she has sent them to eat us up. She's a witch and they are of the Devil." The poor man thrashed as good as he could, but there were just too many of them; so, the Arsenjevas and I, too, seized the whips that were stored underneath our benches and started lashing while standing in the open door of the sled. In the light of the full moon rising I saw the wolves' eyes shine with madness and hunger; icicles hung in their fur and around their salivating mouths. The other sleds caught up with us and the men started to shoot at the beasts, who turned into a howling, bloody muddle of fur, teeth, and bodies. In the evening Menshikov's men boasted about their great bravery, the wolves growing stronger, bigger, and more ferocious with each glass of vodka, until I snatched Daria's sable coat and pretended to be a big wolf. She chased me around the room with a whip, which made the men howl with laughter and even Varvara was in stitches.

The same evening, Daria asked me in the evening, "Marta, would you like to be my lady-in-waiting? Like that, we can be always together and have all sorts of fun. Varvara can be such a spoilsport with her constant nagging. You'll have a room in Menshikov's palace and a salary."

I felt like throwing myself at her feet and kissing her toes, but instead embraced her warmly as a sister would, and answered: "That would be a joy and an honor. I especially can't wait to dress you up as Menshikov's bride." Daria smiled and kissed me back.

Yet the closer we came to Moscow, the less I wanted to think farther ahead than Yuletide. What if Daria's mood changed or Varvara managed to sway her? Even a lady-in-waiting could very quickly be cast aside for some clumsiness or other and find herself alone, poor, and homeless. Daria found me amusing, but I had been surer of my future at the Glucks'. I tried to do as the Russians did and live for the moment, which was easy for them, knowing they would never find themselves on the street the next day. I did have one thing though: just before we left the Schlüsselburg, Menshikov had given me a heavy purse. When I had opened it, it was filled with gold coins that shimmered in the dull gray morning light.

I gasped. "What is that for?" Never in my life had I seen such riches, nor held them in my hand. What could I buy with that? My old life, a thousand times over, I thought. Was a sum like this a mere trifle for Menshikov? The rules of his life never stopped astounding me.

He shrugged. "That's for you to decide. Go shopping if you like and get some dresses and a sable coat or two. Daria knows all the best places in Moscow."

"But why are you giving this to me?" I stared at the open purse, trying to estimate the amount inside. It was too much. "I mean—thank you—"

"Oh, the gold is not from me. I'd never just give things away, you know that." Menshikov winked at me and closed my fingers around the purse. "Close it, girl, and keep it out of other people's sight. Some secrets are best not shared"—he grinned—"but no worries, I'll find out what happened and what the money is for. Until then, spend it wisely."

"Is it from Boris Petrovich Sheremetev?" I called after him, as he gathered his cloak and pulled his fur hat lower onto his forehead, before fighting his way back to the fortress through the thigh-high snow. He turned once and pulled a face, as the men's rivalry was far from over. I smiled. Of course, that was well guessed. Dear Sheremetev didn't want me all at Daria's mercy. After the night when I had held Peter, Shereme-tev had left at once, on the tsar's orders. I couldn't think of anyone else who would make me such a present. I weighed the purse again. If I only knew where my family was, I could free them all and we could live hap-pily ever after. But life was never that easy.

* * *

One morning, after about two weeks in the sled, Daria craned her neck, lifted the curtain, looked out of the window, and ignored our pleas against the cold and the wind. She'd poke Varvara and point at the for-est that lay like a dark line along the fields, or at a certain hill in the far distance. To me, it all looked alike, but she knew the landscape around Moscow like I knew every field and road around my *mir*.

"Stop!" she called, and knocked on the wall of the sled, and the driver obeyed. Her cheeks were aflame and her eyes shining as she pulled my hand up from under the warmth of the fur blanket. "Come with me, Marta. I'll show you something your poor eyes have never seen before."

When she hopped out of the sled, she sank up to her knees into the snow, which made her laugh and push on, forcing me to follow, until the driver plowed a way for us up a hill.

"Come on, don't dawdle," she called over her shoulder, stumbling over the dragging seam of her cloak and straightening up again, her hands red and sore and covered in snow. Up on the hilltop she em-braced me and pointed to the plain beneath us.

"Look," she called, gasping for air. "We are on the Sparrow Hills. And this, Marta, is the world's most wonderful city: Moscow!"

I held my breath: the heart of Muscovy stretched across the whole horizon and offered itself proudly to my eyes. Countless spires and cu-polas sent their own golden light into the hours of the early dusk. The taiga's fresh evening breeze came in from far beyond the city, but it car-ried its sounds and smells with it: Moscow had a life of its own; a life so strong that I felt it right up to the Sparrow Hills, closing my eyes and imagining it. Whips cracked, women laughed, children bawled, and men in the *kabaki* shouted. Animals brayed, water ran over mill wheels and hooves thundered on cobblestone streets and squares. I sensed the food in the kitchens, the sewage in the alleyways, the oils and perfumes in the shops and stalls—all the splendor and squalor. Moscow wasn't built like Riga or Marienburg, all orderly and laid out around a market square. While I saw high city gates, there was no city wall as even Walk had had it, but houses stood jumbled in all sizes, growing rampant in all directions, yet coiling like a snake around its very heart, a group of dark, large houses forming a palace with heavy, high roofs and even more spires and cupolas. All around it lay a belt of smaller settlements and fields that fed on the Moskva and its side rivers.

"It doesn't look at all like Marienburg, Daria," I said.

She laughed. "No. Because it is like nothing you have seen, and certainly not poky little Marienburg, Marta." She pointed to a first settlement. "These are the *posady,* outer settlements, where you'll find the most shops and handymen, artists and gardeners that the tsar has lured to Russia, be they carpenters, rope makers, blacksmiths, painters, welders, or sculptors. Next to it are the mills and the fields that the Moskva floods to give the best fruit and vegetables. But you'll also find the trappers there, the fishermen, and the breeders of falcons, horses, and hounds. Next to them the beekeepers have settled. Wait until you taste Moscow honey."

"Who lives farther out?" I asked, squinting my eyes.

She shrugged. "Whoever. Serfs and peasants. The ants of the Russian empire."

Perhaps my family was there, I thought with sudden longing, if they had been lucky enough to survive. If so, I'd find them, I thought, but Daria pointed to three shiny spires in the heart of the city. "That is the Kremlin, the palace of all palaces," she said in awe. Her pretty face looked like a rosebud in the fur of her collar. "And not far from it, over there, is the *gostiny dvor*. We'll go as soon as we can."

"Why is that?" I asked. "Is it like a market?"

"A market," she said with a snort. "You really have a lot to learn. It's a place of wonder for a girl with a purse full of gold," she said, her eyes locking with mine. I thought it best to be honest and nodded, touching the purse that Menshikov had given me. Daria took my hand and squeezed it. "Don't worry. I know about the money. In the *gostiny dvor* you'll find the most beautiful things a girl could wish for: stalls with gold and silver, Belgian lace, French fabrics, gemstones, fine leather, felts, feathers, studding, embroidery, and so on." She took my elbow. "Let's go and feast. I want to get properly drunk to forget this hell of a trip. Tomorrow, there will be many people to greet. Come."

We stumbled back to our sleds, where Varvara sulked, as her copper pan had gone cold. Rasia Menshikova gave the sign for our departure, and in the evening we feasted our near arrival in Moscow with freshly baked bread, fat salmon, smoked strips of venison, pungent cheese, pastries filled with mushrooms and offal, as well as pickled radish, sour gherkins, and eggs marinated in mustard and cream. The innkeeper's pantry, not to mention his cellar, was empty when we moved on, and as usual I didn't see Rasia Menshikova pay.

The next day we arrived in Moscow.

30

Menshikov's house was the most splendid in Moscow and built of stone at a time when the whole of the city was still made of timber. No wonder the Muscovites only spoke of fire if a couple of hundred houses were properly ablaze. The tsar, I heard, adored the sight of fire as much as fighting it with his own hands, and a new *ukas*—a law—ordered any burned-down house to be rebuilt in stone; those who were unable to afford that had to sell their land. Inside Menshikov's palace, walls were clad in painted leather or covered by huge, heavy tapestries that Menshikov had bought in Holland. Honey-colored parquet adorned the corridors and halls and high, tiled stoves heated each of the hundred rooms, be they in use or not. Daria still called her quarters the *terem,* and had made them cozy with plush-piled rugs from Persia, velvet cushions and fur throws, and old-fashioned icons on the walls as well as smaller tapestries that told stories that Daria, too, had not heard of. We wondered together who that beautiful young girl might be, riding away from her clamoring friends on a bull: "It can't be comfortable with the spiky hair at her naked bottom," I said, making Daria laugh. And why did the young man on another tapestry hold out a golden apple to three beautiful women?

"Just eat it yourself, boy, if they don't want it," was Daria's comment, before I chased her—screeching, laughing, and pleading with me—galloping down the palace's corridors, pretending to be a misfit of half man and half horse that we spotted on a painting. When we both stumbled and fell over each other, Daria gasped, out of breath: "God, you are fun, Marta. Varvara just doesn't get that, as usual."

* * *

My room lay between Daria's and Varvara's: yes, my own room, no poky maid's chamber. It was bigger than our whole *izba* had been and I felt the rugs on the flagstones under my bare feet and brushed the icons' golden frames with my fingertips. My mattress was stuffed with horsehair and the bed linen was scented. Daria gave me my very own slate-and-iron-studded oak chest and watched me fold my clothes inside: her hand-me-downs as well as looted dresses that had been shared between us in Marienburg.

She frowned. "That's no good. You need proper clothes if you want to feast at Yuletide. Give me that purse." She weighed it in her palm after I had fished it out from behind my bedstead. "Good Lord. That is more than I thought. And you really don't know who gave it to you? Alexander Danilovich just would not say," she said, her eyes narrowing. As long as she was not his wife, she could never be sure of his feelings. So far, he showed no sign of wanting to step underneath the bridal crown with her.

"My guess is Sheremetev. He is kind, and generous, but would not want to shame me, just as Alexander Danilovich doesn't want your ladies-in-waiting to shame you," I said smoothly.

Varvara joined us, as she never left Daria and me alone for too long, if she could help it. "Sheremetev, you say? Everybody knows that he has a hedgehog in his pocket; just look at his shabby house, and his old hag of a wife wears last year's fashion. What should a Russian count like him give you gold for?" She, too, weighed the purse with a catty smile. "A maid should never be more beautiful than her mistress," she warned. "Men always have a second thought. Daria, you might have befriended your own undoing. Menshikov has a roving eye."

I bit my lip, as I did not dare to be rude to Varvara. Still, I looked her straight in the eye. Nobody loved me more if I tried to please. If Varvara didn't like me, she should at least know her limits as well as mine.

"Let's go, Marta," Daria said, after passing a long look from her sister to me. "We'll need quite some time to kit you out."

* * *

Daria had made no empty promises: the *gostiny dvor* was a heaven on Earth for women with a purse full of gold. So far, I had only bartered things at the spring fair in my village, and at the marketplaces in Walk and Marienburg had watched wealthy, freeborn people buy trinkets from traveling merchants. Those stalls were there one day and gone the next, while tailors, cobblers, and carpenters would have their shops, but those were not for the likes of me. From Menshikov's house our sled crossed the Red—meaning "beautiful"—Square, snaked its way through icy, busy alleyways, and then stopped outside the *gostiny dvor*.

"You can go into a *kabak*, but mind you getting too drunk," Daria warned the coachman, and pulled me with her, but I stopped in my tracks and looked up, openmouthed: The *gostiny dvor* was no jumble of stalls covered in canvas. It was carefully planned: laid out two stories high and built in brick, just for shopping, every day and all around the year. The entrance and space around was as busy as a beehive. I craned my neck: arcade after arcade housed different shops, and tradesmen flitted in and out carrying boxes and bales. Servants shouted at messenger boys, happy with their little authority, and maids followed their ladies, eyes lowered, yet casting glances at the waiting footmen and burly porters, who hung about at the building's entrance, wolf whistling and chewing and spitting tobacco-stained saliva.

"Come," Daria said, and walked with all the pride that her birth and rank as Menshikov's mistress gave her, head held high and knowing exactly where to go. I followed after, but soon trailed behind for all my looking and touching. The shops sold things I hadn't known existed: ivory and ebony, tortoiseshell and mother-of-pearl, *émaille* porcelain and more pearls, gemstones, silk and velvet, more leather and feathers than I had thought possible. I tried to carry myself as Daria did, but poverty—its scent, posture, and fears—clings to you like leeches in a pond. When spotting me on my own, the shopkeepers guarded their bales of silk with their body, or busied themselves in front of their drawers and shelves of lace and ribbons, lest I'd nick a roll or two. It hurt and I hurried on, when I spotted Daria standing with a lithe man. Both looked out for me, and I braced myself for his same hostile way. But when I stepped closer, his eyes shone like wet river gravel, while the endings of his thin black mustache rose in a second smile. His eyes took measure of me before he kissed my fingers, as if I were a lady.

"Mistress Marta. What a pleasure. I am Maître Duval. Do come in, as I have exactly what you need," he said in a Russian that sounded even funnier than mine and ushered us toward his shop. He made no empty promises. His tailors measured me and in turn whispered with the apprentices. The boys rolled yard upon yard of silks at my feet and held it to my cheeks while I checked my look in a plate of polished metal. Daria and I sipped *tchai* with fresh, thick *smetana* and nibbled on thin biscuits dripping in honey and pistachio while Maître Duval helped me make a choice that flattered me. "The colors of spring are best left to Mistress Daria," he said, squinting at her rosy, fair beauty. "Your skin is like dark gold and your hair like polished ebony. Let's try jewel shades, shall we?" He held swathes of ruby-red velvet and bales of sapphire-blue and burnt-orange silk to my cheeks, before searching in his stockroom for an emerald-green wool cloak. "Another lady's loss is your gain. This is just wonderful for you, as it matches your eyes," he decided, and clapped his hands in joy when I tried it on. Once all orders were placed, he clicked his tongue. "What a lady wears underneath is as important as her gowns," he said, lowering his voice a bit, while holding yards of gossamer-thin and finely patterned lace against his shop's lights.

Daria giggled. "Do it, Marta. You might still teach old Sheremetev a thing or two." When I had paid Duval my due—and certainly far more than necessary—and we finally got to leave his shop under many bows, walking backward, kisses to fingers and demands of further visits, we dropped in with the furrier to choose fox skins to line my cloak. The man asked me to return the next day to see better stock, but for that he generously offered me a matching cap there and then. I wore it as a young lady of good family would: proudly perched to the left, and my hair hidden underneath, and felt giddier and more lighthearted than when pinching some of my father's chewing tobacco as a child. In thoughts I sent thanks and kisses to Sheremetev. Perhaps I should have spent less but having my own money, to spend at will, was simply overwhelming. After all, if I wanted a good life, I had to look the part. How Christina would have loved this, I thought with a pang as the coachman swayed toward us, of course as legless as could be after his visit to the *kabak*. Daria and I pelted him with snowballs to sober him up. As our sled slid through the darkness, the bells of the Archangel Cathedral—Moscow's highest spire—tolled into the lively night. Fresh snowflakes froze on the slush and made the streets and squares slippery: we saw many people fall, which made us laugh even more. The joy of Yuletide was upon us.

In the courtyard of Menshikov's house the groom bowed when helping me out of the sled. He then recognized me and stared, while taking the reins from the coachman. Both men led the horses away, talking and looking at me over their shoulders, smiling, until the dark of the stables swallowed them. Up the stairs, at the threshold of the door, two maids curtsied, and then did a double take with surprise when seeing me. Jealousy spoiled their young faces as they started to whisper, but I would not care. Daria and I linked arms, giggling and joking as we entered the house. As I bent down to wipe the snow off my cloak's hem, Varvara approached, having heard our voices. She came up to greet us as she would one of her equals, with a wide smile and outstretched arms, and the offer of food and drink on her lips. Only in the last moment, when I rose, did she recognize me and stop, taking in my new look. Her face clouded and she dropped her arms, turned on her heel, and went back to her rooms, even though Daria called after her lightheartedly: "Don't be such a spoilsport, Varvara. Stay with us!"

That night I slept with my fox cap on, as having it made me so happy.

* * *

When I lived in my *mir*, the Russian monks counted time since God was thought to have made the world, but Peter changed even that. The years were to be numbered since the birth of Christ; New Year now fell on the first of January instead of early September. The festivities, though, lasted from the beginning of December right through to Epiphany in early January; every night there were dinners, parades, games, masquerades, fireworks, and balls.

"The tsar is in town soon," Daria said one morning, holding a scroll. "Menshikov sent word."

Varvara left for the *gostiny dvor* to buy more dresses and jewelry. I mustered my own gowns, which had been delivered by Duval's boys. I touched the fabric, the stitching, and the lace again and again. Would they be good enough if I were to meet the tsar again? The thought of seeing Peter again unsettled me: Would he remember the night when

I had held him so close, chasing his demons and giving him rest? Of course not, I scolded myself: the tsar had countless arms to hold him, be he in battle or at home.

Still, I remembered hot breath on my breasts and how he had calmed in my embrace, like an upset child. But he probably had forgotten all about it. It was clear what was at stake for Varvara in meeting the tsar again; she was catty and cruel. When a young maid burned one of her dresses while ironing, Varvara had her strung upside down until her face turned blue, before she herself drove sharp splinters of wood underneath the girl's fingernails. The poor thing survived, but barely so. I felt sorry for her, but kept out of it, as I didn't want to share her fate. I thought of Olga's words: Don't help me. You can't. Help yourself.

Two days before Yuletide, Moscow reared like a horse under the lashing of a whip: the tsar, his son the Tsarevich Alexey, and his thousands of men galloped into the city, unleashing a storm of festivities. The city threw itself at its master as a puppy might, clumsy and overjoyed, knowing it would be abandoned again soon.

31

Our sled moved soundlessly as if in a dream along narrow alleyways and the streets leading to the Red Square. The Yuletide feast was held in the Kremlin's main hall with hundreds of people invited. To me, the Arsenjevas looked impossibly beautiful, even though foreign envoys were said to laugh at the Muscovite women, calling them provincial and grotesque. Still, on Daria's advice I wore a dress of flame-colored silk and her maid had braided some strings of her pearls into my loose curls; other than that I wore no jewelry, but was proud of a little golden lace running around my shoulders. "Sheremetev should like you," Varvara said, her eyes gauging me. "The man has no taste, anyway."

The Kremlin towered above the Red Square in all its regal power. It was bathed in torchlight and the warm shine of the lanterns as the shops in the three-story houses all around the square were still busy. In the coffeehouses, which Daria said had opened in Moscow only some years before, every table was taken, and the windows were steamed up from both breaths and brews. Servants ran last errands, girls of easy virtue shivered while waiting for customers, and beggars searched, mostly in vain, for a warm, dry spot for the night. In the morning their frozen corpses would be thrown outside the city walls into clay pits, from where wolves dragged them into the forest.

Daria pointed to the highest of the Kremlin's towers. "This is the bell tower that Ivan the Terrible built after he killed his son."

"He killed his own son?" I repeated in disbelief and crossed myself with three fingers: what a terrible sin.

"Yes. He killed thousands and thousands of people. The whole populace of Novgorod was forced under the ice and drowned, and his son he killed in a fit of anger. He had the tower built to do penance. Whenever his demons haunted him, he'd run up and toll the bell for hours on end."

Varvara giggled at the story, but I looked outside. The Kremlin rose like a dark wall all along the Red Square, a defiant, gloomy fortress clashing with the gaiety of the Saint Basil's Cathedral cupolas right next to it. When we crossed the lowered drawbridge my heart beat faster and I clasped my fan and my purse. I was spellbound and wanted to keep this moment—the moon, the snowflakes, the guards, the torch-light, and other sleds full of gay, beautiful people—forever in my heart. Couldn't I make time stop?

"What happens now?" I whispered to Daria.

She opened her fan and I peered at it: on its silk fabric a picture showed a rosy, chubby blond girl being mounted by a man with a ram's horns and feet. I thought of the lust I had felt in Anton's arms so long ago.

"Now, Marta, the world turns upside down. You wouldn't believe it if you hadn't seen it."

* * *

Shadows gathered in the endless corridors of the Kremlin. They smelled of tallow and smoke as well as the frankincense and herbs smolder-ing in the corners and forced any Russian into awe and obedience, as every stone spoke of the tsar's glory and power. Our steps echoed on the flagstones as we followed a servant to the great hall. The eyes of countless icons hanging on the cold, sooty walls followed me in cold mockery: What was a soul like me doing in the heart of the realm of Muscovy? The courtiers looked like children playing dress-up, moving about gingerly in their Western gowns, breeches, and jackets. A group of popes in long black robes, each adorned with a *panagia*—the golden cross—eyed us with disdain. I could not care less if I looked like a for-eign whore to them. Yet the rooms made me shiver: Was it here that the boy Peter had watched his family being hacked to death; where the Streltsy dragged him by his hair, mocking his mother as a whore? Surely, nobody would want to go on living in a place filled with such memories. But suddenly a pair of winged doors flew open and we stepped into light and merriment and heard music, shouting, and singing as well as a steady, upbeat drumroll. I squinted my eyes at the sudden brightness of the long hall, and Daria said: "Eat, drink, laugh, Marta, and be grateful to be here."

32

Richly dressed people grouped around small tables and the music sounded as light and tinkling as water and not as heavy and longing as the Russian melodies. Servants carried platters groaning with food: whole boar roasted in beer and honey, the snouts stuffed with apples and chestnuts; pies of fish and vegetables in a thick, golden crust; bowls of creamy soup; huge salmon surrounded by walls of caviar, towers of blini and pots of *smetana*. Waiters filled jugs full to the rim: the goblets reached from my fingertips to my elbow. People drank like horses, vodka dripping from their mouths, carelessly soiling their beautiful clothes. I heaped some caviar on a blini; it was so delicious that I had a second and then a third one straightaway. Who knew how long my luck would last?

Daria and Varvara whispered, and I strained my ears. What was going on?

"Look, there is the tsarevich. Alexey has grown up . . ."

I craned my neck with curiosity: Alexey was a boy of perhaps twelve or thirteen years of age and didn't seem grown-up at all to me, but like a child that needed a hug in his simple, dark clothes, with his pale face, his pursed lips, and dark, dark eyes.

"And over there is the widowed Tsaritsa Praskowia with her three daughters. She so wants to marry them well, though everybody knows that Ivan the Idiot, Peter's half brother, didn't sire them," Daria said, and Varvara giggled and answered, "Her court is like in olden times; she lives surrounded by loafers and beggars, soothsayers and palm readers. When

I last visited, a gypsy girl danced for us, naked. Her breasts dangled like the balls of an oxen and her bush spread over her thighs."

I asked for a refill of my jug. What a great night this would be!

The drumroll grew stronger, until a kettle drum took the lead. Everyone was silenced—even the tsarevich stood to attention. The musicians rose in a wave, the doors of the hall flew open, and in stormed a group of men, shouting and cheering, and carrying a sedan chair on their shoulders. The man sitting on it wore a clumsily wrapped white sheet and a childish copy of the tsar's tiara. I stared openmouthed as the procession paraded past me, the men throwing rose petals and paper balls, hooting, blowing on pipes and spinning rattles, and prodding everybody to join in. People bowed to the shockingly ugly and almost deformed man on the throne: That was surely not the tsar? I looked around, wondering what was happening, when I spotted Peter. My heart leaped up into my throat. He was taller than everybody else by a good head or two and dressed up like a sailor in narrow, navy pants, tight yellow chaps, and a short navy jacket with gold buttons, white shirt, and red neckerchief. What was going on? Menshikov smiled and waved. I spotted other known faces, too: princes and boyars who had fought alongside Sheremetev at Marienburg. Just Sheremetev himself I could not see, and I felt strangely relieved at that. When the sedan chair was lowered, Peter bowed mockingly to the throne. "Hail, Prince Caesar!" he shouted, and the crowd repeated his words, the call rising and falling like the tide. "We beg you, let the Drunken Synod begin!" Whoever the toad on the throne might be, the guests knew how to tell the game from reality and obeyed when Peter said, "Drink, all of you, and as much as you can!" He forced a young woman's jaw open and poured a whole jug down her throat. She swayed, glassy-eyed, pale and gasping, but Peter kissed her on her lips, smacked her bottom, and let her go.

I did not like watching this without knowing what was going on, so I asked Daria, "Why is another man sitting on the throne instead of the tsar?"

"I told you. Tonight the world is turned upside down. The tsar is but a Friesian sailor and the so-called Prince Caesar rules." The crowd roared a bawdy song and Peter clapped while they cheered, "The Drunken Synod! Let's start the Drunken Synod!"

I looked for the tsarevich: he was standing by Menshikov, not cheering or singing. Menshikov was nudging him to get him to join in. Daria approached them, smiling at her lover, who greeted her warmly, and then smacked the crown prince again. The boy's eyes filled with tears and he retreated into the shadows of the hall, where the people, the unbridled joy, and wilder and wilder music shielded him from my view.

"Silly man." Daria smiled tenderly when she settled back next to me. "Will he ever propose?" she asked, sounding a bit too casual, while opening her fan.

"Of course," I soothed her.

"I would love to be at home, raise our children and be a good wife to him, living in the *terem*. But like this I have to play by his rules . . ."

"Nobody leaves this room anymore under pain of hard labor," Peter shouted. "Also, there is no more Rhine wine to drink, but only Tokay and vodka. Whosoever cheats has to drink double the measure."

The fake Prince Caesar now climbed on a donkey; his sheet slipped, becoming a loincloth and his worshipers followed him. I almost choked with laughter seeing the half-naked whores, their faces gaily painted and a *panagia* dangling between their bare breasts; blond, angel-faced boys with laurel wreaths in their hair skipped after them, playing the flute and waving flags on which two tobacco pipes formed a cross.

"Patriarch Bacchus, give us your holy juice," the crowd howled, reaching for the rider, the whores, and the boys. It was so funny that I laughed tears: that served the ugly popes with their stinky garlic breath right—too often had I felt their bony fingers pinching my bottom when I worked at the monastery. The Prince Caesar sprayed the crowd with vodka; the people caught the blessing with their tongues, pushing and shoving each other. Some younger princes wanted to kiss the donkey's ass, but he bucked and kicked, so they pulled its tail until it brayed in pain.

The Arsenjevas sat with Menshikov, but just when I wanted to join them, a surprisingly small hand grabbed me around my waist and played with the ribbons of my bodice. Peter pressed me against his broad chest, whispering in my ear, "How do you like my party, *matka*?" My heart somersaulted. He remembered me, and called me *matka*, his old girl. I turned: his face was flushed from vodka, the heat in the room, and the joy all around us, and he swayed. The Prince Caesar rode past and splashed me with vodka. "A special blessing for you, my girl," he roared, trotting on.

My cheeks and my forehead were sticky with alcohol. "Ha! That calls for revenge. Hold the donkey's head, *starik*!" I called.

Peter smiled at the nickname and grabbed the braying and bucking beast, almost throwing its rider off. "Stop it, the two of you. This is a holy donkey, hands off," the Prince Caesar shouted, and tried to hit us with his sprinkler, but both Peter and I dodged him, chasing around the donkey, who shat on the golden parquet. We held on to each other in wild laughter, until I could grab the donkey's head, forcing its mouth deep into one of the huge jugs. It drank greedily and then farted, which left Peter in stitches. "Ahoy, there is donkey wind! Let's all set sail." He ripped off his neckerchief and held it like a sail at the donkey's bottom, but the animal staggered through the hall, crashing into tables, toppling jugs, bottles, and glasses and making people scream. The Prince Caesar whipped the poor beast and downed the last of the vodka.

Peter touched my silk dress. "What a lovely color. You look engulfed in flames. But I hope that is not all you get for a purse of gold in the *gostiny dvor* these days?"

"Oh, no. There are lovely things such as . . ." I stared at him: the purse that Menshikov had given me was not Sheremetev's gift!

He grinned and gave me a peck on the cheek. "It's a low price for the best night of sleep I have had as long as I can remember. I hope you spent it wisely," he said, his fingers fondling my bodice and searching for my breasts without further ado.

I felt heat rise from my belly but slapped his hands. "Careful! Wandering hands get caught in a wolf trap."

He looked at me with shining eyes. "Are you hungry?" he asked.

I followed Peter to Menshikov's table, where I saw the Arsenjevas, Pavel Jagushinsky—who was the steward of the tsar's household—and Rasia Menshikova, who sat much too close to a handsome dark-skinned stranger: beneath the large silk cushions they held hands. Varvara reared when she saw Peter holding my hand, pulling me with him. Her face was pure threat that I tried to ignore. Tonight, or never! Around us settled a motley crew of a giant of a man—"Meet Louis Bourgeois from Paris!" Peter said—two dwarves, and a Moor whose skin was as black as soot. My head spun: Had my life turned into Master Lampert's Tent of Wonders? Peter pulled me down next to him while filling up our big cups again. "These are eagle cups," he said proudly. "I had them made, as all the other jugs were too small for a real stupor." He clapped his hands. "Let's do a drinking game. I had lost *matka,* but now I have found her again and she wears a pretty dress made of flames. Let's toast to that with Tokay. Be warned, I'll whip anyone who drinks Rhine wine."

"To *matka* and her dress of flames," Menshikov said, and everybody drank, even if Varvara's eyes stabbed me from over the rim of her cup, a threatening, dark look that chilled my heart. But I pushed my fear back: tonight, I wanted to be merry. The dwarf somersaulted, which made his face turn green, and he fled to be sick. Peter's dogs joined us, licking his face until the tsar hid under the cushions, laughing and begging for mercy. As the giant spoke with Rasia Menshikova's lover in a foreign language, I met Daria's questioning glance, but then she returned my delighted smile. I had never told her about the night in Marienburg, and now I sat on Peter's lap, feeding him with sweet morsels and throwing food at passing courtiers. He whooped and cheered when I hit my target well, and Daria raised her cup in a toast to me. Thank God I had inherited my father's steadfast drinking nature.

But after even I had started seeing double, the tsar leaped up and grabbed Menshikov by the collar. "Traitor! What are you hiding under that cushion?" he shouted and tugged a bottle of Rhine wine from under his friend's bottom. "I knew it! Rhine wine, that light plonk. You are such a cheat, Menshikov. Sorry, I must punish you. But as you are not an utter dog, you shouldn't drink alone." His eyes locked on Daria and Varvara. "The Arsenjevas will join you. Three eagle cups of Tokay will do for each of you."

Daria passed out and Varvara was sick in her cupped hands before collapsing on the floor. All her finery was destroyed; she had lost one earring, her hair had come undone, and the feathers in it were mere stalks when a servant hoisted her on his back like a sack of barley. Menshikov drank obediently before rising, saluting his tsar, and then throwing his cup at the wall, where it broke in dozens of pieces. Alexander Danilovich's eyes turned glassy and he crashed to the floor like a felled tree. Peter skipped in circles around his friend: all his senses were on a high and he was ready to grab me, when a cushion hit his chest.

"Hey! What's going on?" he shouted when he was hit by a second cushion flying through the hall. It was a cushion fight: the giant hit a courtier and the man fainted there and then.

"Look, Peter," I said. Rasia Menshikova lay with her thighs parted in the cushions and the dark-skinned stranger's buttocks heaved in her, his pants around his knees. Peter whooped and grabbed the man's hips, pushing him on. "Devier, you rascal. Do I have to teach you everything? Don't they even know how to fuck in your country? Rhythm, man!" Rasia Menshikova covered her face in shame when Peter fondled her tiny breasts, pushing them to the right and to the left. "Starboard! Backboard! All men on deck," he shouted.

Feeling sorry for Rasia, I grabbed one of the cushions and hit Peter straight over the head, once and then twice. The cushion burst and it rained feathers, which stuck to his sweaty forehead and hair. I held my breath—had I gone too far? I had whacked the master of life and death in this biggest of all realms straight on the head, and there he stood, feathers and vodka raining! This could mean the spinning mills or death to me or more unbridled fun, I decided, and went for it: "It's snowing!" I laughed, delighted, shaking my locks and spreading my arms, which almost made my bodice burst. "Look, finally some snow and ice for you, and you are its king."

But Peter looked elsewhere. "Just you wait! You'll be hardly better off than Menshikov's skinny sister when I catch you."

Peter lunged at me, but I ducked and ran, shouting, "Well, catch me then, if you can, *starik!*"

I skipped around the Prince Caesar, who kissed a laurel-wreathed boy; a courtier smeared caviar over the naked breasts of one of the whores, then sucking her full, white flesh. The drunk donkey shat some more, swaying pitifully in the midst of the music, the writhing bodies, and the steaming heat. Soldiers watched stone-faced as Peter towered over me and I halted, hiccupping with laughter, panting, my cheeks burning and my blood rushing through my veins, waiting for his next move. He seized me and threw me onto some cushions; it rained more and more feathers, food flew through the air, and the Prince Caesar hung limp in his saddle.

I felt nothing but Peter's hands, lips, and then his heavy body on mine. He spread my thighs and was inside me before I could even catch my breath: How could I refuse the tsar of all the Russias his dearest wish?

33

I woke when a sunbeam tickled my nose. I stretched like a cat and looked around. Where was I? This was neither my bedroom nor even Menshikov's palace. Furs and heavy covers kept me warm in a wide bed and a fire crackled. I opened the embroidered curtains hanging in front of the bedstead: the tsar sat at a table next to the open fire, his back turned to me, in the white light of the window. His feet in their felt slippers tapped on the flagstones while he twirled a quill.

I was naked and my clothes were nowhere to be seen, so I wrapped the sheet around me and slid out of the bed. The flagstones in the gaps between the furs and rugs were cold as I tiptoed my way to Peter and looked over his shoulder. The icy winter light fell on a pile of papers, unfolded or still rolled up in scrolls. Peter hummed to himself and lowered the quill onto the paper in front of him. I peered at it: he sketched something like a large arc. I touched his shoulder and asked quietly, "What is that?"

He startled and jumped to his feet.

"It's only me!" I said. "*Matka*." I used the nickname he had given me at our two meetings.

He calmed; his eyes were as bright green as his belted dressing gown with the fur collar when he stuck one hand into a fur-lined pocket while waving the other breezily over the pile of papers, rummaging in the scrolls, making sheets rustle and fall. "Oh, it's everything and nothing! Just some ideas I have, really, for more new ships and buildings. Letters to write, to friends, soldiers, and other rulers in the West and drafts of laws that may or may not take force. Who can tell with the Russians? I also have to find new taxes and should do away with old ones. Though when in my life did I ever abolish a tax?" He smiled and scratched his head like a boy.

"True. I have heard that you will be taxing the winking of an eye next," I said earnestly.

He looked at me, astonished. "Who says so? Where did you hear that?" Seeing the twinkle in my eye, he chuckled and absentmindedly stroked my bare shoulders.

"Everywhere. On the streets. In the coffeehouses."

"You've been in coffeehouses? Oh! You could be my spy."

"I could," I said teasingly. "But my services don't come cheap."

He arched an eyebrow before asking, "What are they saying there? Don't they love me? If you say yes, I'll abolish that tax on the winking of the eye just for you."

"Well—" I began, but he would not let me talk, sounding impatient.

"Do you know how expensive a war is? Giving my people a space to live, to train soldiers, and to turn Russians into thinking human beings comes at a cost. And all they do is hate me for it. I almost have to beat their children into the schools I've founded for them. But wait . . ." He pulled out a closely written sheet of paper, which was signed and sealed with the gleaming double-headed Russian eagle. A little drying sand still stuck to the scarlet wax. "Here is my last *ukas*: any child of the boyars and free citizens who has not attended school is forbidden to marry. That's a fine rule, isn't it? No schooling, no wedding. I want my people to be educated. I want them to . . ." He hesitated.

"To . . . ?" I prodded him, thinking of Sheremetev's words: *Peter rules as if he's haunted.*

"I want them to think. To think for Russia." I heard pride in his voice.

"But will they still follow you when their thoughts are so free?" I asked.

Peter caressed my tousled curls. "Well, I never! *Matka* thinks and says wise words. Or did you overhear that at one of the parties? But your head is too pretty to be worrying it with such thoughts." Without further ado he lifted me off the floor and the sheet slipped from my shoulders. In two long strides he reached the bed and fell upon me. It all happened as fast as the night before, when I had put his haste down to drunkenness. He gave my full breasts a quick squeeze before he cast off his sleeping gown and made short work of opening my thighs and thrusting into me. As he pushed inside me, he buried his face in my hair and sucked noisily at my neck and breasts like a child. After a few hurried movements he shuddered and fell on top of me with a contented sigh.

I lay still, feeling raw, unfulfilled, and disappointed, his breath hot and unsteady on my aching breasts, when my surprise and my mirth took over. Was *this* the kind of love he had learned from Anna Mons? Was *this* the passion that the Arsenjeva sisters whispered about behind their hands? I so longed for the fire that Anton had lit in my veins, and Peter had slipped off me, all spent, just when I felt embers of lust. He was almost asleep when I playfully grabbed his hair and asked hoarsely, "What about me?"

He raised his head, looking at me with heavy eyelids and half a smile. "What? What about you?"

I gave him a little push and he rolled onto his back. Sweat glistened in the thick hair of his chest, which filled me with a sudden tenderness. I sat astride him.

"Caress my breasts!" I whispered. "Tenderly, and don't stop." My heavy breasts grew even fuller under his touch and my wide, pink nipples hardened, just as my warm wetness found him. He was now all limp and moist but lay just beneath my secret spot. I softly, gently slid up and down on him. My hair fell across his face as I found my own rhythm and began to moan. Peter grabbed my waist, holding it with both hands, just when starlight shot through my veins like a hot, golden rain. I rose up with a short scream and curled up on his chest, panting, and with a satisfied sigh.

He held me tight for a moment, mutely, before he kissed my damp forehead. "My kitten. Are you hungry?"

"I'm starving. I don't know about you, but there was this big man yesterday evening who kept me so busy I could hardly eat." I winked at him.

He pulled a cord and through a door hidden in the wood paneling a chamber boy entered, yawning and rubbing his eyes. He must have fallen asleep standing up. I pulled the sheets over my nakedness. Peter laughed. "No need for false modesty. I can't live without my chamber boys. They know everything about me and you better get used to them."

My heart skipped a beat: *You better get used to them.*

* * *

The boy returned shortly with a tray. A dish was placed in front of me: *pirogi*—pastries filled with chicken and molten cheese—as well as cherries soaked in wine and raisin biscuits baked in honey. The chamber boy poured a dark, steaming drink into a bowl for me. It smelled of sugar, milk, and smoke and had a faintly bittersweet taste that was heavenly and stoked all my senses. I felt like dipping my fingers into the thick, gooey brew and licking them clean. Instead, I sipped it as a lady would.

"What is this?" I asked as Peter returned to his desk.

"Chocolate," he answered, taking a gulp of cognac from a small flagon before stuffing and lighting his pipe. This was how he broke his fast.

"What is chocolate?" I asked, breathing it in again. It was wonderful; I wanted more and more of it.

"The queen of France brought it with her from her homeland, Spain. Chocolate and the dwarves in her entourage are her only comfort, as her husband, the Great Louis, carries on with his mistress who costs him so dearly. Really, the Sun King could fill his stables with whores instead of horses with what he spends on Madame de Montespan." He carried on with his paperwork and I silently sipped the hot, sweet brew. Who would have thought that I could have it better than this poor queen of France? I bit into a sweet biscuit, before dipping it naughtily into my bowl.

I did not return to Menshikov's house after the Drunken Synod. Peter sent for my few dresses and the set of undergarments. The messenger also carried friendly greetings to Daria, which I dictated to Peter's scribe. To my relief her response, read out to me, was quick and warm. She had done me nothing but good.

* * *

The church Masses leading into the New Year were strange, dark, and endless. After the unbridled joy and wild blasphemy of the Drunken

Synod, I was struck by the piousness with which Peter bowed his head in prayer, and I did alike, to please him. Still, my heart was untouched by the priceless icons encrusted with gold and silver, the singing in parts, the prayer books bound in leather and velvet, the sparkling vessels and the splendid robes heavy with gold. It all showed the wealth of the Russian church and was intended to make the believers bow with humility, but could not compare to the cheerful ease of the Glucks' chapel at Marienburg. What had become of them?

* * *

Peter sent fireworks into a sky still heavy with sleep to welcome the New Year. The display was his own idea and he cheered at each bright explosion, each glittering fall of starshine. I stood close to him by the open windows of the Kremlin, stunned and spellbound by the night sparkling with a thousand streaks of color. Peter turned to his son, but Alexey had averted his eyes and looked as if he wanted to stick his fingers in his ears to block out the noise. Peter shoved him and the boy stumbled.

"And you want to be my son, join my recruits, and one day lead my armies, tsarevich?" Peter barked. "Each blast of cannon has you almost wetting yourself. When I think that I celebrated the occasion of your birth with a firework display." He spat at Alexey's feet.

The prince regained his balance. "Yes, and a Prince Dolgoruki was killed when a heavy firework cask fell on his head," he dared to answer.

"There are enough Dolgorukis around, God knows! But if it had hit you instead, I'd have one less worry," Peter said, and turned his mighty back on the slender boy. The courtiers tittered, but I saw Alexey fighting back tears. In the short spell of darkness between two balls of fire, I squeezed his arm. He looked at me, blinking away tears from his long lashes, clearly surprised at kindness from his father's friends. Alexey smiled shyly, surrounded by the shadows of the Kremlin, which were already by then his true companions.

* * *

That same evening, the tsar made me the gift of a pair of earrings.

"Take them, Marta," he said, fiddling with the catch in my earlobe. "They suit you, as they suited my mother."

My eyes widened and I caught his fingers. "Your mother? She, who shielded you with her own body against the Streltsy soldiers when you were a boy, and when they hacked the rest of her family to death?"

"You know the story?" He fixed his gaze on the earring. "Stupid, fiddly thing," he muttered, frowning.

I touched the earrings, which were fashioned into crescent moons and studded with precious stones. They swung with each movement of my head.

"This is too valuable a gift, my tsar," I said, and feigned to take them off.

"They are very dainty. There is hardly any gold," he said. "Keep them, please."

"I am not talking about the value of the gold." There was a brief silence, and I only let go of the earring when he stepped behind me and embraced me.

I felt his hands on my shoulders. "They are yours. That is an order. Do you like them?"

"Yes," I said hoarsely. "I like them very much. No man has ever given me such a present."

"You must have known the wrong men. They are to bring luck to a girl who warms my body and my heart."

I turned to face him. Peter was awaited at a synod dinner; men only this time. In the early hours of the morning, Menshikov, with the help of two servants, would drag him back to his chamber. He kissed me and when I softly opened my lips to taste his tongue, I felt him grow and press against my belly. My hand slid over his brightly embroidered waistcoat to the soft deer leather of his breeches; I loosened the belt and wrapped my fingers around his warm flesh. He sighed and closed his eyes when I sank to my knees, the silk of my robe rustling, and placed my lips around him. He swelled even more and gasped when I took him fully. Peter began to move into my warm, wet mouth, where I sucked him deeper and deeper, tasting his lust and his desire for me. It didn't take long until he dug his fingers into my shoulders and cried out. I swallowed, sat back on the floor, and smiled up at him. My hair had come loose and he stroked it back tenderly.

"Where did you learn that?" He tightened his belt and smoothed his waistcoat.

I laughed. "Well, I was a soldier's wife, after all."

He rummaged in the little pocket of his waistcoat and fished out a coin. "In that case . . ." He tossed the coin into my lap. I held my breath. Should I feel hurt? He grinned. "You said your services don't come cheap."

Well: a coin was a coin, and so I picked it up and bit into it, my expression doubtful. There was a moment of silence.

"Did you think the tsar of all the Russias would give you counterfeit money?" Peter roared.

I did not flinch. "You never know. Who can you trust these days?"

I could hear him laughing all the way down the hall.

Smiling, I dressed for dinner myself, one held for the *damy* of the Russian court. There, a dwarf wrapped in bright ribbons jumped out of a pie in the early hours of the morning. We all pulled him this way and that, making him spin like a top, until he finally stumbled around the room stark naked. He was every bit as adorable as Princess Cherkassy's little lapdog, which was given bowl upon bowl of the sparkling wine the tsar had ordered especially from France.

* * *

Come Epiphany and the blessing of the waters of the Moskva, the magic of the Yuletide festivities was over. Peter hopped impatiently from one foot to the other while the priests had a hole sawn into the Moskva ice and boys, their cheeks pink with cold, swung golden receptacles back and forth, lacing the cold winter air with myrrh and frankincense. It hung in heavy clouds over the ice, and the court gathered around the tsar one last time, still wearied and still half-drunk, but in all its New Year splendor of gowns of silk and velvet embroidered with gold and silver, and furs of sable and mink. Many of the men still wore the flat fur hats of days gone by, and some ladies pulled veils of gold-embroidered muslin over the chalk-white and red of their sleepy painted faces. The tsar looked at them through smoldering eyes: not even this bitter cold that touched the marrow was an excuse for the loathed and forbidden Old Russian style of dress. As the first courtiers stripped off and dove into the hole for a swift dip in the icy waters that was to bless the year ahead of them, Peter was already back in the stables, checking on his men and horses. Everything was ready for his leaving for the field again.

* * *

Peter ordered me back to Menshikov's house without the slightest hesitation, hugging me and promising to be back. "I want you to be safe until we meet again," he said. Safe? He had no idea. I felt sick with dread, for I knew that the lethal jealousy of Varvara Arsenjeva awaited me: if she just found the right moment, I had nowhere to hide. The thought of how she had tortured the hapless maid made my blood chill.

34

Varvara came for me already on my second afternoon back at Alexander Danilovich's house. I was sitting near the fire in Daria's rooms, embroidering a scarf of mustard-yellow wool that I planned to give to her as a present. The wool's soft down grew in between the thick, wiry hair of Persian mountain goats; it was so fine that I could draw the scarf through a ring. It was worth its weight in gold in the *gostiny dvor,* as my now almost empty purse testified.

A flurry of steps echoed in the hall and before I could flee, or hide, the door smashed open against the wall behind. I shrank in my seat: Varvara's hair flamed around her head and shoulders and she wielded a whip. In her fury and self-righteousness, she reminded me of Vassily—how often had she tried to humiliate me? Her real chance had finally come. At first, I froze with fear, as I had done that night in his kitchen, but then hot anger unlocked my limbs. I was not a nameless serf or a maid anymore who had to duck and seek cover, hoping for the best. I had slept in the tsar's arms, however far away that moment felt now—almost as far away as Peter himself was. Who could protect me? No one, I understood. She walked over, her bare feet sounding on the tiled floor between rugs and furs, and raised my chin with the end of her crop. "So you're back after your little stay in the Kremlin!" she said with a nasty smile.

I just smiled back at her and took up my embroidery again, which made her furious, as I had hoped. She screamed, "That's the thanks one gets for picking up dirt like you from the street: stealing my man. Now you'll get it, you whore!"

The whip snapped through the air. I leaped from the chair and rolled over the carpet; God knows I'd mastered the art of dodging blows as a child when my stepmother came for me. The whip tore into the silk cushion, making it rip, and Varvara stared at the damage, as if surprised not to have hurt me instead. I used this short respite to tackle her thighs and knees and she tumbled to the floor with me. Her hands closed about my neck, where her fingers and nails dug into my flesh. I gasped for air as she squeezed my throat tighter; everything blurred and I desperately tried to reach the whip, but her nails seemed to be everywhere at once. I felt a smarting scratch at my cleavage and yelped with pain. In my despair, I grabbed her hair, twisted a strand around my fingers, and tore it out. She howled and lashed at me, but I spun away.

"I didn't take Peter from you. The tsar isn't interested in a strumpet who humps anything with legs. I let you go down a treat in Menshikov's stables, you red-haired nag." I spat the words in her face. She screamed and swung at my head, shoving me backward into the edge of the mantelpiece. My head bashed against it and I felt dizzy as she raised her crop again and took aim.

"When I'm finished with you, no one will look at you ever again," she hissed, gasping for air, her chest heaving and her dress torn from our scuffle. I tried to duck away, and dashed from the fireplace toward the door, but she was quicker, grabbing me by my locks and pulling me backward. I screamed as a red-hot pain seared through my scalp and neck. My head was yanked around and my body followed, as helpless as a rag doll.

"That hurts, doesn't it? There is a lot more where that came from," she said, laughing while pulling me closer to her. Her breath was raspy, but she would not let go of me. "Look at me, before I kill you."

I'm the last thing you'll remember, girl. Those had been Vassily's words that horrible night in the kitchen. In despair, my hands shot up, the nails aiming for Varvara's face. I hit her straight in the eyes and dug in as hard as I could. She screamed and let go, and I gave her a desperate kick in the tummy, which made her double over with pain. Now! I thought, but when I turned to run away, I stumbled over the footstool and fell. As I tried to get to my feet, Varvara stumbled toward me, blood on her face, but still wielding the whip. I was cornered between the stool and the wall, the door so close and still much too far away. I cowered.

Varvara looked deadly: her skin was ashen, her mouth snarling. She placed one foot on my dress's hem, so I could not move. "Stay still, Marta. So I can take better aim," she said. "I'll slice you to pieces and feed you to the dogs. What shall we start with? Ah yes, your face—"

I curled up and raised my arms, folding them over my head, trembling and sobbing. I had gambled and lost. There was no one to save me, with Peter gone and Daria out shopping. But the blow never came. Instead, I heard Varvara whimpering with pain, and a voice shouting, "What the devil is going on here? Can't you womenfolk be left alone for a minute?"

I only dared to take a quick glance, for I couldn't believe my ears: Peter, whom I had imagined far beyond the Sparrow Hills, dragged Varvara backward by her mane. She was spitting with rage and weeping, as her game was up.

"You Fury. Away with you to your rooms," he ordered, snatching the whip. Back to her room? She would finish me off the moment he left for real. My heart stalled with fear; I had to do something: I roughly tore one of his mother's earrings off my lobe. As the catch snapped, blood spurted onto my dress.

I cried out, "Oh Peter, look what she has done!" Tears now streamed down my face, as the shock and the pain were real enough. Blood trickled down my neck and there was an angry red weal on my bosom from Varvara's attack. "She hates me," I sobbed. "She wants to kill me, just because I adore you. Look what she's done to your mother's earring." My eyes briefly locked with Varvara's—she was ashen-faced. I'd show her.

"No," she gasped. "It's not true! I didn't touch the earring."

"My *matka*," Peter murmured, his finger tenderly trailing along my cheek, down to my chest, where my blood blended with my tears. But as I'd hoped, it was the sight of his mother's broken earring that pushed him over the edge. Wielding the crop aloft, it seemed for an unbelievable moment as though he would hit Varvara, who stumbled backward, pressing her hand on her mouth.

Peter's face twitched with rage. "I never want to see you again, witch. Be grateful I am not banishing you to the spinning mills!" The whip sliced through the air, narrowly missing Varvara's head, and she took to her heels, cowering at the wall, next to the fireplace. I sent a little prayer of thanks to whichever God wanted to listen; he richly deserved it. Peter kneeled down by my side, stroked my forehead, and cupped my face, which was shiny with tears.

"My girl. *Matka.* That happened on my account," he whispered, and I shivered as he rocked me gently back and forth, so I threw my arms around his neck and wept and wept and wept, dampening his uniform. I felt him melting toward me. Sheremetev's feeling for my utter helplessness had been my salvation in Marienburg. Now Peter's pity and my show of loyalty and love for him should save me twice over!

"Hush now, shh, shhh . . ." he said clumsily, but not letting go of me.

The door opened and Menshikov and Daria returned, her arms laden with small parcels from the *gostiny dvor*. She cried out and rushed over when she saw the state of me; Peter made sure I could stand, kissing my forehead once more. Then he took some gold coins from a pouch and held them out to Menshikov.

"Here, take them, Alexasha," Peter commanded.

"For what?" Menshikov asked, hooking his thumbs in the loops of his belt. What had gotten into him? Menshikov hesitating before an offer of gold was something none of us had seen before.

"For the girl, of course." Peter pointed at me. My heart was pounding. Did that mean he'd be taking me with him, that I would be his?

But Menshikov kept his arms folded. I dared not breathe. What was he playing at? I'd got the better of Varvara this time around, but if she got a chance before leaving for the monastery, she would kill me. Behind Daria's back, she glared at me, and I cowered close to Peter. Alexander Danilovich shook his head. "Marta isn't for sale, my lord and master." In the silence that followed his statement, I trembled in Daria's arms. What did Menshikov want?

Peter frowned and rummaged for more money. "There you go, you greedy dog, Menshikov. Sometimes I've a mind to take the whip to you!"

I didn't want to be sliced up by a whip, have splinters rammed under my nails, or be strung upside down in a laundry parlor, I thought, but Menshikov knelt and took Peter's hand in his, kissing the tsar's fingers. "I kiss the hand that blesses Russia. My tsar's hand, to whom his underling Alexander Danilovich Menshikov can sell nothing, but only make a present to His Majesty of his heart's desire."

It took me a moment to understand his words, but Varvara sobbed and Daria embraced me. "You belong to the tsar now, lucky girl. Make something of it, Marta," she whispered.

Menshikov beamed and continued, "*Min Her* Peter, allow me to give you the girl Marta as a gift!"

"So be it," Peter shouted as he flung an arm around Menshikov's shoulder, blew me a kiss, and drew his friend out into the hall. "We're going to celebrate," he called over his shoulder to me. "Celebrate properly. Pack your things, Marta, and have them taken to the Kremlin. I'll see you tonight."

Daria and I held each other for a few more moments. When she let go of me, I still trembled, but Daria cupped my face. "You must fall pregnant soon, Marta," she urged me. "That Anna Mons never had a child. It cost her her power and his love. Nothing brings such joy to a man, and a tsar, as a son. Nothing will bind him more strongly to you." I wiped my tears away and kissed Daria on both cheeks. "Your advice is forever in my heart."

Then, I turned to Varvara. She glowered at me, holding her hurting eye. I weighed my thoughts. Yes, she was Daria's sister. At the same time, I knew she would easily bribe a maid who knew her potions, as she had done with Anna Mons, and I would be as barren as Peter's mistress had been.

I stretched out my hand, holding my torn dress with all possible dignity. "Kiss my fingers, Varvara, and I shall ask the tsar for mercy for your sister's sake. Not the spinning mills for you, but a fine, far-flung convent, where you can praise the Lord every morning for the rest of your life." Varvara, sobbing snot and water at the bleak turn her life had taken, choking with anger and her teeth gnashing, kissed my fingertips.

* * *

I spent Peter's last two nights in the Kremlin in his bed. The evening before he left for the field he fell asleep on my breast like a sated child, and in the morning, he kissed me farewell. "You are a free woman, Marta. Should anything happen to me, the master of my household, Pavel

Jagushinsky, will give you fifty gold ducats. You'll be able to build your own life with that."

I opened my mouth to thank him, but stopped myself. "Nothing will happen to you, ever," I said tenderly. "My love will protect you, always."

He laughed as though it were a good joke and nuzzled my chilly hands. "That is good, *matka!*"

When the tsar and his men rode out of the Kremlin gates, the whole city lay frozen, floating in a bubble of ice. The chill reached my heart: Had I been left behind, ready to be forgotten and to be moved on from, as he did with Moscow? I could not allow this to happen.

35

The nobles' palaces on the streets around the Kremlin and Red Square were bereft of masters, who were once more in the field with their tsar. In the *gostiny dvor* womenfolk were serving, and the Moscow *damy* employed Swedish prisoners of war as tutors for their sons. Soon the men spoke Russian with an endearing accent and mastered the latest dances as well as all sorts of other games. The following year some of the oldest Russian families would be blessed with athletic, blond, blue-eyed offspring. My days in Moscow were comfortable, bright, and full of life. All my needs were fulfilled by Pavel Jagushinsky, Peter's master of the household. Yet I felt restless. I had heard nothing from the tsar, who had moved back toward the West to keep the Swedes at bay. Was he simply too busy to write or had he forgotten me? Oh, I knew the whores and washermaids in the camps, and Peter slept well only with skin against his, warming him and keeping nightmares at bay. Or, worse still, was he ill, or had he been wounded? The thought made my heart race. No, I would have heard about that. If fate was proving elusive, I had to seek it out.

* * *

It was one of the first days of spring. The wan sunshine was still grappling for the strength it now gained every day, minute by minute, until it also would rule the night. Rays snuck through the small windowpanes of the Kremlin and made the dust dance above the stack of papers on the desk in the cabinet secretary's office.

The young scribe looked at me uneasily when I held out the imperial double seal. Makarov, the cabinet secretary, who had left with Peter, kept it in Moscow in case of an emergency or *ukazy* during the tsar's absence. "No, Marta. Do you know the punishment for misuse of the tsar's seal? Death by suffocation. They don't just strangle you, they pour molten metal down your throat. Why not simply ask the tsar, if you so want to join his camp?"

"Because I can't write and because he will not grant it. He doesn't want any women in the encampment—beyond what is necessary," I added, blushing.

"Well, that's that, then." The scribe grinned, his arms folded. As stubborn as a mule, this one, I thought, and pushed the seal toward him once more. "You'll come to no harm," I coaxed. "On the contrary."

He got up and looked out of the window onto the busy Red Square: merchants touted their wares; lepers rang the bells on their wrists to clear their way; children ran races, the sedan chairs of the *damy* passed one another, their servants stopping for their mistresses' quick chats; priests had one hand on their head coverings in the blustery wind; people took a break from their daily business in the coffeehouses.

"No," he said, his hands deep in his pockets. My heart sank. In a moment he'd ask me to leave so that he could get on with his work. I thought quickly: the scribe was a young man from a simple background, just like Makarov himself. Hadn't he recently married the daughter of Peter's second stable master? Yes, I had seen her; she was heavy with child. The needs of a young family were plentiful, and I reached into my pouch, but all I found there was an altyn. The coin, worth three kopecks, was the last of my money. It was well spent, I hoped, and would buy the baby some fine lacy linen.

"Prepare the pass and let the tsar's seal be my concern," I whispered.

He looked at the altyn gleaming brightly against the dark wood of his desk, and then slipped it out of sight. The ink dripped thick and black onto a small sponge from the sharpened tip of the quill. He filled a sheet of paper with long, graceful curves. When he was finished, he stretched, winked at me, and said, "I'll just nip into the hallway to see whether the messenger from the West has arrived."

Before he left, he pushed a lump of wax as well as the candle toward me. He didn't want to be in the room to see this in case it cost him his neck. I worked as swiftly as I could with trembling fingers, his fear contagious. Was I sealing my death warrant? The hot wax dripped onto the paper at the very place where the words stopped. Once the layer was thick enough, I pressed the forbidden seal down firmly, so that the crimson double eagle both rose and sank on the thick, oozing mass, proud and threatening.

* * *

I took my leave from my few friends before setting off on my forbidden journey to join the tsar at the front. "You are mad," Daria said, watching me go through my clothes. "What can I do to hold you back?" she asked.

"Nothing." I smiled. "You know me. I have to go. What if he forgets me, or meets someone else to replace me?"

"True. Then do me a favor at least and let these be," she said, taking the lacy underwear and fine gowns from my arms.

"But—"

"No ifs and buts. I'll get you some men's clothes from Menshikov's staff. Though their bosom is not quite as big as yours," she said, giggling. "We also have to cut your hair."

"Absolutely not," I said, touching my beloved locks. "I will pin them up and that will do, together with a flat, Polish hat that I can pull low over my forehead."

"As you wish. But promise me: breast in, belly out, Marta. And keep that cloak closed." I promised and she gave me not only a little money, but better still, a companion who was a good shot: Peter Andreyevich Tolstoy. He was on his way to Peter's camp, from where he was to be sent as an envoy to Constantinople. If he was less than keen on taking a young woman with him through the wild vastness of Russia, he didn't let on.

We left Moscow in late March. When we reached the Sparrow Hills, I halted my horse and looked back, remembering my arrival some months earlier. Smoke rose out of countless chimneys, and domes and spires reached proudly into the dense spring sky. I'd miss Moscow, whatever Peter decided to do.

The snow had melted, and we made slow progress with the muddy roads being torn open by the sheer force of the *ottepel*, the thaw, and the swollen rivers. Tolstoy had to wake the ferrymen from their stupor and kick them down to the river, where the haggard men struggled to keep their flat barges on course under the weight of our load. Waves rolled and splashed against the side of the vessel and last slabs of ice crashed into her. After passing half of the post stations, Tolstoy, his men, and I left the coach route. The rides were long and arduous, but I loved the feeling of the wind on my face as well as the crushing tiredness at the end of a day, weighing my muscles down and making me sleep dreamlessly. I felt strong and made sure not to hinder the men's journey.

The once fertile and lush country had been turned into a barren strip: as in every war, the simple folk suffered most. The *izby* made of mud and straw were ransacked; houses of wood had been burned down and stone buildings plundered and razed, their walls blackened by flames.

Almost two weeks later, at one day's ride from the tsar's encampment, Tolstoy pitched camp for the night near the ruins of a church. All that was left of its *mir* were the foundations of the razed houses and the graveyard, but even the gravestones had been knocked over and desecrated. War knew no respect, not even, or perhaps least of all, for death.

While Tolstoy and two of his men were hunting for our supper, I wandered through the burned-out nave. The chapel's roof was gone and charred, broken beams reached into the sky like bony fingers, and the pews that had not been used for firewood lay toppled and smashed. First green shoots pushed through the cracked flagstones and I spread out my woolen cloak in front of the altar. It was uncomfortable to kneel down in my high riding boots, but I took off my gloves and folded my hands like a little girl. There, underneath the wide-open sky, I prayed to the God who had done so much for me: I placed myself in his hands once more. When I stepped outside, the bushes and tall grass dripped with dew and the white moon was full and high in the sky.

The men and I shared a sinewy winter rabbit for dinner. When we lay down to sleep we used our Cossack saddlebags as cushions and our cloaks as blankets. The night was clear, and Tolstoy and I gazed up at the stars and spoke quietly about our lives until our eyes shut. A soldier whose face had been disfigured by wolves kept guard that night. Ever since the attack he hated the beasts, hunting and killing them, then sewing their tails to his cloak. There was hardly any cloth left to cover.

* * *

Before we set off the next morning I cleaned myself as best I could. Behind the church ran a brook, and I washed the dust and the dirt off my face and fingers, then cleaned my teeth with the roughed-up end of a twig and some sharp blades of grass. Finally, I tamed my curls into a Dutch braid. Neatness was more admired in the field than any lace and finery. I kept my pass at the ready in my belt, as we had to show it to one patrol after the other the closer we came to Peter's camp. Tolstoy raised his eyebrows when he saw the paper's imperial seal, but didn't comment, and I was grateful for that. He found the tsar's encampment on the shores of Lake Ladoga easily, as the small farms in the region had been plundered, the winter crops crudely plucked, and entire forests felled for the building of the tsar's flotilla. As we climbed the slope ahead of the camp the breath of our horses steamed in the cold air. A light rain fell, and the plain stretched beneath us. I had forgotten the sight, the sounds, and the stench of tens of thousands of people living side by side in one encampment. Behind the veil of drizzle, the first fires were lit in the early dusk, and in the dying light of the day a part of Peter's fleet rolled gently on the water.

Tolstoy sighed. "They'll never change."

"Who? What?" I had been trying to spot the tsar's tent, but in vain. No wonder: he'd sleep in as small and shabby a tent as all the rest.

"The Russian army," he answered. "They are savages, Marta. Just look at them. Half of them don't even have a uniform, and if they do get one, it is docked from their pay. Their training consists of eating bad and little food, sleeping on the bare earth, and having their ears boxed by their officers. They have to fight before they know how to hold their weapons. No wonder they scarper like rabbits given half a chance. Peter's soldiers are deserting in droves, didn't you know that?"

* * *

We rode slowly through the encampment. Several generals sat by the fires next to simple soldiers, talking, laughing, and eating together with them. Some of them recognized and greeted me and I spotted a crowd which formed a circle: in its middle, Sheremetev was prowling, breaking up a fistfight between a Tartar and a Russian with a snap of his whip. He lowered his whip, stunned to see me. I bit my lip: of course, he had heard about Peter and me. To my relief he waved and greeted Tolstoy, too. I was feeling less and less comfortable: maybe the scribe had been right, and forging the pass would end up being a fatal mistake. Maybe Peter would send me right back, or I'd find another girl in my place and be cruelly punished. I saw some other women coming out of the washing tent, their day's work done. I warily eyed their low-cut dresses, knowing their hopes and ambitions all too well. One of the women smacked her lips and swayed her hips as we rode by. Tolstoy grinned and nodded at her.

* * *

The flap at the entrance to the tsar's tent was open and the guards were playing dice. My heart raced: there he was. Peter sat around a table with Menshikov and two of his other generals. Their loud calls and laughter told me that they were in the middle of a game of cards.

When I got down from my horse my legs were trembling in the tight riding breeches. Tolstoy watched in silence as the soldiers checked my pass; they couldn't read, of course, but the seal was all they needed to see. I took a deep breath and stepped into the tent. The men stopped their game and looked up. Silence fell when Menshikov grinned, dropped his cards on the table, and cried out, "Queen of hearts, trumps." Then he opened his arms wide: "Marta, you are always good for a surprise. And that's my highest praise for a woman."

The other men, too, relaxed and laughed. All of them, apart from Peter. I trembled inwardly but stood firm as the tsar jumped up, his low wooden stool toppling over. His eyes were dark with anger as he strode toward me. I felt like bolting back to Moscow there and then.

"How did you get here, girl?" he thundered, towering over me.

Menshikov rolled his eyes as I searched Peter's face. His mouth was thin with anger, but somewhere in his eyes was a glint of light. I pushed my luck and shrugged. "I rode. I came on horseback, more than fourteen long days of riding from Moscow to Lake Ladoga."

"On horseback. And how, may I ask, did you get past the guards and the controls?"

I drew the pass from my belt and gave it to him, my heart pounding. This was the moment of truth. Peter unfolded it, studied it with a frown, and then turned and bellowed, "Makarov, come here. Now!"

Sweat gathered in my neck. Makarov, the cabinet secretary, came at a run, and behind him, in the back of the tent, I spotted the tsarevich. Alexey looked glazed with boredom in front of a spread-out map.

"Is that your seal, Makarov?" the tsar asked. Makarov blanched and then reddened, turning the paper this way and that. He finally said, "Yes, sire. The seal is mine, but I didn't issue the pass."

The tsar weighed Makarov's words before he looked at me. I smiled and tucked away a stray strand of hair. "Well, then, let us forget that we have ever seen this paper." Peter chuckled as he held the pass up to a torch and the paper caught fire with a crackle. "It could mean the wheel or the cotton mills for you, Marta. And that would be a shame."

I made to curtsy, but Peter caught my elbow. "Stop. It's such a waste of time. Do you think I have nothing better to do than to watch people bob up and down?" The burning pass dropped into the sand at his feet, where it fell to ashes. Peter stamped out the embers. "Go now, Makarov. What am I paying you for? Try not to despair, it's not you, it's Alexey. The tsarevich is as dumb as an ass," he said. "But together we'll break him in."

Makarov bowed and left. The other men settled down to their cards again, and the tsar and I stood alone in the entrance of his tent.

"You came on horseback?"

"Yes." My cheeks were aflame.

"Alone?" He casually twisted a stray lock of my hair around his finger.

"No, I came together with Tolstoy. It was a beautiful journey. Unforgettable, really."

"A beautiful journey!" Peter snorted. "It is madness for a young woman to do that in these times. Foolish and headstrong, that's what you are, Marta. Do you have any idea what might have happened to you?"

"Nothing that has not already happened in my life," I said. "Taking this risk is part of my duty to the tsar."

His eyes swept over me, taking in my tight-fitting men's clothes. My breasts, now even fuller than before, showed clearly beneath my waistcoat. I had undone the top button of my shirt so that there was a hint of flesh. He seemed to like what he saw.

"And why did you come here? Is life in Moscow so dull for a young woman?" His fingertip followed the line of my throat to my collarbone. My skin prickled with desire.

"I came," I said, "because I wanted to be with you."

"Is that all?" He arched his eyebrows and cupped my face, ready to kiss me.

"No. I also came because I am pregnant with the son of the tsar of all the Russias."

The lights in the tsar's tent burned brightly all through that night.

36

The full moon took my wonder and surprise such as a prince might his due: coolly and haughtily. Through the long, dark tube of the telescope it seemed impossibly close to us. What were those blurred shapes on its surface: towns and cities like ours, or plains and high mountains? Was the moon a mirror of our life on Earth, and why did it shine in the night? I asked Peter all these questions and many more when he set up his telescope for me, after rummaging in the chest that his servants had carried up a hill above the camp at nightfall. He kept all his treasured tools and instruments in it: one of his friends and helpers, General James Bruce, bought them for him in England for outlandish sums. Nothing excited him more: "See what a book of God's marvels opens up before your eyes," he'd whisper. He tried to answer me as well as he could, but finally he said, "Planets are like humans, Marta. There is always a dark side that we do not see. A side made of want and hidden desires."

"Even the tsar does not see it? Don't you know all and everything?"

The moonlight changed his face, even if the clear night sky was sprinkled with stars. "I wish! No. The tsar above all others will never see that other side, as it is so carefully hidden from him. Perhaps it is for the better, though," he said wistfully.

"Well. There's an exception."

"And what would that be?"

"Love. To love is to know the dark side of the other and still want him or her. You are my planet, and I see all of you, and even without peering through some funny pipe into the sky."

He touched my softly bulging belly. "I like you in all your curves. So are you my planet? My Mother Earth?"

"Yes," I said, and gave in to his embrace.

* * *

It was a raucous and cheerful round that had gathered for dinner in the Schlüsselburg. The kitchen served five whole roasted oxen and the servants could scarcely keep up with refilling cups with beer and brandy. Only Alexey crossed his arms in mute protest: he refused to drink his measure. Peter watched the tsarevich and banged his eagle cup hard on the table. "Drink, Alexey!" he ordered. Silence fell and all faces turned to the pale boy. Peter's dwarf, Jakim, tried to lessen the tension by pulling an angry face. "Drink! Drink!" he mimicked with a shrill voice, but Menshikov smacked him so hard on the head that he howled and hid between the pillars. Alexey pleaded with his father. "Please, sir, do not force me to. If I drink so much, I feel terrible and weak in the morning."

"I bet you do. Pull your pants down, so we can see if you're not really a girl. But look at Marta here: she drinks me under the table before she carries me back to my bed. Like that, our unborn son starts off as he should carry on." He patted my belly and then glowered. "Drink! Or I'll have you beaten."

Alexey struggled for courage to speak up against his father. "I am your son as well. I am your heir. You should worry about my health instead of harassing me."

From the corner of my eye I saw Jakim crouching against the wall, pressing his small, fat fists to his eyes and shaking his head in silent despair. I held my breath.

"My heir?" Peter's voice echoed under the vaulted ceiling. Alexey reeled in his chair. Peter drew breath again, the veins on his forehead bulging. "Listen to me. I might die tomorrow, Alexey Petrovich, but you will have little joy in your heritage if you do not follow my example. You must love what makes your country stronger and forsake everything that holds it back. Stop hiding behind stinking priests' robes, like a girl would." Peter grabbed his *dubina*: the knout had so far been lying peacefully beside him, but now he raised his arm. "My heir you will be when you have listened to wise counselors to lighten the burden of your duty. My heir you will be if you spare no effort to secure the happiness of every Russian. But my breath, and my advice, are wasted on you." The *dubina* lashed through the air; Alexey shrank back, sobbing and folding his arms over his head. But Peter was not finished with him. "Nobody is my heir because he was born between his mother's thighs. The tsar suffers most among all Russians. I live for Russia, and one day, I will die for Russia." Peter refilled his cup to the brim and held it out to Alexey and said, calmly, but threateningly, "Drink, or you'll be sorry."

Alexey still hesitated, but Menshikov leaned over, forced his jaw open, and Peter poured the contents of the cup down Alexey's throat. The tsarevich spat, gargled, and coughed, but when Peter wanted to do it once more, I gave him a light shove.

"What?" he asked, the empty and dripping eagle cup in his hand.

I raised my own cup, as if toasting him. "You have spoken well, my tsar. May the day of your death be as far from us as the stars in the sky."

Alexander Danilovich was still waiting to carry on torturing Alexey, but Peter hesitated, and then said, "Leave him. He has already wet himself with fear."

Menshikov wiped his hands on his trousers in disgust and I glanced at the tsarevich. A wet trace led from the buttocks to the knees of Alexey's leather pants and the boy wept, tears streaming down his face.

"Out of my sight with you," Peter ordered, and Alexey fled. The crowd roared with laughter, glasses were raised; the music played again, and the feast continued.

"Marta, the merciful," Menshikov said, glancing at me with caution. I knew what he meant: I had just convinced Peter to allow Rasia Menshikova's wedding to Antonio Devier, the dark-haired stranger, against Alexander Danilovich's wishes. Four times Devier had proposed, four times Menshikov had had him brutally beaten up by his thugs, but Rasia had her heart set on the Portuguese. I raised my glass to Menshikov, and he returned the toast.

After our love the next morning I held Peter tight and felt so close to him it hurt and, above all, close enough to ask a question that pained and puzzled me: "Why do you treat Alexey so harshly? He is but a boy.

Don't you love him?" In a serf's hostile and precarious world, everybody outside our *izba* was a possible threat or even an enemy. Trust could only be placed in the family. We held together where we could. Whom to love, whom to trust if not a father his child? What did the serfs say in their simple, coarse wisdom? "Other people's tears are only water."

He looked at me, amazed, and then shook his head. "I don't treat him harshly. I prepare him for his life as tsar. That's a life without real love."

I frowned. "What are you saying? I love you. And I don't want our child to turn out like Alexey."

He kissed me tenderly, stroking a dark curl from my forehead. "Don't worry. It won't. Alexey was not made with love, but only out of duty and boredom. I never even wanted to be with Evdokia."

"Don't make Alexey pay for that."

"He even looks like her!" He shuddered. "Everything—his sallow skin, the dark eyes, the high forehead, the thin hair, the moody, pinched mouth. God, even the way he walks, this slow gait, is Evdokia's. It drives me crazy. How did she do that?"

"That is not his fault," I said. "He can be like you in other ways. I suppose you have him always with you?"

"It might be too late for that already. In former times not at all. He was with the Lopukins and their popes too much as a child. I was traveling, and learning. See what they have made of him. Half a man!"

I bit my lip. I felt for Alexey, but this was not my battle. Furthermore, I bore Peter's child. I leaned on my elbow for some more pillow talk. "So you never loved her? Evdokia, I mean? Never, ever?" I felt a pang of ridiculous jealousy about the wretched woman. Yes, she had been Peter's wife, but it was I who lay in his bed, while her flesh rotted away from her bones in the convent.

"No, never," Peter answered without hesitation. "The thought of her and our life together gives me goose bumps and I feel sick. My mother chose her for me, as she seemed to fit the bill. Of a lesser clan than the Romanovs, fair of face, pious and seemingly docile—"

"Seemingly docile?" I asked teasingly.

"Every time I came home from the German suburb, she moped and nagged. Once I even brought her a present to appease her. It was a vase that she smashed at my feet, shouting at me, instead of greeting me with a smile and thanking me for seeing her. And as stubborn as a mule. I spoke four hours to her to convince her to take the veil and she refused. Now she is a prisoner in the monastery, where her mind can be as dusty and moth-eaten as her old-fashioned Russian robes."

I kissed his forehead. "Well, if you ever come home to me from other women, I will whip you."

Peter, though, would not smile. "Nonsense. She was my wife, my tsaritsa. It was her goddamned duty to smile at me and be gracious, whatever I did. This, and bear me many healthy sons. I did not expect anything else from her."

To this there was no answer, but I took great care to remember his words.

* * *

After his victory over the Swedes in the first real naval battle of the Great Northern War, Peter was in high spirits. He himself had fought in the thick of it, and Captain Mikhailov and Sheremetev rewarded him with the Order of Saint Andrew. At bedtime Peter tied the blue sash around his chest with childish pride and pinned the diamond-studded order to the threadbare linen of his nightshirt, before he slipped under the blanket. His celebrations frightened even his battle-hardy cronies and the next day Tolstoy left for the Golden Gate in Constantinople, his face pale and drawn.

In truth, a day had not enough hours for Peter. No Russian toiled harder than his ruler as, in Peter's opinion, the only thing that could not be made up for, besides death, was wasted time. By sunrise at four o'clock in the morning he had already written, signed, and sealed a dozen *ukazy*, making his cabinet secretary Makarov smile with the ever steady use of words such as "immediately," "now," "without delay," and "also do not forget . . . !"

Less than two weeks after the battle, the first wooden huts of Saint Petersburg sprouted like mushrooms. Peter gave the conquered Swedish settlements in the marshy Neva plains to his officers. The souls who toiled in the fields hardly cared if a Russian or a Swede gave the orders; their misery just went on and on.

We failed to grasp what these huts meant to the tsar, thinking it might be one of those passing moments, or a fancy he took, before dropping it for something more promising. But to him, nothing was ever more promising than this new city of his. "What do you think?" he asked when he himself laid out the first wooden beams for the Peter and Paul Fortress. "Isn't this just perfect?" He moved them around this way and that, until he was happy. He had but one thought: to hold this earth, may it cost his realm or even his life; never again should either be separated from Russia.

"Why are you founding a new city right here?" I asked him on the evening of the day when we had given the remains of Saint Alexander Nevsky a new resting place on Lust Eland, the so-called happy isle in the soggy marshland all around us, where Saint Petersburg was now founded. I lay tired in his arms, drowsy with vodka; the logs crackled in the fireplace and the flames cast a warm light on my naked skin, which was rosy with pregnancy. I felt strong and safe as never before in my life, for Peter, and for our son. "Don't you have enough cities already? Do you really need another one here?" I teased.

"Oh. Surely Russia has enough of everything? It's all for Russia. My people will only understand much later what I am doing for them." He sighed. "Moscow is dead and belongs to the past. It's the East, Marta."

"Daria loves it for that."

"Daria did not suffer in Moscow what I have suffered there. I hate the Kremlin, Marta." I felt a strain run through his body and I held him tightly until he had calmed down.

"I will never sleep there again. When I have to be in Moscow, I'll be living in Preobrazenskoje, where I grew up," he said, caressing me distractedly. "My new Russia needs a new landmark. I have not chosen the place here in vain: I fought for it and I will offer my subjects a paradise, a New Jerusalem, on the water, dominated by a fortress as powerful as the city's spirit."

"But how will you build a new city? When, and by which means, in the midst of war?"

"You find time and means for what needs to be done, Marta. Such as for love, for example!" He laughed and rolled on top of me.

* * *

Out in the field, I was fully part of Peter's world, even if I was not the only girl to share his bed. But he took the others the way he ate his *kasha* in the morning or peed against a tree. It was me that he drank with, me that he roared with laughter with when I smeared resin and fresh sap on his chair so his bottom stuck to it, or filled his boots half-high with water before he got into them in the morning. I was the one who'd hold him tight when the fits came, or his mad rage, or the blood-soaked horror of his memories overcame him. In my arms, the tsar of all the Russias slept as deeply as a child; I guarded his slumber against his nightmares. When he felt for the hands or feet of the child in my stomach, then no other woman was dangerous to me.

I was the one who carried his son.

37

I sewed infant clothes, slept as much as my body commanded me, and happily gave in to any craving I had: sucking on fresh honeycomb or eating pickled gherkins from the Schlüsselburg's larders. What I liked most though was the sharpness of the Baltic herring: Peter's cook Felten bought the fish in the market near our budding city and marinated them in cream, apples, and onions. This market was a row of ragged booths and stalls, but drew a huge crowd of people, and I followed Felten there one morning in June. The short and stout Dane was in a bad mood, as Peter had roughed him up the evening before: a big round of Limburger cheese had been stolen from the kitchen just when the tsar asked for it. It made me giggle, but Felten still smarted from the routing he had received from Peter's hand.

The Bay of Finland sparkled in the bright sunlight, the first grain stood in the fields, and the earth shone fat and dry. Our low, strong horses thudded along the paths that were torn open by the Russian army's carts, and the ruts and potholes were baked hard by the June sun. I carefully steered my horse around the deepest furrows while Felten moped. "When will we finally return to Moscow, where I have a real kitchen and proper supplies? Just to think of my spices and my vats of stock makes me cry. How should one cook in this wilderness? It's like asking a donkey to play the harp."

I led my horse around the thick stump of an oak tree, a remnant from Peter clearing these forests to build his fleet. "You better prepare for a long, long stay here, and the tsar wants to eat well in his new paradise. We need you for that, Felten," I said.

"Paradise!" Felten spat the word out and then slapped at a thick gnat that sucked lazily on his cheek. Angry like that, he reminded me of the piglets he lathered with beer, mustard, and honey before roasting them on a small flame. Once on the table, their slightly surprised expression, apple in snout, never failed to make us laugh. "More like Hell, I'd say. Is it true that the tsar has ordered forced laborers, prisoners, and souls to build this city, next to the new recruits he has drafted for that?"

I was shooing away a swarm of flies when my horse stumbled in a deep furrow. I held on, just about, but I felt a jolt of sudden pain. The saddle's knob had gored my belly. I kept my voice steady. "Yes. The first fifteen thousand men are to arrive next spring and a second load in August." I stopped and drew a shuddering breath. "For this year, it is already too late for large building works."

Felten sniffed, oblivious. "If I had known that in Holland when I met the tsar on the dockyards, never, ever would I have followed his call. If only I had stayed at home."

I laughed at his despair. "Cheer up! You don't have to cook for all the fifteen thousand workers. In life there can always be worse. Always. Believe me."

He glanced at me, but said nothing. I clenched my teeth, belly still aching from where the saddle had ground into it.

* * *

The wind carried the market's noise and smells to us. Laid out on the bare earth were the first fruits and vegetables of the season; thick pies and cakes; earthenware pots and jars of meat; cheese and bread; bales of plain, coarse cloth; bundles of roughly spun and uncolored wool; as well as roots and herbs that promised to heal all kinds of diseases and ailments.

Felten checked the flashing blades of newly made knives at the blacksmith, and at the pens for pigs and calves—horses were traded somewhere else. He bargained hard for two fattened piglets. The guards bound them by the hooves before hoisting them with sticks on their shoulders. I went ahead, walking with no aim in mind, when all of a sudden I heard a woman's voice rise above all the other noise: "This is usury. You should be put to the pillory, scoundrel."

I stopped in my tracks, heart racing: Could it be? Felten had caught up with me and began, "Mistress—" but I followed the lure of the voice.

"That's what you call filling a pastry? My pigs get more to eat than that and they are as skinny as it gets," the woman said, her back turned to me. The baker defended himself meekly against the weight of her words: no trader sought that kind of attention on market day. I touched the woman's shoulder and she spun around, her eyes scowling. On seeing me, her pinched mouth broke into a wide, unbelieving smile, and I threw my arms open wide. It was her—it was Caroline Gluck!

"Marta!" She dropped her basket and embraced me there and then. For joy I tried not to think about my belly or the sharp twinge of fear. I leaned into her: her cloak and her braided hair smelled of camphor and mint, the scents of their Marienburg home. She finally let go of me, or rather I finally let her go.

"Marta! My God, you are alive. What are you doing here?"

"Where have you been?"

"How is Johann?"

"Is Ernst Gluck here as well? And Agneta?"

We talked so fast and so much that we didn't even hear each other to begin with. I asked after the rest of the family. They lived together in a small wooden house, she said, where the wind whistled through the cracks and crevices of the hastily piled-up logs and Ernst Gluck was working as a teacher. Eventually she noticed my belly. "My goodness, is that already the second for Johann and you? I say—family life becomes you."

I blushed. "No, Johann is dead. I lost the child that I expected at the time."

"Oh, I am sorry. Poor Johann, God bless his soul. But—who then . . . ?" Caroline spotted Felten, who stood behind me with his soldiers. Her voice trailed off as he moodily blew his cheeks; I understood very clearly what he thought of me making him wait but didn't give a damn. Caroline frowned and I bit my lip. Oh, until the end of her days, she'd be a righteous, dutiful priest's wife!

"Well, who else then is the father of this child? Are you married? Why are you here with soldiers? Have you done something bad?"

"Well, no. Not at all. It's not that easy to explain—" I searched for words, as there were truly none for what had happened. When we had met last, unbeknownst to her, I had been pregnant by her son and married to a simple Swedish dragoon. I took a deep breath. There would be time for the whole story later. Better stick to the truth. "My child has a father," I said. "It is Peter, the tsar of all the Russias."

Caroline dropped one of the *pirogi* over which she had fought so bitterly.

"Peter? The tsar! Good God in Heaven!" she said, all pale with surprise, her eyes as big as saucers. "But, how . . . I mean, when . . . this is incredible."

"Milady . . ." Felten said, red-faced from holding a new, enormous wheel of cheese, which he wanted to offer to Peter as an apology for his carelessness.

I embraced Caroline once more. "Why don't you come for dinner tonight? Felten can roast one of the piglets to celebrate. I will send a guard to pick you up."

Caroline hesitated, but couldn't turn down my invitation: her curiosity wouldn't allow it.

All the way back, Felten moaned that he was to give up one of the pigs, until I spurred my pony into a trot. My cheeks were flushed from the sun, the wind, and the happiness of having found the Glucks again. Next to Daria and Peter, they were all I had in this world. I wanted to help and thank them for all the good they had done for me. I didn't ask about Anton, and I couldn't care about him. All I thought of was the joy of meeting Caroline and not the sharp fear of what might have happened earlier on, when my horse had stumbled.

* * *

Our hut was cozy and warm, as the tiled stove burned even in early summer. Before sunrise Peter had already visited the ship docks, sorted out a quarrel between his generals, and finally dictated a long, angry letter to Alexey. Then he had ordered orange trees, camphor bushes, and mint plants from Persia, before drafting and signing an *ukaz* about the general education of the Russian youth. As I pushed the door open he was bent over the ever-changing plans for his city, twirling a quill in grubby fingers and eating a spoonful of cold *kasha*. In a wooden cup, which he had carved himself, a slimy, oily layer floated on the now-bitter residue of *kvass*. His feet tapped and kicked underneath the table and his face and shoulders twitched, but when I entered the room, he looked up and smiled, welcoming the sunshine and fresh air. I shook off my dusty cloak and slipped my swollen feet out of my leather sandals. Their straps had cut deeply into my flesh.

"God, this is good." I sighed, sitting on Peter's lap. When I kissed him, his hand searched for our child.

"What is our young recruit doing? Is he standing to attention?" He nuzzled my throat, which made me laugh. "Hm, you smell good, like fresh air. Has Felten found something in the market? I'm as hungry as a wolf."

"The recruit is swimming," I said lightly. "I think he's going to be a sailor." I grabbed the half-finished *ukaz*. The sight of the heavy rolls of paper covered with thick black ink and the shining, bright red seal where Peter placed his sign, never ceased to amaze me. "Why don't you carry on writing?"

He rested his head on my shoulder and I took in his scent of smoke and leather. "Oh, *matka*. I can command as much as I like, it just does not work. Whatever I say is marred by the stupidity and unwillingness of the Russians. I just cannot do this on my own. I need help."

"Help you? Who could do that?" I asked.

"Someone who is well educated, who can speak several languages. Someone who can be an example to them. But I don't know anyone like that."

My heart beat hard in my chest as a thought struck me. "I think I do," I said. I had found a way to help the Glucks without offending them by offering charity.

"Who?" he asked, amazed.

But before I could answer, a wave of pain washed over me as if a giant had got hold of my body, squeezing me and wringing all life out of me. Fear and agony strangled me; I gasped for air, but my lungs had folded and I felt like suffocating.

"No!" I panted as my skirt turned scarlet with blood. Within seconds its cloth was soaked and a crimson puddle had formed at my feet. The pain blotted every other feeling, and all strength and all life seeped from my body. Peter caught me with a terrified scream and, sobbing, he held me tight when our son was stillborn in the sixth month of my pregnancy.

* * *

The following months blur in my memory and disappear behind a veil dense with grief and deep sadness. It was as if everything I had had no time to mull over before now caught up with me, as I was forced to lie and to rest. The dark thoughts lost no time, but swarmed my soul like locusts, devouring all joy and leaving but a bare, barren soil behind. It felt like birds of sorrow were swooping on me, dulling the light of my mind with their somber wings. Their plumage was as black as soot, and they dug their sharp claws into my heart, breeding in my spirit, laying their rotten, stinking eggs in their nests woven from my despair. When Caroline caught me crying, she embraced me. "Oh, Marta. As harsh as this sounds, only you can rid yourself of this sadness." She was right: no one except the person in whom the birds of sorrow settle can ever drive them out.

Caroline Gluck was always by my side: the Glucks had come into the camp as I miscarried and Caroline had taken over my care, pushing even Peter out of the room at first: "Out! Nothing worse than men in such a situation, gawping like cattle and making the room dirty!" Peter had given them a former Swedish officer's house to live in. She said that he had cried when he tenderly touched the already perfectly formed little fingers and the toenails of his stillborn son. I felt cold with fear. This was my second miscarriage. What if I could not ever give him a healthy child, let alone a son? The birds of sorrow shrieked, and their shrill call made a terrible mockery of Daria's words in the void of my soul. *Nothing binds a man to you like a child. A son.* Caroline fed me hot, thick stews made of bacon and beans, warm bread rolls stuffed with blood sausage, omelets with fresh herbs and dried sweet fruits, which she had soaked overnight in warm wine. Even Felten asked her for the recipe, she told me with a certain pride as she laid hot stones on my feet and folded my blanket over the tiled stove before wrapping me in it. Strength slowly returned to my body, but my soul remained listless. I lay on my bed, staring up at the ceiling and counting the beetles crawling there among the dried tar and the boiled moss.

When I was strong enough, Peter sent me back to Moscow. All my resistance, pleading, and tears would not help; if anything, they annoyed him.

"Please, let me stay with you," I begged, despite knowing the answer.

"You're too weak. In Moscow better doctors can take better care of you. We want you up and running again soon, don't we?"

I could only hope that was the real reason.

So I traveled in comfort, on a litter, and accompanied by a train of coaches and carts, but when we rolled out of the camp I saw a group of young, healthy laundry maids swimming in the river. They showed their bodies without false shame, and their bare, pale skin glowed in the summer sunshine. Which of them would be with Peter, this very night? In a few weeks any of them could be pregnant with his son. I pulled the curtains shut and sank back into the cushions, sobbing uncontrollably and biting my fists until I tasted blood. Peter's favorite dogs, Lenka and Lenta, traveled in my litter, and he had taken leave from them with tears in his eyes. Lenta was pregnant, and I stroked her belly silently and steadily, as if it was a lucky charm.

* * *

I was hardly ever alone, as the Glucks feared I could harm myself. They had followed me to Moscow, as the pastor and the tsar had understood each other immediately. Gluck, being still the upright, learned, and kind man he had always been in Marienburg, on the tsar's orders established the first grammar school in Moscow, which taught philosophy, ethics, politics, Latin, several languages, arithmetic, and physical education. Agneta, the once frail and pale child, had turned into a pretty young girl who made heads turn in the German suburb. Two years after our happy reunion, Ernst Gluck died of a fever and I was to take Agneta in, while Caroline continued to live in the German Quarter of Moscow.

38

I knew from Peter's letters that he had left behind the pain and sorrow of the summer. Did he expect the same from me? Just the thought of it hurt so much, like betraying our stillborn child, but it would be dangerous to forget how Peter had been bored by Evdokia's moping and complaining. I painted crimson onto numb lips, practiced being merry until my cheeks hurt, and wore a new dress of dark green velvet and golden embroidery. As careless and neglectful as Peter was about his own appearance, it wouldn't do for me to not look my best.

He sent for me on arrival. His leather breeches were stained, his shirt reeked of sweat, and he was still wearing the boots he had bought as a young man from his first pay in a Dutch shipyard. When he took them off, his stockings were torn and he happily wiggled his naked toes. "You see, *matka*, even my socks miss you. Nobody is darning them anymore. Their holes are as big as the ones in my heart when you are not with me."

"Have you missed me?" I laughed, my heart beating so hard it almost hurt.

He pulled me close and I felt his breath hot on my throat. "Very much."

"How much?" I sighed.

"Well, let me show you how much." He lifted my heavy skirt and played with the colorful silk ribbons that held my stockings to the lacy silk bodice of my top. I had feared this moment these last few months, and more sharply since his arrival was announced: Would I still feel desire, could I? But heat rose through my stomach when Peter kissed me and lifted me to the coarse table of his living room. He opened my thighs and let his fingertips slide into my wetness before finding my secret spot and gently caressing me until I moaned and opened myself further for him. "It's time we made another child," he said, between kisses.

* * *

In the New Year, Charles of Sweden and Louis of France chased off Augustus the Strong and placed their own protégé, Stanislaw Lesczyinski, on the Polish throne. Peter was stunned with anger, not helped by Turkey readying itself to join the Swedish-Polish alliance and fall into Russia's back. The country, already exhausted by Peter's efforts, now had enemies on all fronts. Was this not his worst fear? How would we survive?

I traveled together with Daria back to Peter's young city. The Peter and Paul Fortress had risen on the shore of the Neva since my last visit. There were many more houses being built, too, even though all building materials had to be brought in from far away. The tsar wanted his city built in stone, and as different as he could make it from the disorder of Moscow; its houses boasting high, regular façades and lining up straight, long streets like pearls on a string, such as he had seen in Europe. Hundreds of thousands of men toiled with bent backs and gnat-bitten flesh, their ankles swelling in the brackish marsh water, fighting to dry out the swamps or force the swelling Neva into canals. Guards would not take their eyes from them: attempts to flee were commonplace.

Our coach had to slow down when passing them, and a suffocating stench gathered in the hot summer air. I examined everyone's features, those hopeless, gaunt faces. Was my father here? Did my brother work among them? But I never recognized anyone, and I listened to the men sing to forget their misery. Hammers and hatchets fell to the ground, on stones, and on logs, all to the rhythm of the Russian songs full of sadness and longing.

* * *

Peter's generals spent the next two years roaming restlessly through the Baltics, taking crucial strongholds and preventing further Swedish attack. After they narrowly avoided an attack from the sea on the still-fragile Saint Petersburg, Peter spent the whole night on his knees giving thanks. I was back in Moscow, pregnant once again. The widowed Caroline Gluck stayed with me, forbidding me to either go out or to drink any wine or vodka: "You will give birth to this child in health, or you will have to deal with me."

She'd forbidden one more thing, but her zeal paled in the face of Peter's passion for me: "You are so warm. If it was possible to get enough of you, I surely would try."

That summer the Red Square sizzled with heat, and even the air in Peter's house in Preobrazenskoje was stifling. Flies clustered in its rooms and the beams crackled with cockroaches. Peter was so disgusted that he had all walls and roofs lathered with fresh, boiling tar, which made breathing even harder.

I was pacing the corridors when the front door was pushed open: a welcome draft cooled my sticky forehead, followed by two soldiers who as good as carried in an exhausted messenger. The man staggered more than he walked. Both Caroline and I retreated into the shadows of the hallway.

The men knocked at Peter's door, and when he opened it, I saw the impatience on his face. Caroline and I listened keenly; any news could mean triumph or defeat. But not a sound was to be heard from Peter's room. I felt faint—what could that mean? Just then, the men came out again, their eyes lowered, and their faces flushed, and I caught sight of Peter looking forlornly out of the window. My heart went out to him.

"Show them the stables and the trough. They can wash themselves and then have lunch in the kitchen," I told Caroline before I slipped inside Peter's room. He didn't hear me and I held my breath, my hand hovering in midair. He was crying, and when I embraced him from behind, his heavy body stiffened before he gave in to my embrace.

"*Batjuschka*. You cry. What has happened?" I softly kissed his shoulder and he leaned on me; I grasped for the windowsill for my knees not to buckle under his weight.

"Sophia is dead."

"Sophia? The Regent, your half sister?"

"Yes. She died two days ago in her convent. Finally."

I buried my face in his back mutely. Sophia, who had relegated her brothers into the shadows of the Kremlin and who had ordered both Streltsy revolts—she, the first woman to ever rule Russia. Peter placed his face in my neck. His tears soaked my skin, his breath burned on my chest, and his body was shaken by deep, desperate sobs. But I also felt another, dangerous tremor going through his limbs. Was that a fit? I sank to the ground and pulled him with me. "Shhh. Come, sit down. Here, with me. Calm down, just calm down. I'm here . . ." I held his head between my breasts and rocked him like a child, softly, to and fro.

It took a long while until he looked up. "She is to be buried in the convent."

"If we find a coffin big enough for her . . ." I muttered, risking a joke.

He chuckled, even while crying. "Indeed! She got even fatter in the convent. I wonder whom she bribed for that. And how did her lover ever mount her? But she was shrewd; so fast and so funny. A ruler, through and through. I feared her, and before I had her imprisoned, I met her alone in the big hall of the Kremlin. She stood straight, but then I had not expected her to curtsy. When I asked her, 'Why did you not kill me, back then, in the Kremlin, when I was but a boy?' do you know what she answered me?"

"No," I whispered.

"'Stupid boy, Peter,' she said. 'All that counts is Russia. Do you think I have not seen that our brother Ivan is an idiot? Who else but you should have ruled Russia after me?' Stability. Continuity—" He wiped his snotty nose with his sleeve, like a boy would. "Yes, let's give her a very deep grave, with neither name nor date. She is not to be mourned and no one shall ever worship her."

I kissed him. "Make that a very deep grave. Deep enough to lodge all the dread and all the demons."

He held me so tightly that the child in my body moved. "Oh, *matka*, why do I have to be so lonely? Why do I always have to be tsar? When Menshikov executed the Streltsy soldiers right outside Sophia's convent cell, decapitating them, or stringing them up by their feet until their heads exploded, leaving their bodies to rot so that the vultures circled the square for weeks on end, Sophia just waved at us, smiling. She never had nightmares. Why me, then? Why do I have to pay?"

I kissed his tears away. "You're not alone. You have us, me"—I placed his hand firmly on my body—"and our son!"

39

Fortune in the Great Northern War swung from the Swedes to the Russians and back, like a pendulum on a clock, and the Red Square was alive as the tsar prepared to celebrate a recent victory: thick, wet snowflakes fell and clung to my lashes and my sable cloak. A thousand torchbearers lined the square, which had been strewn with sand and gravel, steeping the scenery in hues of gold. Cannons shot salute, fireworks lit up the sky in a rainbow of colors, and the steady drumroll almost swallowed the thundering steps of Peter's regiments, who marched underneath the hastily erected wooden triumphal arches onto the square, swinging the captured Swedish flags, the blue and gold cloth torn and burned. In the evening hour the tens of thousands of men formed a single body, calling out in hoarse voices for their *batjushka* tsar. Yet Peter himself was in the thick of it all the time, mingling with his soldiers, standing in the stirrups of his German saddle, which lay on a blanket of leopard fur and red velvet. He waved to the adoring, cheering crowd and I, too, shouted until my voice was hoarse, but just as Peter had finished his first round, our son decided to be born.

The first pang of labor pain almost tore me to pieces; the cramps didn't build up, but hit me like a cart. I gasped for air and the pain cut like a knife into my lower body. Once I was brought to bed—the hastily called-for guards had to carry me more than I could walk—Caroline Gluck was with me, forcing me to rise and pace between the worst pains, and urging me on: "Go on, Marta. He will live. It's a strong and healthy son for the tsar." Her words rang in my ears, monotonous, and steady as the slipping of beads on a rosary, while I bit on a piece of sandalwood that Daria shoved between my teeth. The physician Blumentrost wanted to force me to lie, but I knew how the women in my *mir* had given birth healthily, and it was not by lying on their backs. When only an iron band of suffering held me together, I crouched and then followed Caroline's orders. "Push. Breathe. Press. Once again. And again. Breathe. Hold on. Steady . . ." But the baby wouldn't come. Daria and Caroline held me firmly by my armpits, made me sniff camphor when I threatened to faint, and gently stroked my belly, easing the baby out. I soaked bundles of linen with my blood, and the midwife carried bucket upon bucket of hot water into the room.

By now Blumentrost was not to be held back any longer. "Let me do my work, or the tsar will have my skin as a rug," he said. "Hold her. Firmer! Push! I can feel his head. He's close. Push—stop now . . ."

Somebody screamed like an animal. Lights flashed behind my eyelids and the stench of sweat and blood was unbearable when Blumentrost reached into my body. I wanted to kick him, writhing with agony and rage at my helplessness. He urged me on: "Push once more. Yes! A boy. It's a boy!" Blumentrost sounded as triumphant as if he were the father: he held the infant up into the fading light of the afternoon, spun him around, and slapped him on his bottom, where his skin was still covered with white slime and blood. My son's first cry was strong and hoarse before a merciful darkness closed in on me.

*   *   *

The room was scented with camphor, sage, and myrrh; hot water steamed in the bathtub, and Caroline made my bed with fresh, starched linen and fur blankets before she opened the window wide, pushing the protesting midwife aside. "What a stench! How is one supposed to breathe in here?"

Peter and I endlessly admired the small, perfectly formed fingers and the rosy skin of our son. He had strong, straight limbs and a loud voice; last but not least he drank from my breast like a field marshal. Soon, though, Daria handed the little one to a wet nurse and bound my breasts to keep their firmness and their shape: I belonged back in Peter's bed. My son was baptized in the Kremlin chapel and Peter, who sobbed throughout the ceremony, ordered Makarov to enter his name into the yearbooks of the Moscow Court. Alexey congratulated me in measured words and Peter made me the special gift of Kolomenskoye Palace outside Moscow. It was a palace with hundreds of rooms and as many windows that sparkled in the sun. Built for Tsar Alexis, Peter's father, it had vast hunting grounds—much more land than the monks in our *mir* had ever owned. The thought gave me great pleasure.

* * *

That Yuletide was the happiest ever: sometimes I'd change my disguise three times a night: first dressing as a Frisian maid, then as an Amazon or a Greek goddess. When the festivities ended—normally an hour at which an inky darkness still hid the Moscow rooftops from my sight—I'd slip through the dark corridors to my son's room, where he slept guarded by his wet nurse. I'd lean over his cradle and listen to his breath, entirely content.

At the thaw, I followed Peter into the field. It broke my heart to leave my little boy behind, but there were too many other women who were only too happy to follow the tsar into his tent. I would not have one calm moment in Moscow. My little boy was to follow us as soon as possible, but for the time being I left my four-month-old son in Menshikov's palace under Daria's care. I dictated long letters to her along the way and from the camp, begging her not to forget him in all the disorder of Alexander Danilovich's household. *Do not leave my boy alone in the darkness, as he gets scared. Also, have some warm clothes made, Peter will pay for it. If you need to travel, please make sure my son has enough to eat and drink.*

My little boy died suddenly before Easter in the year following his birth. He had just begun to smile when death got him. "We must have another one soon" were Peter's words. I nodded, fighting to keep the birds of sorrow at bay.

* * *

The following year, I gave birth again. My son was small, yet healthy, but barely outlived his brother. The birds of sorrow nested in my soul: whenever I saw how Tsarevich Alexey grew and prospered, I wondered whether my sons' deaths were a punishment by God for what the tsar's wife Evdokia had to endure.

Daria, who was still unmarried and a maiden by name, gave me some advice. "Only love a child once it can walk, talk, and is strong enough to overcome the first fever."

My beautiful daughter Ekaterina Petrovna was stronger than her brothers. Born in late December 1706, despite Peter chasing war all over his realm, she lived past the sad little milestones of their brief lives. She was a dear child, with an easy smile, blond curls and dimples in her chubby elbows, who walked and spoke early. Between battles, Peter dictated loving letters to me. *Menshikov, too, is not here, and I sorely miss the two faces I love the most in this world. Let our Ekaterina be strong and healthy, so the two of you join me soon. Yesterday a drunk soldier climbed on a rooftop and fell: you would have laughed even more than I did at the sight of it. So yes, I do have fun, but not as much as when you are with me,* the messenger read.

I and Ekaterina joined Peter as soon as we could. When Peter sat with his men in the evening, sharing his worries about the war and the country with them, Ekaterina hid under the table, spinning the spurs of his boots and humming a song, until he lifted her on his lap and fed her from his plate. She took her first steps on the banks of the Neva and Peter was as proud of her progress as he was of the houses of his new city. In the nights, however, the worry about Russia's future plagued him: he spoke in his dreams, shouting orders, or shot up from a light slumber, standing as stiff as a rod, and tried to slip on his dirty, crumpled uniform. I had to force him back into the pillows, soothing him with songs and kisses, so that he could gather strength for the next day, which again should weigh so heavily on him.

Charles of Sweden marched his troops southward, where his trusted General Rehnskjöld defeated both the Saxons and the Russians. At first, the Saxons had been ready to welcome their Lutheran Swedish brothers. But then word about the true nature of the occupation shocked even the Russians: Charles executed all the prisoners on the spot, as he could not feed them. Whole villages were purged; men, women, and children dangled from trees, heads down and their bellies slit open. The crows pecked their eyes, and the wolves chewed their way up from the neck to the guts. Charles's men heated cow's piss and poured it into their bound, helpless victims' throats until the victims burst, or gave no other sign of life, whichever came first. A stream of letters came from Saxony, pleading for help. Peter and his generals were desperate: Was the war lost? They talked until late in the night, every night. Once, when I came to see Peter to bring him hot milk with honey, he crumpled up a letter, his face dark with rage.

"What's this?" I asked, picking the paper up from the floor and smoothing it. It looked important.

"It's a letter from England, written by His Serene Highness, the Duke of Marlborough," he replied, gnashing his teeth.

"You wanted him to mediate between Charles and you, didn't you?"

"Yes. But he declined. Declined! And do you know what I had offered him?"

I shook my head.

"I gave him the choice between the titles of a prince of Kiev or Siberia. But that was not all." He raised his finger mockingly. "So, we top that up with fifty thousand Reichsthaler for every year of his life, as well as the largest ruby ever found, for his duchess loves jewelry and Marlborough is a gambler with huge debts. But that's not enough for a duke, so let's add the Order of Saint Andrew. But His Highness rejects it all." He shredded the letter. "Of course, he refuses. It is much better to know the Swedes are busy here rather than meddling with the War of Spanish Succession. Russia and I are to be slaughtered for the sake of others."

The Swedes settled in Saxony, where Charles waited for his moment. He for sure had more cards up his sleeve: we all knew that. Peter, more worried than I'd ever known him, multiplied his men at the Russian borders, and for the first time in a century the Kremlin, too, was fortified. Though when Peter signed the *ukaz*, he murmured, "It shall go to Hell, this abode of the Devil!" Only a few months later Charles stood in Minsk, which had not seen foreign fiends since the kingdom of Rus grew big, six hundred years ago. Were Russia, and we, lost?

40

I n spring 1708, we struck camp in Kiev, where Peter wanted Ekat-erina and me to be comfortable, so I dictated long lists to Makarov, who from Arkhangelsk sent them west with a ship. Patiently, Makarov repeated to me and Daria the tsar's own orders: "A full English porcelain service, hand-painted with rural scenes, in blue, to serve forty-eight people. Thirteen bales of striped taffeta and several bales of Indian fabrics with various woven floral and square patterns. Twelve barrels of olives and two barrels of anchovies . . ."

I snapped my fingers. "Stockings. The Polish stuff has a run after the first ride. And when I am with Peter, I need warm feet, otherwise I am in a bad mood. That's the last thing he needs now. And you, Daria? What do you order for yourself?"

She didn't hesitate. "Italian balm for my hands, pickled lemons, silk from Amsterdam, and rolls of Brussels lace."

"And a golden wedding ring," I said with a giggle, but instead of laughing she looked like she might cry. I was ashamed to have hurt her and embraced her. "Forgive me. You've been by Menshikov's side for almost nine years. Surely you are as good as married?"

"You have no idea what it's been like," she sobbed. "Menshikov has decided to marry, but not me. He has fallen in love with a Princess Saltykova. The slut is only fifteen years old and last night he told me he wanted to marry her and sire a dozen children, while I should retire to my family estate and await further orders—"

"What? This beggars belief."

Makarov hastily stashed his papers and bowed to take his leave; Daria was so furious that she grabbed a small silver candleholder and threw it at the fleeing cabinet secretary. "Just you run, coward! You men are all the same." Then she flung herself at me. "Oh, Marta. She is young, beautiful, and of a much better family than me. I've given him my best years. Who will want me now?" She pressed her fists against her swollen eyes. "He's crazy about her, because he cannot have her! Her family does not allow him a single second alone with her and he scribbles one horrible love poem after the next to her, war or not, battle or not. I am always available. How interesting is that?"

I listened in silence and picked up Ekaterina, kissing her hair. Daria's tears had smudged her white face paint, which made her look even sorrier. She was almost twenty-five years old, like me. If she still wanted children, she had better get on with it. I kissed her, pulling her onto her feet. "We will find a way, Daria," I said, as reassuringly as I could. "Go home, have a hot bath, and then drink some warm milk with honey, so you can sleep. Trust me, and do not worry." I hope it comforted her, because I certainly didn't believe it myself. Peter and I laughed and drank and carried on so much in Kiev's bright nights that I was sure to be pregnant again soon. But what if he thought of marrying a young princess, for Russia's sake? I could well imagine my fate, as well as Ekaterina's. The thought chilled me like an icy wind.

When Daria's litter left, Ekaterina played at my feet with one of Peter's old pipe stumps and sucked on the seafoam carved in the shape of the Russian double eagle. Her sweet saliva changed it into a bulky, formless clot. The sunlight made her blond head shine silkily; she looked like an angel. I picked her up. "Come. Let's go and see your father," I whispered, and she smiled.

* * *

"What do I care about Menshikov and his women's stories?" Peter looked up from a map he was studying. To the west, the Swedes held Saxony; to the east, the Don Cossacks and their Ataman Bulavin were staging a revolt and the Porte in Istanbul was ready to pounce. Russia was utterly beleaguered, ready to be sliced up by her enemies in a peerless, hitherto unimaginable feast. Had Peter pushed our luck too far?

"Women," he snorted, before continuing to scribble his notes,

which he sent out every evening in all directions. He had already forgotten my presence, but I would not give up so easily.

"What do you mean by that? Daria has given him her best years.
Should she now watch him marry a younger woman?"

Peter shrugged. "But of course. What do you think? Daria has the
worst reputation. I myself have chosen Princess Saltykova for Menshikov. She's a juicy little thing, but horribly well guarded. He has to put a
ring on her finger to get her, as it should be. I shall stand godfather to
each and every son she bears him," He smiled and fingered the ribbons
on my dress. "Perhaps we, too, should get on with having more children than just our sweet Ekaterina?"

I pushed him away.

"What are you thinking, woman?" he roared, but I stood firm. Was
I really only fighting for Daria? For sure I was not.

Peter sighed. "All right. Listen. So far, I did not want an ambitious
marriage for Menshikov, for he shouldn't get too greedy. But he has
proven himself, in battle, as well as in life. I can now reward him without any eyebrows being raised. My love for him is no longer to be called
blind, or unjust. When the times are better, I will also make him a prince
of Russia. For this he needs the right woman by his side."

I was stunned: besides the members of the tsar's family, no one had
ever been a prince of Russia—nobody was born with it; even a tsarevich had to earn the title. Peter leaned in to embrace me, but I trembled
with rage. "Ah. Princess Saltykova is a juicy little thing? Just to be clear:
as long as Menshikov does not marry Daria, you are no longer welcome
in my bed. He is to keep his word. His bloody, bloody word!" I sobbed,
for I put everything I had gained at risk: for Daria, for Ekaterina, and
last but not least, for myself.

Peter grabbed his chair so hard that his knuckles turned white, and I
backed away when he drew breath, his face twitching, betraying deeper
passions than his cold fury. "It's my bed, not yours, Marta. Nothing in
this world belongs to you. Nothing! You are as poor as your bloody
burned Baltics." His words hit me like a cudgel. I clenched my fists. In all
the years of us being together we had never quarreled; no raised voices,
no loud, ghastly words. And now this!

My chest tightened as if it were under an iron band and I held
Ekaterina, who wept and clung to my neck tightly. I felt her heart race

and buried my face in her hair, which smelled of honey and sunlight. I looked at Peter, who avoided my eyes, but stared at his little daughter, pain in his face. "That is not true, Peter. I do own something. I have pride, and my freedom, which you gave me. If you think like that about Daria, what do you think then about me? If Menshikov will not be held to his word, will you? What is to happen to me, with us, if you meet some princess who is a juicy little thing? I prefer to leave, before I am driven away," I said as calmly as I could, then swallowed my tears and turned.

He crossed his arms. "Where will you go? What will you live on?"

I gave no answer and left the room.

"Marta! Stay here. Stay. That is an order," he shouted, but I closed the door behind me. Only once I was in the corridor did all my strength drain from me, like water from one of Felten's sieves. I sank onto my heels, leaned against the wall, and hugged my knees. I gasped and tried to suppress a sob, but then a dam burst and I cried so much that I had to wipe the snot from my face. Ekaterina touched my face with her little hands, her eyes dark with worry, and muttered the few half-words she could say.

Inside Peter's room, I heard wood splinter. That would be his chair then, I thought, or the desk, just as he shouted with rage. I steadied myself, picked Ekaterina up with trembling hands, and went into my room. "Pack my things," I ordered my maidservant, wiping my face. Crying would not help me. What had I done? I might have to give Kolomenskoye palace back, but the jewelry and the gowns belonged to me, I could sell those. And then? I'd have to learn how to read, write, and count. But lesser minds than mine had managed that. In the *gostiny dvor* there was certainly room for another shop. I could become a merchant and afford an education for Ekaterina. She should enter into a proper marriage; a bond in which she was loved and honored. No one was to treat my daughter as I could be treated.

* * *

For two days and nights I heard nothing from Peter. I paced the house while he turned all his thoughts to the threat of the approaching Swedes. By day, he drew up plans for his army; at night, he whored his way through Kiev, striking fear in the heart of the most battle-hardened girls. I swallowed more laudanum than I should in order to be able to sleep. Sometimes I woke drowsily and listened. Did I hear footsteps halting in front of my door? Maybe. I knew that in his anger he could throw bolts of lightning, but then felt sorry at the firebrand he had caused, doing all to extinguish its flames. But not this time. Had we both gone too far? Peter never came into my room—if he had been there at all—and I slipped back into an unhealthy, intoxicated slumber. I suffered like an animal as, despite his words, I still loved him, and it hurt me to see him suffer. Normally, I would have stood by him and Russia in this difficult hour. But now was not normally. My pain at the words that had fallen grew. Of course I had known his temper, but so far I had only mellowed his rage toward others. I had never been at the receiving end of it. I had to do what I had to do, for could I live with him if he did not respect me? I had proven myself a thousand times over.

Finally, there was no reason left for delaying my departure. My chests were packed and tightly chained and locked, as I was to cross the war-torn countryside from Kiev to Moscow. When I asked Peter for an armed escort, he had Makarov reply to me that he could not spare a single man at the moment.

* * *

It was a sunny morning in late August. The golden roofs of Kiev were damp and glistening with dew and I squinted as I stepped into the courtyard of our low, dark house. In my arms, Ekaterina looked around in surprise: we were leaving the only home she knew. There was no turning back, even if I had to force myself forward, step by step.

Makarov and Felten were standing in the doorway, looking so downtrodden that I embraced both of them and pressed small coins embossed with Saint Nicholas in their palms, folding their fingers around the charms. "You have been my loyal friends; please be the tsar's faithful servants in this hour of need. If you come to Moscow, come and see me in my shop."

Makarov shuffled his feet and Felten wiped his eyes with his apron, clean for once, before he handed me a bag of warm, freshly made fudge for Ekaterina. I swallowed and tasted salt. Was I throwing my happiness and my life away? There ought to be another way forward, as there had always been in my life so far. Servants lifted my boxes on the carts;

I climbed into the carriage and reached out for Ekaterina, who would travel on my lap. Don't cry, I ordered myself through gritted teeth: do not cry! I had ample time for that once we had passed the city gates. I waved to the men once more and Felten sobbed like a child.

The coachman clicked his tongue and raised his whip, flicking it over the back of the horses. I was ready to settle in on the cushion, when I was flung forward: the wagon jerked to a sudden halt and the horses dug in their hooves, for the tsar's hand gripped the reins with all its might.

41

Daria's wedding to Alexander Danilovich Menshikov was a quiet, but joyful event. Peter ordered that we celebrate in the European way, and Daria just shrugged her shoulders, when, the morning before the ceremony, I scrubbed her skin rosy and glowing with a pumice stone. "I'd also marry him wrapped in a net. That he becomes mine is all that matters."

Menshikov glowered when he stepped under his groom's crown with a representation of Christ embossed along the golden rim; but Daria was radiant in her dress made of ivory silk and silver thread embroidery and her own bridal crown, which showed Our Lady. The light of the hundreds of candles that Peter had sponsored made her shimmer like the moon itself as she stepped into the dusky little church in Kiev, and I wept with happiness. After the wedding not even the much-too-close Swedish troops hindered us from celebrating as we should with drinking games and dancing. Just before the ashen morning hour we stepped out into a balmy summer night and I felt the dewy grass as fresh as a promise under my naked soles, for I had left my embroidered slippers under the festive table. The afternoon when I had swum in the Dvina had never felt farther away. I shrank back when a first firework burst suddenly above our heads, Peter's very special surprise for Menshikov. He embraced me from behind and whispered the words that glowed in the sky: "*Vivat*. That means: they shall live long, and happily. Look now, the next rocket will spell *Connected by their love!*" I marveled at the light and glory, and clapped my hands with joy, before we all coughed and wiped the soot from our faces.

In the morning, after making love, my breasts were wet with his tears and he raised his head, looking bewildered, when I combed his dark curls from his lined forehead. "You must never leave me, Marta," he pleaded. "I am only a human being when you are with me. If you ever leave, or forsake me, I am but an animal."

The sky was pale blue like a duck's egg when I finally managed to calm him.

* * *

Marriage was not too bad for Menshikov: Daria fell pregnant almost immediately and he pranced about as proudly as the peacocks that he had ordered from Persia for his Saint Petersburg palace on Vasilyevsky Island. Peter stood godfather to Daria's baby boy the following June, offering the child several villages with thousands of "souls" and a bale of fine Amsterdam cloth for his christening robe. But the little one died before he began teething and now Daria and I were linked by a stronger and very different bond.

* * *

By autumn, when the still-supple summer earth was silently preparing for the first great frost, Peter was merely trying to avoid an open battle with the Swedes as long as possible: he lacked the means to win. But then he found an ally to strike fear into the bravest soldier's heart. An ally who had always been by his side, silently and almighty: Russia herself.

When I heard the words for the first time, they chilled the blood in my veins: *Scorched Earth.* I remembered my hunger during the short siege of Marienburg. And the Swedes were to endure a whole winter? There could be no crueler plan.

* * *

Charles was about to march on Moscow, boasting he would dethrone Peter and shatter the Russian empire into small Swedish provinces. Was this to be our end?

Peter stood in his study in Kiev, looking at maps of the Ukraine.

Deep furrows lined his forehead, and for the first time I noticed the sharp lines running toward the corners of his mouth. Dark shadows lay under his eyes and his cheeks were gaunt. When had he last had a square meal? I seemed to have breakfasted, lunched, and dined with Daria all the time in recent weeks. His general major, Nikolai Iflant, ran his finger across a line and explained. "Charles will move his men along here, but the country is hardly cultivated. There are but a few villages, and both the woods and bushes are so dense that man and livestock easily hide in them for months, if needed. Scorched Earth is a Cossack thing, my tsar. When their enemy approaches, they set fire to everything . . ."

"Everything?" Peter asked, his eyebrows arched.

"Everything. The Swedes will have nothing to eat. Winter is coming. Charles marches into frost and famine. I tell you, no army conquers as well as the Scorched Earth and the Russian winter will."

I paused at my embroidery: Peter looked pale, but as keen as an unsheathed blade. His blue eyes were gleaming as he laid his hand heavily on Iflant's shoulder. "That's it, Nikolai. Scorched Earth. Give the order."

My stomach churned, for I knew what this order meant to the little *izby*. As soon as the enemy set foot in the Ukraine, millstones would be smashed to gravel, and all food, be it growing in the fields, waiting in the threshing houses, or stored in the grain chambers—and which was not necessary for the survival of our own army—was to be burned. Fire would devour all houses, all churches, and all stables, bridges were to be torn into the rivers, their rocks and stones damming up the water. Forests and embankments would become a wall of flames. People who refused to follow the order would have to watch their whole village being torched, before they were killed by their own men, Peter's soldiers.

"What will happen to the people who live there?" I dared to ask, my voice husky.

Iflant looked at me. "They will be sent into the remaining forests, along with their cattle and everything they can carry. It sounds cruel, but it's for the sake of Russia. We all pay."

Peter paced the room like a captured wild animal. His old uniform vest hung on his too-tall, too-bony body. What did he live off? Brandy, some *kasha* in the morning, and a few bites of whatever he found in the evening.

"And when the Russian winter comes?" I whispered.

Peter smiled for the first time in a long, long while. "Oh, *matka*. I can't wait to greet him, the Russian winter, this most loyal friend, who does my every bidding. For if we Russians think the winter to be cruel, what will the Swedes feel? They shall be culled like cattle."

* * *

The following night Ekaterina fell ill. She had been coughing for a while, but now she gasped for air, wheezing, and cried, holding her little ear, which was as red as fire inside. We tried everything to lower her fever; Blumentrost bled her several times and, oh, how bravely my little girl held up when the hot glasses were placed on her tender back. She sobbed, but bit her lip and pressed my fingers, which I clenched. The doctors bathed her in ice water and I felt like hitting Blumentrost, but was about to allow her treatment with mercury, when our little daughter died. Peter was numb with pain but threw himself into the preparations of the Scorched Earth plan, disappearing night and day in his study with his generals and advisors. His spirit and his soul were caught in the struggle of Russia's survival. If I struggled to understand his distance to my pain in those days, I heard him dictate a letter to a friend who had lost his son: *I am so very sorry about your loss of a fine boy, but it is better to let go of the irretrievable rather than recall it; we have a path laid before us, which is known only to God. The child is now in Heaven, the place we all want to be, disdaining this inconstant life.* And so, when he clung to me at night, tormented by nightmares, his words reached me, even though he could only speak them to others, and not to me. But if I had been devastated by the death of my little sons, then my mourning for Ekaterina, our daughter who was talking and learning and giving us so much joy, was like falling into a deep, dark well which had no bottom and from which I thought I could never emerge. Soon, I was pregnant again, but where the love for Ekaterina had burned so warm and brightly, a dark chasm of bitterness tore open, which nothing would ever close.

42

Saint Petersburg grew with every month that my belly swelled. Despite the burden of war, Peter insisted on being kept up-to-date with the happenings in his city. The wooden Peter and Paul Fortress had been replaced by a star-shaped structure in stone, ready to brave any attack, and its bastions were named after Peter's best and most trusted men: Menshikov, Sotov, Golovkin, Trubetzkoy, and Naryshkin.

The pregnancy weighed on me and I almost feared the moment of birth, not because of the long hours of pain, but because I would start loving the child so helplessly, and once more be open to all sorrow and pain, should I lose it. Mostly it was Daria who embroidered soft cashmere blankets and sent gifts of rattles and dolls. "Don't give up, Marta. You will have a strong, healthy son, and that will bind Peter and you forever," she encouraged me, forcing me to feel my child quickening. "You must hope, and you must believe," she urged. I was grateful for her support; somehow, only another woman could understand. Peter was once more excited at the prospect of possibly another son. He never mentioned our dead children.

Shortly before I was to leave for Moscow, I lay awake in my bedroom in the little Summer Palace, where the Fontanka Canal met the Neva. My body and my limbs were so swollen that I could not even braid my long tresses and was too impatient to ask my maids to do it. My curls stuck to my face and neck, which were beaded with sweat. My chambermaid was curled up asleep on the threshold, when I heard footsteps; the handle moved and Peter snuck into my room. His eyes lay deep in their sockets and he swayed a bit before he climbed onto my raised bedstead, bit me playfully in the neck, and whispered, "How are you, my beautiful Marta?"

"I'm awful. Look! I can't even comb my hair," I moaned, lifting my swollen hands and wriggling my fingers. He grabbed the silver brush from my bedside table and pulled me up from my bed and across the room to the dressing table with its Venetian glass mirror.

"I'm quite good at combing hair," he offered, and helped me to lower myself on the stool before he worked his way through my thick tresses. My scalp tingled under his firm stroke and when he had finished, my hair framed my face in a shiny, dark cloud. He mutely rested his chin on my head and our eyes met in the mirror. We were as pale as ghosts and the candlelight dulled the outlines of our faces but sharpened our bones. I rose and wanted to lead him to the bed; perhaps I'd sleep better with him by my side, and the sheets of cool, starched linen looked inviting. "Come . . ." I whispered, but to my surprise he held me back.

"No. Put on a cloak. Follow me." His eyes were dark, and unreadable.

"What kind of cloak?" I asked. "Now? In the middle of the night?"

He pointed to my chest of clothes, which was flung open. "Anything, just so you're not in a nightgown." He paused and added, "Something dignified."

Something dignified! I chose a golden-yellow silk cloak that was lined with mink and embroidered with gold threads in a Persian pattern. It fell to my feet, so its deep folds and the belting under my bosom covered my belly.

"That's good. Come now." Peter easily lifted me over the sleeping chambermaid and, once in the hallway, placed a finger on his pointed lips. He beamed now, his face as bright as a jewel. We were like children who planned a prank: What on Earth was he up to? We crept down the staircase and then snuck through the dark Summer Palace, which had a dank smell of the near Neva and of the bitter tar dripping off the torches. I felt the cold of the stone slabs beneath my naked feet, and my mirth and wonder mixed with sudden wariness. What had happened? Had the Swedes advanced so far that we had to flee the city under cover of the night?

Ahead of me Peter pressed down the high, European-style curved handle to a small reception room. I squinted: the room was dark except for the amber glow of the fireplace, revealing Peter's dogs, who snoozed on bearskins, patting their tails weakly as they sensed us. Close by the fireplace stood a priest, wearing a long, dark robe. His feet were in nothing more than a pair of well-worn sandals, despite the October cold, and his hair fell dark and plain and almost straggly to his shoulders, while his beard was neatly trimmed. I bowed my head and he touched the cross on his breast, the *panagia*, in respect. Peter laced his fingers into mine, giving me strength, and drew me closer. "Marta, may I present to you the greatest spirit in the whole Russian empire: Feofan Prokopovich."

So this was Feofan, of whom Peter had so often spoken and whom he admired, even though he belonged to the old Moscow guard and had just returned from Rome; but the number of Feofan's talents was reason enough to promote him. Prokopovich, the abbot of Kiev and head of the city's university, smiled at me: his worn face spoke of warmth and wisdom and his shiny eyes of a swift spirit.

"Now you must also tell me the name of your lady, my tsar," he teased, and Peter smiled. They were clearly at ease with each other.

"That is why we are here. Feofan, this is Marta. She is the sister of my soul."

Feofan's gaze weighed me: I'd rather have this quiet little man as a friend than as an enemy. "And why have you summoned me in the middle of the night, my tsar?" He stroked his beard, yet seemed much less puzzled than me. One of the dogs yawned and turned its belly toward the warmth of the flames. Peter chased it away and kneeled down on the bearskin instead, pulling me down with him, despite my heavy body.

"Peter," I moaned, but he raised his hand.

"Silence. I summoned you to witness an oath, Feofan. Once happier days come for Russia, and once the greatest danger and the threat of the Swedes is turned away, then . . ."

My heart thudded and the blood roared in my ears. Even the child in my body lay still, while Peter, too, searched for words for the unbelievable things he wanted to say. ". . . Then I wish to make use of my freedom since my divorce from the Tsaritsa Evdokia Lopukina to marry Marta."

I gasped. Marry me? It had always been in the cards for Daria, being after all an offspring from an old Russian family, even though she had lived in sin. Menshikov had to marry sooner or later, to sire rightful heirs. Yet Peter had Alexey, and we were good as we were. All anger and all doubt that I had felt in Kiev were gone, blown away far into the east of the realm, ready to be forgotten there, such as an enemy in exile. I knew what Peter was doing for me and what he was facing—the criticism of his family and the aristocracy as well as the scorn of the foreign powers, by whom he so desperately wanted to be accepted—him being almighty or not. Russia feared all change that Peter brought and revered all custom he did away with. Peter would be lonelier than ever with this decision. He'd have but me, I thought, and it made my heart hurt. "Are you sure?" asked Feofan, emboldened by the power of his office and clearly sharing my thoughts.

"Yes," Peter repeated firmly, "I do not fear whatever this might entail."

My heart leaped and I squeezed his fingers. No, he would not fear, ever, and I was determined to join him in that.

Peter spoke solemnly: "Feofan Prokopovich, you shall here and now, testify my oath. Marta, when the times are better, I shall welcome you in the Holy Russian Church, and give you my son as a godfather. I shall marry you, and you shall be known by the name of Catherine Alexeyevna."

I blinked my tears away when Feofan blessed us with three fingers before he left, the sound of his footsteps fading in the passage. Peter and I were alone in the little room. It felt like a fairy tale; I would not have been surprised if the room had spun three times around us. We settled in front of the fire, holding on to each other, talking quietly for a long time until a late, leaden morning light crept through the half-closed shutters of the room. Just before I fell asleep, I murmured, "You do not have to do that, *starik,* you know that? You are everything to me. But I certainly never again expected marriage."

"That's precisely why, old girl, *matka,* I want to give it to you. You have no expectations, which makes it wonderful to delight you. I do not know what the war will bring or what the future holds. But I want you to be sure of my love, and I want you to be safe. My family is a snake pit. The whole world is to treat you and our children"—he felt for the child in my belly—"with the respect you deserve. We are two of a kind." He smiled, nuzzling my shoulder.

* * *

Late the next morning I woke up in his arms. The fire had burned down and the pale sun was high in the sky. Peter breathed quietly and slept calmly, blowing up some of the hairs of his fine mustache. He reminded me of Daria's tomcat when it got some cream, and I chuckled and tickled him. Peter woke and wrapped his arms around me.

"Do you know what you did yesterday?" I asked him softly.

He feigned surprise. "No. What?"

"You proposed to me," I grinned, but I could hardly say those wondrous words.

He leaned on an elbow, his eyes sparkling with mirth. "Do you have any witnesses for this nonsense, Catherine Alexeyevna? No one will ever believe you, you know that, don't you?" *Catherine Alexeyevna*: it was the first time he'd called me by my new name. My joy set Marta alight in a bonfire of love and pride, and Catherine Alexeyevna rose from her ashes. Peter's fingers slid over my swollen belly and between my thighs. "I've often made love to Marta, but never to Catherine. I bet she's an utter vixen. I can't go into battle like that, can I?" he murmured.

My blood flowed faster through my veins and I felt myself going wet between my legs. "Oh no, Peter, I'm already much too heavy. Come and see me in two months, after the delivery," I pleaded.

"Nonsense. We will find a way . . ."

He helped me on my knees and his hands slid over my body, enjoying my full buttocks. I knelt naked, my full breasts lying on the rug, and my stomach stretched, yet I stifled a scream of sudden pleasure when his tongue searched me from behind, hot and moist, finding my most tender spot with ease. "Please," I panted as he slowly began to lick me, spreading my legs farther and pressing my hands to the ground. Peter tasted me with slow, sucking circles, and when I came with a short, joyous scream, he was already inside me, placing his hands ever so gently around my hips and my stomach, feeling our child, as he searched and found his way.

* * *

When I left Saint Petersburg to give birth in Moscow, Peter gave me a worried, long, and loving letter and a sack of money to see me on my way, which Pavel Jagushinsky, the master of Peter's household, tucked into my sleigh at the very last minute.

"What is that for?" I asked, but Peter looked at me gloomily.

"Five thousand rubles, in case any Swede aims better than I hope they do. The money is for the child, and you, should I fall and not be able to keep the promise I gave you."

"I do not want it. I want you to live," I said, pushing the bag away from me.

"Good. That makes two of us," Peter said, forcing the sack back into my fingers. "I, too, am not too much in a hurry to step before my maker."

* * *

The tsarevich Alexey met me in the first courtyard of the Kremlin. He kissed me on both cheeks and lovingly pressed my swollen fingers. "Marta, Your Grace. How was your journey?" His dark gaze grazed my stomach. At Ekaterina's death he had kindly sent me one of his popes to console me—he, too, had loved to horseplay with his little sister, whose godfather he had been—but Peter had forced the holy man to sing naughty, obscene songs before he chased him away, throwing stones at him. Now, Alexey hopped from one foot to the other, his pale skin blotted with ungainly red patches, and he coughed. "The tsar writes me one angry letter after the other. Am I not doing a good job as Moscow's governor? The city and the Kremlin are well fortified, in case the Swedes do make it here. Why is my noble father so very angry with me?"

"Do not worry too much," I said, deciding to hide Peter's fury from Alexey. A good job as a governor? "He does not know his arse from his elbow," Peter would mumble, when he read the orders Alexey had given. "Tons of building material for the fortifications have been squandered, stolen, and sold elsewhere. Has he sent the wagons I asked him for? Have the recruits been dispatched, as ordered? None of it. Oh God. Why doesn't he just hand Charles the key to the city?" The harder Alexey tried, the more Peter found him wanting.

I leaned heavily on the arm of Alexandra Tolstoya, Peter Andreyevich's sister, who had accompanied me on the journey as my new lady-in-waiting, trying to make it safely into the Kremlin across the slippery courtyard.

Alexey padded around me like a young dog, coughing again and wheezing with excitement. "Marta, tell me, did you put in a good word for me? Do you know what people at court say?"

I shook my head, biting my lip.

"If it was not for Marta, we'd suffer endlessly from the tsar's whims."

I took both of Alexey's cold, raw, and red hands: while I was wrapped in a thick sable coat, a matching hat, and brightly embroidered gloves, Alexey was dressed like a schoolboy in a simple, dark knee-length Polish jacket and a crumpled and stained linen shirt. His dark hair fell on his shoulders, long and unkempt, making him look like a priest, and his eyes had a feverish gloss. Did he not understand how risky his words were?

"Yes. Of course, I did put a word in for you, Alexey. Your father loves you dearly." I crossed my fingers in my muff, so that God could forgive me this little white lie. The rift between father and son was already too deep in those days; still, not I, not anyone could have ever imagined what was to happen later. "He will be so proud if you hold Moscow against the Swedes," I added.

Alexey's German tutor, Huyssen, joined us and reluctantly bowed his head, but I ignored him. In Huyssen's letters, which Makarov had read, the shriveled old prune showed off with his teaching—making up half of the subjects he said he taught the prince in—and made fun of me, the washermaid at the tsar's side. Everything about me merited his scorn and created mirth at the German courts: my way of dressing, my style of makeup, and the amount of jewelry I wore.

Alexey embraced me again, but then immediately withdrew. "I should not get close to you. I have a bad cold and you are so close to delivery. I do not want you to get sick before you give birth to my little sister." He coughed again, this time into a handkerchief. When he raised his head, I spotted blood in the fine white tissue.

But I had no time to react to that, as my last thought, just before my waters broke and the first, drawn pain of labor wracked my body, was: Your sister, Alexey? Why ever not your little brother?

Only hours later I held my beautiful, healthy daughter Anna Petrovna in my arms and the dreaded, besotted love of her took hold of me almost instantly. Had I ever doubted that I could feel that again? Fool that I was. She was too much of a miracle.

Sheremetev offered me a beautiful pearl necklace: each smoky gray pearl was as big as a chickpea, and the locket's oval sapphire was as large as a pigeon's egg. It was a surprisingly valuable gift: Had he heard about the tsar's secret promise to me?

As soon as I was strong enough and as soon as the *ottepel* had well passed, I boarded a carriage together with Anna and two maids and headed for Saint Petersburg. I sneakily breastfed Anna and enjoyed the closeness to her little being, kissing and cuddling her at every possible moment. I was determined that she would live, and at every inn I drank liters of warm, almost black beer, to have enough milk for her. God willing, she'd soon have a brother. I smiled to myself.

43

But then fate struck. We were busy with the preparations for Easter in Saint Petersburg when Peter returned from a trip to the Schlüsselburg lying on a stretcher. His advisor, Peter Shafirov, who had accompanied him to the new Ladoga Canal and to the oak forests, which were to be cleared for a new fleet of ships, said, ashen-faced: "He suddenly felt faint and then stumbled and fell." Even though Shafirov's grandparents had already converted from Judaism to the Russian Orthodox faith, Peter still called him tenderly "my little Jew." He now sat in the privy council, an unheard-of rise in fortune for a member of the "chosen people," as they called themselves. He was an exception, as Jews were the one people Peter would not welcome in his empire: "I'd rather have Muslims and pagans in our midst than Jews. They are rogues and cheats. I want to eradicate evil, and not to multiply it."

On his stretcher Peter moaned with pain, and I gave Shafirov little Anna Petrovna to hold, which he did clumsily. I felt Peter's forehead, which seared my palm with its fever. His eyelids fluttered and when I turned his hands in mine, I noticed red blotches on his skin. I cursed at Shafirov. "That's what you get from all this wild partying. Or has he been with a sick girl?"

Shafirov avoided my eyes. I felt uneasy—was there someone I ought to know of? There was no time for more questions: the physician Blumentrost immediately began to treat Peter with mercury pills, which was atrocious: the tsar lay slack in my arms in his sick chamber, where thick, drawn curtains dampened the light and made the air stifling. The pills made him slobber with saliva like a dog, and on his naked feet I spotted the same red sores as on his hands. Were these similar to the ulcers he sometimes had on his loins? Peter was further weakened by each bleeding. He was slipping away, I feared, and I never left his bedside, hoping to catch his every word. Whatever his illness was, I wanted him healed and healthy. Then, two weeks later, he looked at me with a thin, sorry smile on his haggard face. "Perhaps I can never keep my word, Catherine." He whispered, "My bloody, bloody word, as you call it. Maybe I will never be able to marry you."

I knelt at his bedside and kissed his fingers. My tears welled up. "Who cares? All I want is you, here with me." He nodded and tried to come toward me, but dropped back into his cushion, faint and pale. I bit my lip: Would Peter ever recover from this mystery illness? I prayed for it, and my wish was granted: he recovered and rose from his bed, wearing his old green velvet dressing gown and simple felt slippers to look out of the window on Saint Petersburg, where thousands of forced laborers toiled like ants, eagerly, incessantly giving shape to his dream. The plans for the Winter Palace were ready, and even if in the past weeks, as soon as possible but while still on death's doorstep, Peter had still amended them between two letters that had to be sent into the field. As soon as he was strong enough, we visited the different building sites and met the German builders, the Italian sculptors, the French painters, and the Dutch carpenters, whom Peter had lured to Russia that spring with big promises and even bigger bags of gold. When all the snow had melted, a French expert for fountains and canals arrived, as Peter wanted to stage water games, like the ones he had seen at Versailles.

The number of forced laborers rose steadily. Upon approaching the city they were like a dark river whose source was hidden somewhere on the horizon, where the sky met the earth, while its estuary was our city. Only at close range did the stream gain human form and faces. Peter had them guarded ruthlessly, as laborers tried to flee at each stop along the way. Once captured, their leaders were executed, and the rest of the group whipped. At a second attempt, their noses would be cut off. The look of the many gaping holes in the gloomy, bony faces made me sick.

44

It was Shafirov who dared shake the tsar from his sleep. Peter sat up with a jolt, which woke me as well. The milky summer night seeped into my mind, blending reality and the realm of dreams.

Peter held his head with both hands, his eyes searching the room. "What is it? Mother? The Streltsy soldiers?" He started twitching and kicking, but Shafirov lunged forward and held him, dodging the tsar's thrashing arms.

"It is I, my tsar, Shafirov. I have news . . ."

Peter's breathing calmed. "Shafirov, old Jew. Why are you sneaking through the palace at night? What is your news? Spit it out and then let me sleep as any honest man would." He embraced me and I felt his tension.

"The Swedes . . ." Shafirov began.

"Yes?" Peter's voice was alert. "Where are they?"

Shafirov chuckled. "The Swedes are moving south, as they should, marching directly into the Scorched Earth. Our Seventh Dragoon captured a train of food and made thousands of prisoners. The general and six thousand of his men were able to flee, but several thousand carts of food and ammunition are ours."

"So they have nothing to eat? And they move southward?" Peter whispered, his eyes shining. "They will die of hunger." He jumped out of bed, clapped with joy, embraced Shafirov. and pulled him into a short, sharp dance, before kissing him and holding him at arm's length. "Shafirov, my brother. This is the dawn of our new happiness." Both men bumped fists and chuckled, but in the dawn's dull twilight their words crawled like a spider's legs over my skin.

* * *

"What do you think of her? She's a German princess: Sophie Charlotte von Brunswick-Wolfenbüttel."

"Quite a mouthful," I said.

"Is she pretty? Or not? Will she like Alexey? And, more importantly, will he like her?" Peter cocked his head in doubt and studied the picture. It had been propped up close to the window and the morning light fell mercilessly on the face of the young woman depicted. She wore a short, wavy, and powdered wig, her cheeks were glowing brightly, and she was not adorned with any jewelry. A heavy cloak of blue velvet and ermine fur covered her shoulders and her plain-cut dress of light yellow silk. One slender hand held a rose; she smiled with closed lips, but her round blue eyes looked at us blankly.

"She looks pleasant," I said, for to me all these paintings looked the same. Was there a secret workshop, somewhere, that made portraits of nubile princesses to order, following a pattern? "Is it true that she suffered from smallpox as a child?"

"Who says that? Her skin looks as soft as Anna's bottom. And even if she did, good on her if she has survived; scars are not inheritable. She simply has to powder herself more, it's as simple as that. But she is so skinny. Will such skin and bones bear me a dozen healthy grandsons?" he wondered, and shrugged. "Her sister is married to the crown prince of Austria. With those family relations I can happily ignore a flat bosom."

"Good. It's not you who is supposed to touch that flat bosom anyway," I teased him without a hint of jealousy. Vinegar in a woman's voice drives men away. Still, in those times that strange night in the Summer Palace, as well as Peter's oath, seemed like a dream to me. Would he ever keep his promise? I'd have rather sliced my wrists than remind him of it. "You heard that the emperor in Vienna wishes to introduce the death penalty as a punishment for adultery?" I teased him instead.

Peter laughed. "My cousin on the Danube has probably more subjects than he thinks necessary. If I did that, I'd soon be without Russians to rule." He waved at Pavel Jagushinsky, his master of the household, who had been waiting patiently behind us. "Take the painting to the tsarevich's room, so he gets used to her face," Peter said. "She will be his wife. Until then he can go on mounting the thickest and ugliest chambermaids in his retinue, and get into a stupor every day. Marriage will be fantastic for that useless sod."

"Don't say that," I scolded him, as Jagushinsky was listening.

Peter shrugged. "He will marry her and can love elsewhere."

"That is not what you do, I hope?" I asked, arching my eyebrows.

He nuzzled my fingers. "Which other man is so lucky as I am, being with the best of women?"

I smiled tenderly, yet already felt pity for the slender young German princess. Alexey had been unhappy and restless ever since he couldn't prove himself against the Swedes. Perhaps he could appease Peter by fathering a strong son? I did not know what to believe any longer: the tsarevich wrote me cordial and pleading letters, while I heard shocking stories about him that I refused to believe. True, he surrounded himself with flatterers, but wasn't that hard to avoid for any prince? All that was said was malicious gossip, even if I decided to talk to him about his drinking. It was fine to get into a stupor every night. Only it rendered Alexey helpless and sick the next day. This was against the rules of the game according to Peter, who after every feast was the first up and back at work, more eager than ever. Worst of all, Alexey was said to have bragged, "If at last it will happen what is to happen, then I'll put my father's friends and his washer whore on the stake. Just you wait." I kept the words—if they were true at all!—secret from Peter, as I feared for Alexey's safety.

Peter continued talking: "But before I can think of grandchildren, I must marry off my nieces, the tsarevny Ivanovna, Praskovia's daughters."

"Why?" I asked. Praskovia and her daughters lived outside Moscow in Ismailov palace, assembling an olden-style court of loafers and jesters to whom she doled out her charity. When Peter and I approached, the people fled in terror, hiding in the chests and cupboards of Praskovia's household, as the sight of them made Peter furious.

"These girls are pure politics. I want a foreign prince for each of them, in marriage. Alliances are the new way forward, Catherine. No one lives alone." He leaned in to me, burying his nose into my cleavage. "Above all, not me. You are my finest flesh, Catherine. I'm so glad to be back with you. Now my shirts are clean, my boots are polished, and my stockings are mended." He purred like a cat while I played with the unruly little strands of hair on his neck, just above the collar. I relished the moment and we held each other close, until I heard feet shuffle: Peter's master of household, Pavel Jagushinsky, had returned. With his deep-set eyes, his strong cheekbones, and sagging cheeks he always reminded me of a sad old dog.

"My tsar. Doctor Blumentrost is here," he said, and I was startled: Was Peter's treatment not over yet? Was he still suffering from that same strange ailment that Blumentrost would not name, even if I badgered him for it? Was this his reason for staying away from my bed? How should I give him a son if we never had a moment together? I scanned his hands: the red blotches were still there but had paled under the effect of the mercury ointment.

Peter pulled a face. "Blumentrost may go to Hell. Bring him in, Pavel. The quicker he starts, the sooner it's over and done with." Then, he held Jagushinsky back. "Wait, wait, wait. What is this? Your cheek is swollen. I hadn't even noticed. Come here." Jagushinsky did not dare to resist when Peter grabbed him by the hair and bent his head back. "Open your mouth, as far as possible. That's it." He stared into Jagushinsky's throat and wrinkled his nose. "Your breath stinks like a donkey's ass. How does your wife bear your kisses? Or do you mount her when she is too drunk to notice? I shall sort you out." He dragged the stumbling Jagushinsky to the window and did not let go of him, while he rummaged in the top drawer of his little desk, looking for an already bulging bag and a long, thin pair of tongs. Jagushinsky gurgled, begging in vain for mercy. "Open your mouth again . . ." Peter grabbed the tooth, which he thought to be the culprit, with his tongs and gave it a good twist and an even better jerk. Pavel Jagushinsky spat a stream of blood. Peter laughed, let go of him, and proudly held the tooth to the light, turning it this way and that. "Splendid. In the bag with it." Pavel's tooth fell into the little sack filled with teeth: it was more bulging than a miser's purse. When Peter and his friends roamed the streets, taverns, and brothels of the city, both the bag and the tongs were hanging on his belt. If he spotted so much as a swollen cheek anywhere, he'd set to work. Pavel Jagushinsky held on to a chair, lest he collapse, but Peter stamped his foot. "What are you waiting for, Jagushinsky? Let Blumentrost in."

Blumentrost pressed past me with but muttered greetings and Peter opened his arms. "Finally, you come. I have ulcers all over my arse, my cock seeps pus, and pissing burns like hell. What am I paying you for, man? Your cures simply do not help, and Russia needs many heirs. Will I ever be healthy again?" Before I heard Blumentrost's reply, the door closed behind him.

In the corridor, Jagushinsky was bent over double with pain, crying, like a child that had hurt its knee. I gently placed my hand on his cheek. "Ask my *damy* to send for my Circassian maid, Jakovlena, from my kitchen. She has many secret recipes and will surely mix you a soothing paste."

"Yes, Your Grace," he answered, but lingered.

"What else?" I asked. Something weighed on him. He cleared his throat and my heart sank: Jagushinsky surely had to sort out some trouble Peter had gotten himself into.

"The tsar has assigned a new chambermaid to your state."

"Has he now. What is her name?" I made my voice sound even.

"The tsar calls her Boi-Baba. She already has a couple of children, and—"

"And, let me guess, she's pregnant again, isn't she? Do I happen to know the father of that child?" I tried hard not to sound catty.

Jagushinsky blushed with the shame Peter would not feel. I sighed. "Leave it to me, Jagushinsky. I'll take care of her. It's not the first time this has happened, is it?"

He darted away, only too glad to obey me.

I took Boi-Baba in. She wore her thick, dark red hair in a single braid and had so many freckles, you hardly saw her skin. Her wide mouth was always ready to smile, showing strong, healthy teeth. I scanned her waist, but her body was as vast and soft as a cushion, so her pregnancy wouldn't show. She would gladly follow my orders and fulfill her simple but lowly tasks until her time came.

I congratulated Peter laughingly on the strength of his loins, and he smiled, flattered, and bobbed his head; after several bottles of wine and beer he was in a lenient mood. Before he fell asleep in my arms, he murmured, "Whatever I do, old girl, my best belongs to you." He dug his face into my hair like a sow in the straw and, only a breath later, snored heavily. I carefully slid away from under him and stared up at the dark ceiling.

What if this girl Boi-Baba meant something to him, and what if she gave birth to a healthy boy? I had not yet fallen pregnant again, and only little Anna Petrovna lived of my children. I just could not force the sobs back into my throat; my pain was too deep. Iron chains were tightening themselves around my heart and I wept and wept, my body heaving. Only after a long while did I, too, fall into a deep, exhausted sleep.

45

In winter, the Neva clenched its icy fist around Saint Petersburg. Our city froze into a single, glittering crystal, and on a sunny day all life there was caught in a shiny, frosty bubble. Waves froze mid-tide, ships lay enclosed like the skeletons of huge, mysterious sea creatures, and skaters or sleds drawn by souls or strong ponies drew patterns on the uneven surface of the ice, its color pearly against the dense blue sky. On the other hand, it was now much easier to get from one place to another: as Peter still refused to have a bridge over the Neva, each noble family had to build boats and barges. In the summer there were public ferrymen as well, but only the poorest went for free. Russians of standing had to pay one kopeck for a crossing, each way. Perhaps that was why Saint Petersburg grew much more slowly than Peter had hoped: work suffered from both the turmoil of the war as well as the silent, sullen resistance that both nature and man put up against his orders.

In the spring, during the *ottepel,* the ice floes broke with deafening roars and shocking force, tearing us from the exhausted sleep that the still-dark nights offered. The river flooded the paths and washed away the foundations of the new buildings, while the thaw cut us off from the rest of the country. The west wind could blow so violently that the Neva flowed back into the Bay of Finland, its waters swelling, rising, and crashing down in a storm wave on the freshly laid-out fortifications and quays of the young city. The city seemed like a boat lost at sea, ready to be swallowed in the maelstrom of Peter's dreams and desires.

But if the buildings scattered along the banks of the Neva looked like oysters devoid of pearls, the Cathedral of the Holy Trinity was almost finished next to the imposing Peter and Paul Fortress with its bastions and church, and the former market of Nyenschantz with its motley assembly of shops and stalls had moved into a *gostiny dvor*. On Peter's orders, and to satisfy the foreign sailors, a Lutheran church and a guesthouse were built, even if no vessel was allowed into the harbor unless it carried a load of at least thirty blocks of stone and a ton of earth—a levy that made any construction possible at all. Nowhere else in Russia was anyone anymore allowed to build in stone, yet to move the necessary masses of stones and earth to our marshy lands was a horrible task. The building site lacked everything: the forced laborers shoveled the soggy clay soil with their bare hands into their aprons or blouses because they had no proper buckets to carry the mud and brackish sludge away.

Despite the setbacks, Peter and I would hold on to each other, shaking with laughter, when we saw people wading up to their knees in water, carrying their belongings on their back, or paddling on whatever they found, be it a door or an upside-down table. After every flood, Peter himself marked the height of the receding water on the stone walls of the Peter and Paul Fortress, and then had barrels of beer and bottles of vodka cracked open: his city was still standing! The stench of mold would still linger in the roads once both the forced laborers as well as the hired foreign artisans had to go back to work immediately. Rasia Menshikova's husband, Antonio Devier, the head of Peter's secret police, caught a letter written by the French ambassador, Campredon. It was destined for Versailles and made Peter foam with rage: *This city is built on bones. Saint Petersburg is no better than a rotting corpse.*

"A corpse?" Peter first hit Campredon with the *dubina*, his ever-ready knout, tearing the ambassador's fancy new coat and making his cheek bleed. Then, he crumpled up the letter and stomped on it in front of the whole court. "You French fool. Building a city is like waging war. Neither can be successful without sacrificing human life." He again lashed out at the Frenchman, who dared not defend himself.

I wanted to calm Peter down with the help of Pavel Jagushinsky and Menshikov, but the tsar drew his sword and injured both, cutting their cheeks and ears.

Campredon fled, holding his bleeding nose, and complained to me,

sobbing. "It took me twenty-four days to move here on these godforsaken roads. I have paid twelve hundred rubles from my own pocket.
Eight of my horses have died, and half of my luggage has disappeared
without a trace. And now this. *Mon dieu,* what have I done to deserve
this?"

"Keep your anger and your thoughts for the pages of your diary,
Monsieur Campredon, where they are safe from discovery and betrayal," I said dryly, but he stared at me like the pig that found truffles
in his home country's forests. His hand patted his chest pocket, where
he kept his secret little book. Was he surprised that I knew about its
existence?

"*Madame*"—he bowed—"my deepest respect."

* * *

Peter found a kindred soul in the Italian architect Domenico Trezzini.
Even if I did not like the tall man with the arrogant look, the eagle-
like bent nose, and the dark, curly hair that tumbled so vainly over his
shoulders, he at least did not complain about life in Saint Petersburg,
like other craftsmen did. When we visited the building sites, there was
nothing but moaning.

"How should I live and work in this dump? My mind needs space,
and beauty," said the German painter.

"The food is disgusting. I could not expect my sows to eat that,"
cried the French garden architect.

"My delivery of marble and tools is still blocked by customs in the
port. How shall I work without chisels and stone?" asked the Italian
sculptor.

"My workers are nothing but clumsy fools. They can't tell their
asses from their elbows," sneered the Dutchman, who was to build the
bridges over the Fontanka and Moika.

In the coming years Trezzini dreamed and built restlessly, beginning
with the Saint Isaac's Church, the palaces for the ministers, the fortifications of Kronstadt, the Saint Alexander Nevsky Cathedral, the Senate, and simple things, such as plans for even quays and a number of
wooden bridges across the various river arms and dug canals. Where
his work ended, other masters stepped in: the proud Alexander Le
Blond of France, the quarrelsome German Schädel, and Harebel from a

town called Basel, who hated caviar with a vengeance—"Such slippery, glibbery stuff!"—and instead wanted to dunk bread in molten cheese whenever things got festive! Well, each to their own.

When Peter ordered the first few hundred Moscow noble families to move to Saint Petersburg, any excuse was futile, and neither age nor serious illness were allowed to delay the move: the old Prince Cherkassy, the richest man in Russia, begged for a delay as his legs were swollen with gout. Peter's guards dragged the venerable man by his hair out of his palace near the Kremlin and placed him stark naked on the ice of the Moskva, mocking and laughing. His staff started packing up with utmost haste. When a fire destroyed a large part of Moscow, Peter was overjoyed: the burned houses were to stay rubble and ashes—if the homeless families needed a place to stay, they were welcome in Saint Petersburg.

During a festive dinner I overheard Sheremetev say to Peter Shafirov, "Do you know what 'neva' means in Finnish?"

He shook his head, and Sheremetev answered. "It means dirt."

46

The guards declared the Neva's ice safe to bear the weight of sleds and carriages on a clear November morning. The sky was a pale blue, the outlines of the Peter and Paul Fortress looking sharp and almost unreal, and the trees on the riverbanks were heavy with silvery rime. Every breath was a blow to the lungs and the brain.

Eight steeds were tethered to my sled, in which I sat together with Alexandra Tolstoya and Daria, who was pregnant once more. It was adorned with flags, bunting, and silk banners in all the colors of the rainbow and the animals' breath steamed from their nostrils as they chewed on their bridles. Peter stood straight on a small, simple sleigh, his legs wide to keep his balance, holding the reins tightly in his restless little hands. Behind him, the whole court was waiting for his orders, their colorful sleds pulled by horses, deer, pigs, dogs, dwarfs, or souls.

"Are you ready?" the tsar yelled.

"Yes!" A whole excited chorus of voices echoed across the ice and my pulse quickened. Peter raised his arm, his face beaming with excitement, and we held our breath and strained our ears until a cannon shot from the Peter and Paul Fortress tore through the crisp air. Peter's arm fell and he lashed his horses. "Come on, then. The Neva is free for traffic," he cried, and the wind swept the words from his mouth, making away with them.

"Come on!" I drove my horses on with a short crop; Daria and Alexandra cheered and waved colorful handkerchiefs when our sled shot after Peter's, and all the others followed us on the virgin ice.

I slowed down and held my breath as Peter approached the other bank. What would he say when he saw what I had done for him? He stopped his sleigh with a sudden jerk, and stared in silence at the shiny building, rising like a dream before his eyes: walls, towers, and battlements glistened, all made of ice, and sparkling like a fairy-tale castle. It had taken the workmen the whole night to chisel the pavilion from giant ice blocks: its roofs, domes, and spires gleamed like shards of blue glass in the sun, and on the right and left of the entrance of the snow castle stood Peter's Moors. The oiled, black skin of their bare chests was a splendid sight against the purity of the palace, as were their trousers and boots cut from blue and red leather. I caught up with Peter and he turned, slowly, his eyes moist and full of wonder and disbelief. It touched me deeply: he looked like a child at his first Easter. I smiled at him tenderly when he whispered, "Did you do that?"

I blew him a kiss. "Yes. It's a palace fit for the king of snow and ice, my tsar. A gift from your most faithful, loving servant."

He helped me down from my sledge and I carefully set my feet on the slippery surface, then Peter led me inside the ice palace, his face alight with joy. "It is wondrous!" he said, his eyes taking it all in, his mouth open, stunned. Between pillars of ice stood two thrones made of snow, which were covered with leopard skins. Behind them, a red velvet flag embroidered with a golden Russian double-headed eagle draped from the ceiling to the floor, several meters high. Flames danced in a fireplace made of ice, so our backs were warm and cozy, though the rest of the guests froze their buttocks firmly to their seats. Peter and I giggled so much, we almost fell from our thrones, but whoever got up without permission was ordered to drink a potent mix of champagne and brandy as punishment. The musicians had to move their hands all the time, otherwise their fingertips would have frozen to the instruments. Peter made them play a minuet to which our dwarves danced, slithering on the ice with their short, bulky limbs, and tumbling over each other.

I laughed so much that the inside of my stomach turned sour and I had to be sent to bed with colic.

47

Despite the merry Yuletide, the difficult time for Russia was not over yet, even if the Swedes were starving and the Scorched Earth campaign killed them like flies. When I visited Sheremetev in his new Saint Petersburg house, he did not hold back his fear and his reservations.

"For the New Year I wish you health and all the happiness in the world," I said, and tried to kiss his hand, but he hastily withdrew his fingers.

"You should not do that anymore. I certainly do not want to be seen having my hand kissed by you—Your Grace."

I was stunned: it was the first time he had called me that, but I hid my surprise and linked elbows with him before settling in front of his fireplace. As always, I enjoyed being close to him, as I had so much to thank him for. If he had ever hoped that we might be more than friends, and brothers in arms, he never let on. The palace was still almost empty, bar a few well-chosen pieces of furniture. In the room, the walls were bare except for a life-size portrait of the tsar above the mantelpiece. The servants had probably just got the fire going, as I felt chilly and wrapped myself tighter in my cloak of dark red velvet and blond mink furs. A servant served us steaming mulled wine and a tray full of crisp, freshly baked *blinchiki* stuffed with thick pieces of salmon and sour cream.

"Hm, they're delicious," I said, nibbling on a pancake and eyeing the next. "Better than the food in your house usually is," I teased him. "Did you get a new cook?"

Sheremetev blushed. "No, nothing of that sort," he said. Why did my question embarrass him? I wondered but changed the subject. "How long will you stay in the city? Has the tsar issued a new marching order?" I had not seen Peter for several nights, as he consulted his generals and advisors ceaselessly, and afterward his men still had to drink and make merry with him, to make him forget his troubles. Come the early-morning hours he'd be carried to his frigate that lay frozen in the water, where he'd sleep alone, burrowed beneath furs and blankets like in a cloak of loneliness in his tight bunk.

Sheremetev weighed his answer. "How long can we keep the Swedes at arm's length? The last open battle was several years ago now, and Charles has itchy feet. Do you know how close he is to Moscow, despite the Scorched Earth? Only twelve hundred *versty*. Never has an enemy been so close to the city walls. There has to be a battle this summer. A big, decisive battle, which will force either country to its knees, for all eternity." He looked warily into the flames. "But who knows? Next year, we might all be Swedes."

"Don't say that, Boris Petrovich. That is high treason," I said, and took one of his rough, calloused hands in mine. "Promise me that you will not leave the tsar, but will stay by his side, whatever happens. He always plunges himself into the thick of things, you know that."

Sheremetev pressed my fingers. "That's true. Yet if he didn't do that, he would not be our *batjushka* tsar. But you know that I'd gladly take any bullet which is aimed at him."

Just then the door flew open and a small dog, covered with snow, scampered into the room, somersaulted toward Sheremetev, and gnawed at the general's chaps. A young girl chased after the lapdog, picked it up, kissed its head, and then buried her pretty, glowing face in its fur. "He's so naughty, Bobushka." She laughed in a German-sounding Russian. "In town he went for the ladies' heels and the men's boots. Please make sure that your next gift to me is better behaved." She spotted me and fell silent, while Sheremetev blushed deeply: Who else in the world called the successful, hardy soldier Bobushka? I was happy for his little secret, whoever the girl was.

"*You* should be better behaved, Alice. Curtsy, please. This is Marta, the faithful, generous and warmhearted companion of our tsar," Sheremetev scolded, but he winked at her.

She curtsied gracefully, the wide skirt of her simple blue wool dress opening like a flower's petals, and eyed me from beneath her very long, very dense lashes. Her ash-blond hair was loosely braided in a crown across her head and freckles sprinkled her tiny nose. In a stunning contrast to her fairness, the eyebrows and eyelashes framing her amazingly bright blue eyes were almost black.

"I am Alice Kramer, Your Grace," she said shyly. How old was she? Fourteen or fifteen years old perhaps, certainly not any older, I thought with a pang of jealousy. Her body seemed as slim and supple as the branch of a young, strong beech.

"I found Alice lost, hungry, and hiding in the smoldering ruins of a burned-out city of the Baltics. Back then she was still a little girl, but now she's always with me. Have you not seen her before?"

Now it was Alice's turn to blush. I knew the terror she must have felt: hiding in a burned-out city and fearing discovery, while straying among the ruins. And finally, probably going from one man to another as a gift. How alike our destinies were, yet how different. No, I had not seen her before, ever, and I glanced at Sheremetev: How well did we really know our friends?

"Does the tsar know her?" I asked casually, toying with my glass.

"Of course." Boris Petrovich looked in the flames; his face plain.

"Of course," I said gently. Peter knew every pretty face in town. I tried to imagine the slight girl in the tsar's arms but felt no anger. What could she, or anyone, do?

Alice curtsied again. "Your Grace, allow me to retreat," she said, and I held out my hand for her to kiss. When she had left, Sheremetev searched my eyes and said almost inaudibly, "We are on the verge of a great battle. But for the first time in my life I am afraid to die. For the first time in my life I really want to live."

"My friend," I whispered, tears welling up in my eyes, "take heart. Love is a reason to live. Actually, there is no better."

* * *

Before it came to an open battle, Peter's friend and devoted subject, the Russian winter, weakened the Swedes further. As predicted, Charles fled with his troops into a little-cultivated area, where his men collapsed dead or dragged themselves on, famished and frozen. They had eaten their horses long since and carried the saddles on their shoulders, sucking and chewing the leather straps. Their hands were covered in chilblains and poorly wrapped in rags; there was no means of numbing the pain of the sick and wounded, if they got any treatment at all. Limbs of fully conscious soldiers were amputated, and at night, Cossacks crept out of the thicket from where they had watched the enemy, looming at them in the cover of darkness, just as wild animals might. They tiptoed through their deserted villages, knowing every corner, and sliced the sleeping Swedes' throats. The wolves grew fat that winter.

An ambassador of the Cossack ataman—their leader's title— laughed during a meal in Saint Petersburg. "The Swedes have only three hopes in their lives: brandy, garlic, and death." He gargled vodka and spat it to warm his throat for further feasting.

"What does Charles want to do?" Peter asked.

"The Swede will go to Poltava. He is foolish, or desperate, enough to think that if he seizes Poltava, he might as well seize Moscow. As if there was a training ground for the prize of prizes." The wiry little Cossack wiped his mouth with the back of his hand and smacked his lips for more. Peter laughed and grabbed the fattest chicken he could find on the table, sniffed at it, tore a thigh off, and plunked the rest on the Cossack's plate. "Eat, brother. The best food my table has to offer, just for you. Open another barrel of vodka! Are we celebrating, or are we celebrating? Poltava, eh? Well, then it will be in Poltava that we meet. Charles shall eat gravel, earth, and horseshit, take my word for it."

The Cossack shrieked with contentment, a shrill and piercing sound like a war cry—it gave me goose bumps—before he tore the chicken apart, dripping with grease and sauce, and buried his face in it.

I raised my glass, but was full of fear: Poltava it was.

48

In April, when the first flowers blossomed on the dewy green of the meadows, the surviving Swedes struck camp outside Poltava's city walls. A misguided bullet hit King Charles in the heel during the siege. Nevertheless, he continued edging his men on in insane anger, rendering their return to hope and to a normal life impossible. Peter's regiments intercepted a bag of letters sent by Swedes: *We are desperate, and the king closes his ears to even the best advice. He only thinks of one thing: war, war, and war once more. Nothing matters to him, not even victory.* Peter just waited for the right moment, knowing the power of patience. With Russia at his back, he was stronger than ever.

* * *

"No. Do you think I embroider clothes in front of the fireplace in Kiev when you are out in the field? Of course, I'll come with you." I placed my hands on my hips. "No one will stop me from doing my duty, and my duty is to follow you, wherever. Especially now—just look at yourself!"

Peter glowered at me: it was shortly after Easter and we had traveled to Azov on the shores of the Black Sea, to oversee the building of Peter's new fleet. While the air was tangy with the scalding heat of the tar that sealed the timber, and filled with the shrill singing of the saws and the steady, dull beating of the hammers on countless anvils, Peter was bedridden once more after a first walk on the docks: all strength simply seeped out of him, his eyes were bloodshot and his face ashen.

The cure Blumentrost still gave him just would not help: the illness returned in bouts when you least expected it. Peter sweated acid, peed pus, and faltered in my arms. He suffered, but so did I, as I felt like we were battling a faceless enemy. What was going on; was it because of this illness that I failed to get pregnant again, be it with a son or with a daughter?

Peter reeked of putrefaction and sweat, although I every day washed his whole body with tepid water, and now closed his eyes, tired of our discussion. "Damn, stubborn woman! Can't you ever let go? And if I order you to stay away from the battlefield?"

I gently pushed him back onto his bedstead. "I will not be on the battlefield, silly. I shall pray for you back in the camp. And I shall be the first to congratulate you upon your victory. Please, don't make me stay in Kiev. You *need* me. I am your lucky charm."

His waxy fingers searched for mine. "All right, for God's sake. But I do not want to hear any complaints." He sighed.

"Have you ever heard me complain?" I asked, kissing his fingers. When he smiled, his lips pulled back from the gums, like on a corpse. I forced my dread back into a dark corner of my heart, like a wild animal that needed taming. Surely, this was a terrible omen for this all-decisive battle?

"No," Peter murmured, and I held his hand until he fell into a light slumber. The air in the room was stifling: despite the sticky weather Peter would insist that the fortress be heated, as he always felt cold. But just when I rose to open the window, I heard a sound behind me and spun around: Blumentrost stirred from the sofa next to the fireplace. Had he been sleeping there? He looked like a ragged old bird; his frizzy hair was pointing in all directions, and his silk neckerchief and waistcoat had slipped.

"Your Grace," he said, straightening his round glasses and bowing.

"Blumentrost. When is the tsar well enough for him to get back to his horse? Poltava is waiting."

He looked at me and ever so slightly shook his head. My smile froze and I cleared my throat. "What's happening? Share your bad news, Blumentrost. It makes it lighter to bear."

The doctor chewed on the long ends of his mustache. "I don't know what to say. Please." He pointed to the chair next to the sofa, as if I was the guest, and not him. Still, I sat down. The heat of the flames made my skin tingle and I gamely folded my hands and waited.

"His Majesty is very, very ill. He suffers from—" Blumentrost searched for words.

"From what?" I held my breath: finally, an answer! Soon, he would be healthy and I with child again. I'd give Peter what he wanted the most in this world: many, many more sons.

"He is suffering from a venereal disease." He stretched and bent his fingers through the joints.

"A venereal disease?" I repeated the words, lengthening them. "Blumentrost. I am a peasant girl, and speak neither Latin nor Greek," I snapped.

Blumentrost sighed. "All right then. If I must spell it out: the tsar has syphilis. I'm trying to treat him to the best of my knowledge, but there's no cure."

"What are the symptoms? How does the disease make itself known?" I asked, a wave of fear swelling in my stomach.

"Well, to start with, a burning feeling when urinating, blood in the excrement, pus, the—"

I raised my hand, stopping him short. "Has Peter caught the illness from me? Am I to blame for the tsar's fever?"

The German doctor smiled bitterly. "No, Your Grace. When I examined you after the last birth, you were still healthy. You are as strong as a horse, it's a miracle. No. The tsar has caught the illness from a certain Boi-Baba."

"Boi-Baba? But she is one of my maids and pregnant with the tsar's child."

"Not anymore. The tsar had her whipped after the delivery of a daughter, before banning them both to Siberia."

"He had her whipped?" I asked in disbelief, a chill chasing down my spine. "After giving birth?"

"Yes. As a punishment for her having given him the illness. Her husband and her other seven children, too, have been exiled to Siberia."

It had happened in my court, right under my nose. I read sadness and pity in Blumentrost's eyes.

I straightened. "How long has the tsar been ill? Can he be cured? Will the disease affect our children?"

He shrugged. "There is no cure. One can only slow down the course of the disease, no more. It is in God's hands. As for yet unconceived and unborn children—"

"Yes?" I asked eagerly, but he avoided my gaze.

"If Your Grace falls pregnant at all, and if there is no miscarriage in the early stages or a stillbirth, it is a miracle if any surviving children are strong and viable. But we ought to believe in miracles, oughtn't we," he added quickly.

It felt like drifting deep underwater and drowning: the surface above me lured me to light and life, but I was doomed, and incapable of ever getting there. I saw sorrow and compassion in Blumentrost's eyes, which made his words even more unbearable. I leaped to my feet and rushed to the window, tearing it open. The spring air flooded my lungs and the blue sky arched far above the dark Sea of Azov. Yet on the horizon, storm clouds gathered and smaller boats took down their sails so as to not have them shredded by the wind. The seagulls surfed in the strong east wind, piercing the air with their shrieks, mocking me with their beady eyes.

I skimmed my belly: Blumentrost did not know yet that I was pregnant again, for the sixth time. I closed my eyes and cooled my feverish forehead on the glass pane, clenching my fists: I would give the tsar a healthy son. This was perhaps my last chance to do so.

"Yes, Blumentrost," I said, turning, smiling, and gathering my dignity. "One should never cease to believe in miracles."

"Your Grace—" Blumentrost began. I merely raised a hand and then wiped a tear from my cheek. He bowed and retreated; I heard the door being gently pulled shut. Good. No one should ever again see tears running down my face.

49

The truth about the Battle of Poltava is simpler and sadder, but also much grander and more glorious, than any lore surrounding it could ever be.

I stood in the entrance of our tent on that morning in June 1709 and watched as Peter mounted his Arabian steed Finette, a gift from the Scotsman James Bruce. Clouds hung stubbornly in the sky; not even the wind, which bent the treetops, could drive them away. Menshikov held the tsar's stirrups and then kissed Peter's hand; the tsar embraced Alexander Danilovich in turn. I saw them whisper: for God and for Russia, today!

When Peter straightened and raised his arm, all of the tsar's generals as well as forty thousand soldiers kneeled like a single body. His silent gaze scanned the sea of faithful men; a gust of wind caught the red feathers of his hat before the breeze settled in the folds of his mantle, just when the sky tore open and a single ray of sunshine touched the tsar's head. I held my breath: God had blessed him. A stunned, reverent murmur rose from the throng of kneeling men, many of whom made the sign of the cross.

Finette spun and Peter drew breath. Only I knew that he had sat together with Feofan Prokopovich until late last night, writing his speech, polishing every word, until it was shiny and perfect.

"God in Heaven," Peter cried, the wind carrying his words to the very last of his men. The hairs on my neck rose and my skin prickled as I felt destiny close.

"The fate of Mother Russia is in your hands: doom or glory—men! You decide whether our country shall be free or forever enslaved by the Swedish devil. Today, you're not taking up your arms for me. Neither my vanity, nor my quest for glory send you into battle. No. God in his grace has entrusted Russia to me, Peter Alexeyevich Romanov. But the decisive moment has come, and the decision is in your hands, not mine."

Peter steadied Finette, then his voice echoed over the battlefield once more. "Do not be fooled, or scared witless. The Swedish soldiers have no miraculous powers. Their hearts beat, their blood flows, their bodies die. Everything else is a lie and there is only one truth: God is with Russia. And if I know only one thing for sure, it is this." He stopped short, and forty thousand pairs of eyes sought out him alone. "I shall give every drop of my blood for the greatness, the glory, and the fear of God of all the Russias!"

Finette reared, her eyes in her delicate head rolling, and Peter spurred her on. He raced ahead, crouching in the saddle, galloping past his men, who crossed themselves with three fingers. A hoarse cry rose to the sullen sky, and the mass of people as well as the wide horizon swallowed Peter, a vision in a flowing red cloak, embers flying from Finette's hooves. I knew: if he was to fall today, I had witnessed his finest hour.

The Generals Sheremetev, Ronne, Menshikov, and Bruce followed suit and their troops fell into step as one large body, taking up their positions against the Swedes. Only Peter, or so I later heard, was everywhere at the same time, hounding Finette across the battlefield, shouting orders, encouragement, and insults into the foaming mass of fighting men. The tsar was to be seen always, and everywhere: I am sure that only my prayers led astray the three bullets that were intended for him. One tore the felt of his hat; the second dug itself deeply into Peter's breast cross made of solid gold, rubies, and emeralds, a gift of the monks of Mount Athos; and the third bullet stuck in his saddle's wooden frame. Peter himself was unharmed, as if by a miracle.

I know nothing of the battle itself, as when the first injured soldiers were brought into the camp I was too busy with tending to wounds, ladling out dulling vodka to deal with the horror, or holding hands and drying tears of sorrow. Only once the tsar's letter, which he had hastily sent to me, was read to me, did I understand: *Catherine Alexeyevna:*

matka! *God, in His grace, has given us the victory over the king of the Swedes. We have kicked the enemy into the dust; all I want now are your kisses that congratulate me. Come immediately! In the camp, June 27, 1709, Peter Alexeyevich Romanov.*

I wept and downed a goblet of Hungarian wine together with the messenger before I neatened my plaits, washed the blood, pus, and sweat from my hands and face, took off my dirty apron, slipped into my boots, and had my horse saddled.

My horse flew over the plains in the amber light of the afternoon and I felt the child in my body stirring, strong and healthy. My son, too, was celebrating this victory of his father: yes, you should always believe in miracles, Blumentrost. I laughed in the wind, and spurred my horse on further.

Yet I shall never forget my horror at the first sight of the battlefield of Poltava. The plains outside the city's walls were covered with corpses or the maimed remains of what had once been human beings. Vultures already circled in the sky and crows cowered on the branches of the trees, waiting patiently for their turn. Wild dogs dragged body parts away, fighting over limbs. I slowed my mare, for I was afraid to trample any still-living, but wounded soldiers. Bloodstained hands reached out for me and the men begged for a word or pleaded for a sip of water, a doctor, the sight of their beloved or their mother.

One man managed to get hold of my skirt; he lay on his stomach and his breath was heavy and strangled. "Please, milady. Water," he whispered, and I got off my horse. The sight of his wounds was so sickening that I fought the bile in my throat, before searching for the water in a goat's skin in my saddlebags. When I turned, the man had died.

The bitter stench of gunpowder gathered sluggishly over the windless plain, soaking up sweat and blood and squeezing its sweet, sickening smell onto the battlefield like a sponge. I wrapped my braids over my mouth and nose so as not to breathe in the odor of a thousandfold deaths, and kept my eyes fixed on the way before me, or I would either weep or be well and truly sick. But Peter, at this moment of his greatest victory, should find me nothing but beautiful, proud, and radiant: his greatest prize.

The Swedish soldiers who lay nearest to my path, bloodied, starved, and dying, looked no better than skeletons. The Scorched Earth plan and the Russian winter had done their gruesome, thorough work, I thought, choking on tears: I knew that Peter had done what a tsar had to do, saving Russia. Still, nearly seven thousand of Charles's men had fallen that day, and three thousand others went into Russian captivity. Ten thousand men for whom, somewhere, a woman such as I waited and mourned; a daughter like mine, or a son like Alexey, were orphaned; never to know what had happened, never to receive word again. Still, at least for those prisoners the war was over, as opposed to their comrades who had fled alongside King Charles, the haunted man whom God had punished them with as a ruler: twice his horse had been shot dead underneath him, twice he had succeeded in getting away unscathed.

* * *

I spotted Peter from far away, standing tall and proud outside Poltava's walls, surrounded by his generals. A mass of prisoners knelt around him, their faces empty and exhausted, and their gaze as dull as that of animals. They were soldiers as well as the retinue of the Swedish king: servants, musicians, scribes, cooks, doctors, priests, and pharmacists. Captured Swedish flags were stuck crookedly in the ground, their proud blue and golden cloth hanging dirty and torn in the slowly settling haze of dusk.

Peter spotted me and waved, excited like a child: his hair was disheveled, his mantle torn, and the blue sash around his chest, with the diamond Saint Andrew's Order still attached to it, sullied by blood and smoke. His face, too, was blackened by soot and mud, but his blue eyes beamed with pride and joy as he embraced me, before pulling me to the Swedish troops. "Come, look at this, *matka*. What a loot, eh? A marshal, ten general majors, fifty-nine senior officers, and eleven hundred simple officers. And to top it all off, the minister Piper himself." He seized a small, bald man by the scruff of his neck and forced him to his feet. Piper barely came to Peter's elbow; he kept his eyes squeezed shut and trembled with the fear of death. "Charles's chief minister. Well, Piper, we'll find something for a smart man like you to do. Many streets have to be paved in Saint Petersburg, don't they, Catherinushka? Or shall we send him to the mines in Siberia?" Peter kissed me and I tasted leather, sweat, and gunpowder. The Swedish officers averted their eyes—they themselves had been separated for so many years from their families and their beloved—but Peter cried, "Look, you damn Swedes. This is the kind of woman who will bring victory to a man."

Then his gaze fell on the Swedish marshal, who knelt like all the others. Peter frowned. "Are you Marshal Rehnskjöld?"

The man understood his name, and nodded, seeming hesitant and confused.

"Get up," Peter shouted at him. "On your feet, Swedish swine!"

The Swede looked confused but stumbled to his feet. Silence fell, and all eyes turned toward the tsar and the Swedish marshal, who had fooled Peter for so many years and who had made him suffer throughout the campaign, defeating his army left, right, and center. Sheremetev and Bruce exchanged a worried glance and I folded my hands in silent prayer. Please, God, let Peter not sully his glory, his joy, and his victory through a vile, moody crime, I pleaded. The battle was over; killing Rehnskjöld now would be heinous murder. The marshal met Peter's eyes calmly.

"Now kneel again," the tsar snarled.

Goose bumps formed on my arms as Rehnskjöld obeyed, disdain on his face. He was ready to meet his maker, having always fulfilled his duty, however high the price to pay.

I dared not breathe: even the wind had ceased and clouds moved in front of the setting sun. First campfires were lit on the hills around the city, and the air reeked even more of smoke and death as Peter slowly drew his bloodstained sword from its sheath, which I myself had embroidered for him in Kiev. The last rays of sunshine caught on the steel, making it sparkle, as he raised the weapon high above his head.

Rehnskjöld had his eyes closed, and his lips moved. I recognized the Lord's Prayer, which I had so often recited in the Glucks' house.

Peter! I wanted to plead but bit my tongue.

The tsar lifted the marshal's head by his hair, forcing his eyes open. "Rehnskjöld. Do you know how much you have made Russia suffer? A warrior like you is rarely born. In Narva one of your bullets just missed me narrowly," he growled.

I wiped my moist hands on my skirt. When the marshal replied, his eyes were as blue as the skies over Saint Petersburg, and he spoke quietly in the language of Johann: "I ask God for forgiveness for my sins. I'm ready for death, Tsar Peter."

His voice was full of fatigue and Sheremetev closed his eyes, ashen-faced. Menshikov crossed himself with three fingers. Rehnskjöld turned and said some last, encouraging words to his men, then he lowered his head. Some of the Swedes sobbed, burying their faces in their hands.

Peter raised his sword high and higher, but then paused, and took one of the marshal's limp hands, closing his fingers around the sword's pommel. "Take my sword as a sign of my appreciation, Marshal Rehnskjöld. You are a true soldier."

Marshal Rehnskjöld, the fearless hero of countless battles, sank to the ground, dropped the sword, buried his face in the damp, dewy grass, and cried like a child, his shoulders heaving. None of his men dared to touch him, but looked on in mute shock. Menshikov, Bruce, and Sheremetev relaxed, and I laced my fingers through Peter's.

He shrugged and shook his head. "Really. The Swedes are softer than I had thought. What is his problem?"

50

We rode slowly back to the camp and the surviving men followed us in the dying light of the day in a more or less orderly train, together with thousands of ragged, limping, and starving Swedish prisoners. As I had one last look at Poltava, people poured out of the besieged city's gates to plunder the corpses and the mortally wounded, even breaking gold teeth out of a dead man's mouth. Vultures and crows circled high in the sky, ready for a fat meal.

Our camp was lit and people were singing, dancing, and clapping, celebrating the victory. Peter had barrel upon barrel opened, serving wine, beer, and vodka to his men, and Felten robbed the cellars of the town and the barns of the surrounding villages empty to roast enough oxen, lambs, pigs, and chickens and find enough salt fish, cabbage, and flour. At the table, Peter threw away his cutlery and grabbed my greasy hands, holding them up for all to see. "Tonight, we shall eat only with our hands. If I catch one of you carving with his knife, he will be in trouble. Have I made myself clear?" Then he kissed me and served me a crackling piece of pork, dripping with gravy and stuffed with fruit.

The Swedes sat in our midst like islands in a raging sea: they reminded me of Johann, and his gentle manners. None of them farted or burped while they ate, nor did they spit on the ground, but politely turned to the side to pick food out of their teeth. To have a good laugh that evening I had Felten, who hated the Swedes, play the role of the Swedish king. The humiliation drove tears of anger into his eyes and

Peter laughed so much that he fell off his chair, pulling everything from the table in an enormous racket.

In the early-morning hours, when the soldiers and generals clung exhaustedly to their pillows and chairs, Peter handed out the spoils to the victors: Sheremetev got more land and souls around Kiev, and Shafirov—"My favorite little Jew"—was made vice chancellor, a count, and each of his daughters was to marry a prince. Shafirov kissed the tsar's knees, which made Menshikov even more jealous than he already was, but I calmed him, winking and saying, "Alexander Danilovich, surely the light of Peter's grace shines brightly enough for all of us?" Though the more Menshikov got, the more he wanted—such was his nature. Peter himself was promoted as well, and he kissed me. "Now you are the companion of a vice admiral. Are you proud of me?"

In the morning, the child in my body was quiet. I thought of Blumentrost's words and clenched my fists: the infant was my prince of Poltava, a miracle in himself. We left Poltava two days later, as the surrounding land and villages could no longer feed our army, and the stench of death and decay suffocated all merriment in our tents.

* * *

The victorious soldiers of Poltava entered the Red Square in a whirl of thick snowflakes, the ice mirroring their triumph. I myself was not to stand on the balcony of the Kremlin on that day, as I was to give birth in Kolomenskoye. "Give me a healthy son to celebrate Poltava. Please!" he had whispered as he helped me from the sled, tears in his eyes. Moscow was alight with life and joy, and waiting for the hour of birth bored me to tears. I messed up my embroideries and drew figures in the ice crystals on the windows.

So I only heard about Peter riding into the Red Square on Finette, who was adorned with leopard fur, red velvet, shining leather, and a silver bridle. Behind him marched his regiments and his generals, followed by the endless stream of Swedish prisoners, half-mad with fear and worry, and the captured three hundred flags, the weight of the thirty-six Swedish cannons. The crowds were beside themselves; boyars and wealthy merchants such as Peter's friend Count Stroganov invited the tsar and his generals to their houses—Peter and his men never refused. Seven thousand candles burned, each of them seven feet high, and seven triumphal arches had been raised. Once Peter had crossed underneath them all, he reached the throne, where his old crony, the fake Prince Caesar sat, his hair and shoulders covered with snow. Peter laid his hand upon his heart. "With the help of God and the grace of Your Majesty, I have won the victory for Russia at Poltava." The Swedish soldiers thought they had now become completely mad: Who was the tsar, after all? The man in the rough, worn uniform whom they had met in Poltava, or the toad of a man who sat painted and adorned on the throne, giving his court of fools and jesters the sign for the feast to begin?

Daria later told me that the master of ceremonies had to cross the hall on horseback, as there were so many guests, and the colorful ceiling of the Kremlin's festival hall was destroyed, as the men shot round upon round of salute into the air instead of having fireworks.

What she did not tell me, though, others did: Praskovia's daughter, Peter's pretty and nubile niece, Tsarevna Jekaterina Ivanovna, would not leave the tsar's side. Perhaps he was right: it was good to marry those girls off sooner than later.

* * *

A most violent labor began. During the long hours of pain I clung to the curtains of my bed or kicked the midwife who tried to soothe me. When I felt the delivery close, Blumentrost shouted, "Quick, my God, quick! He is lying the wrong way around. I feel the feet." The room went black: I fainted, which mercifully veiled the pain for a couple of seconds. When I came to, I saw Blumentrost's fat hands holding my child's perfect wiggling body to the dull light and the frosty air of a Moscow winter day. A hoarse, strong scream tore through the exhausted, stifling silence of the room. I laughed, and stroked my damp, wet hair from my sweaty, sticky forehead. "He is to be named Peter, like his father!"

Daria busied herself with bed linen and Alexandra Tolstoya washed her bloodstained hands in a porcelain bowl full of warm water, avoiding my eyes. Blumentrost, the ass, turned to the window, checking the child, and then wrapped it in clean linen. He turned and it looked at me, its eyes deep and blue. "I'm afraid that's not possible, Your Grace. It's a girl. A wonderful, healthy little daughter for our tsar."

It took me almost a week before I would hold Elizabeth in my arms. Peter, however, was beside himself with joy at her birth, calling her his little princess of Poltava. She fed her wet nurse empty, was soon as strong as none of my other children had been, and loudly refused to let herself be swaddled.

51

Things were looking up for Russia, as after Poltava, Tolstoy not only negotiated a new peace treaty with the Turks, but also dismissed the rumors that the wounded Charles of Sweden was hiding at the sultan's court as nonsense.

I was in the storage rooms of the Kremlin together with Pavel Jagushinsky to choose furniture for the new Winter Palace in Saint Petersburg, which was still bare, its rooms vast and our steps in the corridors echoing. Jagushinsky made careful note of every chest of drawers, chair, and mirror I liked, though it wasn't too much. Peter's hate for the Kremlin as much as his love for all things new, shiny, and European made for the happiness of many a carpenter in France, Italy, and Germany.

Just before leaving, I spotted a painting that was half-covered with white linen, like a shroud. I frowned. "Is that not the portrait of the German princess that the tsarevich is to marry?"

"Indeed," said Jagushinsky, all of a sudden eager to pack up his scroll and quill.

Not so fast, my friend, I thought, and ordered, "Take the cover off. Why is it here, and not in his apartment, as ordered? He is to get used to her face, pretty as it is," I added.

"The tsarevich ordered for it to be brought here," the master of Peter's household said, sweat beads on his face despite the chill in the storage rooms. I just waved at his helper, who, with one sweeping gesture, made the shroud drop.

I gasped: someone had drawn a horrid mustache above the

princess's lovely moist lips and disfigured her rosy skin with black spots. Worst of all, the canvas was cut all over.

"What has happened?" I asked, stunned.

"The tsarevich practiced his knife-throwing skills on the portrait," said Jagushinsky.

"Does the tsar know?"

"No. Of course not." Jagushinsky mopped his sweat, as anyone would who had hidden this happening from Peter. He'd thrash him with his *dubina,* all right.

"Try to have it cleaned and mended. Then bring it back to his rooms. The talks of the match are proceeding," I ordered.

"Thank you, Your Grace," said Jagushinsky, bowing out of the room backward.

What else, I wondered when I left, was going on that Peter and I knew nothing about?

* * *

At the feast for the name day of Saint Alexander Nevsky in Menshikov's new palace, Peter asked me, "Look carefully at the three daughters of Tsaritsa Praskovia, the widow of my half brother, Ivan. I want a European prince for each of them."

Menshikov had spared no expense for his new palace and Peter was delighted with its splendor. The building on Vasilyevsky Island was the most glorious in the city, laid out with Persian silk, Italian marble, Lybian cedars, Siberian gold, Chinese lacquer work and wallpaper, Delft tiles, African ivory, and English silver. In Menshikov's library, three librarians constantly took care of the thirteen thousand volumes, of which he himself could not read a single one, as well as of his unique collection of maps. The walls of the staircases, the corridors, and the hundreds of private and public rooms and halls were covered with tapestries, trophies, and countless paintings that he bought abroad by the shipload: icons made of silver and gold as well as painted portraits. Daria led me through the long, mirrored passages before the banquet, chatting and giggling as if not a moment had passed since Marienburg, and I saw some flattering paintings of myself and countless ones of Peter at every age.

Finally, Daria stopped, showing me an almost hidden row of smaller paintings. "This is the wall of my grief," she said, and I saw the little faces of her deceased sons, Paul Samson and Peter Lukas. A third child-hood picture showed the delicate, rosy face of her daughter, who was just then bedridden with a high fever. Daria hastily dried her tears, for Peter did not tolerate any grief or sadness on a holiday. I had pleaded for Daria to be allowed to stay away, but in vain. So we walked on, looking absentmindedly at pictures, such as the painting of a naked, beautiful girl holding up a decapitated head and laughing triumphantly. With her round cheeks and dark braids she reminded me of the Ivanovna prin-cesses, whom I should now take a closer look at while we were at dinner.

Menshikov struck the floor with his diamond-studded cane and the first course was carried into the hall; Peter drank from his eagle cup and burped before eyeing the princesses Ivanovna, who wore just about ev-erything they had been able to find in their wardrobe. No wonder the French and Spanish ambassadors had had a good giggle upon seeing them! Still, I moved my long fan made of gray ostrich feathers, ivory, and mother-of-pearl more rapidly: no one should laugh at a Russian princess.

Peter smacked his sticky lips. "Well, which of those girls shall we give to the young Duke of Courland? He is a nephew of the king of Prus-sia. Is there a better way to consolidate our conquests of the Baltics— God bless the day when I set my foot on your land—than marriage?"

Just then, Praskovia's eldest daughter, Jekaterina, rose as smoothly as a cat and came to us, hips swaying and silk skirts rustling. She settled on Peter's lap and took his own cup to her lips. "To a long and healthy life, my victorious uncle." She smiled, her eyes as dark and shiny as sour cherries. She drank and Peter laughed, placing both his hands on her bosom and kissing her naked neck. She wiggled most invitingly, while I pretended to talk to Menshikov.

"By God, it's no wonder I forget too often that you are my niece," Peter said huskily.

"Well, my father was just your half brother." Jekaterina gasped as Peter sucked her swelling flesh in the low-cut dress. I moved my fan, feeling all eyes on me. Of course, Peter had other women, but him being so open in his favor, in my presence, was a novelty. I read the curiosity in people's eyes. Were my days of favor over? Was there a new mistress to be reckoned with?

I tried to keep my calm, but Menshikov stroked his fine mustache that he now sported and murmured, "Watch the little bird. She'd love to be the tsar's wife and order her mother and sisters around. It wouldn't be the first time that a tsar married a so-called close relative. Who knows who really sired those girls? Certainly not Ivan the Idiot."

Jekaterina slipped her hand between Peter's legs. He moaned, until I leaped and dug my nails into her flesh, pulling her hand away. "We are not in a brothel, but in Alexander Danilovich's palace. He was just wondering about a suitable bride for the Duke of Courland," I said.

"Hm, what?" asked Peter, breathing heavily.

Jekaterina eyed me coldly, but Menshikov bobbed his head under his heavy, powdered wig. "If we want to prove the sincerity of our bond to the king of Prussia, we should give his nephew, the Duke of Courland, our most beautiful princess. That would be you then, Tsarevna Jekaterina Ivanovna." He beamed.

Jekaterina stuck her tongue out at Menshikov and pressed herself against Peter's chest. "Dearest Father-Uncle, I only want to give children to Russia. Many, many sons. My mother has proven how fertile we are." She shot me a triumphant look. "I'll be unhappy all my life if I have to leave you, my tsar," she chirped, tousling Peter's hair.

I clenched my fists to stop myself scratching the princess's pink face to shreds. "Fertile? Yes, my princess, your mother bore nothing but daughters," I said cattily.

Peter stopped our smoldering quarrel. "You might be right, Menshikov. But I think we can do better for Jekaterina here," he said, and he embraced her, while studying her mother and sisters: Praskovia just smacked her second daughter Anna hard and pulled her by the hair. Peter grinned and made his decision: "Anna Ivanovna should go. She is to be duchess of Courland. And lovely Jekaterina and I, Alekasha, will visit your galleries together."

Menshikov laughed uneasily, and I smiled serenely, as Peter and Jekaterina left. The sounds coming from the hall's entrance soon after told me that Peter was not even waiting for the darkness of the corridors before he honored Jekaterina Ivanovna with his attentions. I would not look.

The night in the Summer Palace when Peter had promised me his hand, and the closeness we had felt then, seemed like a distant dream.

* * *

Tsarevna Anna Ivanovna was a proud young bride. The Duke of Courland, nephew to the king of Prussia, had originally asked for portraits of all the three Ivanovna princesses, Peter's nieces, but was satisfied with Peter's choice—Anna was a tall brunette with rosy cheeks and dark, radiant eyes—and even more so with his bride's dowry of two hundred thousand rubles. The duke immediately repaid his gambling debts.

On their wedding day, a first layer of thin ice glistened on the Neva and the air was crackling with the promise of snow. Peter and I visited Anna Ivanovna as she was being dressed by her sisters for the ceremony.

Jekaterina just lifted her sister's hair from the nape of her neck and beamed at Peter. "My tsar, what an honor for my sister: What else can a woman desire than to be a happy bride? May God give her many sons."

I felt like slapping her: oh, I would make sure that the young tsarevna got married soon! She was like a bitch in heat, and Peter came ever more rarely, and if so only very halfheartedly, into my bed. What if she, a tsarevna of royal blood, bore him a son?

Peter kissed Jekaterina on both cheeks before also cupping her sister's face. "Anna Ivanovna. You must honor Russia and your dead father, my beloved brother, Tsar Ivan, in your marriage. You marry for your country: keep faith, love your new home, and obey your husband."

"I shall, dearest Father-Uncle," the bride sobbed.

Peter led her up the aisle of the church of the Peter and Paul Fortress. Our breath hung in clouds on our lips as we prayed and chanted, but when the ceremony was to begin, the pope held up his prayer book and said with a trembling voice: "I shall not carry out this marriage, for reasons of faith."

"What is the matter?" The young duke looked nervously at the Prussian ambassador, who rolled his eyes. Nothing here surprised him anymore, I felt.

Anna Ivanovna sobbed, bewildered, and Praskovia rushed to her. "My dove, my little sunshine. Don't worry," I heard her cooing.

Peter rose, grabbed the pope by the collar, and drew his *dubina*. "And why is that, you cursed little pope?" he thundered.

The man bravely spoke up. "In the name of the Holy Russian Church, I refuse to marry a tsarevna with a disbeliever. This is blasphemy and against our law."

"The law? I am the law!" Peter shouted, his voice echoing as he beat the pope twice over the head. Blood dripped onto the colorful marble of the altar and Anna Ivanovna gasped. I crossed myself but Peter threw the pope at his guard. "Scourge him. Thirty lashes for insulting the tsar of all the Russias in front of foreign dignitaries." The Prussian ambassador looked as if he wanted to speak up for the pope, but then changed his mind, seeing Peter's anger.

The bride was in shock: the tears left ugly marks on her carefully made-up, chalk-white face. "Blood on the altar. What a horrid omen for my marriage," she cried. I offered her smelling salts, but Praskovia scolded her. "Pull yourself together—"

"Menshikov!" Peter looked around. "Bring me one of your popes. But warn him of what will happen if he refuses to marry my niece with the German duke."

* * *

All Russian customs had disappeared from the very joyful wedding feast: men and women mingled and instead of the traditional *kournik,* a multilayered dome-shaped pie made of bread crust stuffed with candied fruit, there was a giant cake that looked like Peter's new Winter Palace. We danced through the night and splendid fireworks etched the flaming coats of arms of the Romanovs and the House of Courland into the sleeping skies. The young duke was too drunk to do his marital duty. Three days later, when the newlyweds climbed into their sled to travel to Courland, the new duchess was all wails and embraces with her sisters and mother, with whom she had almost always fought. The hooves of the strong ponies tethered to their sled struck sparks on the hard ice of the Neva pier and colorful flags waved them good-bye in the fresh morning breeze.

But only three days later, Anna Ivanovna, the young duchess of Courland, was back with us in Saint Petersburg, as a widow. Fifty miles away from Saint Petersburg her husband had felt unwell and had gotten out of the sled, where he fell headfirst into the snow and suffocated on his bile under the horrified screams of his helpless young wife.

52

"Tolstoy is certainly the greediest of my ambassadors." Peter snorted, crumpling up Tolstoy's latest letter. "This is the third petition he has sent in a week. Is he not kept busy enough with shopping at the slave market of Constantinople?" Peter chucked the paper ball among other papers, plans, and *ukazy*. "He always wants more gold, more silver, and more sable furs. Either the greed of the sultan at the Golden Gate knows no boundaries, or Peter Andreyevich fills his own pockets."

I rolled on my belly, nibbling on warm *pirogi* filled with *smetana*, nuts, and honey. My pillows in front of the fireplace, where I kept myself busy looking at drawings of new dresses, were soft, but when the logs in the fire fell into each other my lapdog startled. "Silly," I said, and kissed him on his damp muzzle. Peter circled me like an eagle in the sky; I was watching his scruffy boots with the rundown heels and scraped tips coming and going when Peter suddenly stopped and clenched his fists.

He sighed. "I just can't do this on my own anymore. So be it, then. The accursed French and English are right. I shall follow suit."

"What are they right about? Come here to me," I said, patting one of the pillows. Peter rested his head on my shoulder and my lips tasted the cold sweat on his forehead while I tousled his hair. He suffered, and I felt like chasing that quack Blumentrost away to find a proper doctor, one who could heal the tsar.

"I simply cannot rule Russia alone anymore." Peter sighed. "This yoke crushes me."

My fingers halted in their caress. "What does that mean?" I asked, my voice unsteady. Peter had never said anything of this sort before. He certainly didn't mean that it was time for Alexey to ascend to the throne. Did he want to marry a foreign princess? A young woman who could give him sons and always had sound advice to give? His niece Jekaterina's sweet indulgence, as well as her steady demands for clothes and jewelry, had started to bore him, this much I knew. Peter gave gladly, but he would not be asked to do so. In the past few months he had returned to my bed, but at thirty-five I would not fall pregnant so easily anymore.

"In former times, Russia was easy to rule. It was like a simple hut, but now my realm is a palace, with corridors, stories, stairs, and towers. I feel like a boy who has to clear a huge forest with a penknife."

"What do you want to do?" If it was too much for Peter, who on Earth could bear it?

He looked into the flames. "I need a senate. Russia needs many men who lead it, not just one."

"A senate? What is that?" That word sounded better to me than another princess's name. From a small Venetian vial I poured rose oil into my palms and gently rubbed Peter's temples. The fragrance, scented with the last summer, filled the air.

Peter sighed with pleasure. "A group of men who will help me govern Russia; but not men who are chosen just because of their high birth."

"Will they have real power? Isn't that dangerous for you?"

Peter laughed. "My clever, cunning Catherinushka. Of course, only just as much power as I think fit. But they are to find new, fitting laws and enforce them. Complaints about greedy and unjust courts have been flooding in lately." He paused briefly, grinning. "And the senate is going to find me money. Lots of it, for new recruits, for new alliances, for Saint Petersburg. Whoever opens up the most sources of money is the best senator."

"Do we need more money?" I thought of the sheer magnificence with which Peter had furnished our Winter Palace. He twisted my curls around his fingers.

"The tsar always needs money. Though he is never short of it as long as he still has Russia and the Russians. What belongs to them, belongs to me, and I can use it as I see fit. But a senate will be my eyes and my ears."

"And if the senate agrees on something you do not want?" I asked.

"No senator shall ever trust the other. Only hungry bellies and free spirits make for rebellious hearts." The muscles in his neck tensed again and he rubbed his head briefly on my shoulder. "I'd really like to stay here. But I must write the *ukaz* right now."

He stood on the threshold of the secret door hidden in the wallpaper, which allowed him to slip unseen to and from my apartments, when there was a soft knock. Peter raised his eyebrows. "Do you expect a secret visitor, Catherinushka?" he teased me. As I padded to the door, the rugs felt warm under my bare soles. Who could that be?

When I opened the door, the guard helped an exhausted messenger to keep upright. His breath was still flying from his long, hard ride, his cloak was covered with mud and ice crystals, and from his boots filthy, snowy slush melted onto the shimmering marble floor of the Winter Palace. He hit his chest with his fist. "My tsar. An urgent message from the Golden Gate."

"Does Tolstoy want even more gold and sable? Well, tell him that he can't search a naked man's pockets," Peter growled.

The man looked at us, his eyes burning. "It is too late for that. Charles of Sweden is at the High Porte. Tolstoy tried to win the sultan's favor, but in vain. He did not have the means to do it."

Peter pulled the messenger into the room, grabbing him hard. "That is impossible: If Tolstoy did not have the means, what means did Charles have after fleeing Poltava as poor as a church mouse?"

The man almost cried. "That is what we thought. But the king saved his war chest: he is swimming in gold, and furthermore, the brothers Cook of the English Levantine society have lent him money."

"And?" Peter asked, his eyes dark and beady with anger.

"The sultan fears the growing Russian influence at the Black Sea: you are much too close for his comfort in Azov. In the end, Tolstoy forced the sultan to choose; Russia or Sweden."

I bit my lips: nothing good ever came from forcing someone to choose, and sure enough, the messenger carried on. "The sultan replied with impossible conditions, such as handing back the Baltics and Saint Petersburg to the Swedes."

Peter snapped a quill with anger. "This fat toad of Constantinople. I hope Tolstoy gave him the right answer?"

"He did." The messenger sounded meek.

"And?" Peter continued. "What happened?"

"The sultan has locked Tolstoy in the Castle of the Seven Towers."

Peter cursed under his breath.

"What does that mean?" I whispered, looking from one man to the other.

Peter turned to me. "That, Catherinushka, means war on two fronts, everything any leader should ever avoid." He groaned, but then cheered up. "But Russia will not be crushed. Never! Come to Turkey with me. I'll roast the sultan on a small flame and give you the biggest emerald that Constantinople has to offer."

On the same day on which Russia got a senate, it also was at war with the Golden Gate of Constantinople.

53

O h, of course, his whore of a washermaid is going with him . . ."
The timing of Tsarevna Jekaterina Ivanovna's words was ill chosen; they fell like stones into a well into the content silence among the
small circle of people meeting up in Praskovia's house. The servants
were just clearing the second course, and the musicians were retuning
their instruments. The other guests, Peter's closest friends and family,
had been wiping their greasy fingers, and leaned back on the soft pillows. The princess blushed to the roots of her hair when she realized
that we all had heard her.

Peter, who had just been arguing with Shafirov and Sheremetev
about how to raise the funds for the Turkish campaign, looked up. His
mood had not been the best in the past few days, as of all his allies only
Prince Dmitri Kantemir of Moldova agreed to follow him south. Jekaterina must have felt his gaze as heavily as a galley slave feels the whip.
No one in the room dared to breathe; the air was crackling with fear.

Peter looked at me as the public humiliation of Jekaterina's words
made my tears well up. He gently took my hand, and our daughters,
Anna and Elizabeth, too, were trying to comfort me as little girls would,
cooing and caressing me.

Peter rose. "Praskovia, widowed tsaritsa of Russia," he said, and
Praskovia knelt with difficulty on her pillow, adjusting the folds of her
flesh. "My tsar," she murmured, her forehead touching the artfully laid
honey-colored parquet.

"Yes. On your knees—all tsarevny Ivanovna and the duchess of

Courland as well," Peter ordered. The young women obeyed, pale with fright.

Peter led me over to them. "Tsaritsa Praskovia, my sister-in-law. Tsarevny of Russia, my nieces. You are the highest *damy* in my country. I have honored you all my life. But the time has come—" He paused. The princesses were scared witless, not knowing what to expect. What would Peter do: Shave their heads and commit them to a nunnery, or banish them to Siberia? The youngest tsarevna Ivanovna, who was of a simple mind with a flat, pancake-like face, sobbed with fear.

Peter gave me a tender glance. "The time has come to declare my beloved companion, Catherine Alexeyevna, the mother of my daughters Anna and Elizabeth, as the highest lady at the court. Everyone— you, as well as my people—should recognize her as such." He raised his voice and his words echoed in the hall: "Should I not find the time to marry her before the Turkish campaign, or should I fall, so listen to me: Catherine Alexeyevna is henceforward tsaritsa of Russia. To insult her is to insult me. Makarov, write that down," he ordered the scribe, who had already sent one of his men for paper and pen.

I could hardly breathe when Peter blessed me, and before he could prevent it, I fell to my knees. "By God," I whispered, holding his gaze and his fingers, "I will do justice to this honor."

"You better." Peter grinned, then pulled me to my feet and rejoiced. "Music! Is this a betrothal or a funeral? Lazy buggers. Bring the sparkling wine from France. And woe to the one who leaves the room before he is allowed to."

The musicians played a merry tune and Peter bowed before me. "May I ask you for this dance?" he asked, unusually gallantly, before he dabbed my cheeks with a somewhat clean lace handkerchief. "Please stop crying, *matka*. You should be nothing but happy when the tsar declares you his companion and the highest lady in Russia."

That, though, only made me cry more, and I would not calm down all evening.

*   *   *

When I had my chests for the Turkish campaign packed, Anna and Elizabeth were playing hide-and-seek in my rooms. Both girls were tall and strong for their age, but the younger Elizabeth always bullied Anna in one way or the other and I heard her maid of honor cry: "Lizenka. Stop pulling Anoushka by the hair, will you?"

The choice to be with them or with their father, was, as always, terrible, but despite the honors that Peter had heaped on me, life with him was like a walk on the first, brittle ice of the Neva in the early winter. It might carry me on to shining joy and glory; it might also break and allow the black, icy water to swallow me forever.

* * *

Russia had to reach the Danube before the Turks invaded Poland and Moldova, and Peter urged Sheremetev and his troops on. When we left Saint Petersburg in March, a banner with the Holy Cross and the words of Saint Constantine blazed over our heads: *With this sign we are victorious.* Along with Peter and me rode Prince Dmitri Kantemir of Moldavia and his five thousand men, who were hardened by the harsh weather of their mountains.

Next to the prince, a little girl sat on her pony: I had never seen such a beautiful child, with hair the color of a honeycomb and skin like hewn gold. Her eyes were of a curious amber color, but as bright as those of a sled dog, and she held herself upright like a real princess. Peter, too, stared at the child, who might have been eight or nine years old.

"Who is that, Prince Dmitri? War is no place for children. Even women have a hard time convincing me of the necessity of their presence in the field." He winked at me.

Prince Kantemir smiled. "This is my daughter, Princess Maria Kantemir. There is no one at home I could trust enough to leave her there."

"How beautiful she is." Peter stared at the girl, and his look was that of a man to a woman. Maria Kantemir spurred her pony and left the tsar of all the Russias to swallow her dust. His gaze followed her until she had disappeared from our view.

* * *

The early spring sun was burning the meager seeds on the otherwise fertile fields, which worsened the famine after the failed harvests of the previous year. Furthermore, the Ukraine had still not recovered from a plague of locusts. The anger of the people, from whom we took what little they had left, followed us like a curse, but we had to save Russia, even if that meant feeding thousands of men and horses in a famished country. When we reached the Dniester, our wagons were stuck in the torrents or washed away; many horses drowned, and whole charges of gunpowder were soaked and rendered useless. On the other side, the landscape changed to a sea of blistering-hot sand. Its utter desolation swept away our last grasp of reality: our soldiers suffered from sunstroke; hunger and thirst caused hallucinations and nosebleeds. Our troops were beaten by the terrain before they had even fought.

We placed all our hopes on the fertile valley of the river Pruth, which we reached in early summer. Here we could recover from the violent march, we thought, and the evening on which we celebrated the memory of Poltava on the banks of the Pruth was one of the rare happy moments of the Turkish campaign. Peter and I emptied a barrel of sweet Tokay and rolled in the dunes, laughing and gasping, our pores filling with sun and sand. My skin was tanned, my hair was streaked with light, and my body was as lean and supple as before my pregnancies. I took the trouble to dress, groom, and adorn myself carefully for Peter: as always, I had taken all my jewelry along.

We tried in vain to locate the Turkish army. Had those cowards even left Constantinople? Our spies and messengers did not return and we grew all giddy and lighthearted: ha! The cowardly Turk had crawled back into the hole in which he belonged.

"A pity about the emerald I wanted to cut off the fat sultan's neck for you." Peter sighed.

"Oh? Who says you can't still give it to me?" I teased him, and we fell asleep at the table that night, blissfully unaware of what lay ahead of us.

* * *

Instead of the first rays of sunlight the shrill sound of trumpets, the hooting of war horns, and Sheremetev scrambling into the tent woke us: "The Turks! We are surrounded. They are thousands and thousands strong, and well armed . . ." he cried.

Peter tucked his dirty shirt into his trousers while stumbling out of the tent, and I blinked in disbelief at the glowing brightness and the turmoil in the camp. Men were running and screaming everywhere when I stepped out into the day. I held my breath: Was the sight cruel or glorious? We were not surrounded but squashed and lost. Our forty thousand men, who had seemed so mighty in Saint Petersburg, faced almost three times as many Turks and Tartars: it was a sea of soldiers, foaming with hostility. The crescent moon blazed on thousands of red flags, dancing like devils in the hot wind. All the way up to the horizon I saw nothing but soldiers, who looked terrifying with their heavy cutlasses, the shining metal of their breastplates, and the rough skins tied around their shoulders and calves. In their midst, on an elevated litter with pillows and carpets, an incredibly fat man sat under a canopy, as still as an idol. He was covered with jewels, sparkling like a statue in the sun. This must be the sultan.

"Holy Mother. What shall we do?" Peter breathed.

Sheremetev shrugged helplessly as Peter gathered himself.

"To the weapons," he shouted, and shoved Sheremetev. "Take position! Go, go, go! Do you think we have all the time in the world? The tsar is not a sitting duck. I am the Russian bear, who fights and strikes back, until defeat and death." He ran into the tent, calling for his sword, for his armor, for Finette to be saddled.

I embraced Sheremetev; his lean body was shaking with dry sobs. In the past two years he had known neither rest nor respite. "Be brave, Boris Petrovich," I whispered. "Fight. Russia depends on it." I owed him my life at Peter's side and if I saw him today for the very last time, I had to give him strength. "Thank you, for everything," I said. "May God protect you." My heart ached: how very small and helpless the field marshal looked before that wall of Ottomans, running off for his horse and sword. The Turks blew a call to arms into their long trumpets made of shiny metal and soldiers struck large drums: their roll made my skin prickle with fear, as a ferocious and roaring war cry rose to the sky.

In the tent, Peter dictated his last words while being clad in his armor.

"Write, Makarov. 'We, Peter Alexeyevich, by the grace of God tsar of all the Russias, decide the following. Should I be taken prisoner by the Turks, I am no longer the tsar. No ruble shall be paid and no drop of blood shall be shed to save me. If I should fall, give the throne to the most worthy of my descendants.'" He shook his head, thinking about his words. "Even if that's just this damned useless sod of Alexey . . ."

"*Batjushka! Starik!* Don't even think of that!" I cried, and he cupped my face before kissing me hard, and passionately. He looked at me with burning eyes. "At least I have proven myself to you just before our departure. Thank you for all the strength you gave me, *matka*. Thank you, always." He left: the tent flap knocked against the posts and I was alone, kneeling, crumbling under the fear and the pressure and digging my hands into the hot desert, which seared my heart. The sands of the Pruth were the handful of earth which was to fall upon our grave.

* * *

The battle reached me but faintly in the following hours, for I had had a solid dose of laudanum dissolved in wine but, despite my dazed stupor, I clasped a dagger. If I had to, I would defend myself against any incoming Turk, or go out and fight for Peter's life.

54

I woke in darkness. It was a cloudy night and the moon was new, so I needed to touch the pillow next to me to reach out for Peter. It was empty. Outside, the silence was ghostly, and more threatening than any noise that had gone before. My heartbeat was still slow while my thoughts somersaulted. With unsteady fingers I reached for the dagger on the rug in front of my bed and sat up, still feeling dizzy from the laudanum: I had overdone it. How could I have expected to fight in this state? I stumbled to my feet and heard murmurs from outside the tent. Was that Russian or Turkish? Had we lost or won? I wrapped a warm scarf around my shoulders, stepped into the frosty desert night, and almost choked on the stench of despair, death, and blood. My foot struck something that could only be a corpse. I cried out, but all of a sudden a hand was pressed onto my mouth, almost suffocating me. I caught Peter's scent, and dropped the dagger, relieved. His grip loosened and I wanted to embrace him.

"Peter," I whispered.

But he seized my wrists. "We must flee, Catherinushka. Russia has been defeated. Our horses are ready, and we have a guide to help us cross the riverbed. Put on your boots and take your jewels with you. We'll need them to make our way back," he said hoarsely, just as a breeze carried the stench of the battlefield to us, thicker and even more sickening than before. It was as unbearable as the words he had just spoken. I squinted into the darkness: Peter was still in his dirty, torn uniform, booted and ready to mount. The tsar of all the Russias wanted to give heel like a boy who had lost a bet in bear-baiting? What had happened to the brave words he had dictated to Makarov? This was a nightmare. Even Charles of Sweden, our fierce, deadly enemy, would always choose death instead of a shameful peace. I glanced at the so-called knowledgeable Cossack guide, a small, wiry man who chewed on a betel nut. In the moonlight his eyes gleamed like the fires with which beach robbers lured ships to the cliffs. I would not trust that man with a round of moldy cheese, let alone my life, and crossed my arms.

"No," I said.

Peter was stunned. "What? Come on! We need the cover of the night. Lucky that it is so cloudy. No one will see us!"

"Have we surrendered to the sultan?"

Peter nodded sullenly. "We had no other choice."

"So what?" I insisted. "The Turks probably don't even understand what they did to you. What do they know about our supplies? Our General Ronne is already in Braila with his men. From there he'll easily cut off the Turks' retreat."

"Woman," hissed Peter. "You have no idea."

"Oh yes, I do." I gave one of Peter's guards a sign. He rammed his fist between the Cossack guide's chest and belly, making the man groan and double over with pain. "Good. Make sure nobody ever learns why he was here," I ordered, handing the soldier my dagger. The man dragged the guide away, gagging him with his sooty hand.

"What are you doing?" Peter cried. "Now we will never find the way back to Russia."

I locked eyes with him. "Nobody shall ever know that the tsar of all the Russias wanted to run away like a common thief. You would be the laughingstock of all of Europe and you would destroy everything you've ever built."

After a moment of silence, he asked: "What do you suggest then, Catherine Alexeyevna?" How formal my name sounded.

"I am indeed going to get my jewels, Peter. *All* my jewelry. Everything that you in your love and generosity have ever given me. More gems than this fat, greedy sultan has ever seen. Sheremetev and Shafirov are to hand over the loot to him—a gift, with my sincere respect to the ruler of the High Porte of Constantinople, the prince of the Golden Gate. And then—" I grabbed his wrist.

"And then?"

"Then we negotiate," I said calmly, even though my heart pounded.

A wind cleared the clouds and the sudden moonlight made Peter's face look gaunt and his eyes huge and shiny. Peter tenderly touched my cheek. "At heart, you are a man. Perhaps you should rule Russia, not I. At least tonight," he said quickly, weakening his words.

* * *

I returned to our tent, where two large oak chests studded with iron bands and slate stood. I unfolded several Persian scarves on the floor, then dragged the chests to the middle of the tent and tipped them over, their sparkling contents cascading like a waterfall of wealth: pearls and beads, sapphires, rubies and emeralds mounted on breast crosses, hairpins, rings, earrings, bracelets, brooches, tiaras, chokers, and strands of necklaces.

I knelt to eye the treasure and my chest tightened: this was everything I had. Tokens of Peter's love, surely, but also my only security against his whims—such as the constant danger that he would marry a European princess—and the vagaries of fate. What if he were to die tomorrow? I combed with my fingers through the jewelry, untangling the strands of pearls from the other pieces. Peter had always spoiled me for my name day, Easter, Christmas, and of course every time I had given birth. There was the slight tiara made of pearls, rose quartz, tourmalines, blue topaz, and thinly beaten gold, which I had worn in my hair last July, dressed up as a flower fairy, together with the matching necklace and bracelets. I sifted through the jewels as if they were the river pebbles of the Dvina, letting diamond chains and pearls run through my fingers like the droplets of the river of my youth. They were magnificent and the finest Russia ever had to offer. To please me, Peter pushed his jewelers to use larger and more unusual stones, such as green or yellow diamonds, and set them in new ways. I liked my necklaces to reach my breasts or even dip between them, a cascade of dazzling sparkle and wealth. A tiara had to be so big I gladly accepted the ache it gave my head and neck—I held my chin even higher. Each earring had to brush my shoulder, competing with a chandelier's sparkle, for me to consider it proper. After a feast, I loved the cool of the metal on my skin, and often Peter had made love to me when I wore but those stones. I left it to the sultan to break them apart.

I searched and found the earrings that had once belonged to Peter's mother, his first gift to me. I hooked them into my earlobes. A bracelet was made of tiny portraits of Peter, Anna, and Elizabeth, and their faces smiled at me from the diamond-studded frames when I let the clasp snap shut. Just then, I spotted the ring that Peter had given me in Kiev to mark our darling little Ekaterina's first birthday. It was a huge heart-shaped yellow diamond set in a simple band of gold; the goldsmith had worked one of Ekaterina's blond curls into the band. I slid it on my finger, got up, and gathered the rest of the jewels into a couple of bulky bundles. Good riddance, I thought, and when I looked up, Shafirov and Sheremetev were waiting in the doorway.

"Take it all," I said, and soldiers hoisted the bundles on their shoulders.

The small group of men left the camp at the first sign of dawn, which blurred their bodies, blending them with the desert. I watched them leave, and my throat burned with thirst, but my eyes remained dry. Peter stood beside me, silent. When the men had disappeared, he pulled a ring with the imperial seal from his finger, placed it in my limp palm, and closed my fingers around it.

"Let us never forget what you have done today, for me and for Russia. I shall pay back my debts to you, double and triple. Let me also never forget the bravery of Shafirov and Sheremetev. Who knows if they'll come back alive?"

I slipped the ring into the little pouch that hung on my belt. I wouldn't need it until much later.

* * *

The sultan accepted my gift graciously, and with an appreciative clicking of his tongue. Russia was robbed of all and everything in the ensuing negotiations. The Treaty of Pruth returned Azov to the Ottoman Empire, and all Russian fortresses along the Black Sea were to be razed. Peter Shafirov had to stay in Istanbul, as a hostage. He was to join Peter Tolstoy in the Seven Towers, a prison feared for its dank and dark cells.

I gave my word to look after his six daughters and honor Peter's promise of marrying them to a prince each. It would take Shafirov two years and a new peace treaty to regain his freedom, together with Tolstoy.

* * *

When we were close to Saint Petersburg, Peter stopped his horse on a hillside, seizing my reins and lacing his fingers into mine. "Catherine Alexeyevna, marry me as soon as the ice of the Neva melts," he asked solemnly.

The plains lay peacefully in the evening sun, and the star shaped walls of the Peter and Paul Fortress turned crimson in the dying light of the day, while the water of the Neva shimmered green and mysterious. How beautiful my home was; how glad I was to finally return. We had lost the war, but I had triumphed.

"Did you hear me?" Peter asked, but I still had no answer. The evening mist rose from the marshes, hiding the city like a veil and spicing its dew with our dreams and desires.

55

My wedding to the tsar of all the Russias took place almost ten years after the fall of Marienburg, a decade since I had entered Alexander Danilovich Menshikov's tent, when I had dirty feet, wore a torn tunic, and slept wherever I could roll out my bedding.

In my bedroom in the Winter Palace I sat with my legs crossed, touching the soft soles of my feet; the feet of a woman who was being peeled and pampered every week in the *banja,* the bathhouse, before she was anointed with a paste of almond oil and lime juice. A woman who never walked a step too far, and if so, only when wearing velvet slippers. How would the pointed pebbles and sharp stones on the banks of the Dvina today hurt my feet, I thought, wiggling my pink toes with pleasure.

With a light knock, Daria and Alexandra Tolstoya slipped into the room. I peered at them from between my fingers when they curtsied deeply. Oh, God, no! Daria was already wiping tears from her eyes, and I scolded her. "We will cry so much today, do not start already now, will you?"

My chambermaid drew back the Chinese silk curtains from the window and the morning light flooded the warm, cozy room, where the fire in the Delft-tiled stove had been going through the night. I pushed my breakfast of hot chocolate and small pancakes with *smetana* and honey aside and opened my arms. "Let's weep together at least. I cannot believe it, either," I sobbed, and they rushed across the patterned parquet floor to embrace me.

"Come here." I patted my sheets and both of them climbed onto my bed, giggling like girls, even though they were already dressed, coiffed, and adorned for the celebration. Their new brooches with my intricately laced and diamond-studded monogram sparkled as badges of honor on their breasts: Peter had made them my ladies-in-waiting.

Daria poked me and laughed. "Get up, Tsaritsa. You cannot marry in bed."

"Why not? In bed Peter has learned to love me," I replied.

My chambermaid curtsied. "The *parikmacher*, Tsaritsa, to coif you." The hairdresser bowed and entered, carefully carrying the high, powdered wig he had made for me into the room; behind him I spotted the tailor with his two apprentices, and a footman, who carried my wedding dress.

"Eat and drink, the day will be long." I slid from the bed and skipped on my bare feet to the window as a girl would.

Daria and Alexandra laughed with their mouths full. "Dance, Tsaritsa, dance!" they chanted before eating more pancakes with cream. Daria was as chubby and soft as a cushion, due to her weakness for good food.

On the shining ice of the Neva, skaters slid and spun in circles; sleds decorated with cheerful bunting and wreaths and garlands of evergreen skidded along their way. The sky was a dense blue and the white winter sun gave the city a glossy, almost unreal look with trees and bushes hewn of silver and houses built of sheer crystal. It was a kingdom of ice, and I was to be its queen. Trumpets sounded and cannon shots rang out, as Saint Petersburg celebrated our wedding with pride. The joy that unfolded in this crisp morning seized me; I was not only part of it, but was at its very heart. I gave a sob, but Daria chided me, "I cannot do your makeup when you cry, Marta."

"Catherine Alexeyevna," I corrected her, which made me cry even more. That morning I heard my old name for the last time, and in the mirror framed with silver and mother-of-pearl, Marta, the soul born out of wedlock, gifted with a desperate heart and a growling stomach, disappeared forever. Into her place stepped Catherine Alexeyevna, who returned my amazed look with the proud gaze of a tsaritsa. For weeks Peter's Italian barber had lathered my skin with potions of buttermilk, lemon, and vodka to make my shoulders look like the marble from his home country. My hair had been rinsed in a wash of chestnut, beer, and eggs, to give my curls shine and color after the merciless sun of the Pruth, and thanks to Daria's droplets of belladonna my eyes were big and bright.

Daria and Alexandra Tolstoya helped me into my wedding gown woven from silver damask. I gasped when I felt the robe's full weight on my shoulders, but admired its pearl and silver-threaded embroidery of birds, butterflies, and blossoms; thick, twisted cords of silver held a cloak of blue velvet and ermine in place and I struggled for balance when I took my two faithful friends by their hands. "Daria. Alexandra. Promise to help me never forget who I am and where I come from." Alexandra Tolstoya curtsied and Daria nodded, her eyes as round as saucers.

In my reception, Peter, Menshikov, and the admirals Cruys and Botsis waited: Peter had asked the deserving Dutch sailors, who had helped him set up his fleet, to be his ushers. The tsar looked so splendid in his uniform that my heart beat faster. He bowed and held out a flat velvet casket.

"Open it, Catherine," he said brightly. "My mother wore this crown for her wedding. Now it shall be yours, *matka,* and our daughters' after you."

I gasped when I saw the delicate crown inside, with its pearls and yellow and pink diamonds. Peter smiled tenderly as he took it out of the case, and everybody clapped. Only the *parikmacher* made a worried face: How on Earth would he fix the crown onto my wig? But Peter already held out a second casket. "You might wear far too many clothes for my taste, but your neck is decidedly too naked."

I snapped it open and was speechless: on a choker of ten strands, each pearl was as large as a chickpea. It was held by a clasp of the imperial double eagle made of diamonds, rubies, and sapphires. Peter placed it around my neck, kissing my shoulders. "This is the foundation for a new collection." He winked at me as the clasp snapped shut.

I touched the eagle, which covered my whole throat, and said, "The beast is suffocating me."

"Tell me about it," he said, wrapping his arm around my waist and whispering, "Seriously, how am I to tear all these heavy clothes off you?"

The doors to the wider palace were flung open, and the trumpets and drums became deafening. Our daughters, Anna and Elizabeth, flew toward us in silver dresses, their taffeta trains and lace veils flying like gossamer wings. Peter caught them before they could make me lose my balance. "Hey, behave, you little witches, will you, or I will have you thrashed." Both giggled, and Elizabeth tickled his chin and twisted his uniform buttons. She knew that Peter would never raise his hand against her. Oh, if only she were a son, I thought, but reined my thoughts in: not here, not today.

* ❧ и

Feofan Prokopovich blessed our union before God and man in the small wooden church of Saint Isaac. Clouds of incense dulled my mind, sparks of gold and purple danced before my eyes just as they had done so long ago, on my way down to the Dvina, my arms heavy with dirty laundry, and the chants and prayers rose and fell in my ears. The bridal crown floated over my head, and after my vows, Menshikov helped me stand up and steadied me.

After church our sled flew across the frozen Neva to Alexander Danilovich's palace, which bloomed with flags and flowers. Menshikov himself struck the parquet with his diamond-studded staff to let the feast begin. The tall French mirrors on the long walls of the splendid hall reflected our image of unbridled joy a hundredfold. When Peter had drunk three bottles of Moldavian wine, two eagle cups filled with Prague beer, and a carafe of pear vodka, he rose, swaying, and called to my group of *damy,* "Stand up, Anastasia Golizyna. I appoint you Her Majesty's jester!"

The old princess was still chewing her food and pleadingly raised her hands, but he seized her by the hair, dragging her off her seat. "In the middle of the hall with you. Spin, *babushka,* spin!"

She turned awkwardly in the middle of the hall, more or less in tune with the music. Peter grabbed a piece of smoked salmon and threw it at her cheek, where it clung to her chalky, pasty makeup and made her high, powdered wig slip. Peter shouted, "Hit and sunk. Now you, Catherinushka, show the old frigate that you are a good shot." I laughed tears, took a sip of vodka, and threw a chicken wing at Anastasia Golizyna, which hit her smack on the nose.

I whooped with pride, and Peter shouted, "A salute for the tsaritsa, who is as good a shot as the best among my men!" The men drew their pistols and fired into the ceiling; stucco and gold leaf rained down on us. At three o'clock in the afternoon the sun set, and the fireworks lasted all night long, tinting the houses of Saint Petersburg in flaming hues of red, blue, and gold. For three days after, the smell of soot and gunpowder enveloped the city. In spite of the bitter cold, musicians played in the squares and the people danced, wrapped in furs and coats, in the streets or on the icy river and the frozen canals, free vodka flowing in their veins instead of blood.

The following morning, a train of sleds brought Peter and me to the Winter Palace. Menshikov staggered ahead of us to our rooms, shaking a pair of jingles that he had nicked from the musicians and still far too drunk to mind his own din. Peter was holding on to him, and both Daria Menshikova and Alexandra Tolstoya made rude jokes about my wedding night. When Menshikov was about to open the sheets of the bed, Peter grabbed him by the scruff of his neck. "Do not touch my bed with your sooty fingers, you scoundrel," he cried, and shoved his old friend out of the door. "Out, all of you. I must now fulfill my marital duties with my shy bride."

Everyone linked arms, laughing and swaying, and it took a while for their shrieks and singing to fade in the vast corridors of the Winter Palace. The room was warm and the curtains were drawn to block out the winter day. My feet ached and my head spun; exhausted, I leaned against the wall as Peter stepped up to me. "How am I going to take you now, Tsaritsa?" he asked, his eyes sparkling.

"Well, how a good sailor would take his girl, Peter Alexeyevich," I chuckled, toying with the collar of his uniform.

"You asked for it," he said, loosening my skirt. The heavy fabric fell in folds around my ankles. My bloomers followed, and I kicked them aside. He lifted me up as if I were a feather, cupping my buttocks. "My wife has the best ass in Russia. If that is not a reason to marry, I do not know what is," he murmured, sucking my nipples, which burst from my half-undone corset. I wrapped my legs in their silk stockings around his hips, but then playfully pushed him away, pleading, "No, please not. I am still a virgin."

"Let me do something about that, so help me God!" Peter roared; I arched, and he thrust inside me; I tightened my muscles around him and rubbed myself against him. When I was close to coming, I held him back, whispering, "Wait!" He paused and blew softly over my face as I slowly and lustfully satisfied myself. When I sighed and placed my moist forehead to his neck, he laughed. "My tsaritsa. You are a soldier indeed." I held him tightly as he came inside me. For a while we leaned against the wall, panting, before he let me slide to the ground. He stroked the sweaty hair from his forehead and his eyes were as bright as a boy's.

"What now?" he asked.

"Now?" I laughed. "Now we're going to bed. I'm exhausted. And don't you dare wake me up before tomorrow evening."

* * *

Peter held me when I slept deeply, slipping dreamlessly into my new life as tsaritsa of all the Russias. Nothing, or so I was convinced, could ever blight our happiness.

56

Saint Petersburg grew green with the spring, and the trees lining the Nevsky Prospect filled me with as much pride as the stately buildings along the shores of the Fontanka and Moika. Could it really be only a decade ago that Swedes, souls, and swine had dwelt here? When the Neva thawed, foreign frigates danced on the waves next to the boats of the Russian noble families and merchants. Their houses gladly answered the midday cannon thunder from the Peter and Paul Fortress with pistol shots and volleys.

"Just you go to the river," Peter said half-mockingly, half-sadly, when I left for the Neva pier in early May. A new bout of syphilis had made him bedridden for a week; his bloated body made him howl with pain. "Perhaps this Mr. Schlüter would rather see you than me," he murmured.

"Well, after the long trip from Berlin he will be glad to have firm ground under his feet, no matter who welcomes him." In truth I was looking forward to the fresh air, as I was pregnant again. This child was more than a sign of our love; it was a hope for the new city and a new Russia. Should God finally give me the grace of the birth of a healthy son? I prayed for it every night before going to bed.

Peter placed his hand on my belly. "Take good care of the tsarevich," he whispered, and I startled: tsarevich. So far, Alexey still held that title.

* * *

As if the Devil wanted it, a messenger handed a letter from Alexey into my litter when I was about to leave. He wrote from Brunswick, where he was to meet his bride, Sophie Charlotte, and Agneta read it to me. *Your Majesty, I am glad to hear that my father has raised you in rank to be his wife, and that you are with child again. Please always bless me with your grace. I do not dare to congratulate my father, as the tsar has left me unaware of his decision and his happiness. But assure me of His Majesty's liking. I am in your hand—Humbly, Alexey*

It was incredible: Peter had not even told Alexey about our wedding.

"Enough. I've heard enough. Give me the letter, Agneta." Ernst Gluck's daughter now had the age to join my retinue as a lady-in-waiting. "It reeks of stupor and fornication." I grimaced, sniffing at the crushed paper, and pushed the scroll into my sleeve.

We rocked along to the Neva pier, where Schlüter was to arrive. The air in the litter was stuffy, and I moved to the window to fight my rising nausea. When I fixed my eyes to a point it usually helped, but the early midday sun made the stench of the drying swamp around the city unbearable; gnats drew a cruel veil over the laborers and our bearers skillfully avoided the workmen, who were either carrying stones needed for the construction of the Peter and Paul Cathedral, or who loaded barges that lay heavily in the water. The architect Trezzini had carefully planned every one of the cathedral's details, from the pointed tower, which allowed a glimpse of Finland, to the exquisite furnishings in its interior, where from now on all members of the tsar's family should be buried. I looked across the construction site, which was teeming with workers: Would my grave, too, be there?

Just then, directly next to the window of my litter, a man staggered under the weight of his load of rocks. His arms were scarred, dark holes gaped in his skull instead of his nose and ears: he had already tried to escape twice; at a third attempt he would be killed. My stomach turned, and I drew the curtain in front of the window. I could not help him, even if I wanted to.

The quay was teeming with sailors, merchants, and tradesmen; children; girls of easy virtue; and people strolling and checking the wares that had arrived in this city, which was lacking everything. The sweet scent of hot pies and fresh beer drifted into the litter. *Babushki*, old women bent low under the loads on their shoulders, blocked the way as much as herds of cattle and wagons full of barrels and chests. We reached the port just as the frigate from Rostock took its sails down and sailors threw the ropes ashore. Everywhere, galleons and smaller sailboats rocked on the waves and the air smelled of salt, pitch, and smoke. The wind caught itself in colorful flags and bunting all along the masts and ropes, as the ships creaked in their hulls and sailors swiftly climbed from one mast to another, swinging like monkeys on ropes. Voices shouted in all known languages, and seagulls caught the wind in their widespread wings, gliding ahead and diving into the spray before appearing again with fish glittering in their sharp beaks. Agneta gave me a hand before two guards gave me firmer support and I found my footing. How good it was to escape the stuffiness of the Winter Palace and be here, among real, ordinary people. Since my wedding I had not been on my own for a moment, and I missed solitude.

"Who is this Andreas Schlüter?" Agneta asked, smoothing her skirt.

"A German master, who is said to have built a room made entirely from amber for the Prussian king. Peter lured him to Saint Petersburg for a huge sum."

Agneta chuckled when we were joined by Domenico Trezzini, Peter's master builder. I waited a bit, surprised, just to tease him in his vanity, and to see how quickly his hotheaded Italian nature had the better of him. "Trezzini. Why, the man who creates the city of the tsar with his own hands? What are you doing here instead of being at the cathedral's building site?" I asked, when I felt him seething.

"Oh, I'm here quite by chance," he said miserably, looking out at the waves, his brows furrowed.

"What a lucky coincidence then," I said amiably.

"Why did the tsar bring Schlüter to Saint Petersburg?" he burst out.

"Jealous, Trezzini?" I said, feeling quite sorry for him. "The tsar admired Schlüter's work in Berlin and invited him to help build Saint Petersburg."

"Schlüter was caught with his hand in the till in Berlin. Nevertheless, the tsar appoints him as his director of construction and pays him five thousand rubles a year. I have neither such a title nor such a salary."

I tapped Trezzini's shoulder ever so lightly with my fan. "The city is big enough for ten, if not twenty, talented builders such as you and the German. Do not worry."

He bowed, just as Andreas Schlüter appeared on the deck of his ship, counting his belongings, since chests and bundles disappeared all too easily in the hustle and bustle of the harbor. Compared with the men of Saint Petersburg, who after the long winter looked like maggots, or whose faces were reddened by vodka, he was like a young god: his dark blond hair was long and not powdered and the open collar of his starched, pure white shirt showed his strong neck, accentuating his fresh skin and his bright and even teeth. Agneta stared at him, so that I shoved her. "Pull yourself together, Agneta. Close your pretty little mouth. You look like a trout, gawping like that," I whispered.

"Forgive me, Tsaritsa. But I think that only a man of such beauty can create something as wonderful as a room made solely of amber . . ." she said dreamily.

"We have not seen it yet. It is very unlikely that it exists at all," I replied.

The sailors dragged Schlüter's boxes from the ship, while he himself walked over the bridge and stamped on the wharf. "It's good to have solid ground under your feet again." He smiled before looking around. "So, this is the Venice of the North, the paradise of the great tsar?" he asked in German and bowed to me.

I graciously reached out my hand for him to kiss my fingers.

* * *

Trezzini wasn't jealous for long, as Schlüter died in the autumn of the fever, which rose like mist from the reeds around Saint Petersburg. The same illness took my delicate newborn daughter Margarita. After only a few weeks of life, her name was recorded in the saddest of all the court's many lists: the names of my dead children. Peter mourned with me, but I knew that in his heart of hearts he was relieved that it was but a daughter that we buried.

A few weeks later, he came to me and said, "Poor little Margarita. What is done is done and there is no way of questioning God's will. Still, it is time for a healthy, strong son, a strapping recruit for my army."

His lips smiled as he kissed me, but his eyes were sad and serious.

* * *

I met Sophie Charlotte only two years after her wedding to Alexey, when she first arrived in Saint Petersburg. I recognized, from a portrait

I had seen, the strict parting in her thin, blond hair as she curtsied. My ladies giggled, as she was truly as flat as a boy and her face was badly scarred from the smallpox. But her eyes were friendly and mild, her smile came easily, and her voice sounded like a silver bell when she said in German to me, "What joy, Tsaritsa. I have heard so much of your grace and generosity that I pray to be your devoted and loyal friend."

She eyed me curiously: I knew that the whole of Europe gossiped about me. In Paris, Madame, the sister-in-law of the Great Louis, mocked me: "The tsaritsa of Russia is mouse shit pretending to be poppy seeds!" But I opened my arms to embrace her. "Welcome to Russia, Tsarevna. May Saint Petersburg become your home, as it is mine. God bless you and your marriage." The princess leaned in to me like a bird that had fallen from its nest and I offered her a stool next to my throne. "Sit down and tell me about your wedding. Was it splendid?"

She blushed. "Oh, yes. Divine, in fact. We all deeply regretted that you could not keep the tsar company back then."

I hid a smile, for the one who had not regretted this at all was myself. On his wedding day, Peter had dragged Alexey by his hair into the chapel of the Torgau castle, for the evening before, the tsarevich had still clung to his confessor, shrieking shrilly: "Never. I will never marry a heretic. As tsar, I must defend our faith. How am I to do that with a Lutheran woman at my side? This is blasphemy." The pope shielded the crown prince with his body until Peter knouted him, while Alexey got the tsar's fist between his eyes. The next morning, he was wed to Sophie Charlotte, who was allowed to retain her Protestant faith and received twenty-five thousand Reichsthaler, and tableware as well as carriages and horses from Peter—the dowry her impoverished father could not pay. Both men, Peter and the Duke of Brunswick, beamed with joy at the union. Menshikov, I heard, sent a watermelon as a present.

She chattered on breathlessly and a few scarlet spots bloomed on her pale, sunken cheeks. "Well, at least the tsar was with us, and I cried like a fountain when my father led me up the aisle to the tsarevich." Sophie Charlotte had been sold to Alexey just as I had been sold to Vassily, I thought with sadness, just for a bit more money. "On the morning after the wedding, the tsar sat on our bed and chatted with us," she said. The poor girl! Alexey had probably raped her more or less, and then she had to report to Peter about the consummation of the marriage. My eyes grazed her narrow waist and she blushed: there was no sign of a pregnancy. All the courtiers were seemingly engrossed in conversation, but I knew they were straining their ears.

"I'll give you Marie Hamilton as a lady-in-waiting. She will help you form a court," I said. Sophie Charlotte kissed my fingers and Marie Hamilton curtsied, but by the look in her big green eyes I knew that she understood. I was to be fully informed of all the events in Alexey's household and bed. Marie Hamilton would fulfill my orders, as she already fulfilled the tsar's wishes.

57

The guest that Peter most ardently wished to welcome in his city—peace—made itself scarce. For two years Menshikov and thirty thousand soldiers had roamed in northern Germany in order to negotiate peace, but perhaps the German princes were wary of having to feed Menshikov and his men after the Swedes' long years of reign. The wounds of the Thirty Years' War—when almost a century ago the then-ruling European powers were locked in a murderous struggle for supremacy—were yet to heal in the heart of Europe, so that even Peter was impressed when Menshikov pressed further money from Lübeck and Hamburg, which had just been ravaged by the Black Death. Despite all the German complaints, Peter refused to call Menshikov back; one-third of the funds raised paid for the construction of the new fleet.

In May, when the first rays of sun warmed our souls and skin, Peter went to Finland to wage war. When Helsinki gave itself up to the sixteen thousand Russian soldiers, Peter wrote to me from Åbo in early September: *Soon Finland will be purged of any Swedes. The Finnish girls have rosy thighs, but I have not laughed for days. Remain faithful to your* starik, *who loves you so dearly, and come to me, Catherinushka, as soon as you can. Kiss our little daughters good night and tell them that they will have a brother soon.*

I smiled when Agneta paused in her reading: after a short knock, Sophie Charlotte's new lady-in-waiting, Marie Hamilton, hurried into the room. I waved Agneta out and eyed the beautiful Scotswoman who stemmed from the German suburb in Moscow. She, too, was pregnant again, after already having given birth to six children. Who was this child's father: Peter, once more, or the former Streltsy soldier Grigori Orlov? He had escaped the purge of Streltsy regiment by sheer courage and cheek. When he mounted the scaffold, where Peter was waiting for him, ax in hand, Orlov kicked aside the head of the man who had been executed before him and shouted, "By God: Must I make room for myself?" Peter pardoned him there and then, and today Orlov blessed the *damy* of Saint Petersburg. I had heard he was hung like a horse.

"What's the matter, Marie?" I asked mockingly. "You seem out of breath."

"It is about the tsarevich," she panted, laying her slender hand on her ample bosom, but not at all embarrassed about her condition.

I sat up, excited. "Is Sophie Charlotte finally pregnant?"

"On the contrary. Alexey has not slept with her since their wedding night—"

"What?" I turned in shock. That was the last thing I had expected. Like his father, Alexey was not said to suffer from a lack of lust.

"Worse, just this afternoon he asked his confessor how he could rid himself of her and send Sophie Charlotte back to her parents," Marie Hamilton cried.

"And what did the old fool answer?"

"Apparently this can be easily done if you are married to a woman of a faith other than the Russian church, and who is barren. If she does not bear him a child in three years of marriage, he can expel her, the pope says. Otherwise he can baptize her, shave her head, and send her to a convent. Sophie Charlotte does nothing but wail, and when Alexey sees her he throws at her whatever he can grab, be it a chair, a vase, or silver crockery."

I struggled to control my anger, yet rose so hastily from my stool that it toppled. In my heart, I so wished to believe in Alexey—to me, he was still the timid boy whom I had met so many years ago, who smiled at me shyly on the Kremlin's balcony, and whom Peter had left to Menshikov's doing and careless, often brutal tutors. It wasn't his fault that he had not an ounce of Peter about him. Still, he was the tsarevich, and this was more serious than I had thought. "Get my carriage and my cloak. I shall pay a visit to my stepson," I ordered. A servant ran off, his metal-capped soles sounding on the wooden parquet.

"But . . ." Marie began, sounding worried.

"But what?" My imperial green silk cloak was placed on my shoulders, and I felt stronger and empowered to do what I had to do, stretching out my arms and raising my chin. "Dress me up, Marie. I have to look like the tsaritsa."

Marie lay a necklace of multiple strands of turquoise and diamonds around my neck and hooked the matching pendants into my ears. Then she let the bracelets snap shut around my wrists. "Alexey has guests in the Winter Palace tonight," she said carefully, her eyes lowered.

"Whatever that means. Don't you think I have not seen a feast before? Do not worry, I'm used to a lot," I said dryly, as I checked myself briefly in the mirror. Good. Marie curtsied as deeply as she could with her swollen belly. The small staircase of the Summer Palace at the Fontanka Canal was still warm from the day's sunshine when we left.

Our carriage shook on the gravel paths of the garden that Peter had carefully planned. Marie fought against nausea, but I had no compassion and looked out of the window instead. Dusk drew a veil of blue light over the water, and in the balmy, bright summer's night lovers were sitting on the steps of the jetties along the river, talking and laughing. On the quayside, men taught their sons how to swing their fishing rods into the Neva, and the teal-colored feathers of the ducks blended with the river's waves. Saint Petersburg evenings cast a spell like a net, in which we all were caught as helplessly as fish.

* * *

The carriage jerked to a halt outside the Winter Palace. Alexey and Sophie Charlotte had moved into its cold splendor, while Peter and I preferred the simplicity of the Summer Palace with its Delft tiles, low ceilings, and brightly painted wooden walls. It was a house—our house—and not a palace.

I looked up at the imposing façade, Trezzini's masterpiece: torches flickered behind the countless windows, whether the rooms were in use or not. Footmen hurried to my carriage, but otherwise the vast courtyard was empty. When I got out, voices shouted rude songs in the upper reaches and I heard the laughter and shrieks of Alexey's banquet. Suddenly I had a premonition that made my skin tingle.

"Give me your whip," I ordered the coachman, and he passed it to me with a look of surprise. I clenched the silver pommel. "Marie. Show me the way."

Our steps echoed up the large, empty staircase and then along the corridors of gray and white marble; our figures were reflected in the high, gold-framed mirrors along the walls. Soldiers stood to attention at every corner we passed, but no courtiers were to be seen. They were either with Peter in the field, or they used his absence to finally spend some time with their families.

"Should we really do this?" Marie whispered, but I followed the voices and the music, and finally, we reached the small, black marble dining room.

The guards outside the door crossed their rifles with bayonets spiked on top. "No passage, by order of the tsarevich!" barked a soldier with spots as big as bulbs on his face; the other one had hardly any teeth left and gave a grin.

"If you do not want to go to Siberia tomorrow, boys, or be broken on the wheel, then make yourself scarce," I said coolly.

"The tsaritsa," Marie snarled, and both men knelt, banged their foreheads on the floor, and muttered reverences and apologies. When I entered the hall, the first person among the carousing, cavorting people was Sophie Charlotte herself. It was unbelievable. The wife of the tsarevich of all the Russias was serving his drunkard friends beer! Just then, one of them smacked her meager backside. "Ouch! What a bony ass! But vodka is a magic potion: it makes any girl beautiful," he howled, pinching her naked arm. The princess fought back tears, and from the other end of the hall I heard hoots and claps. I felt cold in the pit of my stomach, and I had goose bumps.

"Bring Sophie Charlotte to the tsarevich's bedroom," I ordered Marie, who fought her way through the crowd to the weeping and cowering crown princess.

I myself turned the collar of my cloak up, though nobody noticed me—all were too drunk—and when I reached the other end of the hall, a group of men were gathering around a table, jeering. "Yes! A toast to our crown prince!"

"He takes all hurdles like no other. That is what I call a rider."

"Give her the spurs! Make her whinny!"

Alexey's hair hung loose to his shoulders; his shirt was half-open and glued to his glistening, sweaty body. He wore riding boots, but his breeches hung around his knees and a girl was lying on the table in front of him, her fat white thighs spread wide open. He grunted as he fondled her plump breasts and slapped her buttocks until her flesh turned as red as a cherry. "Yes, my horsey. You must be broken in!" he cried. I felt dizzy; the sight was too awful. Despite all the rough games I had witnessed in the tents, in the field, or in the Kremlin, seeing this girl made me feel like a maid in Vassily's house again, when he came for me on that first, abominable night.

Alexey's companions neighed, whinnied, and imitated the sounds of horses' hooves, before howling with laughter. The girl herself screamed with joy. When I could see her face, her skin was very fair to match her thick red hair, but her tiny eyes and thick nose gave her a mean, callous look. I was about to retreat, when Alexey shouted, "Now witness me making a son and heir for Russia. My father and his whore only manage daughters, and that scrawny German cat can moan to a convent's walls." He rammed into the girl, who squealed and arched her back, her breasts bouncing, their nipples wide and light pink. Without thinking I lashed out, whipping the tsarevich's naked back. He reared with pain and spun around. "Who dares—?" He foamed with anger, but at the sight of me his cock went limp.

"Cover yourself, Tsarevich!" I hissed with barely hidden rage and contempt. The girl sat up, looking at me almost defiantly, while Alexey's friends fell to their knees, their heads bowed. I lifted the crop once more, ready to strike again.

"Do as I say."

Alexey pulled up his trousers and closed his belt, pale with rage. His eyes popped and his lips were pressed together to form a narrow line. "Tsaritsa, what an unexpected honor. Why all this upset? We are just having a little fun." He bowed mockingly. "What brings Your Majesty here?"

"The same thing as you. my wish for an heir to the Russian throne," I said. "Come with me."

He went ahead, blushing with anger. Around us the silence was deafening.

"Where are we going?" he asked as I shoved him through another door.

"Sophie Charlotte is waiting for you in your bedroom. You know the way better than I do." He shuffled his feet, walking as slowly as possible, but I thrust the pommel of the whip in his back. "Move. We don't have all day."

"I do not want to have anything to do with Sophie Charlotte. I love another!" he shrieked.

"Who is the lucky girl?" I asked sarcastically.

"You just saw her. Her name is Afrosinja. She was a washermaid in the Finnish campaign." He looked at me defiantly, but all I did was chuckle.

"Am I supposed to feel close to her for that? You are mistaken, but about many things: I love you, and always have, so listen carefully. It's far better for your health to love and impregnate your wife than some Finnish hussy."

"You're just like my father!" He spat on the parquet of ebony, ivory, and ash. "I love Afrosinja and no one else."

"Your father would have killed you and Afrosinja in his rage if he had just heard you."

I drove the tsarevich to his rooms like a shepherd does with his livestock. There was no one to be seen, but I knew that these walls had ears. "After you," I said curtly as we arrived at his bedroom door. Marie had stoked the embers in the fireplace and Sophie Charlotte sat in bed, almost disappearing behind the vast frame, the curtains, the layers of sheets. Her naked shoulders trembled, her hair was limp and straight, her chest was as flat as a boy's, and a red bruise marked the spot where the drunkard had pinched her.

"I don't want her. She disgusts me!" Alexey screeched, reeling and trying to escape me, but I kept him in check with the whip. Angrily he tore his trousers open: his long, thick cock hung down as limp as a worm. More than ever before he reminded me of Vassily, and I fought my disgust.

"See how the German witch excites me? No wonder we have so many children," he said, mocking me, but on the verge of tears. "She reeks of beer and vodka, like a whore in a *kabak*."

I laughed: "Well, if your Afrosinja smells better . . ."

Sophie Charlotte sobbed, and I hesitated briefly. Was I doing the right thing? "Stop crying. It is for Russia, and for your own good," I said to her, and then called, "Marie!"

The sight of the pregnant Marie, her now even fuller breasts almost bursting out of her loosely laced silk dress, was startling: with her auburn curls, moist pink lips, and lively green eyes, she was a real beauty. No wonder she had shared Peter's bed for so many years.

"The tsarevich needs to sire an heir. Help him," I said curtly, to hide my shame and my horror at what was happening. Marie smiled cattily, showing her small, pointed teeth, and knelt before Alexey. In the doorway, I cast a glance back into the room. Marie Hamilton had pulled her dress from her shoulders, showing her full, white breasts. He gasped when she took him between her rosy lips, closing her mouth around him. The prince clawed his hands into her shoulders and I saw him growing hard again. Somehow, I felt that she was not doing this for the first time and that they had been lovers before.

"Marie," I reminded her in the open doorway, "don't forget: the best belongs to the crown princess." Alexey groaned with anger and disappointment when Marie led him to his marital bed, where Sophie Charlotte cowered in one corner, ashen-faced and hiccuping with fear. I left them to it.

Out in the hall, I sank onto my heels like the peasant girl I had once been, and my tears came. I heard Marie talk and laugh, Alexey shout briefly in protest, and then Sophie Charlotte cry out, again and again. I trembled and twisted my fingers until my knuckles turned white. What I did was for the best of Russia: when Sophie Charlotte bore Alexey a son, I, too, could breathe easier.

Peter, I was sure, would not have acted differently in my place. It was just that thought that made me weep even more.

58

When I joined Peter in Finland, I told him neither about Alexey's problems with his wife nor about Afrosinja, because I had better news to share: Sophie Charlotte was finally pregnant. The tsarevich himself had told me, his face stony, before he, his retinue, and Afrosinja left for Carlsbad to take the waters.

Peter shrugged and said, "With what sort of son am I punished? Oh, why does his weak health not take him from me," before he ordered: "Replace all foreigners in Sophie Charlotte's court with Russians. Her ladies-in-waiting, her jesters, physicians, and midwives: all of them. The child is not to be secretly swapped after its birth, be it a boy or a girl."

Sophie Charlotte pleaded with him to change this cruel order; the ink of her dozens of letters to him was smeared with tears. No wonder—she longed for her familiar ladies in this still-so-foreign court—but it was in vain: she gave birth to her daughter surrounded by strangers whose language she still did not speak properly. It was clear that no one was willing to bet a kopeck on the delicate princess's future. The news of her being brought to bed reached us at Hango Bay and Peter stared across the harbor's gray waters. He looked like the young man again I had met so many years ago in Marienburg: his skin tanned, his blue eyes sparkling, and his dark hair, streaked handsomely only by a few gray strands, disheveled by the wind.

"A daughter!" he spat, handing the letter to Makarov, who stuck it in his leather pouch. "Wipe your arse with it, if you want to. Daughters I have enough myself. If Alexey just wasn't so bloody useless."

I laced my fingers over my stomach: I, too, was pregnant again. The morning light danced on the waves, and the coast of Finland was but a thin blue line on the horizon, where white clouds billowed like sails in the wind. A gull dived into the waves and did not reappear.

Two weeks later we surrounded the Swedish fleet in Hango Bay, and after the battle, the sad remnants of the enemy's ships drifted on the waves: bloated bodies, tattered canvas, and broken wooden planks. Back in Saint Petersburg I gave birth to my daughter Maria—*I have a son called Maria,* Peter wrote jokingly to Menshikov, but the little girl was too weak to survive the day of her birth. Peter kept her birth, as well as her death, secret in the weekly bulletins that were sent to the European courts.

* * *

The young woman was in such haste that she ran right into me; if I hadn't caught her, we both would have tumbled to the ground. I was deep in thought, for Peter had just shown me his Kunstkamera, which was newly founded in the Summer Palace and open for all the people of Saint Petersburg to visit. "Ever since my childhood, I have collected misfits of nature, rare weapons, and memories of my travels and animals of all kinds. Now everyone can see them, *matka,* and learn from it." He pulled me with him between the rows and rows of shelves full of glasses and containers: I saw lambs with three heads, the legless torso of a baby with four arms, twins that were joined at the breast—they made me think of Master Lampert's Tent of Wonders so long ago!—as well as a child with a fishtail and two young dogs that were said to have been born to a sixty-year-old virgin.

"Do you like it?" Peter asked me, full of pride. I nodded, but he frowned. "What's wrong? Are you sad?"

"The Summer Palace was our home. We planned the house and the garden together; from here, we watched our city grow. Now everybody will take a walk in my garden, visit your collection in my salon, and get drunk with wine and vodka in my hall."

"Ah. Don't worry. I'll build you a palace that is much bigger and more magnificent than you can ever imagine," Peter promised before leaving me alone.

So, I heard the hurried steps on the path's gravel, but only when the young woman pushed me, and with a shout of "Damn!" dropped her thickly filled pouch, did I look up. My shoulder ached as she tried to gather up the dozens of scattered coins.

"What a loot," I commented, and she looked up.

"Tsaritsa, forgive me!" The girl blushed. She had refilled the pouch and was about to carry on when I noticed her bright blue eyes and her ash-blond curls.

"Have not we met before?" I frowned.

"Yes, Tsaritsa. I'm Alice Kramer. We met at Boris Petrovich Sheremetev's house."

"Of course! At Bobushka's," I said jokingly. "Are you still in his household?"

"No. His wife got so jealous of me that she forced him to give me as a gift to General Balk," she said, her pretty face darkening. I felt for her: how easily that could have happened to me as well.

"But General Balk is married to Anna Mons's sister. She'll hardly tolerate you under her roof?"

Alice fought back tears. "Indeed. The Balks owed Marie Hamilton a favor and now I belong to her, as her handmaiden."

"I see," I said carefully. "Is that Marie's money? Are you running an errand for her?"

"Yes. I picked up her due from the jeweler Blumenthal. She has sold jewels to him." She sounded hesitant, even if this was nothing new in Saint Petersburg, where Peter's lust for lavish, long-lasting festivals and amusements caused high expenses for his courtiers. Many *damy* shifted the family jewelry to pay for a seated dinner for three hundred or more guests.

"Is Marie Hamilton not pregnant again? Is that her eighth child?" I prodded further, but Alice paled with dread.

"I know nothing about it, God help me!" she whispered, pressing the pouch against her chest. "I must hurry, Tsaritsa, my mistress is a strict woman and I do not want to be beaten and starved." She curtsied and then ran on, her skirts flying.

I walked on, for a last time enjoying the privacy of the Summer Palace's gardens before Peter gave them to the public. Marie Hamilton had been pregnant back then in Alexey's rooms. Had she given the child to an orphanage, or was it raised in the country? Now I was sure that she was pregnant again. But why make a secret of it? I went on, even deeper in thought.

59

Peter and I were sitting by the fireplace in his study while two foot-men tried to create order on his desk.

"Let me show you the palace which I will build for our summers to-gether. You know that I never make empty promises, Catherine," Peter said. He stroked Lenta—he gave all his dogs the same name—and the dog growled softly with pleasure. When Peter gave her an old leather glove to chew, she settled down on the worn tips of Peter's boots. He had taught her all sorts of tricks—taking off a hat, rolling over, giving paw, jumping over a stick—but now she was where she wanted to be, at his feet, warming her hide.

"Can we not simply live in the Summer Palace again?" I pleaded once more. "Only us and our children? Perhaps we can house the Kunst-kamera somewhere else?" I sipped some of my bitter *tchai* and added a good shot of vodka to my cup, as I felt the cold of that autumn to my bones. My last pregnancy had taken much of my strength.

"No. It is no longer just about us, *matka*. We must show Europe that Russia does not fear any comparison; I am peer to all its rulers. Even the Winter Palace seems so small and humble to me. But still, it can be my Louvre, and Peterhof my Versailles."

"Peterhof? Versailles?" I looked at him, confused, but he caressed my hair.

"She who has never seen Paris and the court of the Great Louis can-not understand this. But the tsar of all the Russias can do what the king of France can do. On top of that, Menshikov is building his summer place of Oranienbaum; his palace on the Strelka is already the most beautiful in the city. That dog shall not trump me in the country, too." Peter stood up. "I have been working on my ideas for Peterhof for almost two years, whenever I had time." He got up and searched his desk before cursing and kicking the footmen. "Damn it! If you make order here, I'll never find anything."

Then, he settled beside me on the carpet and dropped a dozen paper rolls onto the floor. "But there was just too much else going on. The new law of inheritance alone has cost me months, and still my nobles and peasants refuse to leave their possessions and property to only their eldest son."

"No wonder. You're not doing anything different, after all." I wanted to bite my lips out of anger at my stupidity. How could I say that?

Peter was mute, but pulled the glove in Lenta's mouth in a playful tug-of-war; she growled and snapped for her toy. Then he sought my gaze pleadingly. "Give me a son, Catherinushka. Only then can I sleep in peace again. I need nothing as much as a son. Just one, please, so I am not completely dependent on Alexey. It's about my beautiful Russia: I beg you." His eyes were dark with concern.

My heart clenched. "If it was up to me, I would give you ten strong sons, my tsar," I whispered, kissing his fingers.

"I know, I know," he murmured, when we heard noise outside the secret door. "The tsar and the tsaritsa are not to be disturbed," Makarov insisted, but between various male voices a woman was whimpering. What was happening?

"That's Shafirov!" Peter strode to the door and looked in puzzlement at the guard holding a ragged-looking old woman, a stranger and Shafirov behind them. "What is it, Shafirov? Can't you wait with the din until supper?"

"May we speak to the tsaritsa?" said Shafirov, who was pale with excitement, pushing his two captives ahead of him. Peter scratched his head, and I, too, was surprised. The woman reeked of sweat and vodka; her gray hair was all dirty and tangled, and her one good eye was hidden behind puffy bags of saggy skin and wrinkles. Her other eye was covered with a dark, dirty linen bandage. She wrung her hands in her shackles and her fingernails were long, filthy, and curved.

I pressed a perfumed handkerchief to my nose. "Yes? What is it?"

Shafirov forced the woman to her knees. "Lower your ugly face in front of the tsaritsa, old witch!" he said.

I rose and the rolls with the plans to Peterhof slid from my lap, rustling. "Shafirov, who are these people?"

"Speak, Uncle Blumenthal," he said to the old man who wore the flat black hat, the black cape, and the sidelocks of the faithful Jews. What had Shafirov called him? Blumenthal? I had heard that name before, but could not remember where. The man bowed to me with a quiet dignity, and then pulled a flat velvet box from his wide cloak. The old woman struggled for breath and silenced, too terrified to whimper, as Blumenthal opened the velvet casket. I came closer and had a look, without really understanding: in it lay the necklace of turquoise and diamonds I had worn when I had forced Alexey back to the path of marital virtue. Peter grasped the necklace with his fist, its splendor dangling like worthless baubles. "Where did you get the jewelry from, man? I myself gave this set to the tsaritsa."

The old goldsmith bowed. "I recognized the noble origin of the piece and turned to my nephew, Peter Shafirov."

"Who sold him the jewelry, Shafirov? And who is the stinking old hag?" Peter asked, pale with anger.

"The old witch is an angel-maker. She ends the unwanted pregnancies of the *damy* of Saint Petersburg," replied Shafirov.

I looked at the disgusting fingers of the woman, while she rocked back and forth in her shackles, on her knees, moaning. Her lips were trembling over her toothless gums.

"And the jewelry?" Peter asked. My throat was dry but my fingers trembled. Where was this leading?

"Well, the jewelry was stolen and sold by Marie Hamilton. She needed money to have a pregnancy ended. Or rather, several pregnancies, if the witch can be trusted."

All was silent and I did not dare look at Peter.

"May I?" said Shafirov, ramming his knee into the woman's back. She fell forward, screaming. "Speak! Maybe you can save your stinking skin," he hissed.

She looked up and her one good eye glittered with greed and envy. "Marie Hamilton is a bitch in heat. And now I, poor *babushka*, should pay for her sins. She used to come and see me every four or five months, crying and lamenting that she could not have the child. God knows with whom she whored. The whole of town, I'd say," she shrieked. "But my work doesn't come cheap."

I avoided Peter's gaze when Shafirov said, "Marie Hamilton has stolen from the tsaritsa more than once and has sold the jewels to my uncle Blumenthal. It was only this beautiful, rare piece that aroused his suspicion."

"How many jewels did Marie Hamilton bring you, Blumenthal?" I asked, haltingly. The reach of the whole story dawned on me only very slowly. He weighed his answer. "She usually sent her German servant, Alice Kramer. Such a dear little thing who would never get in trouble, but she came often. Sometimes just with a ring to sell, sometimes with chains, chokers, earrings, or belts—"

I no longer wanted to hear, and suddenly realized how many of my belongings had gone missing in recent months. How careless I had grown about it, thinking a maid had mislaid a belt, or that my earrings had slipped off my lobes during a wild dance. I, who used to own nothing in the whole wide world?

Peter tore the woman's head up and stared into her one eye. "Tell me, old hag, before I have your tongue torn out of your filthy mouth. What gender were the children you took from Marie's body?"

She looked at him coldly and chuckled, obviously not afraid of what fate had in store for her. "If I am to die anyway, my tsar, I might as well tell you. They were all boys, splendid, strapping sons. And how she sniggered, the Hamilton, when she saw the tiny, chopped-up bodies. You know what she said, more than once?"

I chose not to hear, but Peter nodded.

"'I might be a whore, but I can do over and over again what the tsaritsa can't do even once.'" She toppled backward, howling and bleeding from her nose as well as her mouth, as Shafirov struck her with his clenched fist.

60

Marie Hamilton mounted the scaffold on an overcast day. Both the crown princess and I were pregnant again, but Peter had ordered us nevertheless to witness her execution. Already from a distance we heard the jeering and whistling as Marie mounted a sled at the Neva gate of the Peter and Paul Fortress. I had asked for her not to be tortured, for I had forgiven her both her thieving and her slight. Was she not punished enough? But Peter was not to be swayed in his judgment: Marie had spilled possibly royal blood, and she had to pay for that. Her sled, which was laid out with rotten straw, drew nearer; slight snowflakes fell, and the sturdy ponies slipped on the icy cobblestones. The crowd, which had been waiting since before dawn, shouted obscenities and threw rotten vegetables, laughing and screaming. Marie neither ducked nor blinked when the first rotten cabbage leaf hit her face. Was she crying? I was too far away to tell, but thought I saw traces of ill-treatment on her face after all, as well as a burn mark on her shoulder. Crude hands had shorn off those tumbling auburn locks, which had aroused many a man's desire, and on her bald head cuts and bruises festered.

"God be merciful upon her poor soul," muttered Tsaritsa Praskovia, crossing herself with three fingers. She, too, had begged Peter in vain for mercy for Marie. Sophie Charlotte lowered her eyes and clasped her fingers, while next to her Alexey had leisurely stretched out his legs and munched an apple. He spat out the seeds, hitting his wife's silk shoes.

The wardens lifted Marie from the sled and took her shackles off; she held herself very straight, as if she was on her way to a ball. A woman pushed through the rows of soldiers and spat in her face. "Whore! Child killer! Witch!" The saliva trickled down Marie's cheek, but she gracefully unfolded the wide skirt of the white silk dress that Peter had made her wear in her very last hour. Small black bows adorned the shoulders and waist, but it hung loosely on her gaunt frame. Her gaze skimmed the crowds until it found me: she curtsied very low and I saw her praying for forgiveness before the prison wardens dragged her to the scaffold.

When she looked up, Peter awaited her there. She pressed a hand to her lips in horror, and shrank back, but a soldier stopped her, laughing. "You did not expect that, my girl, did you? The tsar fears he might go out of practice."

The crowd howled as Marie was shoved up the steps, and I shifted restlessly on my throne. Peter gallantly offered Marie his arm and I saw hope flashing in her eyes: Would he pardon her after all? No: the tsar led her to the executioner's block and his hand on her shoulder weighed her down. Her knees buckled and I saw Peter's lips move. Marie sobbed, bowed her head, and leaned forward. Her white neck shone on the rough, dark wood of the block, and Peter turned, raising his hand. The assembled crowd fell silent and his eyes searched mine. I shivered and pulled my fur cloak tighter around my shoulders.

"I cannot mitigate this most severe of all judgments, for that would be against divine and human right. Marie Hamilton, may God forgive you," cried Peter.

Tears streamed down Sophie Charlotte's face and Alexey looked at her briefly and coldly. He was in a bad mood, for Peter wrote him angry, threatening letters every day about just about everything: studies, belief, ardor as the heir to the throne, and of course the state of his marriage. Marie's execution did not seem to touch him in the least. In his retinue I spotted the Finnish girl he had professed his love for, Afrosinja. She curtsied, but I looked back at the scaffold. It was too horrible and yet I could not help but watch. The executioner adjusted his hood and then lifted his sword on Peter's mark. The blade caught the wan light and I heard the crowd gasp and pray. With a single blow he beheaded Marie; a stream of blood squirted high up in the air and her head rolled into a basket filled with straw. The people cried out, and the scent of roast meat rose up to my pedestal: the merchants of Saint Petersburg used the masses and their mood to do good business.

Peter seized Marie's head from the basket and the crowd sighed when we saw her wide, terrified eyes. Very slowly and tenderly the tsar kissed Marie Hamilton's dead, open and moist lips. Sophie Charlotte gagged, and I gave Alice Kramer, who had replaced Marie as my lady-in-waiting, a sign: she stooped and spoke calmly in German to the crown princess. Alexey watched Alice with a glint in his eye: Was it desire or simply curiosity? Whatever, I slapped his arm with my fan made of ivory and silk, lest he had any funny ideas. She and I shared a similar past, so I wanted to protect her in the future.

61

I was not far from the tsar when he turned to Tolstoy, who together with Shafirov had returned from Constantinople, during a feast in Menshikov's palace for the name day of our daughter Elizabeth. "You have always given me the right advice. Help me this time, too," Peter said darkly, and Tolstoy moved closer.

"What is it, my tsar? Has somebody wronged you?"

I leaned back in my pillows. My hour was only weeks away, and my limbs were heavy and swollen.

"Yes. My son Alexey. Everything he does, his mere being, wrongs me." Peter spat and said, "In England, a king once called into the ranks of his knights, 'Will no one rid me of this troublesome priest?'"

"And? What happened to the troublesome priest?" Tolstoy asked with a lopsided smile, as Peter drank deeply of his Tokay.

"The knights went to the cathedral where the man was preaching and slayed him in front of the altar."

Tolstoy weighed the answer, and warned, "Do not act in haste, my tsar. Both Alexey's wife and the tsaritsa are with child. We might be lucky, and nothing needs to be done. Otherwise—"

"But I can no longer bear this waste of space," Peter cried, but lowered his voice at once, as some of the foreign envoys had looked up. "He is an insult, not a son." He glowered, so even Elizabeth stopped playing with her little dog and looked questioningly at her father. I smiled at her, soothingly, and then met the ambassadors' eyes, until they lowered their gaze. For good measure, I sent them the cupbearer and his two companions with a vat of liquor. Campredon, the French ambassador, grimaced when his eagle cup was filled to the brim.

Peter groaned. "The thought that Russia might fall to Alexey haunts me. Let's do something. Now!"

But Tolstoy was not to be swayed. "Please. Wait. For how haughty and demanding can Alexey be, if he has a son and a brother?"

Yes. *If* I, I thought, and checked with myself as I had done a hundred, a thousand times before. Did I feel different during this pregnancy to when I had expected my daughters? Was my belly more pointed than round; was I more or less sick in the morning; more beautiful or uglier, was I sad or jolly? I tried to replace any old-women's tales, any myths and any laymen's advice and all questions and doubts in my heart with prayer.

The tsar studied Sophie Charlotte, his brows furrowed. Neither her marriage nor her blessed state suited her. She hardly ate, and always asked for fresh lemonade, which annoyed him. Her skin was gray and blemished with unsightly pimples and her hair had lost the last of its shine and body and would not keep in soft curls. I pitied her, thinking of the last letter, which, thanks to Peter's secret service, had never reached her father's court of Brunswick. *I am a lamb, which is slaughtered senselessly on the altar of our house. I shall die a slow death, from sorrow and loneliness,* she wrote, and Makarov had read it aloud.

"Sister-in-law of the emperor of Austria or not, I do not know how my stupid son has impregnated this grasshopper again. I would not get a hard-on with that bag of bones," Peter muttered, and Tolstoy said, "Alexey is supposed to have been helped by his mistress." He made an obscene gesture and the two men almost choked with laughter.

I turned around and looked for Alice Kramer. "Where is the tsarevich tonight?" I asked her under my breath.

"He dines alone with Afrosinja. Every evening. They are always together; the tsarevich gave her a big apartment."

Peter lifted his tankard and shouted. "A round for the welfare of my unborn son. And a toast to my unborn grandson." Everyone rose, and I smiled at Sophie Charlotte as she sipped the wine politely and with pale lips. Then I, too, drank deeply, for the wine drove my worries away.

* * *

I paced my little Chinese study with its walls covered with silk and dark red lacquer to ease the last days of my pregnancy. Persian incense burned in the copper pans as it was a clammy, damp October day; even the flames in the fireplace cowered in the draft. For the first time ever I feared giving birth. I was so big: Was I expecting twins? Two sons for Peter, possibly? I forbade myself any sort of hope or daydream.

"Listen, *matka*," said Peter, and read to me what he had just written to Alexey. "'My son. It hurts me more and more to address a lowly being like you as such. I have neither spared my life nor my strength for Russia and my people. So why should I spare your life, which is so unworthy? I'd rather give my throne to a worthy stranger than to an unworthy son.'"

"Is not that a bit too harsh? Don't send the letter just now. Think about it: let us wait for the birth of Sophie Charlotte's child. Perhaps he will better himself . . ." I said, against all reason. I still could not, and would not, give up on Alexey so easily. He had not become the way he was all by himself.

"Oh, you with your heart of gold. No one can ever be so bad that even you might see the evil in him. If I only think of Marie Hamilton. If it was for you, she'd still be alive." Peter tousled my hair.

I shrugged. "Life is too short to be vindictive. Hate and anger just burden the heart and make you lose sleep."

There was a knock on the door and Alice slipped in. "Peter Andreyevich Tolstoy asks to be admitted. Tsarevna Sophie Charlotte is in labor."

"Is it not too soon for her?" I asked, but Peter ordered, "Let him in. What are you waiting for, girl?"

Tolstoy came, together with his handsome Moorish slave, Abraham, whom he had bought at the market in Constantinople, but he himself looked pale and drawn. "I cannot stay long, my tsar. The crown princess is in labor. Blumentrost says it's far too early, but—" His voice trailed off, and Alice shot me a worried glance.

"How can that old quack be so sure about that? Was he present at the moment of impregnation?" Peter laughed mockingly and kicked the logs in the fireplace. Sparks shot up before settling in the embers.

Tolstoy shuffled his feet uneasily. "Rumors are going around in the crown prince's rooms," he began.

Peter looked up. "What kind of rumors?"

"The crown princess is said to have fallen down the stairs. She has bruises all over her body and some of her ribs are broken, says Blumentrost."

I sat down, stuffed a pillow in my back, and put my feet on Peter's thighs. Sophie Charlotte should have fallen down the stairs? She hardly moved anymore. I feared the worst. Peter began to knead my swollen ankles. "Spit it out, Tolstoy," he ordered. "What has happened?"

Tolstoy looked browbeaten. "If you so command: Alexey kicked and boxed Sophie Charlotte so hard that she threw herself down the stairs. Now labor has set in, many weeks too early."

"My God," I gasped. "That's impossible." What had we all allowed to happen?

Peter pushed my feet aside, got up, and went to the small desk. He pressed his seal into the soft lump of wax at the end of the letter to Alexey. When he looked up, his gaze settled on my belly in a silent plea. "The prince has to decide. Either he behaves according to his rank, or he retreats to a monastery." His voice sounded choked and hoarse. "Or . . ." He broke off, and neither Tolstoy nor I dared to look at the tsar. *Or . . . ?* I placed my hands on my body. The child hardly moved anymore, as I had grown so big. My hour was close.

"Call the messenger," Peter commanded, folding the letter.

I knew that this was Alexey's last chance.

62

The following rainy October day, Sophie Charlotte gave birth to a healthy boy. The tsar was present at the birth and held his grandson up in the hazy light.

"Look at him: my heir. Petrushka." He laughed, his eyes shiny with tears, as the child wiggled and clamored for his first feed. He was well formed and in good health, I saw, better than my sons had ever been at the moment of their birth. Peter bathed and swaddled Petrushka himself, giggling and cooing, before laying him in the arms of the buxom wet nurse he had brought in from the German suburbs of Moscow. The little prince was to soak up the new, open Russia with his milk.

"Well, let's get on with it, shall we, my little one?" she asked tenderly, and Petrushka snapped at her large red nipple.

The tsar whooped: "Wonderful. He's already as strong as a bear."

Behind us, Sophie Charlotte stirred in her fever. Blumentrost wanted to bleed her and stood to the ready with his cursed heated glasses in his hands. "Stop it. You are bleeding the life out of her. Serve her hot chicken broth with red wine instead," I ordered, and knelt next to her as best I could despite my belly. "Sophie Charlotte?" I asked softly. She turned her head, but her eyes were glassy; a veil of gray sweat dulled her skin, yet her cheeks glowed unhealthily and bright red. I tried for her hand and her fingers twitched briefly before going limp in mine.

"*Mutter . . .*" she whispered. A maidservant spooned some of the broth I had ordered into her mouth, but the princess could not keep it down.

"See to it that she is not too swathed. Open the windows. Dried fruits soaked in warm wine and chicken broth will strengthen her. Burn camphor in the room. That cleans the air," I told her bored retinue. Sophie Charlotte did not stop bleeding; her fever rose and of the six doctors Peter had sent to her, each was more useless than the last, standing in the corner, muttering and shaking their heads. On his last visit to her apartment, Peter had to be held by two of his footmen, for he had celebrated the birth of his grandson in the past days a bit too thoroughly and could scarcely stand for flatulence. I myself did not see Sophie Charlotte again, as no curse and no evil eye should lie on me when my own hour drew close.

"You go," I said to Alice. "Speak German to her in her last hour, will you?"

When she returned, her eyes were swollen, and her face worn with grief. I told my reader to stop her lecture. "And? Sit down; drink from the hot wine and then tell me."

"Her end is near. Sophie Charlotte is an angel. In her confession, she forgave Alexey everything. She . . ." Her voice broke. I looked into the flames of the fireplace. Our world was not a place for angels.

"What exactly did she say?" I asked.

Alice swallowed hard. "She swore to her priest that Tsar Peter was kindness himself and that Alexey was always a loving husband to her." She slid up to me, digging her fingers into my skirt and burying her face in the folds of my robes. "Forgive me, Tsaritsa. Please, do not send me back to the princess's room. What I see and hear there is just too terrible. I can't bear it." Her delicate body shook and I stroked her hair. Alice was but a shadow of the merry girl I had once encountered in Sheremetev's house. She raised her head and sobbed. "The tsarevna kissed the tsar's hands and took leave from our world. When Alexey came into the room, he threw himself at her feet, kissed her, and fainted three times with grief, until the tsar kicked him and dragged him out of the room by his hair."

Just then, the bell of Saint Isaac's church began to toll deeply, and steadily, before the other bells of the city took up the call, carrying the sad news far out into Russia, all through the long, dark night: Tsarevna Sophie Charlotte was dead. I crossed myself with three fingers. "May God give peace to her soul." Alice sat motionless at my feet, her face buried in her hands. The child in my body lay still, as if listening with us to the bells of Saint Petersburg.

* * *

Peter himself cut open Sophie Charlotte's corpse to put an end to the rumors that she had been poisoned. When the princess lay in the morgue, the tsar himself held his grandson Petrushka over the font. Like that, he chose the boy publicly for his succession, though he did not yet give him a title, neither tsarevich nor prince of Russia. I knew he was waiting and praying.

I did not attend Sophie Charlotte's funeral lest an evil spirit might spread, and my caution was rewarded: I myself gave birth to a strong and healthy son. I wet his scalp with my tears and held him tight, counting and recounting his strong, rosy fingers, and losing myself in the sweet smell of the nape of his neck. "Peter Petrovich," Peter shouted in triumph, holding him up into the light, tears streaming down his face, checking the boy's limbs again and again, kissing the little toes and gazing into the child's eyes of a deep, dark blue, such as his own were. He embraced him, sobbing, and holding him so tightly that the worried midwife had to prise the boy from his father's hands. We kissed, tears of joy streaming down our faces, as cannon salvos tore a hundred and twenty-one times through the Saint Petersburg night and, as if to forget about Sophie Charlotte's death, the bells in church towers all over Russia danced with joy. The next morning, Peter presented me with a suite of Siberian diamonds that took my breath away: the necklace, bangles, brooch, and earrings were shaped like ice crystals. It was the most beautiful thing I had ever seen. When I wanted to thank him, he waved my words away: "A minor token for a woman who has given me everything. Everything—" He choked with emotion and we cried again, together.

That night, I gazed through the open window at the fireworks Peter set loose and listened to the sound of his drumming fading in the streets. He set off to celebrate and the sky turned into a rainbow of colors and a shower of light: I had a son. Finally. My very own beautiful, strapping boy, and Russia had not one, not two, but three heirs.

* * *

"'My father,'" Pavel Jagushinsky read, and frowned, looking at Alexey's letter.

It was the first time I'd returned to the senate after giving birth to Peter Petrovich two months earlier, and I sat next to Peter. I gently steadied his kicking, twitching legs when he heard that salutation. Menshikov, wearing a red coat and a wig of silvery hair, his cheeks looking fresh from the morning visit of his barber, listened up, too.

"'If Your Majesty wishes to exclude me from the succession to the Russian throne, your will shall be done. Please take this yoke from my shoulders. My inheritance crushes me, and my unsteady mind makes me unfit to rule. My body is too weak to steer the country with the iron hand it needs—'" Peter snorted in derision, but I placed my hand on his: Alexey had been diagnosed with tuberculosis, after all. He grunted and Jagushinsky went on reading.

"'I pledge to never seek the crown of Russia. May God protect my brother and give you many more years to live and to reign. The well-being of my children is in your hands. For myself I only ask for what I need to live.'"

Peter raised his hand, and Jagushinsky paused. Silence stretched in the senate. "Give me this," the tsar ordered, scanning the letter. Menshikov watched him with burning eyes. What was going on: Did Alexey really give up his inheritance?

"I can wrap fish in that, nothing else. 'Your will is to be done,'" Peter mimicked. He crumpled up the letter and threw it at Makarov. "For your archives, Makarov. Empty promises and silly phrases."

Makarov smoothed the paper and let it slip between his documents. The senators sat waiting, until Peter spoke in a dangerously low voice. "Tsaritsa Catherine Alexeyevna has given me a healthy son. The question of the succession must be clarified. We are planning a long journey through Europe. Upon my return, the succession shall be determined. Until then—" He suddenly shouted so that the veins on his forehead bulged and his face turned crimson. "Until then, my useless son has to decide: either he shows himself worthy of succession, or he will disappear forever into the darkness of a monastery." His last words drowned in a gargling; he fell from his chair and his face distorted.

I jumped up. "My God, Menshikov, hold on to him. Hold his legs tight!"

The senators had shrunk back, pressing themselves against the wooden paneling or seeking cover behind their chairs. Menshikov weighed the tsar's feet down while I dodged his beating arms. He swiped the tiara from my head, but I managed to press his face into my bosom, where he calmed down.

"The council is over. The tsar needs peace. You will be told how to carry on," I said.

Menshikov and I stayed back behind, alone. The only sound in the room was the tsar's heavy, irregular breathing.

63

When Peter had set off on his first journey through Europe years earlier in search of knowledge and progress, the courts had greeted him with more curiosity than respect. This time he left for Europe to be welcomed as their own: Dutch and British ships protected the trade in the Baltic Sea. Poland, Saxony, and Denmark formed a defensive wall against the Swedes. And another reason for Peter's departure to the West made me smile: his niece, the little vixen Tsarevna Jekaterina Ivanovna, was to marry the Duke of Mecklenburg in April.

Our sleds were loaded with luggage and laid with skins, furs, cushions, and blankets when Peter strolled about in the courtyard, our little Peter Petrovich in his arms. The boy was three months old, strong and full of life, and the thought of leaving him for so long, after all the years that I had waited for him, broke my heart. Snowflakes danced in the icy breeze and the sky was covered with thick clouds. It was late January in Saint Petersburg and so cold that our bodies left warm traces in the crystal air and our breath hung in icicles on our lips. Peter showed his son off proudly to his household, while the nurse followed him, running around him like a headless chicken.

"My tsar, let the prince wear his fur cap. Otherwise he might catch a deadly cold," she begged, but Peter pressed the little one to his chest and sniffed at his neck. "Oh, rubbish. A Russian prince is hardy. Is that not so, my little one? Your mother and I are off, but not for long. Just to kick the Swedish king in the ass and to visit all his former friends. Remember, one must look after one's enemies as much as one's friendships." He kissed our son, and the little one chirped as Peter's mustache tickled him and freed his little hands from the sable blanket into which he was wrapped. "You must not be offended that we leave you behind. I'll take you with me next time. Do not be angry with your *batjushka*—I would never leave you alone if it was not necessary. Look, even your mother will only follow me a little later. We will find you a fine European princess as a bride." Peter nuzzled our son's pink fingers, then sniffed and wrinkled his nose. "The prince has just relieved himself. On my uniform." He handed him to the nurse, who hurried back to the palace with the infant. Peter slung his arm around my shoulders. "It is right that you stay here until our little angel has survived his first winter. Besides, I also like to think that Jekaterina Ivanovna's wedding is not too interesting to you," he teased.

"On the contrary. The tsarevna wanted to marry so badly that I wish her all the luck in the world." I smiled. "Hopefully her husband will survive the wedding longer than her brother-in-law, the Duke of Courland, God be merciful upon his soul."

Peter frowned. "Soon we must also think of a husband for our daughters. Let me have a proper look at that young king of France."

I fell silent, because I was still hurt that Peter did not want me to go to Paris. Instead, I had to remain in Saint Petersburg and then meet him in Germany.

"Why can't I go with you?" I had whined.

"Oh, Catherinushka, you would just be bored there! Besides, I do not have to worry about Russia if you are here as my regent," he had said, trying to flatter me.

"I'd be bored? In Paris?" I had stared at him blankly. I might not know Europe, but I knew that a woman could not be bored in Paris. I suspected the truth and it burned like fire: Peter was ashamed of me. Versailles, like all the foreign envoys, mocked the way I presented myself. I just did what the other *damy* did, and what we deemed fashionable here in Saint Petersburg, which was normally fine for Peter. But now he was eager to be received with all possible honors in Paris: the regent and the little King Louis the Fifteenth should welcome him personally, and take him seriously. At the sight of me, Versailles would suffer fits of laughter, we knew from letters that Campredon had sent to France. When he briefed Peter before the visit to his king's court, he said: "French courtiers change their robes up to five times a day."

Peter was stunned. "Five times? Really? How dissatisfied are the Frenchmen with their tailors?"

"Don't worry, Catherinushka," he said in an attempt to placate me. "I shall share my joy and my memories of the road with you and write you every day." How lovely. I could not wait to hear about the secrets that the River Seine washed into his ear and his stories about the expensive Parisian courtesans.

"Isn't that very ambitious, to look for a son-in-law in Paris?" I asked, to hide my shame and pain.

Peter took my hands out of my sable muff. "Little Louis is a sweet boy, just with too much powder and makeup on his face. But once he grows into a man he'll be just right for Elizabeth. Queen of France, our daughter. What do you think?" He spun me in a circle, dancing wildly among the whirling snowflakes, "I want a king!" he cried, his voice echoing from the smooth, high façades of the Winter Palace. "The king of France for one of my daughters." Just then, we slid on the icy cobblestones and fell into the snow, where we lay on our backsides, holding on to each other, helpless with laughter.

* * *

Two weeks later, fog and frost swallowed the tsar's train of five hundred sleds heading for the West. The last thing I saw of Peter was the royal flag, the crimson double-headed imperial eagle, blazing in the pure white of the surrounding landscape.

Alexey had been gloomy when he took his leave from his father. I could not read his thoughts any longer; those days were long gone. Did he really want to retire to a monastery, or did he just want to win time? A monastery was neither a prison nor a grave, and many a man had swapped the robe against the royal mantle. We all knew that Peter could and would not live forever. What was he playing at? Shortly before he left, I had accompanied Peter to Alexey's apartment. A stupefied and drunken Afrosinja had been dowsing half-dressed in front of the fire. She had jumped up at the sight of us, curtsying deeply, yet sullenly. Peter's dwarf, Jakim, mimicked her clumsy movements and she kicked him, but he avoided her heels with a swift twist, cackling and shrieking like a monkey.

Peter ignored the girl and held the letter that had been read in the senate toward Alexey. "Are you serious about this? You wish to retire to a monastery?"

Alexey kneeled and I noticed bald spots on his skull. "Yes. Please, believe me, my father!"

Peter shook his head and seemed to soften. "You do not know what that means. You're still so young. Think about it again. Then write to me."

Despite everything, Peter was ready to give Alexey another chance, and I loved him for that. Somewhere, deep down, there was still good and hope in Alexey. In spite of everything. I could still see the shades of a fearful child within him, a child that could be helped and educated.

"When do I need to answer?" Alexey asked, somewhat too hastily.

Peter, who had already turned to go, hesitated. "I give you six months, my son. I wish to get an answer upon my return."

I saw relief and triumph flicker over the tsarevich's face as he exchanged a quick glance with Afrosinja. We all knew how much could happen in six months.

* * *

A few weeks before my own departure for the West, I heard a knock on the door of my study. When Alice opened it I heard words in German being exchanged.

"Who is it, Alice?" I asked.

"It is Countess Keyserlingk," she said. I rose from my desk, where I was studying drawings of new robes to be made for me. What a surprise: What could the former Anna Mons, Peter's first great love, possibly want of me? I shot a quick glance at the Venetian mirror that hung over my dainty study table. My slightly slanted green eyes sparkled, and my lips were full and rosy, my throat was covered with diamonds, which also dangled from my ears, and I wore a dress of burgundy velvet that flattered my golden skin. Yes, I felt ready to receive Anna Mons, the woman who all the *damy* and the whores of the realm had feared more than the smallpox.

She was still beautiful; her ashen blond hair was silky and her deep blue cloak as well as her sapphire jewelry matched her eyes. She curtsied deeply. "Tsaritsa. Thank you for receiving me." Her voice was hoarse, and I sighed to myself. Ever since my marriage to Peter, no one ever spoke to me in a straightforward manner, but strewed in my title whenever possible, like seed in a freshly tilled soil, hoping for some harvest. Each sentence was twisted, hiding its true intent or meaning. If the tsar had known nothing but that, how could it be that I was already tired of it?

"Countess, please sit down." I patted on the small sofa next to the hot Delft-tiled oven, when I spotted a young man in her wake. "Who is with you?" I asked, stunned.

"My younger brother, Wilhelm. He has just returned from Europe and is now looking for a position at court. Is there any use in the imperial household for him?" she asked.

The young man bowed. He was as impossibly handsome as the whole Mons family, all fresh-faced, and with an air that spoke of walking barefoot in the grass and skinny-dipping in a river. His dark blond hair was thick and wavy, and his blue eyes were clear as the Saint Petersburg spring sky beneath long, almost black eyelashes and eyebrows. He was tall and well grown, which his tight breeches, the long shiny boots, and the fashionably narrow-cut jacket made clear to his advantage. He bowed deeply, looked up—and smiled. One of his front teeth was slightly chipped, and on both suntanned cheeks, deep dimples formed. It was a smile such as I had never seen before, lighting up his already handsome face as well as the room. All and everything disappeared behind it—Alice Kramer as well as the Countess Keyserlingk—and I had to hold on to the back of a chair, its promise of solace in times of suffering as well as unbridled, lighthearted joy being almost too much to bear.

I blushed, which made me angry. Was I the tsaritsa or a silly handmaiden? He straightened and I looked at his long, slender fingers, where he wore four rings forged from different metals. He noticed my gaze and opened his palms toward me, as if in an offering. "These are my lucky charms, Tsaritsa. A ring of lead for weight in my actions, copper for the warmth in my heart, iron for steadfastness and . . ." He broke off.

"And?" I asked, somewhat tersely.

"And one of gold," he answered, his eyes never letting go of me.

"What does it stand for?"

"True love," he said. "It is as valuable and indestructible as gold, I believe."

A sudden silence hung in the room. I rose and the former Anna Mons curtsied, worry and surprise in her face. Had they angered me, had her brother not done well?

"Your brother can join my daughter Elizabeth Petrovna's court. If he proves himself as her chamberlain, we can take things further," I decided curtly.

He bowed; his eyes full of fresh gladness. His sister wanted to kiss my hand, but I turned away quickly.

"Good afternoon," I said, and left the room, ignoring the mumbled expressions of gratefulness of the siblings Mons. Back alone in my bedroom I leaned against the wall panels and took a deep breath. My heart pounded, but my head was as light as a feather. I suppressed the urge to walk to the window and see them leave, see how this Wilhelm Mons moved. True love, he had said: as valuable and as indestructible as gold.

* * *

A few weeks later I left Saint Petersburg, and my daughters Anna and Elizabeth and my son Peter Petrovich with Daria Menshikova. The city disappeared behind fresh snowfall, which eased the farther we moved west. Reaching the Baltic provinces, I tried to recognize what I could, yet failed. But how confusing I found Europe and especially Germany to be; the number of small duchies and states alone was astonishing. Soon I no longer counted the customs and frontier barriers on which we were held and controlled; our purse emptied quickly in the face of all the tariffs and border taxes. We made swift progress, and the inns were clean and comfortable, so I felt fresh and full of vigor when we arrived in Hamburg in late May. The king of Denmark, Frederick the Fourth, awaited my train of five hundred coaches and wagons, together with Peter.

After the last Swedish attack, Hamburg lay still in ruins and its inhabitants lived in the still-smoldering, razed walls, feeding on berries, roots, and, it was said, stray dogs, cats, and rats. We struck camp in lavish tents, their waxed linen adorned with gold tassels, and my foldable furniture was forged in gilt metal. Peter sent me his barber every day, as he wanted me to shine next to the other ladies. While he and

Frederick tried to agree on a last, joint strategy against the Swedes, I strolled through the city together with my three hundred *damy* and visited the first opera house in Germany: what a difference to the Moscow theater that Peter had tried to establish, where the audience laughed, cried, clapped, chanted, or shouted and threw rotten vegetables, whenever they felt like it, and if it suited or not.

* * *

When we camped outside Copenhagen in the summer, I was pregnant again, and prayed for a healthy brother for Peter Petrovich. What more could I hope for? But things dragged on and we left for Mecklenburg, where Jekaterina Ivanovna and her husband were to lodge us, our troops, and our entourage with their people, but fearing the cost and effort, they fled as fast as they could, sailing or paddling across the Elbe to seek shelter in the free Hanse cities of Hamburg and Lübeck. At our first meeting since her marriage, Peter kissed Jekaterina on the mouth in front of her husband, which made the young duke blush with embarrassment, but Peter poked him and then patted my belly. "Look, Charles Leopold. My tsaritsa is again in blessed circumstances. Aren't you young people stunned by what we old foxes can still do? Better get on with it, man. Let us have a toast to that," he cheered, and emptied the glass, which a page held out to him, in a single gulp.

* * *

We had not heard from Alexey since I had left Saint Petersburg. Why not? I wondered. It would have been wiser for him to keep in constant contact with Peter, showing him his earnest wish to be his heir. I remembered the look that had passed between Afrosinja and him at our last encounter: a look of cunning and connivance. Yet what could possibly happen, I thought, shrugging off doubts and looming fears. Daria Menshikova wrote to me daily, telling me of little Peter Petrovich and his sisters, but also smuggled in word about the tsarevich: Alexey had fallen back into his old ways, and Afrosinja even wore the late tsarevna Sophie Charlotte's jewelry and dresses at banquets and feasts. Didn't he know that he only had these few months? I struggled at his impertinence and recklessness. Sure enough, just before the date of a decision loomed, Alexey did write to us, though I wish he never had: his words were like a rock that was shoved from a cliff's edge, and that kept on rolling, gathering speed and eventually crushing everything in its way.

* * *

I was sitting at my dressing table in the castle of Mecklenburg when Peter entered the room. The high windows were open; fresh air filled the room and made the delicate silk voile curtains billow in the autumn breeze. I felt homesick and lonely: in just a few days Peter Petrovich, my one and only surviving son, would celebrate his first birthday. Oh, to kiss his rosy cheeks, to see him stomp patterns with his little feet in the snowy park, or, even more fun, throw snowballs at the unsuspecting servants and hide behind snowcapped statues, giggling and running back to the palace, where hot chocolate awaited us. Here, the forests lazily turned golden, but their beauty left me untouched.

Peter's arrival in my room was like a fox's in the henhouse. My *damy* scattered and regrouped, all flustered and giggly, but he ignored them; his face had high coloring, his hair, which he had lost in patches after Blumentrost's mercury pills, was made ragged by the wind, and mud stuck to his boots from the military morning exercise. I could not read his face, but when he kissed me, I tasted beer. "Peter, you drank without me. That's against the rules." I laughed, but he sat down next to me on the padded bench in front of my mirror and drew two letters from his worn-out coat. The wax of the seal had turned brittle and fell in crumbles; the paper had been opened, read, and folded again many times. I laid down the silver-studded brush. My heart thumped.

"What is it?" I asked, alarmed. "Is it our son?"

"Peter Petrovich is fine, thank God. But these two letters from Saint Petersburg arrived this morning and they make no sense." Peter frowned. "One is from Menshikov. The tsarevich has borrowed a thousand ducats from him to join us here together with his Finnish whore. Just before, he borrowed two thousand rubles from the senate for the same reason."

"That's a lot of money for one short journey, even if one travels like Alexey," I said. The tsarevich easily trumped Menshikov's needs when on the road. "And? Has he left Saint Petersburg already?"

Peter chewed on his lower lip. "Apparently, yes. He is said to have left the city with Afrosinja, her brother, and three servants."

"Alexey travels with such a small state? Normally he does not make a step without his popes, singers, scribes, barbers, tailors, and jesters."

"It sounded fishy to me, too. But listen to this: the other letter is from my half sister Maria, who is a friend of both Alexey and his mother. She said she met the tsarevich on her way back from Carlsbad, where he took the waters and was on his way to us."

I held the brush out to Peter. "Well, then, everything is in order, *starik*. Come, make yourself useful, instead of moping about Alexey's travel costs."

He brushed my hair nicely and firmly, so that my scalp tingled, chasing away my dark foreboding and fear. Then he stopped and frowned at his reflection in the mirror. "There's something not quite right with the story. Carlsbad is not very far away. If he truly was there, he would have reached us long since. No. The tsarevich has fled Russia."

IN THE WINTER PALACE, 1725

Alexey. In my mind the moody face of my stepson blended with the shadows of the dying night. The day was grappling for strength in the sky above Saint Petersburg; soon, dawn would drop its silver veil on the city. No sound was heard from outside our room. Where were the hundreds of courtiers who had spent the night on their feet? I was back at the windowsill: a frightened, tense silence lay over the Winter Palace. On the forecourt I spotted people gathering; carriages met and sedan chairs arrived, stopping. Were Ostermann and Tolstoy among them? From this distance I was as blind as the moles that we as children had chased out of their holes with smoke, before bludgeoning and skinning them. Traveling traders paid us a good price for their soft, shiny furs, from which they sewed caps and collars, or lined the coats of rich people. Cold air crept through the cracks of the window frames and made the room even chillier, for the fire had burned down. Elizabeth had fallen asleep, literally tired of waiting for the privy council and a decision. Her head was tilted and her pink mouth a little open as she breathed. I envied her for her calm. Well, she had decided to fold for this round of gambling for power and survival. For me, however, this was the last chance to play my cards.

"What are you thinking of, Tsarina?" Menshikov used the salutation as easily as Feofan Prokopovich had only a few hours before.

I turned. How strange: I had seen him countless times, and still could not really describe him. Somewhere in his steep rise from the baker boy selling *pirogi* on the streets to the richest and most powerful man of Russia, the astonishing Alexander Danilovich Menshikov was forever changing face. His coarse features that had once reminded me of a wood carving took on all his sins and shortcomings. He ran his fingers through his hair, still the color of wet sand on the shores of the Bay of Finland. I knew that Menshikov was capable of waiting; I had better watch my back.

"I am thinking of the tsarevich," I said.

"Of your son, Peter Petrovich?" Menshikov glanced at the painting hanging above the fireplace, and Elizabeth sighed in her sleep and then settled again. When my little prince was bedridden with high fever, I had offered God a despicable trade, asking him to take my living, healthy daughters instead. But the heavens had laughed at my despair and punished us with a cruel, swift hand.

"No, of Alexey. Was it not your duty to turn him into a tsar?"

Elizabeth smacked her lips. Menshikov looked at her thoughtfully. What did he see in her? The throne of Russia? Were his ambitions limitless?

"A tsar! How should a man who is a fool, a coward, and a drunkard be a tsar?" he said. "Do you remember when he came back from his studies in Dresden and Peter wanted to see if he had learned how to draw maps?"

"Yes."

"He was so afraid of his father's judgment that he shot himself in the hand. We heard the bang and then he staggered from his room, bleeding and sobbing like a child. A coward, a drunkard, and a fool," he repeated.

"Maybe he was just too trusting?" Menshikov shrugged, but I was not finished with him. "Whom could Alexey have trusted, if not you? Whose example might he have followed, if not yours? You have left him to his weak, cruel tutors, and then the old Russian popes were so clever as to offer him love, warmth, and respect," I said.

Menshikov narrowed his eyes. "You speak of trust? Do you know where Sophie Charlotte fled to, when Alexey beat her up the first time and no one was to know, or no one wanted to know? She came to me, the wicked old Uncle Alexander Danilovich." He slapped his chest. "My doctor put a brace on her broken shoulder and healed her splintered ribs. By God, it is a miracle that her children were born healthily, as Alexey beat her worse than he did his dogs."

I raised my hand. "I do not want to hear this. Not now, at least."

Menshikov bowed his head. "Very well, Tsarina. I am not telling you anything new, really, am I? You know the sorry letters that the poor child wrote home better than me. How strange that her parents never replied, or rather not so strange, because those letters never reached Brunswick, or did they? Sophie Charlotte hung around the corridors like a harbor girl waiting for her sweetheart, pacing up and down the window front, looking out for the messenger from the West. But, alas, he never had an answer for her. And she trusted you."

The gloves were off. "That was something else," I hissed. "If the crown princess of Russia writes to Germany how horrid her life here is, it sheds a bad light on the entire realm. This ought not to happen. The tsarevich's wife is no daughter to any father and no sister to any brother, Menshikov. She belongs to Russia alone."

"Of course. So be it, my empress." The bright light of the morning blurred his features, and I could not tell his thoughts as he brooded by the window. Suddenly he wiped the pane clear, which was clouded by our breath.

"Catherine Alexeyevna," he called. "Come, and look!"

I hastened to him: riders galloped into the courtyard of the Winter Palace, their hats pulled down low into their foreheads and the fur collars of their cloaks turned up. The guard followed them; the imperial green of their uniforms and the gold thread of their epaulettes and buttons gleamed in the bracken morning light. The hoofbeats echoed a hundredfold from the façade of the palace. I suppressed the childish urge to press my fists on my ears.

"Who is this?" I whispered.

Menshikov squinted. "Do you see little Petrushka among them? I don't."

"Must he be with them to be named tsar of all the Russias?"

Menshikov hesitated. "No. Not strictly. But it's better to force everyone to swear their allegiance to the new tsar to his face, there and then." I took those words in before he added, "But it's much more important that they get hold of us. In Siberia we are still far too dangerous for them. It will be the monastery, if they are merciful; the Trubetzkoy Bastion and death, if not."

The men got off their horses and threw the sweaty animals' reins to the running stable boys. A guard looked up at Peter's room and crossed himself with three fingers when the breeze caught the red-hot cloth of the imperial flag with its double-headed eagle, which still danced at the top of the mast: to all of Russia, the tsar was still alive. The wind played along with our lie, our love, and our hope. A man broke loose from the others and motioned them to follow him. Was that Prince Dolgoruki, Petrushka's advisor? The blood rushed from my head. I ought not to faint; the moment of truth had come.

"I'm sorry," I said.

Menshikov waved his hand. "Don't be. You've done everything possible. Now we are in God's hand and can only pray for his mercy."

Just a breath later, a fist hammered against the door. It echoed like shots in my ears, and someone shouted, "Open, in the name of the tsar!" Which tsar, I wondered, when Elizabeth woke up, rubbed her eyes, stretched herself like a cat, and looked questioningly at me and Menshikov.

"What happened?" she asked. "Who is this?"

Menshikov straightened his coat and tied his lace jabot before running his fingers through his hair once more, smoothing it. At my look, he shrugged. "At least I do not want to look like the scoundrel that I am when they arrest me." With a couple of strides he reached the door and turned the key in the lock to open it.

64

Peter was furious. He turned the envelope with Alexey's letter this way and that before snarling, "The dog! He's fooled me. Who, I wonder, posted this letter for him? They'll pay for that. And where is Alexey now?"

I tried to take the letter back, but he would have none of it, folding it up and hiding it in his pocket.

"The heir to the throne has fled my realm. He makes a fool of me in the eyes of the whole of Europe. Behold! The tsar is so terrible that his own son must fear for his life and runs like a rabbit. Oh, how they will laugh in Paris, London, Vienna, and Madrid! I hear their laughter here in Mecklenburg," he said, biting his lips. Then he urged me, "No one must know about it, Catherinushka. It's a secret between us. Oh, this shame. When I get him, I shall cut him off like a gangrenous limb."

"Don't say that," I pleaded.

"Do you know what he wrote to his mother in the monastery? Thank God Makarov catches every letter of importance. Alexey said that once in power he would reverse everything I had done; raze Saint Petersburg, use my fleet as firewood, and reinstall the old customs."

I sat down, stunned at the madness of Alexey's words.

Peter paced the room. "Where can Alexey be? Who gives a coward like him shelter?"

"I do not know, my tsar. Friends perhaps, or relatives?" I wondered. I rose and tried to calm him, but he shrugged me off.

"Friends? In Russia, Alexey is surrounded by nothing but flatterers.

Who wants to call such a misfit his friend? And we have no family in Europe apart from Jekaterina here in Mecklenburg." He brooded by the window, then he looked up. "Oh, Catherine. This is monstrous. Relatives, you say?" Patchy red blotches bloomed on his cheeks as he strode across the room and tore open the door to the hall. The servant who had leaned against it struggled for balance, and Peter shoved him. "Move, man, if you want to keep your dumb head on your shoulders. Get me Peter Andreyevich Tolstoy; then bring me feather, paper, and ink. Quick, quick!"

Peter looked so cruelly determined that I dared not move but waited by the window. He paced on, muttering words, wrestling with his hands, and kicking at the dainty furniture. Finally, he sat and waited in a sullen silence.

"Why are you sending for Tolstoy?" I finally dared to ask.

"Because he is the best bloodhound in the realm, of course. No prey he chases is to live."

I gasped, but he turned his back to me, standing at the window, until there was a knock at the door. Peter opened it and I recognized Tolstoy's familiar, broad figure. "Tolstoy. Saddle your horse. You must find a traitor for me who has fled Russia. I will dictate to you a letter that gives you unlimited funds and free passage."

Tolstoy laughed, thinking that the tsar was joking. "Unlimited funds and free passage? Where has the game disappeared to, my tsar?"

"To Vienna, Tolstoy. Vienna," Peter replied before he pushed me out of my own dressing room and shut the door in my face. I turned to see the look of horrified understanding on Tolstoy's face give way to determination.

* * *

In my bedroom, raindrops drummed against the windowpanes and in the lush castle grounds people out for a stroll hurriedly sought shelter from the growing storm. Young trees bent in the gale and lightning flashed across the sky, making the roofs of Mecklenburg shine as brightly as on a summer's day. To Vienna, Peter had said. What was about to happen?

* * *

Peter abhorred the hunt. He did not own a pack of dogs and only used weapons in battle. Venison was mainly of interest if it filled his plate.

But now he pursued the hunt for Alexey with shocking zeal and devotion. Tolstoy picked up Alexey's trail effortlessly. Under a false name he had spent the night with his so-called wife and a servant in Frankfurt on the Oder, where he bought Afrosinja men's clothes made of dark brown velvet. In Prague, Tolstoy learned, Alexey used the alias of a Polish trader, and by the time he made it to Vienna, Peter had marked his route with small pins on a map of the European countries. He placed his tobacco-brown finger on Vienna. "I knew it," he said proudly. "Alexey is so easy to second-guess. It's a shame what a fool I've begotten."

"How did Tolstoy find him so quickly?" I asked.

Peter laughed. "Alexey gets so drunk every night that everyone remembers both his bills and his misdeeds. A blind man in the night would have traced this good-for-nothing."

Vienna! Alexey had to be more desperate than I had thought. Was he really hoping for the grace of the empress, who was a sister to poor Sophie Charlotte? Or did she not know what her little sister had suffered at his hands and at the court of Saint Petersburg? I would never have given shelter to a man who had beaten my sister to death. But the *izby* of Livonia were not the palaces of Europe.

Peter received the secret report about the nighttime arrival of the crown prince in Vienna and read it to me. "'The chancellor was torn from his sleep at midnight, as the tsarevich begged for an audience. The crown prince of Russia threw himself on his knees, asking for protection for both himself and his companion.'" Here I had to hold Peter long and tight before he had calmed down enough to read on: the tsarevich bent his knee in front of a foreign chancellor! Peter was still shaking with anger as he read further: "'Alexey Petrovich Romanov asks the emperor for the protection of his right to the throne and the rights of his children, but Charles VI also wants peace with Russia and wishes not to interfere with the tsar's family quarrels. Vienna fears a Russian attack on Silesia and Bohemia, so he has asked Prince Alexey and his companions to wait for his decision near the city.'"

Peter's fist clenched so tightly around the letter that his knuckles turned white. "The decision, my son, comes from Saint Petersburg and not from Vienna. Just you wait," he groaned, and brought his *dubina* down on a chair, breaking its artfully carved back.

* * *

Winter came, and I just hoped that the child in my body would not be harmed by all the bitterness and hatred that his father felt for Alexey. Peter's dilemma was clear: he wanted to be perceived as a worthy ruler of a Western empire, while he also wanted Alexey caught and punished. In my presence he sent his Christmas wishes to Vienna, and only on the last page, underneath Makarov's formal words, did he write with his own hand, *Please send Our Son back to us. We will lead him back to the right path with a loving heart; the heart of a father. Your dearest cousin, Peter.*

Yet when Peter received the emperor's reply, I was astonished by the latter's cockiness. At his New Year's reception, Emperor Charles said to the Russian envoy, "As far as we are aware, the tsarevich of Russia has never entered our empire." Peter was fuming, and sent the ambassador two bags of gold. The glare of the coins loosened a number of tongues in the imperial household in Vienna, but Alexey had been first brought to a Tyrolian castle that clung like an eagle's lair to the mountain, and then was spirited away in the cover of the night, together with Afrosinja. No one had seen or heard anything, and no one wanted to say anything. But the tsarevich could hardly have traveled north, toward his father, and so Tolstoy steered his horse toward Italy. He would hunt Alexey down and drag him back to Russia, even if he had to sweat blood.

65

The wet and cold in Mecklenburg made me miss the dry, mysterious winter of Saint Petersburg and the crisp Baltic air. I wished myself on the Nevsky Prospect and imagined the snow in the crystal air and the spotted patterns of ice on the Neva. The short daylight tinted the walls of the palaces and houses in richer hues than ever before, and the people were wrapped in furs, using the few bright hours to go about their business. Early dusk cast a spell on the city and its many sounds, from the shouts of the chestnut merchants, the ringing of the bells at the entrance doors of the *kabaki,* and the crunching footsteps in the snow, to the sleds tracing their way home. Their sharp metal skids struck sparks on the ice, which froze in midair like crystal stars.

And, God, how I longed for my children. Little Peter Petrovich was growing from an infant into a toddler, and for too long Anna and Elizabeth's most faithful playmate was loneliness: the camps of the Great Northern War, where I had always been by Peter's side, had never been a place for them. I knew them to be well and safe, first in my own vast, dilapidated palace in Kolomenskoye and later with Praskovia's motley household. They lived, and their health was a gift from God, I felt—I must have done something right. Still, now I should give birth to another child abroad. I had no choice, but everything inside me hurt.

* * *

On a wet January afternoon I was delivered of a son, Paul Petrovich Romanov. I had rested at an inn in Northern Germany and it was a simple and fast birth: after only two hours of pains the strong little boy lay on the sheets between my thighs. A midwife bathed him, and the prince fed at the breast of a hastily employed wet nurse. The messenger with word of his birth left for Holland, and Peter congratulated me, full of pride on the healthy birth of yet another recruit, while he also announced Paul's birth to the courts of London, Paris, and Madrid. But before those letters had been delivered, our son had already died in the disorder of too many people, luggage, wet cloaks, icy drafts, and overheated tiled stoves. The tender features of my little son were still with me months after his coffin's lid had been nailed shut.

The tsar wrote to me from Carlsbad: *Carlsbad is as funny as a prison; the hills are so high that I hardly see the sun, and the beer, if I find any at all, is warm, without foam, and tastes of cow piss. The worst thing is that they soak me every day like a horse with this filthy water.* When I had caught up with him, we celebrated with a dinner and he beamed. "You know, I'm glad to return home soon. Let's not stay too long in Berlin. Otherwise, Peter Petrovich will grow up before we meet him again." He shouted into the drunken round, "Fill the cups. Three salutes for Peter Petrovich; a toast to the tsarevich!"

Our guests all knew that the rightful tsarevich, Alexey—a grown, healthy, and able-bodied man—was on the run, frightened out of his mind by his own father and threatened by death. Still, they drank obediently to the well-being of a child who had only just taken his first steps.

* * *

Did Alexey know which bloodhound his father had put on his heels? Did he taste the bitterness of Tolstoy's sweat; feel the pain in his limbs after weeks of tireless chase? Tolstoy's hatred, zeal, and disdain ought to have pierced his dreams and poisoned the warm Italian wind when Alexey stood high on the battlements of the fortress of Saint Elmo near Naples. There, in Fort Saint Elmo, with its shady garden scented by almond and orange trees, and its view far over the Bay of Naples, he and Afrosinja hid, and waited. Tolstoy heard that Afrosinja was with child and that Alexey himself was half-mad with fear of his father.

"They have been found." Peter's face was pale with tension, but his fists clenched in triumph. "The emperor believes Alexey to be safe in

Saint Elmo, but in truth he is trapped, like the dirty rat he is. Let me write to Vienna at once. That shopkeeper on the Austrian throne wants to fool me, but I shall teach him a lesson. Let's pay Italy a visit, and I shall take forty thousand soldiers along, just to keep me company. Maybe then His Majesty will be a bit more talkative." He opened the door and barked into the opposite study, where the cabinet secretary was reading the last dispatches from the Great Northern War, which dragged on into its second decade. The Swedes did not give up their supremacy in the Baltics and the western parts of Peter's realm lightly. "Makarov, move your sorry ass, or I'll put it on a stake," Peter called. Was he joking? I wanted to leave, but Peter held me back: "No, stay."

He waved impatiently toward the desk when Makarov came in, a blank paper roll in one hand, quill and ink in the other. For the first time I noticed the silvery hairs on the cabinet secretary's temples as well as the puffy bags under his dark eyes. Having to keep up with Peter without having his giant power was not very becoming.

Peter dictated: "'My cousin, it pains me to learn that my beloved son, who has left Russia without my permission, is in your realm. We ask Your Majesty to make an appropriate statement, and for this we send Peter Andreyev Tolstoy to you, who knows of the tsarevich's whereabouts and will appreciate an encounter with him. We will not suffer any contradiction, as the law of God and of nature is on our side. Russia's next step is in your hands. Your Majesty's most loving cousin—Peter.'" He watched Makarov's quill flying over the paper before sand was dusted over the ink and molten wax sealed it. "Yes, that's good. The scoundrel will understand . . ." Peter muttered.

"Which scoundrel?" I asked, astonished. "Alexey?"

Peter smiled. "No, silly. The emperor of Austria, of course."

* * *

The emperor in Vienna did indeed understand. He weighed Alexey's well-being against a Russian attack on Silesia and Bohemia and soon Tolstoy again traveled south, but this time under the imperial flag. The emperor himself had begged him for mildness with the tsarevich, and during Tolstoy's ride to Naples it rained for weeks, as though the heavens were crying for Alexey's soul.

Alexey waited in Naples with a trembling heart and a brave face.

Tolstoy had words of forgiveness on his lips and treason in his soul. He promised Alexey what he wanted to hear: yes, the tsar loved his son and forgave him; yes, Alexey could hope for a free passage out of Saint Petersburg; he would be allowed to marry his mistress as soon as they arrived in Russia and then live with her in peace and quiet, wherever he wanted to. When Tolstoy wrote to Peter: *It is astonishing how much true love and care the crown prince shows toward this girl,* Peter just snorted in contempt. Yet I thought to myself that Alexey, too, was being human after all

66

We reached Berlin in August. The landscape was lush and fertile, and dozens of lakes sparkled between the green meadows; we passed cool and shady forests as well as clean and tidy villages. Peter's horse trotted beside my carriage, and from time to time he peered into the dim, steamy interior and blew me a kiss. "How do you like it in Prussia? Everything is a bit too clean, huh?"

"Yes," I replied. "So much order would drive me mad, I believe!"

He chuckled. "True. In Russia, this would lead to a revolt."

The farmers stopped their work in the fields when our train of over a thousand carriages passed them by in a cloud of dust and noise, followed by the same number of riders and then again footmen. The land we left behind had been razed as if a plague of locusts had set upon it, but children from the villages ran along with us, staring at a small group of men so tall that their legs and feet hardly fit into the stirrups. Peter had drawn them from all over Russia as a gift to the Prussian king, who loved tall soldiers in his regiments. King Frederick William had had the wisdom to invite in Lutheran refugees from the Palatinate, Franconia, Thuringia, and Austria, as well as many Huguenots from France, and Peter was jealous: Berlin was no match as a city, and yet he had to pay every gifted foreigner dearly to come to Saint Petersburg.

* * *

Seeing Berlin, I could not help but remember the handsome Andreas Schlüter, whom I had welcomed many years ago at the Neva pier. He had built tirelessly for Prussia until he failed to lay the foundations of a tower that was to break through the clouds and fell into disgrace. What else could Schlüter still have done, had he lived? The city peeled itself from the once-dirty, stinking village it had been like a butterfly from its cocoon. Tall trees cast cool puddles of shade and pedestrians out running errands met in coffeehouses, or looked at the wares of traveling merchants. Stately homes rose along the Spree and both the city-castle as well as Charlottenburg Palace were impressive in their splendor and size.

"Peter, my Russian cousin. At last . . ." the king roared as he greeted us. The two big men embraced each other while the queen and I exchanged gentle compliments.

"Sister, welcome to Berlin. How does your niece like it in Mecklenburg? Did you bring a portrait of your lovely daughters? Our Frederick is almost of marrying age." She looked exhausted, as her husband was not called the soldiers' king for nothing, but lived with no comfort, roaming about to look after his standing army of fifty thousand men.

"Are these your ladies-in-waiting?" the queen asked cautiously, eyeing the women behind me. I blushed with shame: as a practical joke Peter had swapped my noble Russian ladies-in-waiting for some rough peasant girls without rank or manners. The sight of the wretched women in their blotchy makeup and slovenly clothes made him roar with laughter. My real ladies were probably at home with their children.

Just then, the young Princess Wilhelmine tugged at the countless iconic images sewn on the hem of my robe. "Why do you have these colorful pictures dangling on the dress? *Les images font beaucoup de bruit*," she noted.

"This is fashion in Saint Petersburg, Wilhelmine. In different places you dress differently," the queen scolded her daughter, but I caressed Wilhelmine's head.

"These icons shall keep me from evil and misfortune, my princess." She could scarcely be older than Elizabeth and seemed bright and gifted.

The king spoke in a strangely abrupt way, as if he wanted to save himself time and breath. "If we survive that damn state dinner today, come to my chambers tomorrow. Simple fare, such as pea soup and roast pork with a crackling crust." He poked the tsar in the side. "And our good German beer, of course. You will need that after visiting

Holland. You can't even water your flowers with that brew. Tastes like piss." Peter nodded, delighted, and Frederick William looked at me kindly. "I do not know how the tsaritsa feels about this, but any bowing courtier I just want to kick in the ass. Nothing better than a straightforward, upright Junker whom I can trust in."

The queen added to her husband's prattle. "My son Frederick is playing the flute beautifully. He might give us a little concert tomorrow night."

"The flute!" the Prussian king spat out. "Crown Prince Frederick should exercise or study instead of playing the flute. I will whack all that fluffiness out of him."

Wilhelmine looked at her father gloomily, but Peter chuckled. "I know what you're talking about, my royal brother. I am looking forward to our dinner."

Peter's gift, the tall Russian men, howled like dogs when they took their leave from their fellow guards, but Peter did not pay attention to them. "Prince Frederick plays the flute, and my son flees, drunk, with his whore all over Europe. Well, what fun we'll have tomorrow night," Peter said when he got into the carriage and knocked his cane's silver knob against the back window, giving the sign for departure. On the way out to Mon Bijou I tried to cheer him up, but he was deep in thought. He uncorked a bottle of Rhine wine and emptied it to the last drop.

Wherever we were, Alexey cast a long shadow upon us.

* * *

"By God, I've never seen anything so beautiful in my life. Has it really been created by human hands?" Peter's fingertips skimmed the walls that glowed in shades of gold, rust, and honey. "How can you work something as brittle as amber like this? Schlüter was truly a master," he said in wonder. The whole room was paneled seamlessly with amber, and the candlelight brought the mosaic images to life, breaking the golden hue into dozens of facets.

I, too, was in awe of its beauty and splendor, and the queen laughed proudly. "We are also stunned each time we see Schlüter's amber room. Nothing compares to it in the whole wide world."

"Oh really? Nothing?" Peter asked, eyeing the amber walls with newly awakened interest. I could read his thoughts but hoped to be wrong.

"Nowhere," the queen confirmed. "This room is my joy and my pride. I wanted to put it into Mon Bijou, where I keep everything that is dear to me. That's also why I offered you the house as a camp."

We had eaten soup and bread and strolled through the castle's corridors until the roast pork would be served, crackling and sweet, and young Prince Frederick was to play the flute for us.

"What is behind there?" Peter pointed to a curtain that covered a wall.

Frederick William chuckled and tugged on a cord. "The pride of my collection." The curtain opened and the king held his candlestick high above his head. "Look."

I saw a statue placed on a pedestal. Peter cheered and the queen giggled behind her fan, but I blushed deeply: a disgustingly ugly man turned his bottom to us, holding his stiff, giant cock in his hands.

"That must be a fertility god. Kiss him, Catherine Alexeyevna," Peter said huskily.

"What?" I whispered, stunned.

"Kiss him. You heard what I said. Like this we can have even more children. Sons, of course," he repeated.

"Really, I do not know if a kiss on a pagan statue will help," the queen said, embarrassed by the situation, and Frederick William, too, hastily tried to close the curtain. "Shall we return to the table?"

But Peter seized his arms, stopping him. "Kiss him, Catherine," he ordered. "Or I will have you beheaded." Peter's eyes went dark, he drew his flat hand over his throat, and our hosts were silent with shock. He would not bear to lose face, I knew, and so I bent forward and kissed the cold stone of the statue. "There you go. Easy!" Peter slapped Frederick William on the shoulder. "My brother. If this is your biggest treasure here in Berlin, I will gladly accept it as a gift and take it with me to Saint Petersburg."

The king was speechless, and I feared the next moment: in Denmark the king had denied Peter a rare, mummified body from Africa as a keepsake. Peter had been so upset that he had broken the mummy's nose off and turned to the king with a sunny smile, the mummy's nose in hand, saying, "Now you can keep your mummy!"

But courtesy forbade the Prussian king from refusing Peter's wish. "Of course. Would you like another keepsake from Berlin?" Frederick William asked, somewhat jokingly. "Porcelain, maybe? Or some vats of pickled herring?"

"No thanks, I have all of that." Peter looked at the queen, his eyes beady with both greed and joy. "But since you ask, I'd like to have the amber room. I'll put it in my most beautiful castle as a sign of the Prussian-Russian friendship. Promised."

"I am not sure—" the queen started, paling and looking around her glorious gold-tinted room, this unique wonder of craft and beauty.

"It would break, my cousin, if dissembled. Also, it takes up a lot of space for transport. At least forty crates or so," the king added, steadying his wife by her elbow. She looked as if she was about to faint. I felt for her.

"Ah, bah. Never mind. If it breaks, I shall have it replaced. After all, I have access to the finest amber once more, just North of Danzig. And do not worry about space in my train. I shall simply leave more people behind than just my tall men. Those were my generous gift to you, after all." He smiled, leaving neither the queen nor king of Prussia any room for refusal.

* * *

We left Mon Bijou two days later. I again felt sorry for the queen of Prussia as I walked through the small palace's perfectly shaped rooms. The glass of the high, polished windows had been shattered and shards lay everywhere. The Persian rugs were trampled, and I spotted burn holes from cigars or carelessly made fires. Belgian damask curtains hung in tatters and the gilded wall panel had been demolished. The chandeliers of Bohemian crystal and the ivory candlesticks were smashed, the Delft tiles lay broken, and soot covered the fine parquet. On the furniture, carving skills had been practiced and the faces in the gilt-framed portraits were cut to pieces by countless knives. Oh, yes, Peter's men had felt at home in Berlin, but we would hardly be invited again.

Our train to Russia contained six more carts. The amber room had been hastily peeled from the walls and packed into forty crates, as the king had predicted. Peter had them opened to check their contents through twice and finally marked them himself with numbers before nailing them shut. Back in Russia, he asked his craftsmen to look at Schlüter's masterpiece and better the room. It was impossible. Peter lost interest and the crates were moved as they were to the storerooms of the Winter Palace, where they gathered dust.

The disgusting idol, however, traveled in my coach, at Peter's behest. I hung my cloak on his cock, but perhaps he did his mysterious magic after all, for when we reached Saint Petersburg with the first autumn storms, I was pregnant again.

Sometimes, when I lay awake at night, listening to Peter mumbling and cursing in his sleep, I thought of Wilhelm Mons and his ring of solid gold: as valuable and indestructible as true love.

67

Alexey returned to Moscow in the bleak midwinter. All along his way Russian peasants threw themselves on their knees, calling him a saint and praying for his welfare. It had been impossible to keep his escape secret, and the tsarevich had become a symbol of hope. Someone dared to rebel against the almighty and often so incomprehensible ruler—but not just anyone: no, it was the tsar's own son.

Peter paced the Kremlin's walls, searching the Red Square: Alexey had to cross it to come to him. The tsar had sworn that his son would receive forgiveness and gentleness upon his return to Russia. He had sworn: by God, the Christian faith, and the Holy Spirit.

He had sworn by his very soul.

Icy Moscow frost glazed Alexey's heart when he crossed the city's boundaries, for he was frozen with fear and had no idea what awaited him. Not knowing is a punishment in itself. Afrosinja had stayed behind, highly pregnant, and cockily demanded consignments of food: fresh caviar, smoked salmon, and sacks of cornmeal for *kasha*.

Four days after his arrival in Moscow, Peter called Alexey before a specially convened council. I myself was not allowed to attend, as Peter feared the influence of my mercy and kindness on him. But in truth, I was glad not to have to witness this farce.

On the evening of the trial, Alexandra Tolstoya came to my rooms carrying a tray of hot wine and savory pastries, but I had no appetite. "What did the tsar say?" I asked her.

"Say? You mean *shout*. All afternoon, all night, until nightfall. Until his voice broke. The council members are deaf, and the tsarevich knelt before them for hours on end, listening to it all, crying and begging for his life."

"What is Alexey accused of?"

"Just about everything," Alexandra Tolstoya said plainly, sipping mulled wine and briefly closing her eyes. "His poor education, his weak health, his cowardice, Sophie Charlotte's death, his fornication with Afrosinja, his choice of mother—"

"His choice of mother?" I asked, bewildered.

"Yes. Forgive me. Only my brother knows about it, and now we, too. And at least in your rooms the walls do not have any ears."

"Tell me," I whispered. Tears of fear were shining in Alexandra's eyes when she said hoarsely, "The witch hunt has begun, Tsaritsa. Everyone who has ever been in touch with the tsarevich or his mother must now fear for their lives."

"But Evdokia has been locked up for years. She has now taken the veil—finally!—and is known as Sister Elena."

"The tsar doesn't care. He is already talking about the Suzdal conspiracy, named after her convent. Supposedly, the poor soul had a lover there, a certain Stepan Glebov. Alexey is said to have written to her and he has visited her. That makes Evdokia also guilty of Alexey's attempt to flee the country. I think she has not even begun to regret having given Alexey his life."

The wind rattled at the closed shutters, and the flames in the fireplace cowered. "What else is Alexey accused of?"

"High treason." Alexandra Tolstoya's dark eyes were big and sad.

"High treason?" I gasped. "But that means . . . He can't . . ."

She crumpled to the floor and cried, nervously, but almost without a sound. "His own son!"

I knelt down next to her and we embraced each other. "Is there no hope?" I whispered.

The shadows swirling in the room made her delicate face seem drawn and aged when she said, "The tsar will only forgive him on one condition."

"Which one?"

"Alexey must tell the tsar the names of all his allies. Each and every one, and he must spare no one. My brother says the tsar will kill them all."

* * *

Only a few days later, my young son Peter Petrovich, who was unwell with a cold and fever, was declared tsarevich and the successor to the throne. I would not leave his side, now that I was finally back with him, but Peter presented him on the Red Square to his two regiments in spite of the bitter cold.

"Can't we wait?" I had pleaded, holding the boy even though he was a toddler who loved tearing between the courtier's feet.

"No, we can't," Peter had said simply. "It's now or never. I'll strike Alexey with an iron hotter than anything he has ever known."

The court flooded in all its finery from the Kremlin to the Cathedral of the Redeemer. As archbishop of Pskov, Feofan Prokopovich led the service. Alexey was ashen-faced as he kissed his half brother's little hand and his knees trembled when he swore loyalty to my son. He kissed my cheeks three times as a sign of peace but avoided my eyes. He must have thought that this was what I always wanted. In truth I hoped that this would satisfy Peter. But Alexandra Tolstoya's words haunted me: *Tsaritsa, believe me, it has not yet begun.* While speakers shouted Alexey's sins from the four corners of the Red Square to the people—"Even when his virtuous, loving wife was still alive, he was fornicating with a creature of the lowest descent . . ." What a mockery! What was Peter thinking?—I felt my child quicken: a brother for the tsarevich, my son? I had never before felt so secure, and at the same time so threatened, at Peter's side.

* * *

During my years at the tsar's side I had witnessed many atrocities. Men had their caps nailed onto their heads because they did not pull them off fast enough upon Peter's arrival. Monks and nuns had their guts slashed because they had dared to call Peter's decisions blasphemous. Old Believers, who claimed Peter to be a German changeling, were smothered with molten metal. But when Peter unleashed the horror in the palace and then throughout the country, he imposed the cruelest of all judgments—dying on the stake—on one man alone.

Nothing had prepared me for the suffering of what it meant to die on the stake. The man's screams tore the air of a crisp Moscow winter day apart, before they faded to a faint whimper at nightfall, after endless hours of pain. His dark blood kept on seeping on the stones of the Red Square, which was true to its name that day, and the stench of his dying drifted into the Kremlin, strangling my soul. Why did this one man have to suffer so much? An officer of the guard whose name none of us had heard before: Stepan Glebov. The answer would have been almost a joke, if it hadn't been so sad.

In his witch hunt, Peter learned that his first wife, Evdokia, despite her monastic seclusion, had not only seen Alexey in secret, but had also begun a harmless little love story. Stepan Glebov was told to guard the tsaritsa but had been moved by her pitiful sight. She replied to his pity with all the passion that had been locked up in her heart those many years. The fire in her had been smoldering, instead of being suffocated by cold, starvation, and endless prayers. Glebov did not burden anyone else under the torture, but Peter had found her tender letters to the man, calling him *lapuschka*, her rabbit's paw. Hadn't she whispered the same nickname in Peter's ear, during the few nights they had spent together? Glebov had to pay for that.

When all of Glebov's bones had been broken and when his flesh was torn from his body with fiery tongs, Peter all of a sudden commanded him to be put on the stake. The pointed wood was driven through the poor man's guts up to his chest. Evdokia howled at the news until her voice broke. After that, she refused to speak, I was told, and her mind drifted off into a realm that lay between the horrible truth and a gracious veil of madness and forgetting. To ask for forgiveness was in vain, so much she knew. Her only sin ever had been to be married to Peter and to not satisfy him.

In those days, even I could not reach Peter, and afterward he was never the same man again. No sleep was ever free from nightmares, and each laugh was haunted and strained. Every feast, every drink only served to make him forget.

* * *

On the night of Glebov's judgment, I went to the locked door of Peter's study. He was still awake: I saw the unsteady light of the candle flames beneath the door. I knocked and his steps approached, but he would not open. Yet I sensed his heartbeat through the wood: steady, and as cold as ice.

"What do you want?" he asked brashly.

I folded my hands, pleading, as if he could see me. "Please, *batjushka*! Let us put an end to this madness, my love. Why are you persecuting poor Evdokia? Hasn't she paid enough for her sin of giving birth to Alexey? You have me, and our children, and the love of your people. We are happy. Have mercy with her love. What can she do to you, and us?"

Peter opened the door and I drew back in horror: sheer madness sprang from his face.

"You ask for mercy for Evdokia? Well, if her lot means so much to you, then share it: I can have you shorn and thrown on a cart to a convent tomorrow. But it won't be Suzdal, where she was, with its sweet air and warm sunshine, you can be sure of that," he snarled.

From somewhere far inside the palace I heard footsteps approaching, halting, and then hastening away in the other direction. I pressed myself against the opposite wall, horrified. I, too, had not slept that night, because every second of slumber invited nightmares in. I could only pray for the souls of those who were near and dear to me. The tsar had already sent his half sister Maria to the dank cells of the Schlüsselburg. Anyone could be next, even myself and my children.

Peter stepped across the corridor and seized my elbow. His face came close to mine. I smelled his bitter breath but did not flinch and met his eyes. There was no escape.

"You ask for favor for the horny goat who fucked Evdokia? I'll tell you one thing and listen to me well. A tsaritsa remains forever and ever the tsar's wife, untouchable for any other man. And you want me to change my judgment for Glebov?"

I swallowed hard, struggling for composure and courage. I had never seen him so threatening. "Yes. Show mercy. Please."

Peter hesitated. He reeked of the long nights spent in the torture chambers, their dampness and dread; I also sensed cold smoke and the strong, cheap vodka which he drank by the barrel together with his companions. He grabbed me by the hair and bent my head back. I howled with pain and my heart raced: Was this it? "Catherinushka. Just to please you, my dove, I have thought again about the judgment for Glebov. Do you want to hear my decision?"

"Yes," I said. I ought not show my fear; Peter was like a bloodhound in those days.

"Well, then. I'll have him wrapped in a fur coat, he'll get socks on his feet and a cap on his head." He grinned.

"What on Earth is that for?" He held me too tightly for me to move away and forced me back against the wall, cupping my head in his hands. It felt as if he wanted to crush my skull.

"Silly. The warmer a man is on the stake, the longer he lives, and the longer he suffers." He laughed, shrill and sudden, and tried to kiss me, but I pushed him from me, disgusted.

"What's wrong with you, my little tsaritsa? You are not normally so squeamish, are you?" He looked at me mockingly.

I looked at him and felt his fingers, which had caressed me so often and had held my hand, promising me marriage a lifetime ago, against all odds. What had I sworn to myself back then? I would not fear, even if it hurt. I would not fear, for his sake.

"You stink," I spat at him. "You reek of the blood on your hands. Do not dare to touch me." I choked and wiped his taste from my lips. He stared at me and his silence frightened me more than his anger.

"As brave as ever, aren't you, Catherine Alexeyevna?" In cold fury, he turned and slammed the door of his study shut.

It took me a long while before I moved away from the wall and stumbled along the corridors to our son's room. He slept in his little bed, which Peter had fashioned in the shape of a boat, his nurse curled up beside him, his little hands holding one of her fingers ever so tightly. "Go and sleep," I said, gently shaking her and taking her place. "It's my turn now." Little Peter Petrovich's cheeks were rosy and round, and in his sleep his lashes cast a shadow on his face. At least he was spared this madness.

* * *

Alexey did not ponder whom he could sacrifice to save his own skin. The names spewed out of his mouth like water from a spring. The majority of them were shockingly familiar to me. Peter's oldest friends as well as the tsar's half sister Maria; Evdokia's family and an Old-Muscovite bishop: the latter confessed without hesitation that he prayed nightly for Peter's death. To him, Alexey was the only legitimate heir from a marriage desired by God. I knew that he was not alone in the Russian church, but no voice rose to defend him. Peter should have his skin rather than theirs.

The weeks and months of the persecution swamped our lives as icy and dark as the wintry Neva in their cruelty, and I chose not to know, witness, or remember. When their bones were broken on the wheel, Peter's oldest friends spat at him: "Despot! The mind needs freedom to evolve, it can't be dragged there in chains. You strangle us in captivity and terror."

Peter was stunned into silence and cold fury. Others were condemned to blows with the knout or forced to do heavy labor in mines or to build canals. The bishop still had the strength to curse Peter before his death on the wheel: "Son of the Devil, you curse upon our country. If you lay a hand on your son, his blood shall come upon you and yours, to the very last tsar. Fire and death upon your dynasty: God have mercy upon Russia. Curse the Romanovs!"

Alexey had to witness the torment of his loyal friends; he could neither eat nor drink, and had hardly slept since his condemnation. The heads of his allies were stuck on pikes on the Red Square and their empty, horrified eyes stared at the passing crowds. In their midst, on a quadrangular scaffold, hung the corpse of Stepan Glebov, Evdokia's lover, still on his stake. Crows pecked at his eyes and wild dogs tore his limbs off at night, dragging them into the alleyways.

I resisted the dark lure of evil, but I watched helplessly as it got hold of Peter, casting a spell over his heart and turning it to stone.

* * *

A few days after Glebov's death on the stake, I left my rooms, together with only a young page boy. I still did not like the Kremlin's dark corridors; their shadows as well as the icons' cold eyes scared me. All of a sudden I strained my ears: Were these steps coming toward me? I halted, and heard cutlasses clink. My heart raced. Was someone being arrested again, did Menshikov set off on a bear hunt, or was it the guard patrolling the castle? In those days, every sound and every movement could mean death. I was trying to hear more when a guard came around the corner, led, to my surprise, by Antonio Devier, Rasia Menshikova's husband and head of Peter's secret service. He bowed, and the soldiers knelt in spite of their weapons. Only now did I see the woman in their midst; a slight person dressed in black, her head veiled. She had to be a nun, as her long robe was woven of a rough, dark twine.

"Tsaritsa," Devier said, and the woman lifted her veil, eyeing me coolly.

"Whom are you talking to?" she asked, and I immediately recognized the tall, rounded forehead and her eyes, dark as coal and of an unhealthy shine. Her long, narrow nose above her fine, bloodless lips and her waxy skin that never saw the sun, on her shaven head, boils and chilblains festered. Her fingers clenched the seam of the veil, as if she were about to grab something—or someone. When she took a step toward me, I noticed her dirty feet in her worn leather sandals; her toenails were long, curved, and discolored.

Yes, she did look like Alexey, or Alexey looked like her. Evdokia —or Sister Elena, as she was now known— had been called in for interrogation. She scorched me with her gaze, as she took everything in: the gray pearls braided in my thick, dark, glossy hair, my sable-lined blue velvet cloak, as well as my warm boots made of embroidered leather. I felt ashamed: this woman should wear my clothes; this woman was to bear Peter his children; this woman should see her son ascend to the throne. The silence in the corridor became unbearable and I found it hard to breathe; Devier looked from her to me, unsure as to what to do. It was not God's will: those words came into my head and my shame abated. What remained was compassion for a wasted life and so I bowed my head. "Be blessed, Evdokia." Her gaze drifted from me into the darkness of the empty corridor: there was no more life in her heart, no more fire in her mind.

Devier cleared his throat. "Men. Let us go." Soon, Evdokia's footsteps were lost in the musty cold of the Kremlin and oblivion swallowed her. Peter soon moved her to a convent near Lake Ladoga, where she shared her humid cell with a mutilated dwarf; the tsar also had her tongue cut out. She was to receive no visitor and to hold no conversation; even writing letters was forbidden. She lived her life as a shadow, and the punishment that Peter gave her was time: endless, empty, dripping time, years and decades of it. I tried not to think of her, as it scared me witless.

At least she had loved once more by meeting Stepan Glebov: truly loved. For what had happened to my own feeling for Peter? Had it also fallen victim to the witch hunt for Alexey and his allies? I roasted in hellfire in those days, yet emerged feeling as raw as never before. How was I to live by his side, and to love him as I should? I could only try.

68

We stayed in Moscow until Easter. Peter exchanged colorful painted eggs and blessings with every courtier, and the tables in the Kremlin were laden with *kulitsh*, a sweet milk-baked Easter cake, and the delicious *pasha*, a pudding made of fresh cheese and pickled fruits.

Alexey sat at the table, but would not eat; his clothes hung loosely on his thin body. He seemed to me like a man made of glass who'd shatter at a mere touch. Peter, I guessed, was far from done with him. The tsar kissed me and asked with a full mouth, "When all the boring ceremonies are over, can I come to you tonight?"

I tried to forget the horror of the past few weeks and agreed. He slept tightly snuggled up to me, his hand resting on my body. In the morning he listened with a little tube to the heartbeat of our unborn child.

The feast ended the following day when Peter let the whole company clear the paths in the Kremlin's park so that we two could walk there before a restful little sleep. We both laughed at the pale faces of our guests, who were struggling to shovel the snow fast enough to keep up with our steps.

Anna, Elizabeth, and my little Peter Petrovich threw snowballs at them, and whooped with joy when they hit my fool, the old princess Anastasia Golizyna, straight in the face. "Hit and sunk," cheered Peter, spinning wildly with our son. "Come, fly with me, my son." We clapped and cheered as Peter fell with the little boy into the snow. They both started to make an eagle, until the tsar felt sick and vomited in the snow.

It rained on Easter Monday and the water washed the blood together with the last snow from the stones on the Red Square. I thought the horror had ended.

* * *

The Great Northern War had been raging for almost twenty years and at last, Sweden seemed to give in, and the struggle for supremacy in the Baltics was settling in Russia's favor. Everyone was tired: the generals, who had been crisscrossing Russia and Europe for years; the soldiers, who had forgotten the faces of their families; the nobles, who told their sons to flee instead of serving the tsar's army for life; the small landowners, who were burdened with high taxes; the souls, who could never hope to buy their freedom; Peter himself, who finally wanted to look from Peterhof over the Bay of Finland and say, "This is forever Russia." Above all, Sweden, which no longer had a ducat in its treasury, was tired of the madness of a king who was a stranger to his own people. Everybody wanted an end to the war. In May 1718, Peter Shafirov, General James Bruce, and Baron Ostermann were sent to the island of Åland to negotiate a peace. But the war had lasted so long that no one knew its cause anymore, which made peace difficult to make. Shafirov and his companions came back to Saint Petersburg, their hands empty, and the war continued, but on Swedish soil alone.

* * *

Spring comes to Peterhof, the one-story castle with its light yellow walls and white trellises on the Bay of Finland, in May. The last ice, as well as the remnants of dirty, slushy snow, has melted, and the mild air chases any memory of the cold. Fountains spew water as a marvel of pipes, canals, and nozzles pump salty seawater up from the bay into the gardens, where it dances, sparkling, for our pleasure. The young trees that had grown in the orangery blossom and bear fruit, and the sea sparkles in front of the long terraces. Stairs of gray marble lead down into the park, which Peter himself had planned so it is possible to catch a glimpse of our pavilions: Marly, the marble house with its straight, strict beauty, and Mon Plaisir, a simple structure and our first true house in Peterhof. How often had we waited there for the boat coming from Saint Petersburg? Most of the time its passengers were soaked to the skin, thanks to a sudden shower above the Bay of Finland. The ladies' makeup dripped off their faces, and the musicians shook the water from their instruments. Peter and I laughed tears at the sight of them, all while sitting warm and dry inside Mon Plaisir. These happy days were gone forever, for it was one morning in May in Mon Plaisir, among the growing light of the day, the lush meadows and the dense forest, that we waited for Alexey.

69

Ilooked out on the troubled waters, just to avoid seeing Afrosinja. She sat on a low stool, her face calm, but her loose, long hair flashed around her head like the flames of Hell. She had given birth just a few days ago, but Peter had the child immediately killed. I blinked to chase away my tears and tasted the sea salt on my lips.

Gray gravel crunched under the soldiers' feet when they marched Alexey toward Mon Plaisir. Afrosinja exhaled sharply, propping her chin in her chubby hands. She had not seen Alexey since their separation in Bologna a couple of months ago; Peter had sent him to the Trubetzkoy Bastion in the Peter and Paul Fortress upon our arrival in Saint Petersburg. I shuddered. The complete darkness of their cells shrouded the inmates' minds and dragged them into death and despair. No man left those torture chambers in one piece or alive, and if so, only to climb the scaffold.

Peter was standing with his legs apart, as if keeping his balance on a ship, his hands folded behind his back, when we heard the knock on the door. Afrosinja straightened herself and I held on to the windowsill, as if to tell myself that there was still life and beauty out there. If I only took one step toward Peter, I would fall and crumple.

"In with the traitor," cried Peter, and soldiers placed themselves to the right and left of the door as two bullish men dragged Alexey in. Behind them I could see two more soldiers. Alexey's head hung listlessly, and he had, if at all possible, become even leaner. Could he still stand on his own? The light blinded him, and he raised a hand weakly in front of his eyes. Afrosinja eyed her lover coldly and Peter curled his lips. "Is my son so dangerous that he needs six men to guard him? Look, he is trembling like pig's blubber. Leave us."

Alexey cowered, burying his face in his bony hands. "The light. I can no longer bear the light. Father, I beg you," he pleaded.

"Shut up," Peter told him. "I'll decide when you can talk." My fingernails dug into the windowsill. Alexey's sobs shook his exhausted body.

"Look up," Peter coaxed. "See who is here."

Alexey spotted Afrosinja only now. He gasped and wanted to embrace her, but Peter cruelly pushed him back. Alexey staggered and Peter seized his elbow: he probably did not want Alexey to fall and die in a stupid accident. No, he was not to escape him.

Afrosinja looked at Alexey, who wept in Peter's steely grasp. "Afrosinja! Are you all right?" He looked at her body, which was still heavy, but clearly no longer pregnant. "What happened to our child?"

She shrugged with a sullen face.

Peter interrupted Alexey. "You can save your breath. I drowned your child like an autumn kitten and Afrosinja proved to be an upright and loyal subject of the Russian empire."

Alexey stared at his mistress. The dawning understanding in his dark eyes was awful to see. I understood that Alexey—the fanciful, moody, haughty tsarevich—had really, truly loved her. Seeing Afrosinja there, sitting calmly among us in Mon Plaisir, hurt and tortured him more than any interrogation so far might have done. He buckled under the weight of her betrayal. His strength melted away and his whole being dissolved in the spring sunshine of that May morning. I felt like choking and crossed my arms, so as to not reach out for him.

"No," Alexey whispered. "Not you, Afrosinja."

"Hand me the letters, Afrosinja," Peter reached out and Afrosinja fished in her cleavage for a bundle of letters. She gave it to him with a bland smile and I felt like smacking her, but instead I kept my arms crossed.

"Catherine Alexeyevna, dearest stepmother," Alexey cried. In the mercilessly bright light of the morning the skin stretched yellow and waxy over his skull, his ribs showed underneath his skin where his shirt was torn, and his face and neck were bruised and swollen. Someone had raised their hand against the tsarevich! I tried to smile at him encouragingly, but my lips would not listen to me. Instead, tears rolled down my cheeks.

Peter watched us from the corner of his eyes, waving the wad of letters. "Alexey Petrovich Romanov. Did you write these letters, and did you ask Afrosinja to burn them?"

He nodded meekly.

"Instead, she has kept the proof of your betrayal on her bosom. Close to her warm, soft flesh." He held the bundle under his nose, sniffing at it with delight.

Alexey sobbed. "Why are you so cruel, my father? How have I ever wronged you, apart from being born as your son?" Afrosinja sat frozen on her stool, but Peter strode up to Alexey and kicked him hard, so that he toppled onto the marble floor.

"I will fell a just judgment. Do not dare to suspect me of anything else."

Alexey was bent double with pain. "I'm lost," he gasped.

The sun warmed my fingers: the light, I had to stay close to the light, I thought desperately, and licked my cracked, salty lips as Peter circled Alexey like an eagle in the sky would a mouse. He read the first letter and shook his head. "In spite of all the effort that we have made with your education, you still have impossible spelling and even worse handwriting."

Afrosinja gave a little laugh while mute tears ran down Alexey's face. Peter leafed through the letters. "Ah. Here is a letter to the emperor in Vienna. Let's see what you had to tell the sot: 'As Your Majesty has heard, the bastard son the washermaid has given my father is sick with fever. My father does what he wants, and God does what he wants.' What do you think of these words, my washermaid?" Peter mocked, looking at me. He knew where it hurt. "What, in Alexey's opinion, might God want to do with our bastard son? Let him perish, perhaps?"

Breathing hurt me, the air cut into my lungs, and hatred spread in my veins, poisoning my heart with its venom. Alexey hated my son; he wished for my boy to die. I avoided his pleading eyes. There were things I could not forgive. Peter knew that. He was like a puppeteer, pulling all our strings.

Peter did not wait for my answer but opened the next letter. "Ah, this one goes to your cousin Jekaterina Ivanovna in Mecklenburg.

Listen to this, it's just too amusing: 'I hope for an uprising of the Russian troops in Mecklenburg, which puts an end to my father'—" Peter paused.

Alexey was deathly pale. "Father, please, I have no strength."

But Peter was unmoved. "Just one more, for fun's sake. Oh, it is addressed to the senate of Russia! Listen carefully: 'My father's cruelty has driven me out of the country. Why does he hate me, but loves the children of his second wife? My half brother Peter Petrovich is weak and puny. He can die at any time and the tsar himself might leave us at any moment. I am destined to rule over Russia. Do not hand me to oblivion. It shall not be your harm.'"

Peter paused and then read slowly and clearly. "'If I am to be the tsar, then I shall leave Saint Petersburg forever and return to Moscow. I shall burn the fleet, dissolve the army, and drive away all the strangers beyond the borders of our country. I will honor the Church and our God.'"

The silence in Mon Plaisir was deafening. I knew that with these words in writing, Alexey would not stand a chance. There were only the two men, locked into a struggle that fate in its whims had brought upon them: father and son. Alexey lay on the ground as if dead, and Peter towered above him. Afrosinja had buried her head in her arms and I dared not move.

"Sit up, Alexey Petrovich Romanov," Peter ordered. Alexey forced himself up when Peter said solemnly, "As the tsar of all the Russias I accuse you of high treason. Do you admit your crime?"

I held my breath. Alexey looked at Afrosinja, but I read neither hatred nor anger in his eyes, only pain and loss. She met his gaze, also crying now. Alexey's sallow features broke up and twisted in pain and shame. "I do, my tsar and father," he whispered, and his words were almost lost in the waves washing over the pebbles on the shore outside Mon Plaisir.

That moment, I split in half. One part of me stayed at Peter's side in Mon Plaisir, as his faithful wife, despite all the hateful events. This woman would always belong to him and loved him out of a long, happy memory. She breathed the same air as he did and shared his bed if he were still to ask for it. She shone in the brightness of his light so no one dared to approach her; no one heard the hollowness of her heartbeat.

The other woman, though, broke free from the appearance that Peter and I so carefully kept, and she retreated quietly within. Peter would not get hold of her, no, never again, for she settled silently in the depths of my soul. For a long time she drifted there like a boat without a rudder, lost on the stream of my life, until one day: when another man's love would moor her in a last harbor, a spot so full of beauty and belief, passion and peace, that she could have never imagined it.

At moments I still taste the scented air of Mon Plaisir on my lips, and I hear the wind of Peterhof whispering those words of wisdom about the color of snow, the taste of tears, and the vastness of the sea.

70

On the morning that Alexey's fate was to be decided, somebody lightly touched my shoulder, but I slept equally lightly in those days.

"Tsaritsa. You have a visitor," Alice whispered.

My heartbeat quickened. A visitor meant nothing good at this ungodly hour of the day. "Who is it?"

"Boris Petrovich Sheremetev. I said it was too early to receive. You are not presentable."

I climbed out of bed and chuckled. "If there is one man in the world who has seen me in a less than presentable manner, it is Sheremetev. I'll be right there."

I glanced across the quay and the river to the dark, brooding walls of the Peter and Paul Fortress. A beautiful June day was dawning: boats danced on the green waves, and the early, bright sun made the river sparkle when the iron Neva Gate opened. I saw a group of men leave the fortress and step on the barges that awaited them.

I frowned. "Should Boris Petrovich not have already taken his seat for Alexey's tribunal?"

Alice nodded mutely.

"Hand me my dressing gown. Hurry," I said, running my fingers through my hair as a makeshift comb.

Sheremetev stood by the window in my antechamber, his narrow shoulders slumped and his neck crooked. He looked small, and very alone. My heart went out to him: What would have been if things had taken their course otherwise? He had loved Alice and had been forced to give her away. When I approached, he knelt with a sigh, as his gout pained him. I pulled him up on his feet, kissing him three times as a sign of peace. He blushed and adjusted his coat. "Tsaritsa, thank you for receiving me at such an early hour . . ."

Alice had stoked the embers in the fireplace and Sheremetev shuffled closer to the flames, hoping I would not notice.

"I do not know how you feel, but I am so cold. Come, sit down with me," I said, settling on the sofa by the fireplace. He smiled at me gratefully—the warmth of the fire lessened the pain in his swollen limbs—but I knew I had to help him further.

"I have not seen you for so long, Boris Petrovich. Does my old friend come to me only if sorrow weighs him down? But I have to warn you. If your son wants to grow a beard or your daughter wants to wear breeches, I can't help you. Or do you want to own lands that belong to Menshikov? Forget about it." There, that made him smile.

"If only it were so easy."

"What is it then?" I asked, taking his hand.

"Tsaritsa," he said, "I have devoted my whole life to my tsar and shall do so until my last breath. I'll fight for Peter, I will ride, I will sail, I will even learn"—he smiled briefly, before carrying on—"and kill, as I have done many times before." He wheezed between sentences. "But I cannot watch a father judge his son. For the verdict on Alexey is already settled."

If Sheremetev, the man of honor, said "the verdict is already settled," then it must be true. I bit my lip. "Tell me how I can help you."

"I asked to be freed from my duty as a judge at the tribunal, but the tsar has beaten my messenger with his *dubina*." He buried his face in his hands; his white hair as thin as a spider's web. When he looked up, he was weeping. "It is a yoke I dare not carry. This verdict is against every law of God and nature. A father who wants to try his son, asking for the help of the church and the courts. I cannot die in peace if I am to be part of this. I don't like Alexey. Among all the bad people of Russia he might be the worst. But still . . ."

I pondered his words. "Go back to your palace, *otez*. I will sort it out."

I leaned in closer to him, breathing in his bitter scent of age and near-death. "Are you sure the verdict is already settled?" I whispered, as in those days the walls had ears.

He looked at me, his eyes veiled. "Maybe not for the church or the tribunal. But in the tsar's heart—yes."

* * *

When he left, I had another look at the opposite shore: the boats had crossed from the fortress to the admiralty, where Alexey's trial was to take place. The ferrymen leaned against street lanterns, chewed tobacco, and watched the girls passing by, whistling and catcalling at them. Children gathered around them, eyeing the barges and pestering the men with questions. I stepped away. As long as men like Boris Petrovich Sheremetev lived, there was still hope for Russia. In the tsar's heart—yes. So he had said.

* * *

But the tsar's heart is in the hands of God; only He can find the just answer to all questions, wrote the court of the Russian church, which refused to pass a judgment on Alexey. For them, the Old Testament, in which a father punishes his misguided and errant son, opposed the New Testament, which preached forgiveness and love.

Peter was furious and called for a secular tribunal; a hundred and twenty-seven Russian dignitaries had gathered in Saint Petersburg. I myself saw him only once during the time of the tribunal. He took me by surprise, coming to Peter Petrovich's playroom. I was pushing a small wooden boat across the parquet floor and my son made the sound of wind, waves, and thunder. "Boom!" he cried, clapping his hands, and I flipped the boat over as if it had been struck by lightning. He whooped and I embraced him, smelling the June sunshine and the first apples on the trees in his hair. I spent too little time with him alone and had been robbed of milestones in his life. I held him closer, but he fidgeted and shouted, "Father! *Batjushka!*"

Peter and Alexander Menshikov stood in the doorway, all booted and ready to leave. Peter lifted our little boy up: how small and vulnerable he looked in his father's hands. Had he ever held and kissed Alexey like this? The answer to that question frightened me out of my mind.

"I see you've won a naval battle, Tsarevich?" asked Peter. Our son nodded, his cheeks flushed with pride, and placed his hands trustingly on his father's chest. "I am very proud of you. Let's go to Peterhof soon and you can choose a boat for yourself."

I rose, forcing myself to sound cheerful. "Where are you going so early in the morning?"

"To the fortress. The court needs more evidence of Alexey's betrayal," Peter said casually.

"More evidence?" I folded my hands on my belly. It was a mere few weeks until I would give birth again. Menshikov laughed and playfully pinched Peter Petrovich's cheek. "Thirty lashes with the knout loosens every tongue."

My stomach churned and I stepped up to Peter, but he caressed my hair. "This is nothing a woman in your condition should worry about," he said, but I searched for his fingers, enjoying this rare moment of confidence.

"Peter, I beg you," I whispered. "Don't do this. Do not sully your glory with blood from your blood. Do not torment the flesh of your flesh. Ban him. Send him to the sawing mills, to the mines, or to a monastery. But do not let his death come upon us and our children."

Peter looked at me, his face guarded. "Menshikov, call the tsaritsa's ladies. She is not well, and she needs rest," he ordered. Before he left, our son pressed against him once more and he kissed him tenderly. Peter would not look at me anymore and my heart knotted with dread.

* * *

After the first interrogation by the tsar, Alexey had to rest for three days, Alexandra Tolstoya told me. Only then was he strong enough to meet his father once more. Evil and cruelty lured Peter into their dark arms, and he was intoxicated by his power and the stench of sweat, fire, and blood in the torture chambers; the long hours in the Trubetzkoy Bastion fogged his brain. Whatever Alexey said, sighed, or sobbed, Peter used for his cause, and against his son. He was to stop only when there was nothing more to confess, or if nothing could be confessed anymore.

After another day and countless hours of agony for Alexey, Peter had convinced the tribunal of the prince's high treason: Alexey was to be publicly executed. Peter himself did not pass the death sentence; he left it to the court he had called upon to judge his son.

Prince Alexander Danilovich Menshikov was the first to sign the verdict with a cross beside his name. Peter's own hands were clean. But what if there was something else to know? Perhaps Alexey had not bared his soul completely yet, despite all the tortures? Somewhere in Peter's vast realm a group of conspirators might just be waiting for the right moment to free Alexey! Seagulls shrieked above the Trubetzkoy Bastion, lifted by the breeze toward the Bay of Finland, as Peter and his men took the barge from the Summer Palace's jetty, one last time, on the afternoon of the judgment.

I knew them all. Peter Shafirov was already sitting in the boat, staring at the water, while Prince Trubetzkoy chatted to him. Tolstoy and Menshikov shared a passage with the tsar, who held his balance on the boat, wide-legged. Why did they go and see Alexey again? What for? He had confessed. The verdict had been passed.

When the darkness of the fortresses' star-shaped walls had swallowed Peter and his men, I knelt below a small icon of the Virgin Mary. My fingers trembled as I folded them, searching for words in my memory when I prayed for Alexey's soul. Alice blended me a potion of hot wine, St. John's wort, and laudanum, which brought me some hours of restless sleep, plagued by nightmares: I gave birth to a monster, which Peter welcomed as his child without hesitation.

71

When a fist banged against my bedroom door toward midnight, I sat bolt upright, drenched in sweat. Was I still dreaming? Alice's face was ghostly pale. "Who can that be, mistress?" she whispered anxiously. "Are they coming to get us?"

There was another knock on the door, hard and demanding. But then my fear gave way to anger: if the Devil himself was at the door, I should offer him a glass of vodka before he took me. "We shall see," I said, padding across the floor, and opened the door. I shrank back, yet placed my hands on my hips. "Alexander Danilovich. What's gotten into you?" I hissed.

Menshikov leaned heavily against the door frame, as if his legs were no longer carrying him. Behind him crouched a cripple, holding a lantern, which cast an unsteady light, drawing out their shadows on the wall. I could not see the guard's face because of his hooded coat, but that was probably for the best. Menshikov seized my wrists. "Catherine Alexeyevna, come with me. Please. Right now. He's going mad," he stammered. He reeked of sweat and blood, his eyes lay deep in their sockets, and his face and arms were speckled with dark spots. I freed myself from his grip, and ran a finger over his skin and sniffed at it.

"This is blood. Have you been in a brawl? Has something happened to the tsar?" I asked. Instead of an answer, the ragged cripple raised his lantern and I stifled a scream. Menshikov's entire cloak was soaked with blood.

"Come, I beg you," he whispered. "Come quickly."

"Not alone," I said, suspicious. "Alice, put on your cloak," I ordered the girl, and slipped into my boots.

We followed Menshikov and the crippled prison guard down to the river. In the white hours of the night, mists veiled the Neva, thickening into fog on the other bank. Once we were on the barge, the dewy swathes swirled around my ankles and soaked the hem of my nightgown. The magic of these hours no longer touched me. A night that was not dark mirrored the madness in Peter's realm.

Alice squatted on the planks as the cripple drove the boat forward with steady pushes, the water giving way silently. Menshikov and I stood mute and very close together; he twisted his fingers to stop their trembling. When we reached the Neva Gate, Shafirov stepped out of the shadows and helped me disembark, while Menshikov lifted Alice onto the pier. We walked along narrow passageways into the darkness of the Trubetzkoy Bastion; water dripped from the roughly hewn, cold gray walls and pooled on the uneven stone floor. Tar dripped from the torches, hissing, and rats scurried into the shadows. The place reeked of blood and death, and Alice's fingers clung to mine like a drowning man's to a plank until we halted at an oak door studded with iron nails. Its small window was shut and locked. Was this a trap? What if I couldn't even trust Menshikov anymore?

I pulled my cloak tighter around my neck as the cripple unlocked the door and retreated into the shadows. The door shrieked on its hinges, a sound that made my blood curdle, but I raised my chin and took a step forward. In the corner of the dingy, windowless cell lay a man on a bunk, apparently asleep, with a blanket hastily drawn up to his chin. The unsteady flames of two night-lights danced like the spirits of the wretched beings whom these walls had swallowed. My eyes had barely adjusted to the dim light when another man threw himself at me, clasping my knees. I staggered, but Menshikov caught me. "Menshikov! Help," I cried when I recognized Peter's dark head. He buried his face into my cloak, sobbing, and soaking my damp nightshirt with his tears, his sweat—and blood. When he looked up, his eyes rolled into their whites, his face twitched, and froth covered his blue-stained lips. I reached out, as if to comfort him, but just could not touch him.

"Catherinushka," he moaned. "Thank God! I did not do anything, do you hear me? It wasn't me, whatever they say. Help me. It is not my fault," he cried, his pleas resounding from the cell's bare walls. "Help me, help me, help me—" He bent forward, rocking and howling like an animal.

"Give me a hand, Menshikov," I said, and we dragged Peter to a stool. He embraced my waist and I felt his hot breath through my dress.

"Now you're here, everything will be fine. I did not do anything. It was not my fault," he stammered again. Alice knelt, taking Peter's hands in hers, and I went over to the bunk. Only then did I spot the man sitting next to it, with his head buried in his hands. I touched his shoulder. It was Tolstoy, but his face was empty when he simply sighed and slumped once more. The blood in my veins thickened with fear, and I had a foreboding that made me want to turn on my heels and flee. Instead, I leaned over the bunk and looked closely at the man who lay there. It was Alexey, and yet it wasn't him. His skin was blackened, and the eyes bulged from their sockets; the mouth was open, the jaw slack and broken, and the teeth cracked or missing. The swollen tongue hung to the side, a bit of its flesh torn. His nose was thick and twisted, and the ears were half ripped off his head. No, he did not sleep; he was dead.

"Alexey," I whispered in shock, struggling against my rising nausea and trying to stroke his eyelids shut. But they would not close and stared out at me, charging us all with his death. When I tried to pull the blanket from his body, Tolstoy held me back. "For the love of God, don't, my tsaritsa," he begged. "You're pregnant."

I shrugged him off, but Alexey's state made me recoil in horror, despite Peter Andreyevich's warning. Menshikov held me tight until my head stopped spinning and my nausea dwindled. Alexey's flesh had been torn from his limbs with burning tongs and all his bones had been broken on the wheel. Their ragged, sharp ends pierced his skin, which was blackened from burn marks and streaked with whiplashes at his knees, hips, and chest. On no battlefield had I ever seen such a sight; no wild animal treated his prey this way.

"Good God!" I panted.

Peter raised his head from Alice's lap. "I've done nothing, believe me!" Alice held him and he sobbed like a child at her breast.

I overcame my disgust and dread and stroked Alexey's thin, straggly hair. "Now you have peace," I murmured. Tolstoy sucked his teeth when Alexey's head came loose from his body and rolled to the side, like a ball. He had been beheaded! I pressed my hands against my mouth, aghast, but Menshikov stopped me from running away.

"It was the tsar who did it," he whispered. "Peter was beside himself when Alexey died during the second torture. It was a miracle that the boy had lived so long, with God or the Devil's help. Peter was so furious that he grabbed my sword and beheaded Alexey's dead body. Now he's going mad." I heard Menshikov yet did not understand him. My teeth were chattering, and I felt searing pain in my lower belly. Was I going into labor, here, in the midst of this horror?

"Catherine, what should we do?" urged Menshikov. "Alexey must be laid out in state, otherwise there will be rumors that the tsar killed him."

"There will be rumors? What else could by now be the cause of his death?" I said, choking on the words. Menshikov ruffled his blood-stained hair.

"A stroke, maybe. Or his weak chest? Everyone knows that he was in poor health . . ." His voice trailed off. If he himself could not come up with a convincing cause, how did he hope to deceive Russia and the whole of Europe?

I bit my lips until I tasted blood, thinking hard. "Alice," I then said, gently. Peter was still crying in her lap, dampening her skirt.

"What about her?" asked Menshikov.

"You go get the garrison's doctor, his medication, and his tools," I ordered, and minutes later she returned with the man who obviously had been chased out of bed, for he wore his nightcap, and under his cloak I spotted his bare legs and feet. He bowed, peering at the corpse on the bunk. "Give us everything we need to tend to wounds," I said, taking his doctor's satchel. "We also need alcohol. Lots of it. You are free to leave, but forget what you have seen, if your life is dear to you."

Menshikov pushed him back out and I unscrewed the bottle of vodka and passed a coarse thread through a needle's wide eye. Then I went to Alice and took her hands in mine. I felt her fingers tremble.

"Alice. I must ask you for something. It is monstrous. But both of us, the tsar and I, will never forget it if you help us tonight."

"What is it, mistress?" She stroked Peter's hair as if he were a child. He leaned against her, breathing heavily.

The dread I felt caused me heartburn. "Please wash Alexey's body with the vodka; clean him and settle his bones back into their place. He must look like a man again." She wanted to rise and step over to the corpse, but I held her back. "Alice. You will also have to sew his head on again." I spoke very softly, as if I myself hoped not to hear those horrid words. In the cell's dull twilight Alice nodded slightly, mutely, and I held out the needle and thread to her. She went to Alexey's bunk, her nightdress rustling, her shoulders hunched, clutching the vodka, a rag, and the needle. Tolstoy silently rose to leave her his place next to the corpse.

"Help me, men," she whispered as she sat down. When Tolstoy and Menshikov turned Alexey so that his shoulders rested on her knees, his loose head placed in her lap. Her gaze met his wide stare and she gagged, but made the first stitch through his blackened skin, sewing the throat to the trunk, placing a knot after each stitch and cutting the thread with the sharp, small knife from the doctor's satchel. With each stitch her fingers became steadier, and she worked in silence while we looked on. Silent tears ran down her cheeks, dripping hotly onto Alexey's dead face. In the candlelight Alice looked so mild and mournful that the men around her cast down their eyes in shame.

* * *

The day's first colors were beginning to fill the white night sky when Peter and I took the boat back to the Summer Palace. The water swallowed the rudder with a hollow splash. Peter clenched my hands in silence, numbing my fingers. Only when we reached the palace's footbridge did he raise his head. "Tell me I'm not an animal, Catherinushka. Tell me," he whispered, as the morning light fell into his red, exhausted eyes. "Tell me you will stay with me, always," he pleaded, clutching the hem of my skirt, as the waves sloshed against the bow of the boat. While I cast about for words, he peered up into the sallow sky and then cowered in the boat. "Do you know what the executioners back in the bastion swore? That Alexey's soul had fled his body in the form of a crow," he said, sinking his face into his hands. When I wanted to console him, he leaped to his feet. The small vessel swayed as he shouted, threatening the skies with his fist: "I will get you! Just you wait! All of you—" His heavy, pained breathing filled the silence around us. The Neva streamed toward the Bay of Finland, the pale night drifted away, blending into a bright day, and the first rays of sunshine warmed me; I helped Peter toward the two footmen waiting for us at the bridge, and in his bedroom handed him a heavy sleeping potion.

* * *

The following evening, Peter celebrated the ninth anniversary of the victory of Poltava. He laughed and cheered as never before and forced more people than ever to keep sleep, and his demons, at bay by their sheer presence. I felt hot as I sat covered in heavy robes, jewels, and the pasty makeup I had applied on his orders. Peter drank like a horse, downing one eagle cup after another, but I secretly poured every second glass of my Tokay away. The feast of Poltava blended with Peter's name day, and in the days that followed I endured long Masses, suppers, fireworks, parades, and drinking games. The envoys from all over Europe were forbidden to mention Alexey: he had died as a traitor and nobody was to mention his name ever again once the funeral had passed. I saw the French ambassador, Campredon, eagerly writing in his little book.

* * *

Alexey's corpse lay in state underneath a white canopy in Trinity Church. His coffin was guarded by a tall, bulky soldier whose real task was to hinder anyone coming too close. A magnificent Persian silk scarf had been wrapped around Alexey's neck: no one should ever see Alice's fine stitches. The people passed by the former tsarevich in dull, dumb adoration, praying silently and wiping their eyes. The court itself was still drowsy from the recent days' feasts. Menshikov leaned toward me and whispered, "In my head, the drinking songs mix with the hymns, so I had better shut up." During the service, Peter was in floods of tears, his hands clenched in prayer. When Feofan Prokopovich read about Absalom, a traitor to his father, King David, he had listened intently. Once the service ended, Peter stepped up to Alexey's coffin: he swayed and held on to its edge until he regained his balance, then kissed Alexey's cold lips, which would never doubt Peter's vision ever again. Then the tsar straightened, his cheeks flushed and his eyes fresh and awake. He looked ahead, over the crowd's heads, far ahead into the future.

72

Tolstoy was made a count as a reward for hunting Alexey down, and the only person I would have wished flogging and torture for got away unscathed: Afrosinja married an officer and led a life of peace and prosperity. In Hell, I hoped, she would get a just punishment for her heartless treason.

Two months after Alexey's death I gave birth to a daughter. "Next time it's a son, Catherinushka," Peter said lightly, as little Tsarevna Natalya clenched his finger. "She is strong as a bear." I made Alice Natalya's first lady-in-waiting, and as she held the little girl, I spotted icy strands in Alice's ash-blond tresses. The night of Alexey's death had stolen her youth.

* * *

The first flakes tumbled from the sky throughout the night as we celebrated Saint Andrew's Day in Menshikov's palace on Vasilyevsky Island, his sole property. The first dishes were just being laid as the double doors of the gilded hall opened and a messenger slid in. He was soaked to the skin, caked with mud, and could barely fight his fatigue.

Menshikov got up, while Peter toyed with the colorful, speaking birds that Tolstoy's Moorish slave Abraham Petrovich Hannibal was showing him: Peter treated the man like family and had even sent him to Paris for his studies. "Give me a drink. Give me to drink," cried one bird.

"Shut up, shithead!" the other replied.

Peter roared with laughter and filled the birds' trough with vodka. "That should make them even more talkative."

Menshikov reached the messenger, listened, and placed his hand over his mouth in amazement. His eyes searched for Peter, who just tugged the bird's red and blue tailfeathers. "What a beautiful present! Thank you. I'll keep them in Mon Plaisir," he said. Abraham bowed, and the muscles played under his dark, velvety skin; some ladies sighed softly.

The messenger drank thirstily from a glass of beer and chewed on a pork shoulder bone as Menshikov made his way through the crowd to Peter, who looked up. "Why this sourpuss, Alekasha?" He grinned. "Are you jealous of my birds?"

Alexander Danilovich bowed. "My tsar. Your enemy, the king of Sweden, Charles the Twelfth, is dead."

Peter went on stroking the colorful feathers of the bird nibbling on his shoulder. "Dead? Charles of Sweden? That's not possible."

"Dead. He laid siege to a fortress in Denmark, and a bullet hit him in the heel. His soldiers carried him with them for days, but the wound was festering. He died of sepsis."

Peter handed the bird to Abraham, turned to the hall, and slowly clapped his hands: once, twice, and then three times. The music stopped and the voices hushed.

"My cousin, the king of the Swedes, has passed away," he cried before he triumphantly punched the air. "Charles the Twelfth is dead. Russia's enemy is no more." His words fell like stones into a lake and drew circles of astonished silence. Charles had been part of our lives for so long; a world without him seemed unthinkable. Peter grabbed his eagle cup with both hands. "The dark clouds have drifted; long live the light," he cried, ready to drink deeply.

But before the guests could join his toast and his merriment, somebody gave a desperate sob. Peter spun around, his face dark, and I caught my breath. At a table near us sat the most beautiful woman I had ever seen. She wept, but her tears did not dull the luster of her almond-shaped amber-and-gold-speckled eyes; her heavy honey-blond tresses had come undone and her full breasts rose and fell with anguish.

"Why are you crying, girl, when the greatest enemy of your fatherland has died? Do you mourn the dog?" Peter thundered, but she bore his blazing look of anger.

"I do not mourn our enemy. On the contrary," she said, her voice as pleasant as a bronze bell.

"Why then do you grieve?" Peter towered above her and she rose; their eyes locked.

"I weep, for peace is now farther away from us than ever before. What else other than confusion and delay can follow on Charles's death, my tsar?"

Peter's eyes softened. "What is your name?" he asked before gently wiping a tear from her cheek.

"Maria Kantemir, princess of Moldavia."

Peter kissed her fingers. "Princess. Does your beauty surpass your wisdom, or is it the other way around?" Her long black eyelashes cast shadows on her cheeks, which had the color of wild honey. Peter did not let go of her hand, but cried, "Let us drink to the wisdom of the princess of Moldavia. And let us weep for peace, which is ever more elusive."

Everyone obediently sobbed into their cups and drank, yet I eyed Maria Kantemir. I remembered her well from our campaign at the river Pruth, so many years ago. Back then she had been an unbelievably pretty child, but promises of this sort were easily broken by illness or an early death. Tonight, the feathers of Abraham's birds paled in comparison with the princess's beauty.

"God protect us and give us peace," she said, toasting Peter, never once taking her eyes off him. The colorful birds shrieked, and their cries rose to a storm in my ears, swallowing the music and the cheers and laughter of the crowd. How could I ever have feared Peter's other mistresses, or his niece, the child Jekaterina Ivanovna? This woman, I knew, would make me suffer as never before.

73

God gave us peace, though only after the confusion and delays that Maria Kantemir had sensed: the new Swedish queen, Ulrica Eleonora, first turned to England for help. Admiral Norris dutifully attacked Russian bastions on the shores of southern Sweden, but a stray dog was the only casualty of that skirmish, and a bathhouse burst into flames. In the first spring following Alexey's death, the second Peace Congress of Åland began.

* * *

Yet there was to be no peace in my heart: when the *ottepel* thawed the land and the mind, my little son caught a fever. One day after the first, angry scarlet spots appeared on the skin behind his ears and on his arms, Peter Petrovich lost consciousness. I did not leave his bedside, but struck up camp in his bedroom, talking to him, washing down his hot skin, kissing his face and fingers, and fanning him with cool air. When I sank on my mattress on the floor, exhausted, I would start praying, offering God a quiet, desperate trade. He could take everything I had, or everything I might ever have wanted to have, if he only left me my little boy. I heard myself whisper despicable words that might have turned the Almighty even more against me. "Take me. Take Anna, my God. Take Elizabeth. Take them both, take us all, but please let him live." The sight of his slight, feverish body robbed me of my mind; in those hours my tears never dried.

Peter was on his way back from Peterhof: if only he came in time, and soon, to be with me. The next night I never stopped praying, but when day broke, my son could not hear me anymore. His eyes were glassy, and he squinted as if the light hurt him. His skin was so flushed that every touch of mine left a white mark on his hot, tender body. Neither my words nor my love reached him; his little fingers lay slack in mine. Blumentrost wanted to bleed him, and Menshikov held me back with all his strength so I did not whip the quack.

In the evening my little son took his last, tormented breath. Peter Petrovich, the tsarevich, was dead. When his narrow chest no longer rose and fell, I heard someone scream. It sounded like an animal in the slaughterhouse and only later did I know that this had been me. I remember nothing, not scratching my own face bloody nor tearing out tufts of my own hair. My hands and arms were bloodstained from smashing my fists against the walls, breaking mirrors and cutting myself with the shards, all over my body, just to dull the pain in my soul.

It was Peter who brought me back to my senses with his own pain and sorrow: it was impossible for him to comfort himself with God's will at this loss, which was too overwhelming. It was clear to all that my little Peter's death was God's punishment for what we had done to Alexey.

As I lay over our son's little body, cuddling, caressing, and kissing him, the door flew open. The tsar still wore his muddy boots and his face was blackened by rainwater and muck. "Petrushka!" he cried, taking us both in his arms and holding us so tight that I gasped for air, before I gave in to the closeness and the pain. When he let go, he lifted Peter Petrovich's corpse, carefully, as if our boy was made of glass. Tears streamed down Peter's face when he pleaded, "Tell me that you're alive, my little angel. Do not leave your father alone. I do so need you. Petrushka. Tsarevich. Say something." Peter sobbed, strangled by grief, looking at the deathly pale small face: our son looked like he was hewn from ivory. The tsar drew him close, pressing the body against his huge chest, then looked to the heavens and let out a scream that made the pope, who crouched in the corner, cross himself with dread. Peter cradled our dead son, his broad shoulders heaving with sobs. "Come back, Petrushka, come back to me," he wept as he slid from the bed to the floor, still holding our dead boy. I crawled to him, blind with tears, crouching with him and our son. So we sat for a long time. I would not stir, just breathed in the faint scent of Peter Petrovich's hair, which already started to wane. His skin turned waxy, but I still squeezed his fingers, hoping he would answer. But it was in vain. The tsarevich was dead, and with him all our hope.

It was Menshikov who dared to take our little boy from us. I snarled like a wildcat and slapped, scratched, and bit him, but he would not let go. Finally, it was the tsar who led me to my rooms, where my ladies awaited me, already dressed in black and thickly veiled.

Peter himself did not stay: where he went, I did not know.

Alexander Danilovich Menshikov and Peter Shafirov took care of the tsarevich's funeral. The tsar, so I heard later when the madness lifted from my mind, locked himself in his rooms for days, refusing all food, but gorging on bottles of brandy and vodka, which Pavel Jagushinsky smuggled in. The birds of sorrow nestled into every corner of my soul, clawing themselves into my heart, and when their chicks hatched, their wings bore not feathers but hooks. More than once I thought of taking my own life. Why could God not leave me this one child, just my son, whose life meant so much to Peter and me, and a whole country and its countless people?

He, and Russia, needed an heir.

* * *

Weeks later, I woke in the late morning and heard a noise from my study. When I walked over, barefoot and in my nightshirt, Peter was standing by the window. My heart leaped: he was still there; he was still with me. "My love?" I said quietly.

He turned and I startled: it was Peter, and yet it wasn't. His face was swollen, and his eyes were bloodshot, with pupils as pointy as a pinhead. He must be drunk or in some other sort of stupor, I thought. He laughed bitterly. "Do not worry, Catherinushka. We are both as ugly as the night. Peter Petrovich has taken all beauty with him to his grave." He reached out for me. "Come here now."

He was right, I knew: I only kept the birds of sorrow at bay with vats of vodka, and I had to drink a lot before they sullenly clawed their way back into their nests, leaving me in peace. I stepped up to him at the window, taking his hand. His fingers laced into mine; it felt like in the olden days.

"What are you watching?" I asked.

"Them," he said. "Alexey's children."

Between the rosebushes, Alexey's son Petrushka played with his older sister. The children had stretched a rope between two statues and were jumping, playing pony and ringmaster. How healthy they looked; laughing and their cheeks flushed by the fresh air. Peter thought the same as I did: meanwhile, the maggots ate our son.

"Why is my grandson so strong and handsome?" he murmured. Since Alexey's death, nobody had dared to speak of him. "And look at his sister. She is pretty, the daughter of the German scrawny cat, with shiny hair and straight, white teeth."

I leaned in to him. "Do not hate them just because they're his children," I whispered. "Raise them to be good children of your house. Their father is not their fault."

The children's laughter and joy blended with our heartbeats, but Peter shook his head. "Their birthdays shall not be part of the court calendar. Petrushka shall never be tsarevich. And it's enough if he learns to read and to write. More is not necessary. Alexey's son is never to rule Russia," he decided, his voice sounding like ash. He freed himself from my embrace and stepped away.

"Peter—" I began, but he shook his head.

"God has punished me too much for me to broker an accord with him. I am in Peterhof, should you look for me." The grief in his voice still hung in my heart long after he had left me. I closed the curtains, shutting out the bright spring light, but the fabric would not stifle the children's joy. I spooned much too much laudanum into warm wine and went back to bed, though it was near noon. In my dreams the shrieking of the birds of sorrow sounded like children's laughter.

* * *

Peter hid the death of our son from the weekly letters to Europe, but the news spread like wildfire. Of course, he knew what I knew, and what everybody knew, and what was thought all over Russia and Europe: eye for eye, tooth for tooth, son for son. The world saw our little Peter's death as a punishment for Alexey's suffering, just as we ourselves did. No one dared to say this, however, bar one of Menshikov's monks, who was boiled to death in a great cauldron. The cruel punishment did not erase the bitter truth. After so many years, and so many children, the tsar of all the Russias had no heir.

* * *

Peter left, as he had said. I knew he would not spend his nights alone but dared not inquire. Never before had I felt so frightened of losing everything I had ever cared for. My mind turned and twisted like a caged weasel, not finding any way out. Going forward made me invariably reach a dead end.

* * *

In autumn, the Congress of Åland failed for the second time to end the Great Northern War. Pavel Jagushinsky, James Bruce, and Ostermann once more blamed the Swedish queen, Ulrica Eleonora. "She does not wish for peace and is as stubborn as a peasant girl," Jagushinsky said at a dinner. "A woman on the throne, what an idea! She should have her husband crowned."

I slapped him playfully with my fan. "I do not see why a woman's rule should be worse than a man's?"

He shook his head. "I beg your pardon, Tsaritsa, but women cannot keep their minds together. They scatter their thoughts; a hundred things have to be done at the same time. Women are like chickens who jump at five grains at a time."

Peter winked at me over his spoonful of lamb's stew, smacking his lips. "What do you think, Ostermann?" he asked his chancellor, amused.

"I agree. Women cannot tell important matters from trivial ones. As a man you set your mind to one thing and you succeed. Therefore the tsar is a tsar."

I did not want to spoil the merry hour with a fight, but I sensed that we all thought the same: the tsar was a tsar, but he had three healthy daughters, and no son.

Peter's niece, Duchess Jekaterina Ivanovna, fled Mecklenburg at the arrival of the British soldiers, together with her little daughter. I also heard that her husband, the duke, had regularly beaten her. So she happily moved back in with her mother, the tsaritsa Praskovia, and in the goodness of my heart I raised the little Mecklenburg princess together

with my daughters. It was a small thank-you to Praskovia, who had oc-
casionally looked after Anna and Elizabeth when I had to follow Peter.

Alexey had been buried for almost two years when Peter, in a brief,
private ceremony, gave the title of Tsesarevna to both Anna and Elizabeth. My heart soared for them, who were now crown princesses of all
the Russias; Anna, already a young woman and all dark curls and blue
eyes like her father, winked at me when I wiped away more than one tear;
Elizabeth, who was a gangly twelve years old, smiled, her teeth shiny like
pearls and her gaze as lively as a bird's, as Peter cut the gossamer-thin
veil of a mantle from her shoulders, thus marking her as having come
of age. Of course, we all knew that they were only placeholders for
another little brother to be born, but their bright faces and their proud
demeanor gave me endless joy.

* * *

In the following May, England retreated from the Baltic Sea for good,
and peace talks began for the third time in the Finnish town of Nystad.
I had not bled for three months in a row: had the hurried encounters
for which Peter had just about found time and desire helped me once
again to blessed circumstances? I counted on my fingers until I could
be sure: the child was to be born in the autumn. I had to tell Peter the
good news—we would laugh and be merry, just as in olden days! I rang
the silver bell on my bedside table and Agneta hurried in, her cheeks
flushed and her eyes shiny. I swung my legs over the bed. "Agneta,
you're getting lazy. If your dead mother knew, she would make you
sweep the stove as a punishment." Agneta giggled, but hid something in
the folds of her skirt.

"What do you have there?"

She blushed. "Nothing, Tsaritsa. Just a little book."

I held out my hand. "You are as red as a cherry, so it cannot be quite
so harmless. Give it to me, even if I cannot read."

She handed me the book, which was bound in beautiful crimson
leather. "Well, there are lots of very colorful pictures in it," she said, and
giggled.

The cover smelled of jasmine and sandalwood and when I opened
the first pages, the pictures were indeed more than colorful. I turned

the book this way and that and blushed. "Ohhhhhh, that looks very difficult! Do people really do that? Where did you get this from?"

"It's from China, and in the *gostiny dvor* it is worth its weight in gold. Look here, Tsaritsa." She opened the book at a page where a man was being pleasured by two girls at the same time.

"I must show this to the tsar. He will be enchanted. I'll give it back to you right away."

"Shall I dress you, Tsaritsa?"

"My cloak will do. I have something to tell him anyway."

Her gaze skimmed my belly and she beamed.

* * *

I paced through the secret corridor leading to Peter's rooms and looked at other pictures in the sinful book. Unbelievable: I had to try *that* with him! When I pushed open the secret door to his antechamber, the footman, who slept curled up like a kitten on the tsar's threshold, rubbed his eyes and stood, somewhat embarrassed, to attention.

"Tsaritsa! I do not think the tsar is ready to receive," he stammered. I slapped him on the shoulder, laughing. "Boy, I've seen the tsar very often other than ready to receive, so make yourself scarce and go eat some hot *kasha* in the kitchen."

But he blocked Peter's bedroom door, blushing. "Tsaritsa, I beg you. Do come back in an hour." A stunned silence reigned, then I heard sounds from Peter's room: laughter, and low talk. Was that him, or someone else? My heart chilled.

"Step aside," I ordered curtly. "I can hear that he's awake."

The young man's shoulders slumped, and he obeyed. What else could he do? The room was dusky, as the dark green velvet curtains with the golden embroidery filtered the light. It took a moment for my eyes to grow accustomed to the twilight; I heard Peter mutter and I tiptoed to the bed. Golden thighs were wrapped around his heaving hips and a pair of hands clasped his neck. His whole body rose and fell; he groaned and panted. The woman who took him spurred him on with endearments that made my ears burn.

"*Batjushka!*" I said. Just the night before I had put his haste and absentmindedness down to his many tasks. In truth, he had wanted to save his strength for someone else. "Peter!" I said, this time louder, and he spun around, slackening at my sight. That served him and his whore right!

"Catherinushka! Who let you in?" he asked, sounding helpless. I was long since used to Peter's infidelity with hundreds of girls, who remained name- and faceless. He was the tsar: so it was, and it could not be otherwise. This, however, I knew, was different. While Peter seemed embarrassed, Maria Kantemir let her taut thighs linger on the tsar's back; her slender fingers played in his frizzy gray chest hair. She smiled at me, her full lips parting and her peculiar, gold-speckled amber eyes as narrow as a cat's. The honey-colored tresses spread like rays of sunshine on the pillow's starched linen and her breasts were full, high, and round. She made no effort to cover herself, but said cheekily, "Tsaritsa, my everlasting fidelity and devotion. *Batjushka,* you giant of a man. You crush me. Let me move." She then purred.

"Of course, my princess," Peter stammered, throwing on his old green housecoat and coming to me.

"*Matka,* why do you come here so early?" he asked unhappily as he saw the tears in my eyes.

"I wanted to tell you something, my tsar," I said, swallowing my tears.

He led me to one of the windows. "What is it?" He glanced back at his bed, where Maria Kantemir watched us with raised eyebrows.

I leaned closer to Peter. "I am once more pregnant with a tsarevich for the realm."

He squeezed my arm. "How wonderful, Catherinushka. Splendid. Shall we celebrate that this evening?" I beamed at him, but then he said, "Is there anything else you wanted to tell me?"

"No, but—"

"Well, then—"

Maria Kantemir lay on her belly, her chin propped in her hands, letting her golden calves swing.

"I will see you in the evening, at the table," he said, steering me toward the secret door: I was given my leave. My cheeks burned with shame, and from the corner of my eye I saw Peter stepping to his bed and pulling Maria Kantemir's hips upward. "I should have you whipped, as cheeky as you are," he growled, "if your skin weren't so delicate."

She laughed and rolled onto her back. "Come here. Where were we?"

The door closed behind me and I asked the young footman, "Who gave you the order not to let me in? The tsar, or Princess Kantemir?"

"The princess Kantemir."

"And you obeyed her?"

He did not dare to look at me.

* * *

Only once I was back in the corridor did I notice that I was still clutching the naughty Chinese book. My knees buckled and I sank to the ground, wiping the tears off my cheeks. True, my shirt was of silk instead of coarse wool, and the floor beneath my feet was made of fine wood instead of bare earth. But other than that, little had changed in the past twenty years. I was helpless against fate. My son was dead, and a younger woman lay in my husband's bed. My past was gone and there was no future. The shadows of the corridor gave life to the colorful pictures in the book: in the flickering candlelight the women's bodies looked like they were carved from gold. I slowly tore page after page from the book, ripping them to shreds.

74

The very cold spring brought the first of what would be four years full of hail, devastating storms, and famine to Russia. Locusts plagued the land, devouring all grain and then even the stubble. Villages were haunted by hungry wolves and bears, and the village councils had to prepare for an autumn and a winter of strict planning and precise rationing. Everywhere in the country Alexey's ghost was spotted. Where he stepped, so we heard, flowers blossomed, and grain sprouted. Peter had the people who spread such nonsense knouted or killed.

* * *

My unborn son was to become a child of the peace. In September 1721, Andrej Ostermann finally negotiated peace between Russia and Sweden, which ceased all claims to the Baltics in eternity.

When Peter arrived back in Russia in the early morning hours, he rushed straight into my bedroom, shaking me awake and shouting with joy. "Catherinushka, wake up! Do you know what has happened?" he cried, jumping up and down on my mattress like a child. I rubbed my eyes, still sleepy, and heard Peter more than I saw him, but sensed his excitement, the sea and the wind, as well as his sweat after the long ride.

"What is it, *starik*?" I was so glad that he wanted to share a moment with me! He pulled me onto my knees, our heartbeats sounding as one, there, on the crumpled sheets.

"Listen," he said, raising his finger. I held my breath just as the first bells of the city began to toll into the black stillness of the night. The sound tore the sky over Saint Petersburg as all the other bells joined in, their joy resounding in my heart.

"These are the bells of peace, *matka*. The peace of Nystad. The war is over!" Peter rejoiced.

I gave a sob, as the war had lasted what seemed to be my whole life. "Peace!" cried Peter. *"Mir!"* He leaped out of my bed, ran to the door, and tore it open. The young guard wanted to throw himself to the ground when he saw Peter, but he caught him. "You. Give me your gun, then you can still kneel down. You do not need it anymore, because it is peace!" Peter ran to the window with it and struggled with the curtains. I laughed as I saw him tangled in the heavy fabric, and together we pushed the window open and Peter shot the weapon up into the velvety sky of his city. People gathered on the quay and looked up to the Winter Palace: scared, yet full of surprise, as Peter shouted for more ammunition. He reloaded and shot a second salute: I held him around his waist, so as to lessen the weapon's recoil.

"Do not be frightened, you asses!" He laughed. "Peace, we have peace! *Mir! Mir!* The Great Northern War is over," he cheered, his voice breaking, and his words drowned in the volleys that now answered his own from all over town. The church towers of Russia carried the news into the country, and people ran out into the streets in their nightgowns, dancing, laughing, and embracing each other. They grabbed everything they could find, as long as it made a mighty racket: drums rolled next to the rattling of pots and the clinking of swords, sickles, and scythes. Just a moment later, fireworks lit up the sky above Menshikov's palace. Peter watched with damp eyes. "My Alekasha. Let us go to him. Now, at once!"

Down on the quay, musicians were playing, and those who saw Peter knelt and tried to kiss his feet. In the midst of that raging mass of people we set out in a ferryboat to Vasilyevsky Island, and the waters of the Neva were aflame from the bonfires lit all along the riverbanks. A Russian calls "peace" and "the world" the same word, *mir,* and the joy about the peace of Nystad was louder than any battle cry, but it sounded like the sweetest song.

* * *

It took Peter three full days to sober up enough to think about a suitable celebration of Nystad in the cities of Saint Petersburg and Moscow.

His fingertips were still charred from the fireworks he had sent into the sky, and his arms ached from tirelessly hitting the drums when he reached for paper and ink. "Let's start. I only want to hear fabulous, unheard-of ideas," he ordered. "After all, this is the end of the Great Northern War." Maria Kantemir slid into the room and settled next to him. She was dressed as was the custom in her country, and the narrow tunics and embroidered leggings suited her as well as her heavy silver jewelry. Her scent of musk and patchouli clouded my spirits: my *damy* whispered that she blended her perfume with some drops of her very own moisture to make it more bewitching. Peter placed his hand on her knee and gave her his list of ideas: "Have a look and tell me what you think."

She read and tilted her head. "All this sounds nice, but it's not quite enough. A ruler like you must add a strong, almost divine note." Her amber eyes, speckled with drops of gold, challenged him.

"What do you suggest?" Peter urged, as if pearls of wisdom were about to drip from her full lips. From under my lashes I watched the others, Peter's friends, pupils, and advisors, who were also the companions of my life: Alekasha Menshikov, of course. My savior Count Sheremetev, and Count Tolstoy, with whom I had faced fate so many years ago, disguised as a man, and whose hair had since turned as white as snow. How did they bear themselves toward Maria Kantemir? We had fought and feasted together; many times, I had saved them from the harsh punishments that Peter could pass so easily in his anger. Thanks to me, their estates had escaped confiscation, they had avoided banishment to Siberia, and their lives had evaded death on the scaffold. But gratitude and loyalty is a wall easily eroded by the first wave of disgrace, I thought, as I saw how eagerly they were leaning in to listen to Maria's words. She held the tsar's brain captive between her thighs and they nodded at her words, be it out of fear, courtesy, diplomacy, or true belief and admiration.

"Come as Poseidon, the god of the sea. Sail on the fleet that you have created up to the city you founded. Celebrate all your achievements, my tsar. We can think of Moscow later."

Peter beamed at her. "My beautiful Maria. How clever you are." He kissed her and she pushed him away, her alluring smile full of promise.

"Later, my tsar," she murmured, lowering her dark lashes. My fingernails dug into my palms as I smiled approvingly. This woman was more dangerous than hail, fire, and plague put together. I placed my hands on my swollen belly, and the unborn child answered with a small kick. Whatever Maria Kantemir planned, it was I who bore the tsarevich underneath my heart. Any word would look like bitter jealousy and drive the tsar further into her arms. Only the sweetest of joys would do—given that I got half the chance for it. God just had to be by my side.

I cannot fault Maria Kantemir's work in planning the celebrations of the peace of Nystad. We sailed up the Neva like an image from a dream: the foaming waters a mottled green and gray; the brilliant, blinding white of the sails of the hundreds of ships, frigates, and boats; the air bright with thousands of flags, banners, and bunting; and the shores black with people. I looked like a real tsaritsa, wearing a dress of shining blue-green silk, my glossy, thick hair all piled up, and wearing emerald combs in my hair as well as a heavy choker around my neck. Under my bosom, too, I wore a belt of emeralds and sapphires to distract the gaze from my already-heavy stomach.

"You shine like the sun, Catherinushka. No wonder that even the magpies are jealous," Peter teased me after the holy Mass as we rode through town for the whole evening before we went back to the palace to change for a masked ball: I looked like a Dutch peasant woman, with flowers in my hair and a blue-and-white-patterned dress, while Peter had dressed as a sailor from Friesland. So we mingled with the fools, the fairies, the shepherds, and the Persian princes until the early hours of the morning. I felt happy and strong, until Peter forced Maria Kantemir onto a divan near my throne, pushing her robe all the way up to her naked hips, spreading her thighs. The little bells that she wore on her ankles and wrists clinked softly as he began to lick her. Her fingers laced through his dense hair, like poisonous snakes in tall grass, and she let her head fall back, her eyes closed. She came with a hoarse warrior's cry and rose to kiss Peter's moist lips, before she whispered some words into his ears. He smiled and snatched a bottle of vodka while flinging her over his shoulder. She hung as limp as a young cat when they disappeared in the corridors of the palace.

* * *

A week after the celebrations of Nystad I began to bleed in the early-morning hours and my little son was stillborn in the first days of October. Peter's face was as ashen as the morning when he came to see me. After my body tore, my heart broke as well, seeing him like that.

"What happened, Blumentrost?" he asked the doctor, avoiding my gaze. Blumentrost shrugged helplessly. "I do not know, my tsar. It was a healthy and strong boy, but the umbilical cord was wrapped around his neck. He suffocated in his mother's body. That's why birth set in so early."

Peter briefly covered his face in his cupped hands, his shoulders slumped. He would not look at me, but rose, as if he had heard enough.

Blumentrost, however, held him back. "My tsar—"

"Yes, what?" Peter asked impatiently. Where was he off to so quickly? Had Maria summoned him and he would leave me here, weak and alone in the morning? I sensed the birds of sorrow setting upon me. The thought seared my soul.

Blumentrost sighed. "It was a difficult birth, my tsar. The tsaritsa has lost a lot of blood—" I would not hear his words, but was too weak to place my hands over my ears. "I think it is better if the tsaritsa does not have more children."

The enormity of what had been said built up between Peter and me; every word was a stone in a high wall growing between us. Twelve times God had given me the chance to give Russia an heir. Twelve times I had failed. That night Peter, I heard, attended a feast in Menshikov's palace together with Maria Kantemir. Menshikov had arranged seats of honor in a little tent set back from the crowd where she drank from the tsar's glass and he fed her tenderly with little bites from his plate.

75

A few days later, when I dressed for the Te Deum in Trinity Church, Peter came to my rooms. I was still weak, and my ladies helped me with everything: "Keep going, my *damy*! I just want you to be sure to make the tsaritsa beautiful as never before." He winked at me and gave me a secretive smile.

"Am I not beautiful enough for the reading of the peace treaty?" I asked, as Agneta twisted my hair in thick braids around my head. I forced a smile into my voice. He gave me a peck on the cheek.

"You never know what the day still brings," he said. "Agneta, adorn the tsaritsa with the necklace I gave her at our wedding." I was amazed, but Peter placed the heavy choker on my throat; the pearls cooled my skin, and the colorful gemstones in the wings of the Russian double eagle sparkled in an unspoken challenge.

Peter tilted his head. "Not bad. Now the red velvet dress."

I had wanted to wear the imperial green silk, but he raised his hand. "Silence. Do not contradict me in front of your ladies, or else I'll have you whipped, *matka*," he joked. "That's good. Let us go."

He led me down into the courtyard, where our sleds were waiting. The servants jumped from one foot to the other because of the early frost. In the sled, Peter asked: "Do you think I need this wig?" He had placed it haphazardly on his head, and his own hair, streaked with gray, hung out here and there above his ears and his forehead. I nodded and he shrugged. "Oh well. So be it. But I feel like a monkey," he growled.

* * *

Peter was unable to listen to Prokopovich's well-spoken words during the long Te Deum, his feet tap-tapping the floor. I looked questioningly at Alexander Menshikov, but he, too, just shrugged, and I forced my thoughts back to Feofan's words, which were like pearls on a string, echoing from Trinity Church's golden, domed ceiling. "I wish we already knew what our tsar has done for us . . . for do we ever want Russia to suffer the same fate as the Greeks and the Greek kings?" I shook my head, without knowing what their fate had been. Alexander Danilovich did the same, and I stifled a giggle. We were both so simple.

But just as the crowd settled in a last prayer, Prokopovich gave Peter Shafirov a sign by touching the *panagia* on his chest. Shafirov rose: the once spindly man had grown into a powerful, self-indulgent prince. His blue silk jacket emphasized his bulk and the tight trousers clung to his heavy legs, and even if the bows on the tips of his shoes made him look like a fool, he was a dangerous man: his five daughters had married into the best families in the country, he did business with Menshikov, and he was said to have offered a sapphire necklace to Maria Kantemir. When Shafirov took a scroll from his sleeve, Peter drew me to my feet.

"Thanks to the tsar's glorious deeds, we have left behind the age of darkness and Russia has found her place on the world's stage." Peter's fingers stuck to mine, and my eyes met Menshikov's gaze. Alexander Danilovich clearly understood not only that something very important was happening, but also that Peter Shafirov had trumped him. I straightened my back, which still hurt from the hours of a labor that once more had been in vain.

Shafirov cleared his throat. "The senate begs the tsar to take the title of an emperor. You have risen from the East, now be a ruler of the West! Tsar Peter, become our Peter the First. Tsar Peter, become Peter the Great, father of your country, emperor of all the Russias."

His last words were swallowed by jubilation: music roared, and Feofan made the sign of the cross over Peter's head. Peter gave Shafirov the kiss of peace, looking surprised and embarrassed, and raised his hand. Silence fell in the church. "I cannot help but accept this honor," he cried, and I felt his pride and joy: a tsar was an archaic title for a ruler of the East and more akin to a king. He had risen in rank and had shifted Russia once more to the West. "*Vivat* the emperor and the empress of Russia!" Voices thundered a thousandfold through the church and across the square, reaching the Neva and blending with the hundreds of volleys fired by the ships' cannons before the waters carried the news far, far out into the world. I was empress of Russia: *Imperatriza*.

* * *

In the following weeks the Neva began to rise. First, the waters reached the steps of the moorings, before lapping the quay. The following morning, neither horses nor carts could pass the flooded streets. Come nightfall, the courtyard of the Winter Palace and the castle's ground floor were underwater. Footmen and servants barricaded the building with bags of sand, but a whiff of musty dampness was tangible only a few hours later. Dark clouds gathered on the horizon and it began to rain. The sea raged into the river, tearing down houses and carrying away walls. Soon the bloated corpses of animals and men, women and children drifted in the flooded streets and disease and plague festered. Peter had dykes built, and the people carried the water from their houses by forming chains with buckets and vessels of all sorts, yet clinging to their way of life, playing cards on the roofs of their houses and wading through the thigh-high waters to their flooded *kabak*.

Nevertheless, with the first snowfall Peter celebrated Saint Andrew's day in all its splendor. Again, Menshikov had invited us to his palace, as Peter loved the splendor without having to foot the bill. That evening, our sleds made their way through the wonderland that Saint Petersburg now was, horses snorting and bells jingling at their harnesses. Snow fell slanted in front of the glowing lanterns, and all of Peter's hopes and dreams for his New Jerusalem had come true: all wooden, shabby structures were replaced by tall façades of palaces and the houses of merchants or burghers alike, three or four stories high and with their windows lit. Church spires rose in the night sky. Pillars and posts along the quays and the bridges were snowcapped. The barriers of the wide roads and prospects were raised and people were out and about everywhere, clad in furs. The air smelled of roasted chestnuts, grilled meats, and mulled wine. Peter sat next to me, all warm underneath the bearskin the footman hooked up to the left and right of the sled's door. I saw his face glow as he took it all in, such as I did. He had willed this beauty of a place from nothing, I thought, and I had been by his side. I, not anyone else, least of all Maria Kantemir. Nobody could take that from us. Once at Menshikov's palace, however, that feeling dissolved like our breath steaming up in the sudden warmth of fires and candles— thousands of them—and dozens of damp furs and cloaks being cast off: Maria Kantemir leaned close to Peter while eating, whispering, and telling him cheerful stories about the floods. He laughed so much that he pleaded for mercy, so she seized her whip and lashed Peter's fools on their legs.

"Don't you see? The tsar wants to laugh at the flood. Get on your boat, or I'll teach you a lesson." The fools hastily turned a small table upside down and hopped inside it, looking like two castaways on the Neva. Maria Kantemir circled them, whip in hand, looking as danger- ous as the wild cats in her homeland's mountains. Every time she came close to the boat the two fools paled with fear and acted more and more wildly.

It was not until Peter raised his hand and gasped, "Enough, enough, I cannot laugh anymore!" that she gave them leave. When she sat down with a haughty smile, Menshikov kissed her fingertips.

* * *

When I returned to my rooms, Agneta saw my sullen mood and helped me out of my heavy dress, my underwear, and my linen without ask- ing any questions. She didn't need to. Everybody knew. When she unclasped the jewelry from my earlobes, my throat, and my wrists, I breathed a sigh of relief. The tiled stove warmed the room pleasantly, and I looked at my bare, beautiful self while Agneta cleansed my face with rosewater; in the twilight of my room, I saw the bed that Peter had avoided ever since I last gave birth. All reason for him to see me there was gone. I should not give him an heir, but rumor had it that Maria Kantemir laced Peter's drink with love potions made from either the ground horn of an African animal or the dried, crushed sex of an In- dian tiger, so he would take her three or four times any night. I had also heard that she had not bled in the past months, which frightened me. I closed my eyes; the November moonlight flowed into my heart.

Agneta, though, had heard something else: "My empress," she said, smiling, "the people say that the latest flood is the fault of this Moldavian witch." She rubbed my shoulders with jasmine oil and I breathed in the heady perfume. "The whore Kantemir is said to have called the waters. When she took her barge to the Winter Palace last week, the people bombarded her with horseshit."

For the first time in weeks, I laughed, and Agneta joined my cheerfulness. It made me ready to face the world. Had my place in Peter's bed been taken—in his bed, and his heart?

I neither could, nor would allow this to happen.

76

All of Europe, bar Austria, recognized Peter's new title as emperor of Russia: Vienna had not forgotten the manhandling at the moment of Alexey's flight.

But Peter's gaze turned to the East, as his ambassador to Isfahan, Prince Volynsky, spoke in the senate. He looked impossibly groomed compared to most of the senators, whose hair straggled beneath their wigs; their skin was veined and red and they picked their noses, flinging their findings in all corners of the senate. Volynsky's dark hair fell well-oiled to his shoulders, he was cleanly shaven, and his fingernails were spotless and short. Compared with him, the other senators looked like savages.

"Welcome home, Volynsky. You look like a true Persian. Do you still eat pork? If not, I'll have you flogged." Peter was only half joking, I knew, but the senate laughed obediently. "What is going on in Persia? Tell me all about Isfahan."

Volynsky hesitated. "I have some good news. More and more trade leads through Russia, and we have been able to largely suppress the attacks of the Cossack tribes along the riverbanks. This ensures safety for the sturgeon fisheries as well as the transport of caviar."

"And the bad news? Or will you bore us with talk about fish eggs for longer?"

Volynsky's face turned grave. "Russian trading stations have been attacked and the whole country is in turmoil—I am glad to have made it across the border. The shah of Persia was overthrown . . ."

"And why didn't you say that sooner?" Peter cried, and lashed out at him with his knout, tearing the silk sleeve of his Persian overcoat and drawing blood from Volynsky's pale skin. "Who has started the rebellion, and when?"

"Afghan rebels have occupied Isfahan. They burn, plunder, embezzle, and kill. Their wild customs spread over the land, and there is no more law; no one knows what is right or wrong."

Persia was important, I knew; gold, silver, copper, lead, oils, tints, cashmere wool, silk, fruits, and spices were loaded on barges before the wares traveled on and to be weighed with gold. What better moment could Russia choose for an attack and return with a rich loot? Peter stroked his mustache and grinned. "You really did not deserve the knouting, Volynsky. Take it as a sign of my love. The next time I want to chastise you, just tell me it has already been done." Then he frowned. "All right. Let's get going. Where are the rebels located? Only in Isfahan, or all over the country?"

* * *

One month later, Russia declared war on Persia. The country was still exhausted, the princes cursed at having to leave their families and estates again, but I alone was elated: the campaign would allow me to escape Saint Petersburg, where all and everybody watched me, waiting with bated breath: Would I be ousted? Also, the simple life we led in the field, with only a tent and not a palace to share, had always allowed Peter and me to find each other again. There, I was sure, Maria Kantemir could not harm me. I pondered Blumentrost's warning when I had Alice pack some light, lacy undergarments and nightshirts: blast him; I would fall pregnant a thirteenth time in my life and all would be well. My spirits were high when my chests were packed as this time, for once, I did not leave behind an infant on whose life Russia depended. My daughters, Anna and Elizabeth, were young women, and little Natalya was strong and healthy.

* * *

On the eve of our departure I paid Anna and Elizabeth a visit to take leave from them: sometimes it felt as if saying farewell was the only reason I ever saw them. Their rooms were a picture of peace: Natalya was being comforted on her wet nurse's full breast, her cheeks rosy and her hair thick and dark. She was soon to be three years old. Anna embroidered, sitting close to an open window, and compared her own botched stitches with her maid's fine work. When she spotted me, she flew toward me.

"Mother, how wonderful of you to come. Ever since I heard about the campaign to Persia, I thought I would not see you again." She blushed slightly. "You know, there's so much to speak about."

I embraced her. Why did children grow up so fast? Had not I just given birth to her, a year before the Battle of Poltava? She was almost fourteen years old and had inherited Peter's bright blue eyes as well as his fair skin and dark hair. I knew what she wanted to speak about: the young Duke of Holstein had been asking Peter for one of our daughters' hand in marriage. Anna, as the eldest, felt that she was entitled to this engagement, though I knew that the young duke had fallen in love with Elizabeth. At his last visit he'd sailed up and down the Neva, hoping to catch a glimpse of her; but each time I had sent Anna out onto the balcony. Finally, he had stuck to his proposal to either princess.

"Let me look at you," I said, and spun Anna by the waist until the pink silk mousseline layers of her dress flew like gossamer wings. Her ladies laughed and clapped, and Elizabeth looked up from her chess game against Wilhelm Mons: my heart skipped a beat. It had been so long, with all the travels and troubles, since I had seen him. How comfortable he seemed in the presence of the princesses, my daughters. Still, he had that air of gaiety and ease about him that no court manners ever could destroy.

"Really, Anna, as silly as you are, no peasant in his *izba* would want to marry you, let alone a duke!" Elizabeth chided, and I frowned.

Mons faced Elizabeth at a small table, and the captured chess figures lay alongside the board of ivory and ebony. He said, "Really, Tsarevna. Is there a greater joy for a young woman than to marry a young man of standing and fortune?"

Did he tease her? She blushed and her fingers silently twisted a pawn on the board.

I watched them closely, which was a pleasure—I could have looked at his stunning face and smile all day long. No wonder that at court more than one person joked about my daughter's closeness to him. So far, I had not given heed; but where there was smoke, there was also fire.

"Do you not want to wish me farewell before I go to Persia?" I asked, trying to ignore Wilhelm, who rose and bowed. It was impossible. His skin was tanned as if after a long ride and his hair a bit disheveled. Time took no toll on him; if anything, it made him more handsome. A couple of fine white lines caused by laughter had settled well around his eyes and in the corners of his mouth.

He smiled, showing the tooth with the little chip missing—what had that been, a brawl or a bit of gravel in a piece of bread? "Tsaritsa. May the sun shine on you and your happiness for many years to come," he said. I saw so much warmth and understanding in his eyes that my soul and my spirit soared toward him. Yet I nodded curtly and turned my back on him.

Elizabeth watched us and then rose to curtsy sullenly. "I'll be glad to greet you, Mother. But I needn't wish you farewell; it is said that you are staying here in Saint Petersburg?"

Her words hit me as painfully as an arrow in a Cossacks' ambush. "Who says that?" I asked, struggling for composure.

Elizabeth shrugged. "Everybody. Father, and the court."

She stared behind me and curtsied even lower than before: I turned and Peter stood on the threshold, together with Maria Kantemir. They had spent the last days in Peterhof—our Peterhof!—planning the campaign, and she looked like a beautiful savage. A tight tunic fitted over embroidered silk trousers, yet was slit to just below her breasts, showing her softly curved belly and a heavy silver belt; her wrists appeared too slender for her chunky bracelets. Instead of being painted white, the skin of her face was lightly tanned, and she fed the small monkey sitting on her shoulder with nuts and dried fruit. Daria Menshikova knew that the princess bathed naked in the Bay of Finland before drying herself off on the pebbly beach outside Mon Bijou. The water—a mirror of the gray, wild sky—was tamed by her presence and even the waves lapped her toes obediently.

"My tsaritsa," Peter said smoothly, "what luck. Now I can take leave from all the ladies close to my heart."

Elizabeth lowered her eyes, while I felt but a heartbeat away from Wilhelm Mons. I sensed him with all my being and it kept me steady. Anna hushed; she lacked her younger sister's guts, but suffered with me.

"Take leave? Why is that? My chests are packed . . ." I began, but Peter stopped me short.

"At your age, such a journey is no longer becoming to a woman. You will be my worthy steward here. Who else could I trust so much?" He gave me a peck on the cheek, his lips and his mustache skimming my skin. Elizabeth pressed herself against him, and Anna curtsied, before he lifted Natalya up.

I felt utterly helpless: my life and my love slipped away from me, just as the silver sand of the Dvina had run through my fingers on washing day. If he left for Persia with Maria Kantemir by his side, I was lost, and might as well have my head shorn here and now, ready for the monastery he would choose for me upon his return.

"I shall be gone for a while. Keep me in your heart and in your prayers, my empress." Peter bowed more formally and kissed my hands, but then as he turned to leave, the monkey jumped from Maria Kantemir's shoulder and seized some of Elizabeth's chess pieces; it nibbled at the queen, but shrieked with disappointment at it not being edible, and chucked it to the floor.

My daughters' ladies threw themselves on their knees to pick it up, but Maria Kantemir's voice lashed through the room: "Come here!" The monkey swung himself back on her shoulder and Peter kissed her on the mouth.

"Already quite imperious, my lady," he chuckled, and she looked at me, her eyes glowing like those of a wild thing looming out of the dark at a campfire. Her threat was clear: upon his return, Peter should not be my husband anymore. I curtsied lower than anyone else when they left the room together. There was no time to lose.

77

My Circassian maid Jakovlena understood the order: I had sent for her at a very late hour, in secret, and she had come to my rooms from Felten's kitchens. Her gray hair was tousled from her sleep in the warm ashes of the fireplace, yet despite her advanced age her skin was smooth and fair, an inheritance of her tribe, who sold their daughters for the highest price to the court in Istanbul. Her people had tamed the smallpox: fathers scratched their baby daughters' skins and trickled droplets of blood laced with cowpox into their veins. The illness that the babies caught was much milder than the smallpox and saved them for a lifetime from that disfiguring and often fatal disease. Jakovlena had never wanted more than to work in Felten's kitchen, though I had richly rewarded her for her many services over the years: her stone house stood in the third street behind the Moika, and I had not only paid for her daughter's education, but had also given the girl good pin money; her two sons were officers of Peter's regiment.

"Persia," Jakovlena said, weighing the word. She would pack what little she had this very night. "At your orders, my princess." Then she slipped away, another dark shadow in the bright night of my city, gliding effortlessly between worlds just like the secret she was.

On the pier, the day broke bright and blue and seagulls hovered, hoping for rich pickings. The air was alive with all the languages of the giant empire that Peter ruled. Our three-masters had a long hull but a low keel, as this allowed for an easier journey to the Caspian Sea without the many shallows and sandbanks in the streams holding us back.

Flags fluttered in the wind; watchmen kept an eye on the cargo, and the crowd was buzzing. Sailors swung from mast to mast, their wives wailing and their children pale and sad; ship boys ran last errands; jugglers with colorful birds and monkeys were asking for money or pilfering food and purses; and merchants sold pots, knives, ropes, tools, lucky charms, icons, potions against seasickness and other ailments, crooked daggers and swords. Through the colorful hustle and bustle I saw Peter on his horse from afar, studying a map together with his Cossack leader, while Menshikov shouted orders.

Only when I was very close to him did Peter spot me, taking me in blankly. His face twitched, which could be a sign of anything: anger, or mirth. Did the sailors suddenly slow down the loading of the goods and guns? Any man or woman with red blood in their veins held their breath, watching us. I steadied my mare and led it close to Peter's stallion. The horses nuzzled and chewed each other's bridles. Menshikov hid his smile behind a cough, while Peter reached for his *dubina*. I held my breath and sought his eyes before saying in a low voice, for his ears only: "You do not really think that I'll let you go to Persia alone?"

His fingers slid from the knout's pommel. "No. If I'm honest, I did not believe that, *matka*. I'd rather believe in black snow."

I smiled and spoke up. "My tsar, forgive my tardiness and my delay. Where shall my chests be loaded?"

Peter hailed Ambassador Volynsky, who was busy riding up and down the quay. His fine Arabian steed suffered in the still heat of the morning: its nostrils foamed, and mosquitoes clustered in its eyes. "Volynsky. Let the empress's luggage be loaded on my frigate. And see to it that she has everything in her cabin she might need," Peter ordered.

Volynsky wisely hid his surprise, but when I felt ready for a last joke with Peter, a sedan chair made of painted wood, the flag of Moldova waving on its roof, was set down next to us. A narrow hand pushed the curtains aside. Peter chewed uneasily on his mustache, and Maria Kantemir looked at me in surprise, when Peter bent down and kissed her. "Take good care of yourself, my darling," he murmured. Then he said to me, "*Matka*, we'll see each other on board." He galloped off and Menshikov winked at me, bowed at both of us, and followed Peter, his horse's hooves sending sparks into the morning air.

Maria Kantemir and I were alone in the midst of the crowd. I stood in my stirrups. "Since when do you come in a litter? Even your empress comes on horseback," I said curtly.

Her gaze was mocking when she stroked her loose honey-colored hair from her forehead. "My empress, have you not been told? How shameful," she said, and, despite the sunshine, a frost settled on my heart. I dreaded her next words: "I am pregnant with the son of the tsar of all the Russias. He does not want me to ride."

* * *

I took care to be always seen on deck and have a friendly word for everybody, be it a lowly sailor or an admiral of the fleet. I took my seat at the table together with Peter and Volynsky and followed our progress on the map: the Moskva met the Oka, a stream as wide as the sea, with densely populated banks and lush, fertile fields behind. Wherever we anchored, the villagers came down to our ships with musicians and gifts such as freshly slaughtered cattle and poultry, barrels of beer and brandy, still-oven-warm loaves of sourdough bread, eggs, and vegetables. Peter took it all with tears of gratitude in his eyes, assuring the people of his grace. They suffered a second summer of famine, and the hungry gaze of the pale, much-too-skinny village children followed our ships upstream.

When we reached Nizhny Novgorod we were stranded on Volga sandbanks and the hot summer air cupped our ship on the slushy, muddy waves. Ashore, Peter spotted Tartar scouts, looking grim with their deep-set eyes, high cheekbones, and smooth tresses as black as a raven's wing. Their quivers were long and hung across their shoulders, and I heard that they rode their ponies tender before feasting on them. They were a lazy and predatory people, so that Volynsky doubled the guards on board.

Maria Kantemir made an unbelievable fuss about her pregnancy, yet the sight of her frightened me, for her now clearly pregnant belly was more pointed than round, and her skin was blotchy and blemished, which meant she carried a boy. The journey on the sea doubled her morning sickness. I prayed for a storm so she would vomit her black soul out of her body. But Peter was so worried about her that I made sure to ask every day about her well-being. "How is the princess of Moldavia? Has she had a walk today? Let me send her my Circassian maid, Jakovlena. She knows all sorts of healing herbs and potions."

But Maria Kantemir would have none of it. "You do not really think that I am drinking a tea that the tsaritsa has sent me?" she had snarled, pouring the hot brew on Jakovlena's bare feet. Only when her sickness would not abate did she accept my help, and after a while she even sent for it.

Beyond Kazan, the water gained speed; the rapids carried our boats, but with the Cossacks and Kalmucks about, the riverbanks were deserted. We anchored on a peninsula close to the city of Tsaritsyn; I had my glass already filled to the brim when Peter stepped out of Maria Kantemir's cabin. The night air was still as hot as the Devil's breath, and I had washed myself down with lukewarm water to freshen up. My skin was scented with rosewater and jasmine, a potion that Jakovlena blended for me. Peter buckled up his belt and ran his fingers through his sweaty hair, while Maria followed him on deck. She clearly hated making love with him in this hot weather and in her condition; in the pale light of the full moon her eyes lay deep in their sockets. She settled between Peter and me, refusing the fresh fruit with a sullen shake of her head, but Peter forced a grape as big as a walnut into her palm. "Eat that. Here. In front of my eyes," he commanded. "I want a healthy son. Children are born strong when their mother is well fed," he joked, then pinched my cheek. "When you were pregnant with Elizabeth, you ate like a horse, didn't you, Catherinushka? So, let us have a toast to the strapping recruit that our beautiful Maria is expecting. A strong son for Russia." He drank deeply from the fresh, foaming beer and burped. Maria paled and pressed her hand to her mouth.

"Princess, was the tea my maid Jakovlena brewed you not helpful?" I asked, sounding worried and kind. Maria nodded, but gagged again.

"You're sending her remedies through one of your ladies?" Peter asked, and I lowered my eyes. "Yes, my tsar. No one knows more about a healthy birth than my Circassian maid Jakovlena. And on a troublesome journey like this, one must take no risks."

"Oh," Peter said, and pulled a fishbone from his teeth before cleaning his fingernails, stained by gunpowder and tobacco, with it. Maria Kantemir poked listlessly at the fish that Felten's men had caught in the afternoon. "You mean the journey does not help the princess's pregnancy?"

My eyes filled with tears. "After what I have suffered, I know how strenuous a campaign can be for a pregnant woman," I said haltingly. "That is why I wanted Jakovlena to look after Princess Kantemir. It's for Russia, after all."

Peter kissed my hand. "Do not cry nor worry, my wonderful Catherinushka. This child will be born in good health."

Maria Kantemir stared at me, her eyes, shining in the moonlight, as dangerous as a snake's, but Peter had made his mind up: "Dearest, as soon as we reach Astrakhan, you will strike up camp there and this Jakovlena will be in your state."

She wanted to complain, but before she could I cried out, "No, my tsar, I need Jakovlena. Without her herbal tea I cannot sleep. Do not take her away from me, please, I beg you."

Peter hesitated, but Maria Kantemir said, "All right. I shall settle in Astrakhan together with Jakovlena. Her brew does help me."

Hot tar dripped from the torches and hit the black surface of the water with a hiss as Peter patted my hand briefly. "So you can't sleep? What a worry. Well, once we are standing in the field, you'll be so tired that you will no longer need Jakovlena and her drinks. Now it is all about the healthy birth of the tsarevich."

The tsarevich. My heart skipped a beat, and Maria rose and kissed the tsar with a catty smile. "Allow me to retire. The prince needs rest," she said, laying a slender hand on her stomach. How far was she gone? Four or five months?

Peter and I sat for a moment. The torchlight speckled my skin with golden hues, and I moved closer, so that he could inhale my scent of jasmine and rosewater. As I filled his cup my hair fell loose and shiny over his naked arm, and his eyes gleamed in the moonlight. "Who would have thought, Catherinushka, that we would be in the field together once more," he said, brushing back my curls and sliding his hands over my neck down to my bosom: its flesh shimmered rosily through the delicate linen of my dress. I slid off my chair and knelt in front of him; he sighed as I tasted him before climbing on top of him. I rode Peter first slowly and then faster, and he came with a muffled scream, throwing his head back, his gaze searching the moon and the stars.

Afterward, he raised his jug to me. "It will be a son, won't it, Catherinushka?"

"Of course, my tsar. To the tsarevich's health," I toasted, and the clouds across the moon hid the look in my eyes.

* * *

My Jakovlena stayed behind with Maria Kantemir in Astrakhan, the city of a thousand turrets, fragrant fruits, and lingering moonlight. I kissed the old woman three times as a sign of peace when she took leave from me. "Peace be with you, mother." I repeated the Persian greetings the ambassador had taught me.

"May God guard you and yours, Tsaritsa. You're a good woman," she replied, heaving two saddlebags heavy with gold over her shoulders. She was able to retire in wealth. Jakovlena would not turn to look when she left, and I knew that I should never see her again.

78

We slaughtered, baked, and brewed outside Astrakhan's walls. The Russian traders, who felt safeguarded by our presence, sent us melons, apples, peaches, apricots, and grapes. In the stifling heat nearly twenty-three thousand foot soldiers joined us on our march to Derbent on the Caspian Sea, and more than a hundred thousand men followed us from farther across the country. But fatigue, heat, hunger, and thirst robbed them of their senses and our supplies were too puny for all of us, even if we quartered each ration, as a dozen of our flat cargo boats sank in a storm on the Caspian Sea. Felten and I oversaw the slaughtering of thousands of starving horses. It was horrid, but thanks to their meager flesh our men had the strength to move on to Baku.

In the evening, after I had treated the last cases of sunstroke and burned skin, I asked for Peter's Italian barber to come to my tent.

"What can I do for you, my empress? Do you need fresh talcum for your body? I still have a little bit of powder. But your perfume from Grasse has unfortunately dried up." He gladly sipped the cup of cold, sour milk I offered him.

"None of this, Maestro. Cut my hair."

"I beg your pardon, my empress?" In his eyes a woman without a long, full mane was not a woman, I understood.

"My hair hinders me in this heat and in the sun. My scalp steams. Off with it," I said.

He hesitated, got up, and wanted to reach for the jug of water.

"No," I decided. "The water is too valuable. Cut it off dry, just like that." His fingers stroked over my scalp. "Go on," I encouraged him, smiling at us in the mirror. He raised my tresses and placed his blade at the nape of my neck, where I felt its cool, sharp metal and enjoyed the brief sizzling sound with which each curl fell to the tent's bare earth, until the barber cleaned his blade and wrapped it back into its leather sheath. Like a woman of the mountains I wrapped a scarf around my head in a turban, allowing me to spend the whole day with the troops.

At nighttime, Peter's gaze was empty. "We cannot go on to Baku, *matka*," he said, exhausted. "The men would not survive the thirty-day walk. Let's return to Astrakhan," he decided. "I shall be with Maria, in time for the birth of the tsarevich."

"To the tsarevich and his mother, Princess Kantemir." I raised my glass and emptied it in a single go.

* * *

The house in Astrakhan lay eerily quiet. No children were playing on the flat roof; no women sat on pillows in the cool of its shade, sipping tea and chatting. No servants were running errands, filling the air with the patter of their bare feet and the jingle of the silver bells tied to their ankles. Even Maria's faithful guard of Moldavian soldiers was nowhere to be seen.

Peter and I rode into the shady courtyard, followed by the cook, Felten, and two dwarfs who sat on asses. Birds swarmed through the air; their wings made the mulberry leaves rustle. Water fell into a basin inlaid with colorful, shiny stones. Goldfish swam, but the surface was covered with algae. In the heating pans in the corner of the courtyard the ashes were cold.

"Hello?" Peter called, but everything remained silent. I got off my horse and washed the dust and the heat from the long ride off my face, despite the algae and the water's sour stench. Suddenly I had the feeling of being watched and looked up to the gallery. Did a slight, veiled figure slip into the columns' shade?

"Maria?" Peter got off as well, walking ahead. As I followed him through the dusky rooms his steps echoed in my heart. He pushed open the door to the room where he had taken leave from Maria Kantemir so tenderly just a few weeks ago. A suffocating stench of sweat and camphor took my breath away. Peter gasped, covering his mouth and nose. I had a look around: pillows lay scattered around a divan made of *kilim* rugs, and on a low table inlaid with ivory stood a silver tray with a cup of mint tea. I dipped my finger in the drink: it was cold and an oily film locked its surface. The marble floor was covered with silk rugs, and in front of a folding screen I spotted a bowl filled with yellow slime. Filthy sheets had been cast off the empty bedstead, as if someone had hurriedly stood up. Peter fought for breath and called again, "Maria? Where are you, my love?"

My blood pulsed with fear and caution when we heard a noise, and we spun around: a woman stepped out from behind the folding screen. She was densely veiled and said huskily, "I am here, my tsar." The veil stifled her voice, but when Peter stepped up to her, looking delighted, wanting to lift it, she seized his wrists. "Let it be. I can do that myself. I'm used to that by now," she said with threatening calm. I lingered in the shadows; my heart raced when Maria Kantemir threw off her veil and stepped naked into the merciless light of the Persian morning. Peter gasped with horror and shrank back. I, too, only just suppressed a disgusted cry when I saw what Jakovlena had achieved.

The smallpox had had a feast with the stunning beauty of the princess of Moldavia. Her honeycomb hair had fallen out, except for a couple of straggly strands, and her scalp was covered with scabs and bruises. Her skin was gray and pale, the once even features blemished by deep, crater-like scars. Thin, pale lips barely covered her gums where once an alluring full mouth had been. The pox had ravaged her body, too: her breasts hung flat and wilted over her pointy, sharp ribs; on her arms the illness still festered—she scratched on the blisters and pimples—and on her legs an ashen skin stretched over her long bones.

"What happened to you, Maria? Our child—" Peter began, scanning her waist. I bit my lip and clenched my fists: her tummy was flat. Maria Kantemir had lost the child she expected from my husband, the child that would have put an end to my happiness and my life as I knew it. Peter stood as if struck by lightning, but she suddenly turned and pounced at me like a wildcat. One of the soldiers just about held her back, but she fought his grip, spitting and biting with rage while I ordered curtly, "Get the tsar out of here; he must not contract smallpox."

Felten and the soldiers dragged Peter out of the room. At the door, he turned, and I read sheer dread in his eyes: only he looked at me, and not at Maria. What did he see? A tall, strong woman with her hair cut as short as the thorns of desert thistles; the mother of his children, the companion of his years, the empress of his realm. He left me to it.

"Hold her," I ordered the soldier coldly. He grabbed one of the sheets and seized the princess. I stepped up to her. I had won the game that she felt so safe playing.

"Princess," I asked gleefully, "what happened to your beauty? And the tsarevich, the child on which we had placed such hopes? How dreadful! Who could have guessed that the pox was raging right here in Astrakhan?"

She spat out and I shrank back, just about avoiding the poisonous saliva. "Devil of a woman! I know that your maid passed me the disease. She bled me one day and then I caught a fever and the smallpox. You are to blame," she shrieked, before she was strangled by sobs. "My son was to rule Russia."

"Save your breath," I said. "You get even less than you deserve. If it is Jakovlena's fault we'll have her tortured until she confesses."

Maria Kantemir howled and wanted to strike me once more, but the soldier held her too tightly. "She ran away, just like everyone else, when I fell ill. I gave birth to a stillborn child on my own. Nobody wanted to help me," she cried. "Just look at me!"

"I am looking at you," I said. "Is that not what you had in mind for me? Being cast aside and forgotten?"

The soldier pushed her away, wiping his hands in worry and disgust, and we hurried out: Maria Kantemir's crying and cursing rang eerily through the vaulted gallery as we left.

Peter had already returned to the ship; the courtyard was empty. I myself locked the door to Maria's house and let the key slip into my pocket where it should be forgotten. With Volynsky's help I hired an old woman and told her to push plain food and water through a flap in the entrance gate, as if feeding a cat. If the bowls were untouched several days in a row, the house was to be set alight.

But I certainly hoped that Maria Kantemir would live for many years to come.

79

The war against Persia ended in the following autumn. A messenger interrupted one of Alexander Danilovich Menshikov's splendid masked balls with news of the victory at Baku. Before midnight struck, more than a thousand bottles of sparkling wine were emptied, and the only peaceful year of Peter's rule began.

* * *

I so wanted to recognize the man, but after all these years it was almost impossible. He knelt, and I saw only his back and his calloused hands. He was partly bald, and his sandals were stuffed with straw for lack of proper shoes.

"Look up," I said, and he did so, trembling with fear.

Peter's fingers drummed on his armrest. "And? Does he tell the truth? If the dog has lied, I'll have his tongue torn out."

The man moaned and curled up even more.

"Let me look at you." I stepped down from my throne and stooped. Neither the guards nor Peter, Anna, Elizabeth, or Wilhelm Mons—without him, my daughter barely took a step—let us out of sight. The man trembled like pig's blubber but met my gaze. His thin blond hair reminded me of my father's, but he had my stepmother's deep-set eyes and gruff lips.

"Are you telling the truth, man?" My voice was torn with raw feeling, and he spoke with rotten yellow stumps instead of teeth in his mouth.

"I swear by God Almighty, Marta: I am your brother, Fyodor."

Fyodor was a coachman on the road between Saint Petersburg and Riga, where he strapped himself to the carriage's roof, watching the luggage or looking for scoundrels and obstacles. The sun beat down on him, he was soaked by rain, or his buttocks froze to the cart. When a fellow traveler had threatened him with a good hiding, he had shouted, "I am our empress's brother. If you hit me, you'll have to pay for it." In his stupor, he was dragged to Saint Petersburg.

"How is Christina? Is she alive?" I asked. The question tasted of days long gone by.

"Ah. She brought us nothing but shame. Mother caught her with a man and gave her a hiding. She ran away and today she is a whore in Riga." He looked as if he wanted to spit, but the sight of the Winter Palace's marble floor made him change his mind.

"What happened to the rest of the family?"

He pulled a face. "Maggie married a shoemaker in Riga. The man makes a lot of money but sets the dogs on me when he sees me."

"How did Father die?" I asked him.

"Our new master killed him, just after the first famine."

My poor father. "And Tanya?" My voice was hoarse. "Your mother?"

Fyodor grinned. "She moved in with our new master. He liked her, in spite of her years."

"I am still not sure," I said, searching his face. One more question, to quench all doubts, forever. "Which animal attacked us, and you crushed its skull with a stone?"

He thought hard, lines furrowing his ruddy forehead. Silence fell in the small throne room. Then his face softened, and he said, "It was a snake, sister."

* * *

Peter showed himself generous: my brother and sister, Fyodor and Maggie, received a pension, but my pleas on Christina's behalf fell on deaf ears. He giggled when the soldiers led Fyodor Skawronski away. "A whore in Riga. No, really, Catherinushka," he mocked me. "I'll send her to a convent where she will be looked after. Now forgive me, this thief and scoundrel of Menshikov has been trying to cheat the imperial buyers once more—" He left, merrily lashing his boots with his *dubina* as if to train it for Menshikov's back.

Anna also took her leave; my eyes met Wilhelm Mons's gaze when he bowed and followed Elizabeth. I quickly looked away.

Once they had gone, I waved Jagushinsky closer. "Pavel Ivanovich, is it right that the tsarevna Elizabeth is with the young Mons at all times? Does that seem disreputable?"

"It does not *seem* disreputable, it *is* disreputable, my empress," Jagushinsky said cautiously.

I pondered his words, then rose and smoothed my skirt. "I am grateful for his services," I decided. "But Elizabeth is to be given a state worthy of an adult tsarevna. Mons is to be my chamberlain from now on. At my age, I should be beyond suspicion." I playfully slapped Jagushinsky's shoulder with my fan. "Now off you go, the tsar is waiting for you. Do not worry: the *dubina* is already busy enough for today."

I watched him go, my heart clenching. Was I asking for my own undoing? Nonsense. Wilhelm Mons could easily be my son: my handsome, healthy son.

* * *

The yelling and shouting coming from Peter's rooms could be heard from fifty feet away; I heard Menshikov and, in between, the high-pitched voice of Peter Shafirov. I hastened my steps: Had Alekasha gone too far this time? Inside, Menshikov and Shafirov were rolling on the ground, kicking, beating, and biting each other like two drunkards in a *kabak*: fists flew, and bones cracked. Peter himself circled the two men and lashed them with his *dubina* wherever he could. "Stop it, you scoundrels! Fighting in front of your tsar as if I was one of your whores, how dare you?" he bellowed, as Menshikov grabbed Shafirov by his hair, while the latter bit his arm. I threw myself at Peter, holding him back. "*Starik!* What's the matter?" Shafirov sobbed while checking his torn, richly embroidered coat and Menshikov sat down, panting. Pearls and silver threads were scattered all over the room. His wig was mussed, the curls coming undone.

Peter placed his head on my chest, gasping for air. "Both are liars and cheats, Catherinushka!" he said. "Thank God I can always trust *you.* Menshikov should have had his bones broken on the wheel a long time ago for all his lies and frauds."

Menshikov, who could cross Peter's empire from Riga to Derbent and spend every night on an estate of his own, pulled himself up. Every Russian knew a different story about his greed, as he wished to be rewarded for every service rendered, be it in rubles or kopecks, a noble horse for his stables, or a beautiful girl for a night. He had more titles and honors than hair on his head, his food was prepared by French cooks, his princely carriage was pulled by ten horses, and at times, Daria wore more magnificent jewels than I. Nevertheless, I would not forget a friend who had done me good. In Saint Petersburg, a man was either a plaintiff or an accused, and fortune would not stop to smile at my old friend. If Menshikov fell in disgrace, and was duly punished, none of us was safe from Peter's wrath.

"What's the matter?" I asked.

"Menshikov has sold the Russian troops stale bread and thin soup. The money for supplies is dangling in diamonds around his wife's fat neck instead. More, he stole fifteen thousand souls from the Cossacks, and now I have to quench an uprising." Peter spat furiously.

"Well, I have heard worse. Is not Menshikov always Menshikov?" I reminded him, and Alexander Danilovich dared a smile, but Peter was furious, pointing to the door. "Out! Both of you. Shafirov, I'll check on your business. If you leave town without my permission, I will execute you and your family on the spot. And you"—he pointed his *dubina* at Alexander Danilovich—"Menshikov! Your bitch of a mother conceived you in sin and shame and you shall die in sin and shame. Yes, you shall end where you started!"

80

Daria Menshikova came to see me the same evening, just when we—my ladies-in-waiting, Wilhelm Mons, and I—listened to my reader at the fireplace. The book was of slippery content, and my younger ladies giggled. Peter's illness hindered him from knowing them as well as he would have done in earlier years, I thought. In the past few weeks his suffering had worsened and his swollen body made him scream in pain.

My eyes were drawn to Wilhelm Mons; I could not help it. He lay on a chaise longue and looked into the flames, which gave his skin a golden hue. His long, well-shaped legs were stretched out, and crossed. Did the reader's words make his heart race, as they did mine? Were his lips, which smiled so easily, demanding when they touched a woman's mouth? He moved, folding his arms behind his head, and sighed, while looking in the flames. How was it to be caressed by these long, slender fingers; those hands that he so casually folded beneath his head? Again, it was easy to imagine him out in the open, sleeping under a starry sky and being content sitting around a fire. I forced myself to take my eyes off him when Agneta whispered in my ear, "Daria Menshikova is waiting for you in the Chinese Cabinet, my princess."

In his struggle for survival, Menshikov used the strongest weapon at his disposal: the memory of my youth and the friendship with Daria. If we met today, we ate sugared violets and made idle marriage plans for our living children, mourning the dead. As I rose, Wilhelm Mons sat up. "Follow me," I said briefly.

I felt him closely behind me. If I stopped, would our bodies touch? Instead, I hastened my steps. This was not to happen.

In the Chinese Cabinet the candlelight brought the birds painted on the colorful silk wall coverings to life. Daria paced the small room. At the sight of me, she threw herself to her knees, grabbing my ankles, but I embraced her.

"Wilhelm, give your handkerchief to Princess Menshikova. No woman is to be left weeping," I scolded him playfully. Daria sneezed as loud as a farmer's wife into the silk cloth; her hair was tousled, and the tears left unsightly traces on the pasty white makeup she still ordered from Venice.

"Sit," I said, and Wilhelm pushed a dainty, silk-covered chair closer, which creaked under her weight.

Daria rummaged in her cleavage and handed me a small roll of paper. "Alekasha won't tell me what's going on. He smashed our green salon to pieces and the cook got the hiding of a lifetime. As I left he went for the Delft tiles in his study. He sends you this—"

I unrolled the scroll, on which there was only one sentence, its ink smeared by tears. "Read it to me," I told Wilhelm, who stepped up to the fireplace.

"'What am I to do?'" he read out slowly, looking up, astonished, but Daria's and my disbelief was palpable. We stared at each other: the powerful Prince Menshikov knew no further.

She clasped my hands. "Please, Catherine Alexeyevna, by all that once linked us, by all that we once loved. Help us."

"What should your husband do, Daria?" I asked, chuckling, after a moment of silence. Wilhelm watched me, a slight smile playing in the corners of his full, soft lips. He leaned against the silk walls as casually as if they were those of a stable. His presence made me lighthearted, and so I said: "Well, quite simply, Menshikov is to follow the command of his master and become what he was earlier. Tomorrow night, at a supper with me and some friends. Will you join us?" I asked her but looked straight at Wilhelm.

Daria took my words with her into the frosty winter night.

* * *

Our dinner was simple, and Peter ate in sulky silence. He needed more money, but already took his tenth share of even a torn fisherman's net being pulled through Russian waters, however big or small its haul. "Can you think of something else that I could tax?" he asked me testily.

"Let me think. Homesteads, cattle, wood and bricks, houseware, crockery, cutlery, sleds, carts, beehives, ponds, rivers, mills, even *banjas* are already taxed."

"Yes. Everything I see when I cross my country," he admitted grumpily.

I dipped my spoon in my soup, fishing for cabbage and pickled gherkins. "How about taxing vegetables for floating in a soup?" I asked.

But Peter said, "Already done. The only thing that is not taxed is the air for breathing."

"Well, then . . ." I said, holding my breath.

Peter chuckled and raised his glass. "To you and your power to always make me laugh." His eyes were moist; the candlelight hid the icy streaks in his hair and smoothed the deep lines in his puffy face. Wilhelm, who waited on me, refilled my goblet so that I could answer Peter as I should, when we heard a racket from outside the room: banging and a familiar voice shouting, "*Pirogi!* Hot fresh *pirogi!*"

Peter listened, surprised, as the doors flew open and in marched Menshikov, dressed in rags and barefoot despite the cold. A too-large baker boy's cap slipped over his eyes, and he toted pastry on a large tray in front of his belly. "*Pirogi! Pirogi!* Buy with me, the baker boy, Menshikov." He shoved his tray at Peter. "Eat, puny little prince. Everyone knows that that witch of your half sister Sophia doesn't let you have a square meal!"

I held my breath. Peter's eyes wandered from his friend's face to the steaming, fragrant *pirogi,* and back again. He tasted one. "Hmm—still as good as in olden times, Menshikov, you scoundrel!" He laughed, and Alexander Danilovich knelt, tears filling his eyes.

"Will you forgive me, my heart?" he whispered. "I have failed you. But if you flog and behead all scoundrels in your empire, you'll soon have no subjects left."

Peter threw the pastry to his dogs, who leaped at it, and embraced Menshikov, sobbing and laughing at the same time. "Do not cross me again, Alekasha, for otherwise I must have your hide, as sorry as I'd be."

Menshikov sat and the men chatted, drank, and laughed as if nothing had ever happened. From behind my chair, I felt Wilhelm's closeness, breathing in his scent of musk and sandalwood. I felt as helpless as a doe who senses the hunter approaching. So I heard only faintly, as Menshikov said to Peter, "But you ought to keep an eye on that cheat Shafirov . . ."

* * *

The following morning an adorable boy was sent to my room; his skin was like chocolate, and on his crimson velvet cloak Menshikov's coat of arms was embroidered. He bowed and opened the heavy jewel case he carried, showing a tiara, necklace, and earrings made of flawless diamonds of such size and fire that they had no par in Peter's treasury. The child chirped in broken Russian, "With gratitude and adoration from Alexander Danilovich Menshikov." I gladly accepted Menshikov's beautiful present. He had given me so much, why not these gems, at such a moment in life? I sent the boy to Abraham Petrovich, Peter's Moor, where he would want for nothing.

* * *

A few weeks later, in Peterhof, Peter sent for me after we had spent the morning together.

The tubby stable cat had had kittens and our little Natalya was besotted with the blind, clumsy bundles of fur. She sat on Peter's knees when he asked: "Which one do you want, my girl?"

The morning sun set Natalya's auburn curls aflame and my heart tightened with love. Soon she was to receive her first lessons.

"Can't I have them all?" she asked, astonished, and Peter cupped the five kittens in his large hands. "Of course, my little angel, you *can* have them all, but perhaps your sisters might want one as well?"

Natalya thought for a moment. "All right. But only one."

"Open your skirt, we'll put them inside. But let's take the mother cat as well. The kittens still need her," Peter said. The cat dug her claws in his hands when he turned to me. "Are you coming?"

"Not yet. Elizabeth breaks in the stallion that the king of France sent her. I'll watch."

"Hopefully she will not break her neck before we marry her off to Paris." He chuckled and stepped together with Natalya from the darkness of the stables into the bright spring sunshine, where Alice already waited for them. She took Natalya's free hand, and the little girl skipped and played angel: they disappeared in a swirl of light.

Elizabeth noted my presence at the ring with a polite nod. I watched her force her will upon the stallion and knew she had not forgiven me for taking Wilhelm from her. She would be a good queen to France, even if Versailles had grown curiously quiet in recent months, if only she ever became the princess she was.

Peter and Feofan Prokopovich awaited me. The priest leaned against one of the study's walls, his dark robe blending with the paneling. The room's scent of dust, paper, ink, and tobacco was laced by a salty breeze and sunbeams drew patterns on the Persian rugs. I kissed Feofan's *panagia*, and he blessed me with the sign of the cross. What duties did Feofan have in Peterhof? His manifold talents never ceased to astonish me; he wrote plays as well as the history of the Great Northern War, together with Peter, every Saturday morning. He read the works of scholars, whose names I could scarcely pronounce, in their own language: Spinoza, Descartes, Bacon, and Leibniz, to name just a few that I cared to remember. All his work was done for the tsar's honor and glory, who had made him a "Father of the Fatherland."

Peter looked up from the paper he was reading with a tender smile. "*Matka,* come, sit down with us two old men. We'll talk some nonsense together."

I felt Feofan's gaze not letting go of me, but I closed my face as only we souls knew how.

"We were talking about freedom," Feofan said.

"I like to talk about it! *Volya!* To do what you like; isn't that the dream of all of us?" I laughed.

Feofan scolded me. "My empress, you speak like the soul you once were. But freedom means not to do whatever one feels like, but to be delivered from all ideas that hinder our souls' well-being."

Peter placed his muddy boots on the table. I frowned: What was Feofan going on about? He chose every word carefully. "There are laws of the heart and of nature. God decides on them, or his chosen ruler. The tsar is a father to his people. With God's help he takes decisions which we can't fathom immediately."

"Get to the point, honorable Feofan," Peter said.

"The tsar has no son," the pope continued. "So he will and must decide alone upon the succession when the day comes."

"Let that day be far from us," I said.

"Indeed." Peter chuckled and got up, shaking his legs. "Thank you, Feofan Prokopovich. I will tell the empress alone what I have to tell her. But you showed me the way."

When Feofan had left, I clenched the carved lion heads of my armrests and Peter looked at me in silence. I could barely hold myself back: Which of his bastards would he appoint as his heir? He had an army of sons born out of wedlock. My chest hurt, and I stepped to the window: the room was silent bar the ticking of the room's clocks that were set to chime together.

Outside, on the bright gravel of the terrace, Elizabeth stood with Wilhelm, her cheeks flushed by the ride. He laughed politely at what she said but kept his distance. My gaze skimmed the park's treetops and the fountains, whose water sparkled in all the colors of the rainbow, and then slid out toward the leaden sea of the Finnish bay. Peter stepped behind me, embracing me and nuzzling my neck.

"Catherinushka. I've learned that a woman's body does not do my bidding," he said, sounding sad, his words cutting my soul like a blade. "God has denied us a strong, healthy son. I cannot be angry with him, for wrath shall not spoil my old days. But you and I, we always stuck together. You have been faithful to me, always; your words were to be trusted, as were your kindness and your grace." His voice cracked. I leaned my head back on his shoulder and closed my eyes so as to not shed the tears I felt coming. Was he sweetening the bitter pill for me?

"I want to thank you," he breathed into my ear. "Are you ready for this?"

I opened my eyes and the light poured painfully into my mind. "Ready? Whatever for?"

"To be crowned. Next year, in Moscow, as soon as it is warm and sunny. If I die before my time, you can carry on my work," he said, his eyes not leaving my face. "Are you ready? We are both old. I want to thank you for everything."

We are both old. His words rooted in my soul, but before they could hurt, I nodded. He laughed, delighted, as he bit me playfully in my neck. "I am so proud of you!"

Wilhelm looked up to our window. I felt his gaze like a caress and stepped away from the pane. I am not that old as yet, I thought, when Wilhelm watched with burning eyes as Peter lifted my chin and kissed me.

81

Peter Shafirov trembled like an aspen's leaf when he mounted the scaffold, barefoot and dressed in a hair shirt: he had been found guilty of treason and embezzlement of public funds. After the weeks in prison he looked again like the young, bright man he had been before his greed got the better of him. Alexander Danilovich sat beside me: spinning the diamond-studded knob of his walking stick. To celebrate the day his former friend was to be beheaded, he wore a new wig.

For April, the Moscow air was unusually stuffy, and a small crowd had gathered on the Red Square. After three years of famine the people looked gaunt; their eyes lay deep in their sockets, and their heads were mere skulls. I knew the whispers: *God punishes the murderer on Russia's throne. We pay for the tsar's sins.* The Moskva carried hardly any water and in some parts of Russia travelers were told not to spend the night alone in an inn, for otherwise they might end up as a juicy stew. Shafirov sobbed when he saw his five princess daughters soaking their handkerchiefs with tears. I searched for Peter's eyes, but he looked at me blankly.

The night before, I had searched my drawers for the leather pouch which had hung on my belt at the Pruth. Inside lay the ring Peter had given me back then, when Shafirov had risked his life for Peter and for Russia, going into the sultan's camp. "Let us never forget what happened today," Peter had said back then. When I had placed the ring on his desk last night, he frowned.

"What is that?" He had turned the ring back and forth, so that the candle flame caught the fire of the flawless ruby.

"The ring you gave me at the Pruth twelve years ago," I reminded him. "You said that we should never forget what Shafirov did for Russia."

Peter had slipped the ring in the pocket of his old green velvet dressing gown. "Go back to sleep, Catherinushka. It will be a hard enough day tomorrow." He sighed.

* * *

Peter stood up on the scaffold, his face unreadable; in a cruel joke the executioner pulled Shafirov's legs away as he was about to kneel down, so he wobbled like one of Natalya's toys on what was left of his belly. The people jeered, while the executioner adjusted his red hood to see better through the narrow slits cut for his eyes. The ax flashed in the morning sun; Shafirov's lips moved in a silent prayer, and his wife, the slender, sour Baroness Shafirov, fainted as the steel fell.

I closed my eyes—and heard the crowd gasp: when I dared a peek, I saw the ax stuck in the wood next to Shafirov's head. He cowered at the executioner's block, ashen with the sheer dread of still being alive. Menshikov flicked some mucus from his nose and grunted with anger. "Really, can't a man like Shafirov even afford a good hangman? Fool."

Up at the scaffold, Makarov handed Peter a scroll, and the Kremlin's walls threw the tsar's words back at us: Shafirov had been pardoned. A sigh went through the crowd, the Baroness Shafirov came to, and when Shafirov took his seat in the senate later that day his eyes had seen death. His physician had to bleed him twice until he felt truly among the living again.

* * *

In the evening, I found the ring of Pruth lying among my bottles of perfume, my makeup, and my brushes and combs, though Peter never said a word about it, ever again.

* * *

The summer brought long, bright days and I returned to Peterhof: Peter helped me on my boat, kissing me, calling me by my old nicknames. It was as if his love for me was refreshed, twenty years into our togetherness. As the wind filled my boat's sails, I saw him merge with the gray stone of the Summer Palace's jetty, waving me good-bye. Yes, I felt the peace and safety that I had longed for since so long, but also the unrest and the wish of yet more to come. Was that the other woman, deep inside of me, stirring? I willed her to be quiet. In Peterhof, I knew, Wilhelm Mons awaited me already.

* * *

After the stifling heat of the city, the sight of the barren, famished land pained me: for the fourth year in a row, the barns were bare, and starved bodies lay at the roadside, as no one had enough strength left to bury them. Instead, Peterhof was a quiet paradise: the treetops had grown beyond the palace's roof, the fountains sparkled from afar, colorful birds darted through the air, butterflies tumbled in the reeds, and I heard the little monkeys I kept in Marly shriek.

As I set foot on the jetty, Wilhelm Mons was there to greet me. I slipped on the wet planks and he caught me, his fingers closing tightly and his four talisman rings cutting into my flesh. I bit my lip to not cry out, as it was a sweet pain that came together with what I had most longed for: the touch of his hand. When I looked up, confused, his gaze was deeper than the sea around us. Words of gratitude died on my lips; something long forgotten stirred in my heart, and the sheer force of that feeling took my breath. My other self, the woman who had hidden in my heart ever since Peter had questioned Alexey, rose from the shadows of my soul, and before I could stop her, she stepped out into the sunlight and replied to Wilhelm's longing with all her heart.

Nothing happened but our fingertips brushing, and my skin was scalded by his touch. I walked up to the palace but would not turn to look at him; no, not yet.

That same evening the first of many messengers from Saint Petersburg reached me. Peter wrote to me as he had not done for years: *Matka, where are you? The palace is so empty without you, and no one makes me laugh. I play with Natalya every day, because of all our daughters I find your soul, your wit, and your beauty in her. What prince will be good enough for her, one day? Otherwise, I wander from room to room and find you nowhere. But rest well in Peterhof: it's wonderful to grow old with a loved one—*

I stopped the messenger short. "Enough, man, you have a long ride behind you. The gamekeeper has brought pigeons up to the house, go get yourself a good plateful."

He handed me the crumpled note and bowed. "Does the tsaritsa have an answer for His Majesty?"

"Perhaps tomorrow," I ordered, waiting for his steps to fade away. I knelt down at the library's fireplace, which was lit to fight the morning chill. I held Peter's letter to the flames: they licked hungrily over the dry paper. The first words to be swallowed were those of Peter's last sentence, *To grow old*. His black writing twitched and fought against the fire, but I crouched, patient as a peasant girl, and watched the paper fall to ashes. Suddenly I had to laugh. I laughed and laughed—a laughter to scare a sane man witless.

Catherine Alexeyevna was not *old*, Peter. She was young, strong, and beautiful: she who loves, lives, my husband. My laughter turned into tears, and all of a sudden I was crying, cowering on the rug, sobbing and clawing the pile, all my despair and the shock of the past catching up with me. I wept until I curled up like one of Natalya's kittens, there, in front of the fireplace. When I awoke, I shivered. A summer storm had torn open the windows; rainwater pooled on the floor, and cold, salty air filled the room. My rug was soaked, too, and the light yellow silk of my dress clung to my body. I tried to pull myself up onto a chair, but it toppled and fell with a clatter. The door flew open, and I saw the man whom I had hoped and loathed to see.

"My empress," said Wilhelm, his voice unsteady. "I heard a sound. Have you hurt yourself?" Had he guarded the door, watching over me? How else could he have been here so fast? He reached me in one or two steps, while I sat still: my hair fell loose and tousled over my bare shoulders, where my dress had slipped in the restless slumber.

Wilhelm knelt next to me; his fingers skimmed my cheeks, touching my mouth like a butterfly's wings. I greedily closed my lips around his fingertips and tasted the salt of my tears. He kissed my damp cheeks and muttered, "The color of snow, the taste of tears, and the vastness of the sea." I closed my eyes, giving a choked sob.

He embraced me, holding me close: since when had I been longing for this? Ever since I first met him? "We mustn't—" I started, aware of the danger and the madness of this.

"I know," he replied, as the yellow silk of my dress tore like parchment paper, and his hands cupped my full breasts before he unlaced me; my nipples hardened under his lips and tongue, my body aching for his caress. As he searched my wetness with the tip of his tongue, slowly and softly, taking all his time to taste me, I cried out, lying on my back, splayed naked in the bright daylight, and he would not allow me to cover myself.

"You are so beautiful, Catherine Alexeyevna. The most beautiful woman under the sun, so full, soft, and warm." His words made me ease; his lips found each fold of my flesh and let no part of me escape; his tongue soft and moist, his fingers supple, his hands strong. I opened my legs wider and wider, my hips coming toward him, his face and then his cock. He was so big and hard that I gasped when he came into me, filling me out, as open and wet as I was, and then pulling me on his lap while he knelt. I gave a muffled moan to have him so deeply and still feel him grow, but he placed his hand on my mouth.

"Move," he whispered.

"I can't," I gasped, but he made me, and a new wave of lust came over me, riding him until I felt sore with pleasure; in my ecstasy I bit his fingers with the four rings bloody as he shoved them in my mouth when I came, and then I licked the crimson sweetness of his flesh like a kitten would some cream. In his arms, I was a woman once more, not just an empress. I struck all weapons in a defeat sweeter than any victory could ever be.

* * *

It was late afternoon when I walked barefoot to the window to close it. It was raining again, and the door, too, was battered by the wind. How reckless we were: we had not even shut it before making love. This was madness—if Peter knew, it would be our undoing. He had tortured, maimed, and killed for so much less than this betrayal of everything we had lived. I turned, my heart racing and some raindrops wetting my cheeks. My body ached where Wilhelm had touched me, yet I already yearned for more. It felt as if I belonged to him. He napped on the rug, breathing softly, sated, his cheeks rosy and his open lips smiling, and I lowered myself at the wall next to the fireplace and sat looking at him: he was my husband, my son, my youth, my love, my life. I took wood chippings from the basket next to the fireplace and rekindled the flames, just as I had learned as a girl. Sparks fed on the dry straw I had stuffed between the logs, and I cowered on my heels and hummed a little song as I guarded Wilhelm's slumber. How wonderful life was; I neither wanted to sleep, nor to cover myself or eat. My love refreshed, warmed, and nourished me. I knew this must never happen again.

* * *

The following months of my life forever belong to Wilhelm. How we lived our love so fully, I do not know. A special God protects lovers: we shared every heartbeat, every thought, every hope, and every fear. At the glorious Peterhof dawn we crossed the park down to the sea and bathed in the bay, splashing and laughing. We moved among the trees until they spun around us; the sea breeze crusted the salt on our skins and blue clouds piled up at the horizon while we sipped of the scented summer rain. Among the trees, and on the soft earth of the ground, Wilhelm and I became one creature with two heads, four arms, and four legs. What sounds like a monster from Peter's Kunstkamera was the most beautiful state of being I was ever to know. The summer in Peterhof was our world, and this world was good and great.

* * *

Elizabeth avoided me. She ate with her sisters in their apartments, kept to her ladies, and when I met them in the park she walked away. The sea breeze blew the fountain's water droplets in a rainbow in front of her colorful skirts, which faded among the trees as she left me behind.

One morning, I paid her a visit in her schoolroom: the blue silk curtains were drawn, and the books' polished leather bindings gleamed in the sunlight. In one corner of the room stood a man of glass, on which the girls studied the human body. He was cross-eyed, as one of his ceramic eyes stared at me, the other one down to the globe at his feet, ever since Elizabeth had torn it out, and Madame de la Tour, the governess, had not twisted it back in. Next to the piano of German make I spotted Anna's silver music stand, for she had singing lessons to please the young Duke of Holstein. The wind ruffled her music sheets, despite the hooks of ivory holding the paper down.

This sound did not bother Elizabeth: her head was bent studiously as she wrote a note. I snuck up to her; some curls had loosened from her ash-blond plaits, and the nape of her neck was touchingly childlike. Before I knew what I was doing, I caressed her head with more tenderness than I had truly ever felt for her.

Elizabeth started. "You!" she hissed, and the look of her eyes, which were as lively as a bird's, pierced me.

But I asked in a friendly fashion, "What are you doing, Elizabeth? How diligent to still be here after your lessons with Madame de la Tour."

"I have not written in my diary for so long and the weather is not nice enough to go riding anyway," she said. I looked outside, where a light wind swept the sunny treetops. What could I say to her? It was clear that she wanted me to go. So I cast a glance at her sheet of paper, and while I could not read her writing, I noticed how strong and slanted her letters were. This was not a child's hand, but a woman's.

82

Peter sent me letter after letter to Peterhof, and every line spoke of love and longing: *Unfortunately, I cannot be with you, Catheri-nushka. My old illness plagues me more than ever, and I am glad to spare you the sight of me. My stomach is as bloated as a horse's, and the pain binds my chest with iron straps; the ulcers on my legs make every step a pain. At least Alekasha has given me a magnificent stallion. So I drink to forget the pain and go riding, even though it takes three footmen to lift me in the saddle.*

* * *

When the summer turned into a damp autumn, I returned to Saint Petersburg with a heavy heart. At least Wilhelm was with me, and I remember having the sailors tie up my barge on a bend of the water well before town. I gave them two hours' leave and was with Wilhelm once more. "This has to be the last time," I said, as his fingers slid into me before I could even undress. "If we do this in Petersburg, the tsar will kill us both."

"If I have to die, I want to die for you, with you" was his answer. He pushed me on my bedstead and turned me, raising my hips, and slid in me. His holding me down and closing my legs while thrusting in me gave me more strength than I had thought possible. I bit the cushions to not make a sound yet wanted to cry for more with every breath.

* * *

Just when I would have been as happy tending the fire together with Wilhelm in a little *izba,* I had to plan my coronation. Was I but a soul after all? I felt utter dread: never before had a tsaritsa been crowned; the Moscow ceremony should make the importance of Peter's step clear to everybody, be it a wealthy prince or a pauper in his vast realm. My spirit, my body, and my soul dreaded the weight of the crown, and Peter must have felt my unease when he drew me close in his study in the Winter Palace. "Do not worry," he said. "I shall be with you, every step of the way." He smiled, misunderstanding my nerves. I winced, as I longed so much for Wilhelm that I wanted to avoid Peter's touch. But then I gave in and caressed his tousled hair. The table was covered with drawings for robes, uniforms, and jewels.

"Look. We drive from Menshikov's house to the Kremlin, crossing the Red Square, which will be full of flags. The way to Uspensky Cathedral is not long, but all the people should see you and it must be unforgettable." He rustled with his tobacco-stained fingertips in other papers. "Here: the list of the people who will carry your train. I have, of course, thought of Sheremetev—"

If anyone deserved to be with me that day, it was Boris Petrovich, I thought, but asked: "And who, my tsar, shall crown me? Feofan Prokopovich?"

Peter dropped the scroll, placed his hands on my bare shoulders, and kissed my forehead. His voice quivered as he said, "No, Catherinushka. I myself shall crown you, and no one else."

* * *

That night, I sat on the broad sill of my bedroom window: darkness had fallen like a curtain on my splendid city of glistening snow. Wilhelm pulled the floor-length sable coat off my naked body, pressed me against the pane, parted my thighs, and slid into me. My calves pressed against his shoulders and I bent against the window that was dripping with our breath, sweat, and lust. Wilhelm forced me deeper among the velvet curtains to muffle my sighs, moans, and then a cry. He forced me still, feeling my heart race against his, his mouth laughing as he kissed his own taste from my lips. We lived our love shamelessly, as if there was no tomorrow—the fear of discovery, and what might happen then, made our feelings even stronger and our passion more burning.

But the boost of life and pleasure was as heady as no lasting happiness can ever be.

* * *

Peter set the date for my coronation at the end of May. "No other month is golden enough to celebrate this day," he said at a meal during which his two dwarfs wrestled, the Moor Abraham Petrovich being their referee. I ate lots of caviar, as Wilhelm had told me that it was good for love. When I looked up, he gave me a tender smile, which made Peter frown. My heart chilled, as Peter asked lightly, "How is the young Mons doing in your retinue?"

"Very well. I have not heard any complaints," I replied, feeding Peter with a *blinchiki* of smoked sturgeon.

"Mmmm, delicious." He smacked his lips and sucked my fingertips, then drizzled lemon juice over my neck and licked it off my skin but stopped short when he noticed my diamond necklace; Menshikov's gift. He frowned. "Such stones are rare in my kingdom. Who gave it to you?"

"Alekasha. He was so grateful to me for my advice," I said merrily, but Peter shook his head.

"*Matka.* You before all others should not accept gifts, and certainly not from Menshikov. No reproach against him must ever besmirch you, don't you understand? There must be a person in my kingdom who is untouchable; and I wish this to be you." He sounded upset.

"Of course. How thoughtless of me. Come now, *starik,* this is not an evening for harsh lessons. Drink with me." My tenderness soothed him, and I refilled his jug to the brim. My body ached for Wilhelm, who stood behind us. But tonight, I had to be Peter's wife.

* * *

The robes and uniforms for my coronation were delivered from Paris, but my crown was made in Saint Petersburg. The Nevsky Prospect was cloaked in fresh snowfall when we first visited the jeweler: Peter did not want him to travel with his valuable work. The slight man and his apprentices bowed, moving backward into the small cabinet when the guards manned the door. Peter and I sipped tea with vodka from dainty china as the casket was placed in front of us.

"Put the cup down, or you'll spill everything," Peter warned me tenderly, and the jeweler glowed with pride: "Are the most gracious Majesties ready?"

Peter nodded, and the man blew his cheeks as he unlocked the box but ordered: "Light more candles. I want this to sparkle as the sun, the moon, and the stars." I almost had to laugh, as he sounded so taken with his work.

"More than a million rubles, just for your crown," Peter murmured, kissing my fingers. Goose bumps covered my arms: one million rubles was an unimaginable sum, enough to feed generations of Russians in their small, filthy, stinking *izby*. I blinked my tears away: the crown was a miracle and so different from the jeweled domes I knew. A border of diamonds sparkled at the lower rim. Each stone was as big as a hazelnut, resting on an ermine saddle so as to not press into my forehead. Gray, pink, and white pearls alternated with diamonds on the arches forming the upper part of the crown, while in between, sapphires, emeralds, and again diamonds sparkled. The splendor was topped by a ruby cross; the stone at its heart was as large as a dove's egg, spewing crimson and gold sparks.

"Can I try it on?" I asked hoarsely, but Peter looked at me, horrified.

"A crown is not a cap or a hat, Catherine, which you *try on,* but a sacred sign of the power that God in His grace grants you. You may wear it only once you have been anointed. No water in this world can wash the blessed oil from your forehead: only then are you ready for a crown."

* * *

Back in the sled, dusk blotted the fading light of the early afternoon. Peter pushed his hands into my sable muff, lacing fingers. "Thank you for always being with me. I will make it up to you." Candles burned behind the windows on the Nevsky Prospect, and in the lanterns along the canals. The snow glowed under the clear, star-studded sky, as shiny as Wilhelm's eyes after making love. Could I hope that he would look at me forever and ever? A thousand eyes watch a tsar's wife. Stepan Glebov had paid the highest price for loving Evdokia, and she was but a discarded, cumbersome woman to Peter. Me, however, he honored in a way that no tsar had ever honored his wife before. It wasn't even worth thinking about what he'd do to us. Still, I just could not let go of Wilhelm.

That same evening, I ordered Maître Duval from the *gostiny dvor* to the palace: he had moved his business to Saint Petersburg. While all my robes were made in France, I wanted to sew Peter's coronation coat myself, stitch by stitch. I ordered many *arshin* of sky-blue taffeta from Paris and chose silver braids to fit the knee-length jacket. Out of coquetry, I settled upon flaming red silk thread for the stockings. The price that Duval quoted me made my head spin: one silver thread alone could pay a dragoon's salary for two years. Yet I did not hesitate, and when Maître Duval got his order book out, I said to Wilhelm: "Sign it in my name, will you?"

* * *

At the end of March, Saint Petersburg's noble families left for Moscow. Last icicles hung in the trees lining the Nevsky Prospect, but a milder air and the first rays of sunlight spoke of the near spring. An endless train of carriages and wagons crossed the countryside: thirty thousand people were on the road at a time. Boats used the early arrival of the *ottepel* to sail to Moscow, and children ran with the ships, waving and cheering. Clouds rolled over our heads, and the wind blew the worries and the shame I sometimes felt from my heart, scattering them in the vastness of the realm. Often I had to retreat to my cabin: everything was too much to take in. Twenty-five years ago, in another life, a man had bought me for a piece of silver. Now I should be crowned tsaritsa of all the Russias. Sometimes Wilhelm would slip into my cabin, holding me tightly and whispering sweet nothings until I could breathe again. My fear was mirrored in his eyes, but he kissed me until his strong, steady heartbeat calmed me: How should I do without him? He supported me, felt for me as no man had ever done before. Was there a chance for us to be happy together, I thought, just when I saw the thousand turrets, spires, and towers of Moscow. It was not my city, but the place of my most splendid hour. Yet the brightest sun casts the darkest shadow.

* * *

On the seventh day of May I climbed into the golden carriage on the innermost courtyard of Alexander Danilovich Menshikov's house. Peter himself steadied me in my heavy gown. My hand trembled as I placed my fingers into his. "Stand tall, Catherinushka. Have no fear," he reassured me, but I felt dazed and the weight of my velvet robes crushed me. Peter had insisted on the much-too-warm fabric, and the high-necked dress was stiff as a board with gold embroidery. Some of my twelve page boys, who held my train, lifted it, so that I could get into the coach. The boys, all of them sons of Peter's faithful helpers, looked adorable in green velvet and matching caps adorned with white ostrich feathers. I gasped under the sudden pressure of the diamond clasps on my throat, but cannons thundered and the bells of the city called; the gates opened, and as soon as my imperial coach rolled into the Red Square, cheers and clapping arose. The guards stood to attention, trumpets were blown, and drummers rolled a fast, upbeat rhythm. The musicians of Peter's two regiments were playing a tune when two swallows buzzed by my carriage, their beady eyes mocking me. The twelve mares pulling my carriage reared, and the coachman sweated in his silk livery. My hand rose all by itself, and I smiled and waved. There was no turning back.

Outside Uspensky Cathedral, the newly created Cavalry Guard, which Alexander Danilovich was part of, awaited me, while Sheremetev reached out to steady me. He murmured, "I am so glad, my lady, I could die."

Suddenly, all the colors were even brighter, the music even gayer. Step for step I made my way through the nave of the cathedral. The court had had to purchase tickets for the event, and a sea of familiar faces turned to me, but I looked straight ahead, to where General James Bruce stood, holding my crown on a velvet cushion, beads of sweat glistening on his upper lip. I struggled to sit at Peter's side in my stiff robes but tried to copy his calmness and dignity. He briefly winked at me, but then turned stone-faced, looking straight ahead.

Feofan Prokopovich read the Mass as the archbishop of Novgorod, and with the help of my cavaliers I knelt before him. His voice echoed in the silence of the cathedral, and if I had felt unbearably hot before, chills now chased over my skin. The twelve young page boys pressed their foreheads onto the cathedral's cold stone floor. Silence ruled, in and outside the church. Feofan Prokopovich drew a cross with warm, fragrant oil on my forehead and muttered his blessing.

The world spun: only Peter stood still, the calm in the eye of the storm. He had done nothing but this for his whole life, I understood when he lifted the crown, its gemstones catching the light, and I sensed him more than I saw him. The crowd sighed longingly; the blood roared in my ears when the weight of the crown sent a sharp pain through my tense neck down into my rigid shoulders, as I placed my fingers in Peter's. I wanted to kiss his feet, but he did not allow it. "*Starik*," I murmured, and the pain ebbed away as I stood. Music flooded the cathedral. Perhaps I only then gathered what he was willing to share with me. Tears streamed down my cheeks, leaving traces in my thick white makeup. Peter held the scepter to his breast and raised my hand in his: together, we had lived and loved, and together, we ruled.

The court rose for the final blessing and the choir's voices carried my gratitude out onto the squares of the city, to the glare of the gold coins that Menshikov had thrown at the crowd and the gurgling of the fountains, which spewed red and white wine. The festivities lasted a week, and then the whole court, with its servants, families, livestock, and luggage, left again for Saint Petersburg, as Peter planned to celebrate his name day on the Neva with sea games and a new round of celebrations.

83

"Now I have gone too far." Peter flinched. "As soon as I have battled one pain, I feel a hundred others rearing their ugly heads." His face was flushed, as he had been bedridden for the past four months. Blumentrost called upon other doctors for advice, which worried me. If a quack admits his uselessness, things are serious. Doctor Bidloo arrived from Moscow, but finally it was Doctor Horn who drained almost a liter of blood, urine, and pus from Peter's bladder.

Wilhelm instead brought freedom, wind, and sunshine with him, telling me funny stories about the estate with the five thousand souls I had given him. To him, ten days were long enough to gather the adventures of a lifetime. "I can't wait until you come and see me in the *datcha*," he said—that was how he spoke of the little palace close to the Bay of Finland, as if it were a hut. "Do you still know how to get an egg from under a chicken's bottom? Are you good at milking?" he teased me.

"I've forgotten it all." I laughed.

"You'll have to start from the beginning then, with me, in the stables," he said, and I chuckled, going on my knees, opening his breeches.

I sensed his hesitation. "Come," I whispered. "I command it."

His eyes shone like jewels as I, the crowned tsaritsa of Russia, took him slowly, fully, in my mouth, as if I were a maid. His lust was the only realm I ever wanted to rule.

* * *

But when autumn came, Peter asked for supper in my rooms. I ordered his favorite food from Felten—pork sausages with sauerkraut, fresh flatbread, and cold beer—and adorned the table with evergreens from the Summer Palace's garden.

As Peter came in with Jagushinsky, Makarov, and Menshikov, Wilhelm waited on me and Daria Menshikova and Agneta: the more, the merrier, I thought. My dress was of simple dark green cotton, yet I wore Menshikov's necklace to flatter him. When Peter entered my room he gave me a dark look.

"Are you in pain?" I frowned, but he would not answer, so I filled his plate to the brim and broke the bread. He did not thank me, but I chatted all the more. Then, after an hour's mute chewing and gloomy looks, Peter growled, "Tsaritsa, what time is it?"

The table fell curiously silent as I reached for the delicate watch hanging on a gold chain around my neck: a gift of Peter's from back in Berlin. "Only nine o'clock, *starik,* so there is a lot of time left for food and joy."

But Peter lunged at me and tore the chain from my neck. I gasped with pain as the links broke and the ladies screamed. Peter thrust the watch's diamond hands forward so roughly that one of them broke. "You are mistaken, Catherine Alexeyevna," he shouted. "It's already midnight, and all but you, me, and him"—he pointed at Wilhelm—"are to leave."

My heart pounded and I felt sweat tingling on my neck and armpits. Yet I smiled and said, "Your wish is our command. Good night, my friends." I clapped my hands, yet I saw the dread in our guests' faces and felt faint with fear. Wilhelm stood as still as a statue, his face pale with dread. He steadied himself on the back of a chair, his knuckles turning white. Only the crackling of the logs in the fire was to be heard as Peter's dark gaze went from me to Wilhelm, and from Wilhelm back to me. I sat down once more, sipping from my wine. My calm goaded him and made him unsure, just as I had hoped. He pulled a letter from his chest pocket; the paper had been read and folded many times, and some of the wide, slanted letters were smeared by tears. Peter looked at me, full of contempt, before throwing the letter at Wilhelm. "Unfortunately, I have married an uneducated washermaid. Read, you vain monkey!" he thundered.

Wilhelm's fingers trembled as he read soundlessly before looking up. He fell on his knees, gasping for breath, wrung his hands, and stammered, "My tsar. That's a shameless, mean lie."

Peter did not leave him any time for more but struck Wilhelm in the face with his clenched fist, knocking him over. I called out in horror and leaped to my feet, but Peter grabbed and shook me until my teeth chattered, before he shoved me away, staring at me, full of hate. "I have married you and made you an empress. I have crowned you, and this is how you thank me? Rotten to the core you are, even proudly wearing the spoils of your corruption—" He lunged and tore Menshikov's necklace from my throat, and the priceless diamonds rained down on the rugs in a sparkling shower when Peter pushed me against the wall's paneling.

Wilhelm crawled to Peter, kissing the rough leather of his boot tips, sobbing and pleading. "My tsar, for all the love and all the honor that you have given my family, please do not believe this. I would never besmear the tsaritsa's name, or ever betray you."

"Son of a bitch!" Peter kicked Wilhelm several times in the face, chest, and belly, making ribs and cheekbones crack and breaking his strong, white teeth. Wilhelm moaned and spit blood. He bent over double with pain. I did not move, cowering against the wall. "Do not dare to name the tsaritsa together with your damned brethren. All of the Mons will pay for this!" Furious, he seized a Delft porcelain water jug and hurled it against a Venetian mirror, smashing it to pieces; I ducked as shards flew. "This, Catherine Alexeyevna, shall be done with you and yours," he cried.

I crossed my arms. "Fabulous. You have just destroyed one of the most exquisite pieces in your household. Do you feel better now?" I knew that he would take any fear or pleading as a sign of guilt. I held his gaze as he pulled me close, and I saw doubt there; doubt that might save me, if not Wilhelm.

"Damn you and your guts, woman!" he hissed, before he turned to the door. "Guards, to me!" Four tall men stormed into the room. Had they been lingering outside, waiting for the tsar's signal?

Peter pointed at the crouching, bleeding Wilhelm. "Arrest that man!" he ordered breathlessly. "Throw him into the Trubetzkoy Bastion. Torture him until he confesses his theft and embezzlement from the tsaritsa's treasures. I shall have the proof I need."

"No!" I gasped, and Peter caught me as I fainted.

84

On the day of Wilhelm's execution, I made sure to be seen practicing together with my daughters and a dance master from Paris, hiding my pallor with scarlet cheeks and glittering jewels. "I heard of a new minuet from Paris, teach it to us!" I clapped my hands and ate sugared violets to force my lips into a smile. The master showed us the series of steps, and Elizabeth repeatedly glanced at me. I thought of the slanted writing that had sealed Wilhelm's fate: but no, I told myself, that was impossible. She was my *daughter*. As Wilhelm was dragged from the Trubetzkoy Bastion to the scaffold, I moved to the light, floating melody and danced across the pieces of my broken heart. But then Peter's guards entered the ballroom: I was to attend the execution.

* * *

The people were eerily quiet as the whole Mons family was led to the executioner's block. Wilhelm himself could not walk anymore. Crude hands had thrown him onto a sled filled with rotten straw, and from there he was heaved onto the executioner's broad shoulders. Peter would not let me out of his sight but I smiled at him, eating more sugared violets until my teeth and my cheeks hurt.

"Well, Catherine Alexeyevna, what do you feel now?" he asked, beady-eyed. I tightened my fur collar around my neck and shrugged.

"I took him for a trusted employee. If he really stole my jewels then he deserves a just punishment," I said, looking at Wilhelm, feeling ready to faint. I had asked God in vain for strength for this very moment. My

452 ⚜ ELLEN ALPSTEN

love was no longer a man, but a miserable lump of flesh as the men dragged him up the steps to the scaffold. He sighed and fresh drops of blood left a last trace. I knew that he had not betrayed me or our love, despite Peter's torturers doing their cruel trade to the best of their knowledge.

"Oh, yes," Peter mocked me. "He stole the crown jewels, as you know very well. I even have proof of him embezzling your funds."

He shoved a piece of paper in my hand and I unfolded it. It was my order for the fabrics for Peter's coronation gowns that Wilhelm had signed in my name, at my order. The clothes I had sewn with my hands, as a sign of my love and gratitude.

"He signed his undoing, the young Mons." Peter smiled. "Look. Look well, Catherinushka."

Wilhelm whimpered and I dug my nails deep into my palms. I loved him; loved him too much, and yet did I not love him enough? Why did I then not confess and join him on the scaffold there and then? If I had ever despised Afrosinja for sacrificing Alexey, then so much more would the thought of my own silence haunt me until my dying day.

Peter tore me to my feet, shoving me closer to the scaffold. "You can't see well enough from here," he snarled, and I staggered along, straight to the block, where Wilhelm's body hung. He could no longer lift his head, and I was glad of it, for I could not have borne his gaze.

Peter kissed my cheek and shouted, "The tsaritsa wants to see up close how the common thief, Wilhelm Mons, traitor of her trust, is being judged!"

A murmur rose from the crowd; they knew all too well why Wilhelm had to suffer. On Peter's sign his men started, and I could not hold back anymore. My tears flowed freely, blinding me and blotting the sheer horror of Wilhelm's death. I know they broke him on the wheel; they slit him open and tore his guts from his body, roasting them on a spit and feeding them to the crows in front of his eyes, before finally beheading him. Peter held me in an iron grip and let me weep until Wilhelm, my wonderful Wilhelm, so full of life, love, and lust, was no more.

85

Oh, yes, Peter knew. In the following days he forced me to the scaffold again and again; our sled would stop where Wilhelm's corpse still hung. His limbs had been torn off by wild dogs, his eyes pecked out by birds. "Come on, Catherinushka, we'll stretch our legs," Peter said merrily, steering me so close to Wilhelm that my skirts brushed his butchered body. I obeyed but chatted about trivial matters until it got to be too much for Peter himself. "You and your damn courage. If my generals had but a sliver of that, I would have won more wars," he growled as he pushed me back into the sled.

I cast a last glance at Wilhelm's beheaded torso and took leave of all the love left in my heart. The sled jerked forward, its silver bells jingling in the frosty air. A gust of icy wind hid the scaffold in a cloud of fresh powdery snow.

The same evening, I left the dinner table in Peter's rooms early. My heart longed for the stillness of the night, as I needed all my strength for the days to come. Peter already had forbidden his ministers to obey any of my orders and had sealed my treasurer's office. I had no money left and ran up debts with my ladies.

Alexandra Tolstoya loosened my hair, unclasped my jewelry, and unlaced my dress. In my bedroom, a few candles were alight: Had someone already been here? I slipped out of my soft shoes, holding on to my dainty bedside table, when my hand skimmed glass. Had I ordered a sleeping potion? I raised my night-light—and heard myself scream; the candle slipped from my fingers and hot oil spread; first flames licked at my sheets.

Alexandra Tolstoya rushed in. "Milady, what happened?" She suffocated the flames by stomping on them and tearing a sheet from my bedstead.

I sobbed and gasped, pointing to the night table.

"Oh my God, the animal!" she whispered.

Next to my bed stood a tall glass in which apples were kept in vodka during the winter, which in Saint Petersburg one could buy in any *kabak*. Yet no fruit floated in this one, but the head of my beloved Wilhelm. His blue eyes were wide open and his lips pulled back from his gums in agony and fear. He stared at me; his gaze pleading, but not accusing.

I gagged with disgust and tears. "Take that away, Alexandra," I stammered.

She lifted the glass, gagging and with unsteady fingers, but when she turned around, Peter stood behind us, towering. We both shrank back, horrified, as he took a deep sip from his brandy flask, swaying. "Your room is so bare, Catherinushka. What's wrong with a little jar next to your bed?" His tongue was heavy and lilting. "Alexandra Tolstoya, whoever moves this glass will pay with their lives. With regard to your faithful service, I commend you to place it where it belongs," he added, slurring his words.

Alexandra looked at me, but what could I do?

"Put it down, Alexandra," I muttered, and curtsied. "How kind of the tsar to think of the adornment of my room." Was that it, had he punished me enough?

No.

Peter pointed at me. "And now, Catherine Alexeyevna, I'll think about what's going to happen to you." His cold, hard eyes made me shiver. He had already won, and I had lost everything: What else could he want? Alexandra made me a sleeping potion and in my nightmares Wilhelm's eyes filled a sky like stars of darkness.

No one at court was ready to wager a kopeck on my future at Peter's side; my destiny was sealed. The only puzzling thing was *what* might happen exactly. To which convent should I commit myself, shorn and lonely? Or was there a cell prepared in the Peter and Paul Fortress, where he would torture and kill me as he had done with Alexey? Under the first blow of the knout, I would confess all that I was accused of, and gladly more. I had suffered when giving birth, but could not bear deliberate physical pain. I remembered surrendering to Vassily without putting up a fight. Only Menshikov would not forsake me, secretly sending me letters and small gifts to lift my spirits. Agneta told me with tears in her eyes what Peter had said in the senate: "I will do to her what England's King Henry has done to Anne Boleyn."

"What did he do to this Anne?" I asked unhappily. "And what was her offence?"

"She was an adulteress, Tsaritsa," she whispered, before drawing her flat hand across her neck.

* * *

It was almost midnight when I made my way through the dark, secret corridor that linked Peter's rooms to mine. The night-light just about helped me find my way without stumbling over a sleeping footman's body. I pressed my ear against Peter's door: he was in there with Tolstoy and his chancellor, the German Baron Ostermann. Their voices were muffled.

"My tsar, do not act rashly; please think of the betrothal of Tsarevna Anna to the Duke of Holstein," Ostermann mumbled.

"I do not see the link to the tsaritsa's crime. Just answer me: convent, exile, or death?" Peter asked angrily.

I chewed my fingers and held my breath. The light at my feet flickered.

"Well," Ostermann said, "the duke could dissolve the engagement if the bride's mother had a bad reputation. With all due respect, the courts of Europe talk enough about the tsaritsa as it is. What if the empress were to be charged with adultery and beheaded? That would put an end to any of your daughter's marriage plans." For once, I felt like kissing the wry German who normally was no one's friend.

"Ostermann is right. Not only is Anna Petrovna's engagement at risk, but we would also not find a new suitor for Tsarevna Elizabeth, once Versailles turns her down," Tolstoy added.

I heard wood breaking, and Peter curse. What did he kick and smash in his anger; his desk or his chair? There was a moment of silence. "How are the marriage plans with France coming along?" he asked.

"Not at all," Tolstoy said. "King Louis is silent—insultingly so. The duc de Chartres, also a possible suitor, married a German princess a few weeks ago without even telling us. Will a king take what a duke despises?"

I pressed my ear so hard against the wood that it burned.

"So be it. I'm waiting. But her hour will come, and it will come soon."

I heard the cold fury in Peter's voice. I tiptoed back to my room, my heart racing and sweat trickling down my neck despite the chill in the passage. What had I sworn to myself the night in the Summer Palace when he promised me marriage? I would not fear.

* * *

Two weeks after Wilhelm's beheading, the betrothal of my eldest daughter, Anna Petrovna, to the young Duke of Holstein was announced. He gave a concert beneath the windows of the Winter Palace and the musicians' fingertips and lips froze to their instruments. Afterward, we crossed the Neva in sleds, and read the Mass in the Holy Church of Trinity. Feofan Prokopovich blessed the rings, and Peter placed them on the young couple's fingers. During the feast, the ball, and the fireworks, I was the radiant tsaritsa, for all to see, with my very last strength. Yet my mind would neither let go of Wilhelm's mutilated body, nor of Evdokia's miserable life.

* * *

The palace was treacherously peaceful in the first, dark hours of the day: How long had I knelt there in the cold splendor of the corridor outside Peter's door? My fists were scraped raw from banging on the door, my stomach growled, my hair was tangled, and my cheeks were scratched and bloody as I had wept and pleaded myself hoarse. Finally, I heard him stir on the other side.

"What do you want, Catherinushka?" he asked warily. I sat up. At least he called me *that*.

"Forgive me, my tsar, *batjushka*!" I was strangled by sobs. "I beg you on my knees. *Starik,* darling, love of my life, please. For all that is dear to us. Our children, Russia—and for all we've been through." The door opened but a crack, and he looked down at me.

"You deceived me," he said bitterly. I wiped the tears from my cheeks, as helpless as a child, and sat up: it was true, as simple as that.

"Yes. Forgive me. But I do not want to fight with you, my beloved. I want to make you happy, as always. I miss you; everything about you. Take me back into your life, into your heart. Only there do I have a home. You are my husband, my brother, my father, my home—"

He opened the door a little further, peering out, and I could see his face. His skin was pasty and his eyes swollen. "I do not know, Catherinushka." He sighed. His hesitation frightened me more than any judgment passed in raging anger. Peter could fling rash flashes of lightning, but when he saw the firebrand he had caused, he put out the flames. Snot and tears ran down my face, and I shivered with cold and tiredness.

"Come in." He sighed again, and pulled me to my feet and into his room. The curtains were closed and it reeked of liquor, sweat, and smoke. His favorite chair was pushed in front of the fireplace. Had he sat there, his feet close to the fire, listening to me pleading on the other side for hours on end? He sat down again, and I crouched on a pillow at his feet. Peter looked at me, and I was careful not to interrupt his thoughts. His face was unreadable and changed by the shadows cast by dawn.

"What is it with you women?" he said, shaking his head. "Anna Mons made a fool out of me. Evdokia deceived me even in the convent in which I stuck her, but still besieged me with her letters. At least you cannot write, Catherinushka. I will have my peace. Maria Kantemir did not keep her pompous promise of a son for Russia." I held my breath as he dipped his hands into my dark, shining curls, wrapping a strand of my hair around his finger. "But you, Catherine, you have betrayed me at the very moment when I shared my highest good with you. Why did you do this?" He sniffed at my hair. "Hm. You're still beautiful. How often were you pregnant with a child of mine? Twelve times, if I'm not mistaken." He uncorked the brandy bottle that stood beside him on the floor and took a swig. "Twelve children, and you are still so stunningly beautiful. But what will the convent's chill do to you? What will you look like, bald and gaunt?" He drank deeply. "What's worst is that in the end, you, too, did not truly understand me. Don't you know how lonely a ruler is; how cold the throne is on the skin of my arse and how far away I am from anyone who is close to me?"

"I've always been with you. I am always with you. I will always be with you," I whispered. The flames warmed my bare arms, yet I had goose bumps all over my body. "Can you not forgive me?" I had done once what he had done a thousand times. In Russian fairy tales, houses rest on three stilts; was the palace of our love but leaning on the one pillar: my love and fidelity?

He stared into the fireplace. "No. I cannot forgive. But I have not decided either what to do with you. Go to bed now, *matka*." His voice did not allow for another word.

I rose, but took his chilly, slight hands into mine, and whispered, "I have borne you twelve children, Peter Alexeyevich Romanov. Can you imagine what it means to give birth twelve times?" I asked him. "None of your soldiers has suffered like that or has risked his life so often for you. And do you know why I did that? Just for love, my tsar."

He gazed mutely into the flames. I let go of his fingers and his hand fell limply into his lap.

At noon the next day, Pavel Jagushinsky picked up Wilhelm's head from my bedside table and brought it to the Kunstkamera, where it was to be housed.

* * *

Evil spirits and memories haunted Peter more than ever; his jealousy seared his soul, making him restlessly roam his empire. Every day I was unscathed meant hope, but in its uncertainty the passing time was also a punishment. Every day I heard new and wild stories from my *damy*.

"Imagine, the tsar passed a house where a wedding was being celebrated. So he knocked at the door, sat down at the table, and drank more than anyone else."

"Yesterday, the tsar visited the Ladoga Canal and drank until dawn with the architects."

"No, he is at the Ironworks of Olonez, where he chased a blacksmith from his anvil, just to smite six hundred pounds of iron himself. He asked to be paid for his work, and bought a pair of long socks at the market."

He was everywhere at the same time, just not in Saint Petersburg, with me.

* * *

Peter returned to our city in February. His old fever seized him more violently than ever and he did not even recognize me by his bedside. Few people were admitted and I ordered that little Petrushka, Alexey's son, was not to come to the Winter Palace from his godfather Prince Dolgoruky's house: the sight of him would upset Peter unbearably. My orders were listened to once more. I knelt there, hour after hour, or lay down beside him, cuddling up close, whispering memories into his ear. He quieted and his breath steadied. I embraced him and fell asleep.

Menshikov came to the sickroom in the early-morning hours on one of the following days and opened the window. When the clear winter air streamed into the room, Peter reeled in his fever, but my weight held him down.

"What made him suddenly relapse?" I asked.

Menshikov filled his long pipe and set it alight. "Well, I wouldn't call that *suddenly*, my empress. When we left the ironworks of Olonez, the tsar already felt cold, despite the new socks he had earned." We both smiled, then he turned serious again. "Yet he pressed on, straight for Saint Petersburg. It poured with rain; we followed the shoreline, so as not to get lost in a storm, and heard screams coming from the water—" Menshikov blew a few rings into the air, their thin smoke dissolving. "Some sailors were in distress. Before I could hold back the tsar he had already jumped off his horse—"

"And then?"

He shrugged. "What would you expect? He jumped into the icy water, without the least regard for his own safety or health, and swam out to save the men. Once he had brought their boat ashore, they drank like fish, round upon round of hot spirits, before the tsar got back on his horse. The storm still raged, but we pushed on. He felt feverish before we reached the first of the city's barriers."

Blumentrost entered the room. "My empress, perhaps it is better to leave the room for a moment. The mercury cure is not for Your Majesty's eyes."

I refused. "I'll stay, Blumentrost. Someone must hold his hand to comfort him."

Menshikov smiled. "A true empress, as always."

When Blumentrost opened Peter's blanket, I pressed my hand to my lips, fighting the bile that rose in my throat. The skin on his swollen belly had blackened, as if rotting away alive. Spots and ulcers covered his groin, and when the doctor pressed his side ever so lightly, Peter roared with pain and rose from his feverish sleep.

"He suffers from kidney stones, Your Majesty," whispered Blumentrost. "I'll have to work together with Paulsen and Horn."

Peter's puffed-up body and the stench in the room made me choke, but I took a deep breath and lifted Peter's head tenderly. "I'm ready."

Blumentrost reached for the mercury ointment and pills.

* * *

"How is he now?" Menshikov slipped back into the room after a few hours of sleep.

What should I say? For days Peter hovered between life and death. His gigantic body had been weakened already by so many struggles: the tsar, our life, and our death, just as he wanted it to be.

Makarov looked shrunken in his black coat as I waved him close to me, by the window. "Makarov, I fear that Blumentrost is killing the tsar," I whispered. "Please send a messenger to Berlin. The king of Prussia has a fabulous physician, Herr von Stahl, of whom Peter has often spoken. Bring him here, cost what it may."

Night fell, and servants drew the curtains shut, thus hiding Peter's suffering from his city. Candles were lit, and the warm scent of beeswax as well as the richly spiced Persian incense that smoldered in coal pans softened the stench of the disease. To Peter, the room's shadows were alive with the people who had accompanied us along our way and who had gone ahead into the underworld. I heard Peter mumble, "Mother, do not cry. I am coming. Sophia, leave me alone. And Alexey, you use-less boy—" He groaned and wanted to turn around, but Blumentrost would not allow it. Peter settled on his back again but narrowed his eyes. "Sheremetev. There you are. Actually, it's all your fault—" I sobbed to drown out his words as Feofan Prokopovich entered the room together with a simple pope. Peter made his last confession for the third time in those days.

I wept so much that I fainted several times, both out of fear and of sorrow. I would not master either feeling.

When the tsar was too weak to speak, Feofan Prokopovich, Menshikov, and I formed a tight circle around the bed. I knelt once more so as to be closer to him. Peter's gaze slipped away. The bells started tolling and people gathered on the quays and the Nevsky Prospect for prayer. What did they wish for? For Peter's death, or for his recovery? Did I myself know what I was hoping for?

He opened his eyes once more, searching my gaze. "You love me, don't you? Say that you love me, always," he whispered, his lips dry and cracked.

I nodded, tears streaming down my face. "More than my life!"

He sighed. "You better had."

I smiled and placed a finger on his lips. "Do not talk, dear. All will be well." A glance passed between the doctors, Blumentrost, Paulsen, and Horn. Peter whispered something and Feofan Prokopovich bowed to his lips, frowning.

"What does the tsar want?" I asked, my voice unsteady.

"His Majesty asks for paper and pen," said Feofan, his face plain. Menshikov rummaged in the tsar's desk. Was I mistaken, or did he take longer than necessary? His future, too, was at stake. Finally, Prokopovich folded Peter's fingers around the quill. Black ink dripped on his starched sheets. I heard the feather scratching over the paper, and Peter's throttled voice. "Tsarevna Anna Petrovna. Bring my Anoushka to me, my dear eldest child—"

Anna? How would she be able to handle little Petrushka's claim and keep his godfather, the greedy Prince Dolgoruky, at bay? A tsar dying meant past and present hanging in a balance. The wind got stronger, whistling around the Winter Palace's walls. Who had really heard his words? Neither I nor Menshikov followed his order. Feofan crossed himself in silence.

Peter's dainty fingers tried to roll the paper, but the scroll slipped. All of Russia held its breath.

"Oh, my God." We spoke his last words together.

IN THE WINTER PALACE, 1725

As Menshikov opens the door, the corridor outside our small study is full of men. I spot the members of the synod, the senate, and the admiralty. In one night we have fooled them and all of Russia. I rise and ready myself for the nasal voice of Prince Dolgoruki, arresting us in the name of Petrushka, the new tsar, Peter II. I fold my hands in silent prayer and close my eyes. But the light is so bright, it pierces my closed lids. Am I already dead?

"Tsarina," Menshikov says huskily, and I look up. The men of the privy council kneel in front of me: Ostermann, Tolstoy, and Jagushinsky—all of them. Menshikov stares at me with bloodshot eyes and looks like the scoundrel he is after all.

I straighten up. The icons on my dress jingle like a wind chime, and my jewelry sparkles in the candlelight as I speak. "The great and gracious Tsar Peter the First of Russia has passed away. We are torn by grief and numb with pain. For We, Catherine Alexeyevna, empress and tsarina of Russia, are aware of the responsibility which God places on Our shoulders." My voice fills the room as I lift my right hand. "We swear to do justice to God's grace, and to love all Russians as Our own children. We will righteously reign, and trust in your experienced advice and guidance." I look into the privy council members' eyes, man for man. The choice is theirs: rule with me or perish with me.

Menshikov is the first to decide, swift and cunning, as always. If there was muttering of discontent among the princes, the boyars, and, above all, the church, he would call upon the army; the planted bayonets will quench calls for resistance and turn doubters into most fervent supporters. "Hail, Catherine Alexeyevna, tsarina of all the Russias! Hail, the tsarina," he thunders, and the council joins his cheering.

The call goes forth in the corridor, the courtyard, our city, and finally all over the country. Above the Winter Palace's gate, the flag with the double-headed eagle is lowered to half-mast. From the Peter and Paul Fortress one hundred and one cannon shots tear the morning air, the bells of the Trinity Cathedral toll dully, and then all the churches of the city follow: the tsar is dead; long live the tsarina!

Feofan Prokopovich has returned, just in time, as is his custom. He kisses my fingers and swears his loyalty to me; Makarov unrolls the hurried *ukaz* that proclaims me tsarina. The princes Dolgoruki come into the room, clutching Petrushka's hands. They must have torn the boy from his sleep, as the young prince blinks, confused by the many candles. His hair is tousled, and his feet are bare. I feel no remorse: Alexey's son is still so young, and his time will come. The Guard secures the steps and stairs before which many hundred voices roar, "Hail Catherine! Hail the mother of the nation, hail our tsarina!"

Their generals kneel; countless times I had sat with them by the campfire, celebrating their victories and lamenting their defeats. I tended to their wounds at Poltava and spooned thin soup into their bowls underneath the beating Persian sun. I was always there, as long as they could remember. I had protected them, their goods, and their families against Peter's wrath. At his side, I had learned what it took to rule Russia. This was the way it should be: Peter is dead. My beloved husband, the mighty tsar of all the Russias, has died, and not a moment too soon.

Time held its breath briefly in the upper reaches of the Winter Palace.

EPILOGUE

Excerpt from the diary of
Jean Jacques Campredon,
French Envoy to the Imperial Court
of Saint Petersburg,
16 May 1727

I've just returned from the palace, where Prince Menshikov told us about the tsarina's failing health. In all the years since I am in Russia for His Most Gracious Majesty the king of France, I have not seen so much grief in the people's faces. Even Menshikov is stricken, and he better ponder his future. For what will happen to him, once the tsarina passes away, only two years after the death of Peter the First? Menshikov has more enemies than hair on his head, and in his grandeur and ambition ignores this fact blithely. He betrothed his daughter to the tsarevich Petrushka, but engagements are made to be broken. Oh, there will be a lot to write about in the coming weeks, I'm sure!

The tsarina is dying, and one can only marvel at the divine will which has raised her so far, so unbelievably far beyond her birth. Even my queen, who came from humble Poland as Princess Maria, is impressed by her, although she of course would never admit to it. The tsarina wanted the king of France as a husband for her own daughter, the tsarevna Elizabeth. But a washermaid's daughter on the throne of France? *Mon dieu.*

At the great tsar's funeral, she claimed the throne by her sheer mourning and despair. How may one woman have so many tears, or maybe we just do not meet any decent women anymore? Tsar Peter had loved her. But had she loved him truly so much that her tears at his wake could be trusted? He was too terrible. Only a few moons earlier Wilhelm Mons had been beheaded, and there was no doubt about the nature of his crimes. But all was forgotten at the tsar's funeral: her ladies-in-waiting, their faces thickly veiled, tried to hold her back, but she threw herself to the ground, clawing herself in the two coffins and howling like a wounded beast. It took her weeks to let Feofan Prokopovich close the dead tsar's coffin at all. He lay in state surrounded by the signs of his greatness. Then, just five weeks after the tsar's death, the little tsarevna Natalya died at the age of only seven years. The Lord gives, and the Lord takes. The young lady-in-waiting Alice Kramer fell victim to Natalya's death; her mind clouded and she took her leave. The court gossiped for days on the princely pension the tsarina paid her. What had the true nature of her services to the tsar and tsarina been?

On the tenth day of March 1725, both young Natalya and her father, Peter I of Russia, were buried in the Peter und Paul Cathedral in his glorious city of Saint Petersburg. Tens of thousands of soldiers of all regiments gathered at dawn on the ice of the Neva; thirty-two hundred noble horses were tethered around them, chewing on their silver bridles. Twelve officers carried Peter's coffin and eight general majors held up the canopy of green velvet with its golden tassels, shielding the coffin from the snow. Peter's closest friends and the high dignitaries of the empire held a piece of the coffin cover each, the snowflakes mingling with their tears.

Once the funeral was over, everything quickly reverted to an everyday life. The tsarina broke the court mourning to marry her daughter Anna to the Duke of Holstein in a most splendid wedding. The bride left Saint Petersburg, wailing and weeping. Tsarevna Elizabeth is still unmarried, and she does everything possible to spoil her reputation. She is a beauty—*parbleu*! I have never seen such a cleavage, not even in Versailles—and her only faults lie in her behavior and her nature. Unfortunately, I am too old and not a guard, so she doesn't look at me. I was right to dissuade my king from marrying this princess. Her morals would have even surprised Versailles.

Menshikov says the tsarina's lungs were swollen, but only two weeks ago, at the first signs of the *ottepel*, I rode with her and could hardly keep up as she chased through the woods. At a river, she made us dismount, walked down to its shores, and slipped out of her shoes. We watched her picking up pebbles and talking to herself. She felt the cold of the water, wading into it with bare feet, before she turned, frowned, and asked, "Do you hear the horses on the road? What could these men possibly want?" I turned, yet there was nothing to be seen.

She is still a fine woman, with very graceful movements, a bright, clear mind, and always of wonderfully high spirits. No wonder the people love her: the tsarina has never forgotten where she came from, but I believe she is bored without the tsar. Already in the morning she dips five warm pretzels into a heady, hot Burgundy, as to get a swift boost. On the first day of April, she had the fire bells rung and watched how the people rushed to the street in their nightshirts, but there was neither fire nor flood. To make up for her prank, the tsarina served vodka for free and no one was allowed to go to bed before noon, just as if Tsar Peter was still alive. God, how I feared and hated his feasts; sometimes the eagle cup is part of my nightmares. Many times, I have prayed that His Majesty King Louis should call me back to Paris. Why did I ever learn Russian?

Restless lights wander behind the Winter Palace's windows. Menshikov, who knows so well how to sow and harvest, can call on us at any time.

Horsemen gallop out of the palace's gates. The tsarina has not waged wars, she has not plundered, and has razed neither cities nor countries. These were two good years in Russia; we lived happily and created new happiness. Blumentrost, the quack, teaches at the Academy of Sciences, and the Saint Petersburg gymnasium is open to gifted children from all over Russia. Last year Vitus Bering carried on with his travels. Only the tsarina herself never learned how to read or to write. "An old mule does not turn into a horse, Campredon," she said to me.

The carriage of the Counts Skawronski enters the Winter Palace: Are they well and truly the tsarina's lost family? Everybody wants to belong, and even a tsarina should not die alone. After being pregnant twelve times with the tsar's child, only one daughter and a supposed brother hold her hand in her very last hour. Her pain comes in waves, so it is said, and sometimes so violently as to strangle her.

After my supper. The month of May brings the first brighter nights to Saint Petersburg, their darkness turning milky, which never fails to enchant me. The city is awake, the palace is lit up. If I am to report to Paris later tonight that the tsarina has passed away, we will again have a Tsar Peter, Petrushka, the young son of poor, haunted Alexey. When I looked for sealing wax in the drawer, I found an old leaflet, which I had forgotten about:

One could forever and ever praise the merits of the dead Tsar Peter, the greatness, the uniqueness, the wisdom of his rule. But his work brought pain to all the people who came close to him. He disturbed peace, prosperity, the strength of his empire. He violated the dignity, rights, and well-being of his subjects. He mingled insultingly in all matters: from religion to the family to the holy church. Can one love such a despot? No, never. Such a ruler is nothing but hateful.

There is a knock on the door. It must be the court's messenger: a tsarina does not die as a woman, but as a ruler, even if she was always much more a woman than a ruler. I ready myself to leave. Had I ever before spotted the silky sliver of blue hair setting the Neva apart from its shore at dusk? This night, the fireflies dance for her alone. My duty calls me, but before I go, I read through the leaflet again.

Can one love such a despot? No. But a man, who also happens to be the tsar?

The tsarina had made her choice.

ACKNOWLEDGMENTS

I first discovered Marta/Catherine when I was aged thirteen, reading Leo Sievers's fabulous book *Germans and Russians,* which charted the millennial history of these two countries and its people. That was it for me: writing about Marta's incredible destiny was an all-encompassing endeavor. I was never able to thank Lindsey Hughes, professor of Russian history at the School of Slavonic and East European Studies, UCL, for her outstanding oeuvre *Russia in the Age of Peter the Great*—it was my bible while writing *Tsarina*. Nothing would have happened without Jonny Geller and the amazing Alice Lutyens at Curtis Brown, agents par excellence and best guiding spirits, who took on the gamble that *Tsarina* was. The day you first answered my query letter, a heron settled in my garden—the most auspicious of signs! Thank you, too, to the elegant and capable Deborah Schneider of Gelfman Schneider/ICM Partners, literary scout Daniela Schlingmann—a fine woman of the first hour— and the whole fantastic foreign rights team at Curtis Brown for spreading the word further. Hats off to my first international publishers and editors such as Faiza Khan at Bloomsbury, Charles Spicer at St. Martin's Press, Francesca Cristoffanini from Planeta DeAgostini, as well as Dr. Nora Haller and Tilo Eckhardt at Heyne PRH. You are the magical core "Team Tsarina," and always happy to welcome others into your ranks. Special thanks to Charlotte Collins, who first translated the prologue, as well as chapters 1–8, from the original German manuscript. It gave me a brilliant base to work with and the courage to write on, as words are a movable feast and like clay.

A brief word for the sake of historical accuracy: the beginnings of Marta's life are shrouded in mystery. She emerges from the mist of time when she took a position as a maid with Ernst Glück. While Field Marshall Sheremetev captured her at the siege of Marienburg, I blended his persona with Peter's crony Fedor Matveev Apraxin later in the manuscript. It was Apraxin who took the Baltic girl Alice Kramer in. Likewise, Alice Kramer was called Anna, as were Rasia Menshikova and Alexandra Tolstoya. Other than that, I took very few liberties with happenings and timelines: the Petrine era is incredibly well documented. Also, Marta's tale could only have been invented by life itself.